THE
MOUNTAIN WHISPERS

ALI SPOONER

THE
MOUNTAIN WHISPERS

ALI SPOONER

Affinity
Rainbow Publications

2020

The Mountain Whispers
© 2020 by Ali Spooner

Affinity E-Book Press NZ LTD.
Canterbury, New Zealand

Edition First

ISBN: 978-1-98-858872-8

Editor: Angela Koenig
Proof Editor: Annette Mori
Cover Design: Irish Dragon Designs
Production Design: Affinity Publication Services

ACKNOWLEDGMENTS

I would like to thank my fans for following my stories, providing great feedback, and encouragement. Writing wouldn't be so much fun without you. Thanks to Affinity, Irish Dragon for the cover art and the team of editors, readers, and publishers who continue to help me grow as a writer.

DEDICATION

For Chas, my nephew and real-life Mitch. I hope someday we will share some of these adventures. Love you...MOST!

TABLE OF CONTENTS

Chapter One   2

Chapter Two   7

Chapter Three   11

Chapter Four   27

Chapter Five   40

Chapter Six   59

Chapter Seven   142

Chapter Eight   155

Chapter Nine   175

Chapter Ten   205

Chapter Eleven   231

Chapter Twelve   263

Chapter Thirteen   279

Chapter Fourteen   308

Chapter Fifteen   315

Chapter Sixteen   324

Chapter Seventeen   346

About the Author   349

Other Affinity Books   350

Y'all ain't gonna believe this…

CHAPTER ONE

Eli Fortner pulled into the driveway of her Florida home and was surprised to find her best friend Carol's car parked in the drive in the middle of a workday. She had completed her road trip early and had driven straight through to surprise her partner, Sara, when she came home from her shift from the hospital. Little did she know she was the one about to receive the surprise. Eli pulled her truck into the garage and walked into the house through the kitchen. She assumed she would find Carol and Sara sitting in the kitchen, or out by the pool on such a lovely day, but music from the bedroom caught her attention.

With each step closer to the master bedroom, the betrayal of her partner and best friend became as clear as day. She could hear loud moans of pleasure emanating from the room, and when she walked in, the two women were entwined, engaged in passionate lovemaking. She and Sara had been living together for three years, but Carol had been her best friend since high school and had been her college roommate.

"What the hell?"

Her voice startled the two women on the bed, and Carol gasped in surprise. She blinked twice and stammered, "I didn't think you were coming home until tomorrow?"

"I wasn't scheduled to return until then, so I thought I'd surprise Sara with an early homecoming, but I can see the surprise was on me."

Sara pulled the sheet over her naked body, but would not meet Eli's eyes.

"This doesn't surprise me from her," Eli glared at Sara, "but you, my best friend for almost thirty years. Seriously, Carol?"

"I never intended for this to happen. You've been spending so much time on the road, and Sara and I would get together when she was lonely. It just seemed to grow from visiting as friends to more."

"I was working to support this family," Eli growled. "How long has this been going on?" She watched as her best friend hung her head.

"About six months. I wanted to tell you Sara and I had fallen in love, but I haven't found the right time or words to tell you."

"Well, it seems you just did. I'm leaving now, before I do something I'd live to regret. I'll be back in three hours, and I want you both gone." Her glare fell on Sara. "You can come by Saturday afternoon, and I'll have your belongings packed and on the driveway. Leave your keys on the counter in the kitchen." She turned to leave, then stopped and turned around. "Both of you."

†

3

Eli stormed out of the house, and as tears welled in her eyes, she backed her truck out of the garage. The pain from the betrayal of a long-time friend hurt worse than the loss of the woman she thought she loved. Eli and Carol had been through so much over the years. She couldn't believe what she had just discovered in her home. Rage burned deep inside her, and she needed to find a safe method of burning it out.

She drove to the beach and pulled into one of the public restrooms. Her suitcase was still in the backseat. She opened it to take out shorts, a T-shirt, and her favorite running shoes. Eli changed and dropped her dress clothes in the truck before walking to the beach.

Angry cries from a seagull made her look to the beach where several birds were fighting over scraps of food leftover from a visitor. "I guess I'm not the only one pissed today," she spoke to the birds. The victor grabbed the last piece of bread and took off in flight, followed by the others in hot pursuit. *I won't chase after Sara, or Carol for that matter. It's time for me to move on.*

†

After stretching, Eli started down the beach in a slow jog along the wave-packed shore, steering clear of the soft, thick sand that would slow her down and further ignite her fury. She needed speed and distance to burn out the storm of emotions running through her body. Her heart pounded in her chest as her feet thundered down the beach. When Eli realized she had been in full-out sprint for several minutes, she slowed her pace and turned to see the restroom on the roadside. It was four miles from the one where she parked. *Damn, I've never covered that much ground so fast.* Eli turned and began walking toward her truck as the sun began to sink to the horizon. The sea breeze felt cool as it caressed her sweat-

4

drenched skin, leaving white salt stains on her dark shirt. *Man, that felt good, but not a good time to be without something to rehydrate.*

†

When she reached her truck, she kicked the sand from her shoes and climbed inside to go in search of something to quench her thirst. Eli pulled into the first convenience store she came to and stopped briefly at the beer cooler. *Would taste good, but not what my body needs right now.* A look to the left brought her to the sports drink section, and she pulled out two of her favorite flavors. She cracked one open and took a long drink before walking to the counter to pay. *Damn, tastes good.* She sat her drinks down on the counter and pulled out her wallet.

A young cashier with pink and purple streaks in her dark hair smiled at her. "Can I interest you in some lottery tickets? The first drawing of the week is tonight, and it's over a hundred million."

"Why the hell not? Give me five quick picks and two of those scratch-off games, but I only want winners," she joked.

"Winning tickets coming up. You'll have to come take me to dinner if you win the big one," the young woman replied, flirting with Eli.

Eli chuckled. "If I win tonight, you can pick anywhere you want to eat."

"I'll hold you to that," the young woman said with a wink as she handed Eli her change. "Good luck."

"Thanks, my luck has been shitty today, so maybe this will change it." Eli left the store and walked to her truck. As she climbed inside, her stomach growled. Eli didn't feel like eating but knew her body well enough to understand it would be persistent with its complaints until consuming some

5

calories. Passing fast food restaurants, she drove off the beach and stopped at a small Greek shop for a chicken pita, fresh-made hummus, and a Greek salad.

†

Eli let out a deep sigh of relief when she pulled into the drive and there were no other cars in sight. She opened the garage door and drove inside, closing it behind her. After removing her suitcase from the backseat, Eli walked around and grabbed the bags holding her dinner and the lottery tickets. She placed the bags on the kitchen counter and took her suitcase into the master bedroom. Disgusted by the sight of the unmade bed, she stripped the linens and tossed them in a hamper. *I wonder how many times I've slept on sheets they made love on.* The thought threatened to bring her anger back, so she pushed it from her mind. *No need to worry about it now.* Taking clean sheets from the closet, she remade the large bed. *All fresh now.*

Her stomach growled loudly, reminding her of the dinner that awaited her in the kitchen. "Time to eat."

After eating she glanced at the scratch-off tickets and decided they could wait until after she showered and got comfortable. *Thirty minutes won't change the outcome.*

The hot water pelting her skin relaxed her, and when she pulled on shorts and a T-shirt to sleep in, Eli decided to call it an early night. The tickets were forgotten for the moment. A quick email to her boss to confirm the next day off and she climbed between the crisp sheets. She worried the emptiness of the house and the emotional angst would make her toss and turn all night, but Eli felt a strange sense of ease and drifted into a deep sleep.

CHAPTER TWO

Eli rinsed off in the shower the next morning and poured a travel mug of coffee. Her first stop would be to purchase boxes from a moving company. The sooner she could get Sara's belongings out of the house, the faster she could move on with her life. There was a surprising bounce to her step when she reached the store and came out with a large stack of moving boxes and a roll of tape. As she drove home, her thoughts returned to the day before and, strangely, she would miss her best friend more than her lover of three years. She carried her purchases into the house and began assembling the boxes.

The closet was the logical place to start, and Eli took great joy in ripping the clothes from the hangers, not bothering to fold them before tossing them into a box. Shoes came next, and Eli took a large garbage bag from the kitchen pantry, and stuffed them inside. Sara had loved to shop for shoes and had three times as many pairs as Eli. Heck, she had at least two pairs in her own closet which were twice as old as the relationship Sara had so easily tossed away. Some things were just too hard for Eli to give up on. A lover who betrayed her wasn't one of them. She sat on the side of the bed. *Was there a sign I missed that Sara and I had problems? We seemed to be coasting along on cruise control, so where did we go wrong?*

Eli's eyes scoured the shelves of pictures from various vacations and events they had attended. They were both smiling and appeared to be in love and having a good time. She glanced at a half-full box of scrubs and then walked over to the shelves and dropped each framed photo into the box. Eli left only one picture on the shelf. She was standing between Carol and Sara on a beach in Jamaica. Shaking her head, Eli picked it up and dropped it into the box. Three boxes down and she was ready to tackle the dresser. Grinning, she pulled out the top drawer and dumped it into an empty box. "Damn, that felt good." Laughing, Eli emptied the rest of the drawers into boxes and moved into the bathroom. "Not much here to worry about." She was giddy and on the verge of breaking out in song as she tossed her fancy electric toothbrush and bottles of perfume into a box of matching underwear sets.

Done in the bedroom and bath, Eli walked through the rest of the house. Other than a few pictures, there was little left of Sara. The furnishings, appliances, and other small items were all purchased before Sara moved in with her. Returning to the bedroom, Eli looked at the boxes. Three years together and Sara had amassed six boxes of their life together. Eli taped the boxes closed and carried them to the foyer. She would carry them out to the driveway on Saturday as promised.

Her eyes landed on the counter by the garage door. A simple silver "S" key chain sat next to Sara's garage door opener. Eli had forgotten about it, but Sara hadn't. Carol's keys struck Eli in the heart. It was a picture of the two of them from their college graduation. They both wore smiles that said they were ready to conquer the world and make it theirs. Beneath it was a simple note scrawled in Carol's handwriting. *I'm sorry.*

Carol had always been her rock, and nothing prepared her for this betrayal. Nothing ever could.

Her emotional dam burst and tears ran down Eli's face. Her body slid to the floor, and she buried her face in her hands as her tears turned into uncontrollable sobs.

When her tears abated, Eli walked into the bedroom and changed into running clothes. Running had helped clear her head yesterday as it had many times before and she hoped the physical activity would work the magic again.

†

Eli locked the door behind her and began walking. Thirty minutes later, she was in a full run, her body soaked with sweat. She stopped to take a drink of water and felt a stream of sweat run down her spine. Physically spent from the exertion Eli felt an emotional high releasing her tension with every drop of sweat that fell silently to the asphalt.

†

Returning home, Eli walked to the refrigerator and plucked out a fresh bottle of water. She took a long drink and placed it on the counter. Her eyes landed on the scratch-off tickets, and Eli reached into a bowl, took out a quarter, and began scratching off the hidden numbers. Two fifty-dollar symbols then several odd denominations until she reached the

9

final block. Her fingers worked frantically to reveal the third fifty-dollar symbol. "Bingo," she shouted, then reached for the second ticket. "No way," she mumbled as three five-hundred-dollar symbols came in to view. She remembered the flirtatious young clerk who had sold her the tickets and her promise of dinner if she hit the big one. It wasn't the lottery win, but she would give the clerk two-hundred and fifty dollars of the winnings for bringing her good luck. Eli tucked the two winning tickets and the list of quick pick numbers into her wallet. She would shower and take a drive out to the beach to cash in her winning tickets and grab some seafood. Eli hoped the young woman was at work so Eli could share her winnings. It wasn't quite what she had promised, but she felt confident the young woman would accept her gift and allow her to bow out on dinner. She was way too young to take out on a date, and Eli wasn't into one-night stands.

CHAPTER THREE

Dressed in her favorite jeans, black leather boots, and a Garth Brooks T-shirt, Eli drove to the beach. A cute smile welcomed her when she walked into the store.

"You're back," the clerk purred.

"You fulfilled your part of the bargain and sold me two winning scratch-off tickets," Eli replied as she pulled out her wallet. "Now it's my turn to share." She handed the two tickets to the clerk.

"Awesome, you won five hundred and fifty dollars. I can pay this out here if you'd like."

"That's why I came out here."

"Cool," the clerk replied and opened her register. "Do you mind a few twenties?"

"They spend just as fast," Eli said with a wink.

Blushing, the young woman counted out Eli's winnings and handed the bundle of bills to her.

Eli accepted her winnings and then began counting out two hundred fifty dollars and handed them to the clerk. She glanced at the woman's name tag. "Not quite millions, Emily, but I think this should buy you and a friend a nice dinner."

Emily's face turned into a pout. "Does this mean we aren't going to dinner?"

"I'm afraid not, sweetheart, but thanks for changing my luck."

Emily spotted the remaining ticket in Eli's wallet. "Did you win the big one?"

Eli chuckled. "I forgot to check for the numbers."

"Give it to me, and I can run it through the scanner for you."

Eli handed her the ticket and waited.

Emily scanned the numbers on the ticket. "Oh my God. Oh my God, it was you," she screamed. "There was a solo winner of a hundred-four-million-dollar pot, and you have the winning ticket."

"What?" Eli took a step back. "Are you playing with me?"

"I swear to God; you are the winner." Emily printed out the winning numbers and then showed her the numbers on the second line of her ticket. "See for yourself."

Eli looked at the numbers and felt faint. She grabbed the edge of the counter for support. "Holy shit, you're right."

"You are the first big winning ticket, I've sold. Can I get a picture?"

"What? A picture? Sure."

Emily raced around the counter and snapped a selfie with Eli. "You have to contact the Lottery office in Tallahassee to arrange for this payment. Congratulations." She was beaming with excitement. "What's your name?"

"Eli Fortner," she replied still stunned. "Thanks, Emily." Eli placed the ticket in her wallet and rushed out to her truck.

"Holy shit," she repeated as she fired up the engine and pulled out onto the street.

†

Eli rolled down all the windows and opened the sunroof to let the fresh air rush into the truck. *I'm a millionaire.* She drove down the beach and pulled into a parking lot to watch the sunset. Eli picked up her phone and was about to hit the speed dial for Carol and then stopped. Instead, she dialed her brother who would be driving home from work.

Mark answered on the second ring. "Hey, Sis, everything okay?"

"Yes, Mark, but I need you to pull over to the side of the road.

"I'm at a gas station pumping fuel. You sure everything's okay?"

"Yes and no."

"Hang on a sec."

Eli could hear him replacing the nozzle on the pump and climb into his truck. "Okay, I've got you on speaker, and I'm sitting down. "What's going on?"

"The good news is I won the lottery for a hundred-four-million-dollars."

"Are you shitting me?"

"No, Baby Bro, I'm serious. I just found out, and you're my first call."

"That's fantastic news. Wow, it's freaking incredible. Why am I your first call instead of Sara?"

"That's the bad news. I arrived home from a business trip yesterday a day early, and I caught her and Carol in bed."

"What the fuck? Carol, your best-friend-since-the-beginning-of-time Carol?"

"Yeah, it was quite a day yesterday. I lost my lover and best friend in a matter of minutes."

"I'm so sorry, Eli, you deserve better than that. What a piece of shit. I know you probably took Carol's behavior the worst. Are you okay?"

"I should be devastated, but you know I feel an odd sense of relief. And, I just won a shitload of money, so I can start over and do whatever I want."

"Damn straight you can. I am happy for you. You have a lot of planning to do. Payments or lump sum, yadda yadda." He chuckled. "I'd stay anonymous if I were you or every long-lost relative will come a knocking on your door."

"That's a good idea. Hey, would you mind if I drive up tomorrow and you can help me plan?"

"You know you're welcome anytime. Come tonight if you want."

"I can't. I promised Sara I'd leave her stuff out on the driveway tomorrow. I'll put it out early and hit the road."

"You're a better person than me. I'd light her shit on fire."

Eli broke out in laughter. "The thought has crossed my mind more than once. Screw it. I'll put her boxes out tonight, pack a bag, and head your way. Maybe it will rain tonight."

Mark chuckled. "That's the spirit. Have you eaten yet? I'm grilling steaks."

"I'll grab something on the road, so don't wait on me."

"I'm gonna toss an extra on the fire for ya, so just eat enough to hold you over."

"Deal. Love ya, Bro."

"Love you most. Drive careful. I've never met a millionaire so don't cheat me out of the pleasure."

"You got it. See you in about four hours."

†

Eli started her truck and drove home to pack a small bag and place Sara's boxes out in the driveway. An hour later, she was on the road driving north.

Food, I need food. Eli pulled into a drive-thru and ordered two cheeseburgers, fries, and a large drink. She unwrapped the first burger, cranked up her stereo, took a bite, and returned to the road.

The trip to her brother's was an easy route, and one she had made many times. She finished her meal and sang along with the radio, and as the miles slipped away, she began to dream. For months she had scoured the internet looking for the perfect piece of property in western North Carolina. Eli kept returning to the same listing for weeks. The two hundred acres was perfect. A small cabin was high on the mountain, and the property met all her requirements. A fast-flowing stream, abundant springs, mature hardwood, cleared land for pastures, and garden spaces. All it needed was her. The price was way out of her range, but the photos of the property called to her. *Stop the presses. The price didn't matter anymore. She could afford the property and many more.* Her grin widened, and her foot got a little heavier.

"Damn, I better set the cruise, or I'll start my new life paying a speeding ticket."

Eli's phone was synced to the truck, and she scrolled through her contacts until she reached the number for her realtor in Asheville and hit call.

Jenna, her realtor, picked up after four rings. "Hey, Eli, what can I do for you?"

"Sorry to call so late on a Friday, but I need you to work on a cash deal for the Brewer property."

"Seriously, Eli?"

"Yes, it was out of my price range, but I'm coming into some money soon, and I want that property."

"I'll contact the broker tomorrow and start working out details. Can you swing a down payment next week if it's needed?"

"It won't be a problem. Just let me know how much you need."

"I'll keep it as low as possible. The property has been on the market for quite some time, so I'm betting the seller is motivated. I'm ready to wheel and deal for you."

"Thanks, Jenna, keep in touch."

"I'll let you know as soon as I've got a deal in the works. Congratulations, Eli."

"Thanks, Jenna. I look forward to meeting you soon."

"Likewise, Eli. Goodnight."

A green road sign came into view. Montgomery was only thirty miles ahead.

†

When Eli turned onto I-85, a light rain began to fall, and she realized it had been several months since she had seen her brother and his family. Time seemed to pass quickly, and she was eager to see them and her Blue Heeler pup, Cruz, they were raising for her. The pup had been a gift for Sara, but Cruz had not bonded well with her and became aggressive toward her, nipping her several times. Maybe the dog sensed something Eli had failed to notice. Sara had become jealous of the bond between Cruz and Eli, so Mark agreed to foster the pup to work on her behavior. They had two medium-size dogs who would give Cruz playmates and keep her in line. Sometimes though, it was hard to tell who the Queen of the Castle was. Mark's two sons, Mitch and Brad, also worked well with the rambunctious young pup, but it was Mark's wife Laura who welcomed her into the family.

Eli understood Cruz was a handful to deal with and from a high-energy breed who loves to have "work" to do. Herding was in her blood, but she would retrieve a thrown ball until she was ready to pass out from exertion. Eli planned for her to move to North Carolina, where she would have acres to run and play. Eli would have plenty time and love to shower onto the pup she missed so dearly.

The rain ended, and the rest of the short drive went quickly. The boys must have been in the front office of the home playing videos, because as soon as her lights flashed in front of the house, Mitch and Brad came barreling out of the house.

†

"Aunt Eli," Mitch cried out. Her eighteen-year-old nephew swooped in and wrapped her in a bear hug.

"My goodness, you've grown another six inches," Eli exclaimed as he released her.

"He should have. Mitch eats everything in sight," younger brother Brad reported.

"Mitch's not the only one who has grown. Damn, I have to look up to you, too, now. That is just not right." Eli hugged Brad, now fourteen, and stepped back to look at them both. "You sure have grown."

"Naw, you're just shrinking, Aunt Eli," Mitch teased.

"I am far too young to be shrinking!"

"Not according to Dad. He says you're older than dirt."

"He does, huh? Do I need to remind him he's only three years younger?"

Mitch grinned. "Naw, we already know he farts dust."

"Stinky dust, too," Brad added.

"Well, it is a family trait, and I bet the two of y'all keep right up with him."

"Don't cha know it," Mitch said. "Where's your bag? I'll carry it in for ya?"

"The bag's in the back seat, but you better let your little bro get it. You have to carry this old lady inside."

Mitch laughed and picked her up before she could stop laughing. She smacked his arm. "Put me down, ya goof. I was only teasing."

Mitch placed her on the ground. "It would have been a piece of cake."

"Maybe so, but I can't have you damaging my frosting."

"Now who's the goof? Is it true you're a millionaire?"

"I will be as soon as I go to Tallahassee to claim my jackpot."

"Wow, I've never met a millionaire." Brad grinned, and his braces flashed in the glow of the streetlight.

"Holy cow, when did you get braces? Oh my gosh, both of you?

"Two months ago."

"I reckon it was way past time to visit."

"We've missed you," Mitch said, as he swung the door open and Cruz came flying through the house.

Eli knelt and hugged Cruz, who was licking her cheek. "Oh, I've missed you too," she said between fits of laughter. She placed her hands on the sides of the dog's face. "I hope you're ready to go to North Carolina."

"You're moving to North Carolina?"

"Yeah, Mitch, I hope to soon."

"Hey Big Sis," Mark said as Eli walked into the living room.

"There's Florida's newest millionaire," Laura said from the couch.

"I know, will somebody pinch me to prove it's not a dream."

Brad reached over and pinched her arm.

18

"Ouch, you didn't have to take skin," she cried out.

"Nope, you're not dreaming, Eli" Mark chuckled. "You have got to remember who you're around when you say stuff like that. These two knuckleheads adore you and will do anything you ask."

"I've already found out. Mitch was all set to carry this old lady inside. It seems their dad told them I was old as dirt."

Mark chuckled. "I may have mentioned it on occasion. Are you ready for some steak?"

"You know I can always eat your cooking."

"I'll put your bag in my room," Mitch said and disappeared.

Eli frowned. "I hate taking over his room."

"He would sleep out in the fort we built him to have you spend the night. I don't know why he loves you so much."

"The same reason you do," Laura said as she walked over and hugged Eli. "You have to ignore all this manly testosterone. I've given up trying to understand any of them." She winked. "Come on let's get you some food."

"We saved you some tofu, Aunt Eli." Brad giggled.

"Alright," Eli responded and punched him in the shoulder.

"Ouch, what was that for?"

"The pinch, and not eating all the damned tofu."

"You're safe, the Tofu Queen was off duty tonight." Laura smiled. "There will be plenty for the boys tomorrow though."

"Plenty what?" Mitch asked as he returned.

"Tofu." Brad groaned.

†

The group sat around the table as Eli devoured the delicious steak. "I can't believe the fort is still standing. What is it, about ten years old?"

"You and Dad did a great job. Brad practically lives in it after school."

"You used to also, before you learned about girls." Brad rolled his eyes.

"I don't think I need to remind you about all the girls who text and message you," Laura told her youngest as she ran her hand through his hair.

Mark smiled at her. "They must have gotten the chick magnet gene from you, Eli. Good lord knows I didn't have girls knocking down my door."

"You got the one that counts." Eli winked at Laura.

"That's why I love you, Sis. You say the sweetest things." Laura walked to the refrigerator. "Can I get you a beer or a glass of wine?"

"A cold beer would be great."

"I think I'll join you."

"I knew you would." Laura handed them two beers. "O'Doul's for the boys?"

"Oh, heck yeah, we have to celebrate," Mitch reminded them.

Laura brought three low-alcohol beers and passed two of them to her sons. They popped the tops and raised their bottles. "To the first millionaire of the family," she toasted. "Has it sunk in yet?"

Eli placed her bottle on the table. "I don't think it will until I have the check in hand."

"When do you plan on going to Tallahassee? Do you need a bodyguard? I'm on Spring Break next week."

Eli looked at Mitch. "I'd love a bodyguard, but is that how you want to spend your spring break?"

He shrugged. "Dad can't get time off, so it beats hanging around here."

"Well, you know, Destin isn't too far off the path to take a side trip."

Mitch's head popped up. "Are you serious?"

"What about your little brother?"

"He's already signed up for a baseball camp. So, it's just you and me."

"Okay with you two?" She looked at Mark and Laura for confirmation.

"Good thing you won the lottery. You haven't seen him eat. You're going to need big bucks to keep him fed. Tofu is our cheapest option here."

Eli looked from her brother to her nephew. "I promise you no tofu next week unless you are having withdrawals."

"Not a chance." He gave her his sweetest smile. "Can we get sushi?"

"Absolutely."

Laura shook her head. "Did you change the sheets on your bed to get rid of the boy funk?"

"Yes, ma'am, she's all set."

"Thanks, Mitch. I hate kicking you out of your bed."

"No problem Aunt Eli. I'm just glad you're here."

"Me too. I can't believe how long it has been."

"Time flies."

"Speaking of which, you boys need to hit the sack. Brad has a ten o'clock game tomorrow, and I know you'll both be hard to get up in the morning. Say goodnight and hit it."

The boys groaned but kissed everyone goodnight.

"I'm going to bed and let you two dreamers have some time together," Laura said.

Eli smiled. "I won't keep him up too long."

"Thanks, he can be the biggest bear to get out of bed on a Saturday."

"Love you, too, honey." Mark smacked her butt as she walked by.

Cruz walked over and placed her head in Eli's lap. "She's missed you, too."

Eli stroked her head. "Will it be okay for her to go to North Carolina with me? I know Laura and the boys have grown to love her."

"They have, but she mopes around for days after you leave. We love her, but she loves you more."

"I could use the company."

Mark sighed. "I'd be lying if I said I was sorry Sara was gone, but I know it has to hurt."

"I guess love is blind. I didn't see this coming, but I think it was perfect timing if ever there was such a thing for a breakup."

"Stupid bitch will regret her actions once she finds out you're a millionaire. I bet she begs you to take her back."

"She can beg all she wants, but I'm not looking back. Time for me to live for me."

"I'm happy to hear that. You've worked hard all your life."

"We both have. Do you think you'll be ready to retire soon? More importantly, do you still want to move to North Carolina?"

"Yes, to the move, but I'm not sure when we can retire. Laura is still a few years away, and the boys are still in school."

"Would a million dollars help to speed that along?"

Mark's head snapped up, and he scowled. "I can't take your money."

"Well technically, it's money from the state of Florida Lottery, and I can use it any way I want. I wish to give you the money to pay things off and provide a nest egg and college tuition for the boys if they go."

"No, Eli, it's just not right."

"I will be forever offended if you won't accept it. I need the last of my family near me and money will never be an issue for any of us again."

"Mitch has already asked if he could move in with you next year after he graduates. He loves you just a bit."

"I'd love to have him as a partner until the rest of you can join us. I could use all the muscle he's gained. Do you still want to take a crack at building a log cabin?"

"Love to, yes, but I'm not sure if I'll have the skills to do it."

"I called Jenna on my way and asked her to work on a deal for the Brewer place. There's a beautiful building site, around four thousand feet which would be ideal for you."

"I know you've told me about the place before. It sounds almost too good to be true."

"If you can decide on a plan, I can have a builder start on the cabin, and if you want to finish the inside yourself, we will make it an option."

"It would be nice to have a shelter over our heads right away."

"Trust me, with all the ideas running through my head you will have plenty of opportunities to build structures. Chicken coops, smokehouses, barns, spring houses and more."

"Damn, I don't think I'll sleep a wink tonight."

"You better get some rest. We have big plans to discuss tomorrow after the game."

Mark looked down at Cruz who still had her head resting in Eli's lap. "Kiss your mama goodnight and let's go to your kennel."

"Goodnight, baby girl. Mama loves you." Eli kissed the dog's head and accepted a lick to her cheek. "Maybe you can go to the ballgame tomorrow." She looked at Mark.

"She goes every week. I think Mitch enjoys playing fetch with her more than watching his brother play."

Eli stood and stretched, then hugged her brother. "Goodnight, Baby Bro. Love you."

"More. Come on Cruz, let's call it a night. See you in the morning, Sis."

†

Eli walked into the bedroom and opened her bag to pull out her hygiene kit. As she walked past the office, she could hear Mitch talking in a low voice. She tapped on the doorframe with a grin. "Kinda late for a call isn't it? Goodnight, Mitch."

He rolled his eyes. "Goodnight, Aunt Eli."

Eli brushed her teeth and tossed back the covers. The sheets smelled fresh, and would feel great on her skin. She slipped out of her jeans and opted for a T-shirt and shorts to sleep in. Eli covered her body with the sheet and stretched her arms above her head. Her brain swirled with activity, and she worried Mark wouldn't be the only one with busy brain tonight.

†

Mark crept into the bedroom, hoping to keep from waking Laura.

"I'm awake, so you don't have to trip over something trying to be quiet." A soft chuckle came from the bed. "I thought for sure you two would be up for hours."

"I think we were both tired. Eli dropped another bombshell on me, though that might keep me awake all night."

"Goodness. What now? She's not pregnant, is she?"

24

"Ha! Wouldn't it be awesome if a mini Eli was running around?"

"So, don't keep me in suspense. What else?"

"She's giving us a million dollars of her winnings to pay off bills, build a nest egg and college funds for the boys. Eli wants us to live with her in North Carolina."

"A million dollars? Are you kidding?"

"Nope, I told her you had a few more years until retirement and the boys would need to finish school before we could consider moving."

"With this kind of jumpstart, we could afford to move after Brad graduates. I'm sure Mitch wants to go already."

"Maybe next year after graduation, and this summer if she's ready for him."

"If it weren't for the boys' school, I'd be ready to go now. I'm getting burnt out on all this political crap."

"I know, sweetie. I've moved around so much, I don't have a hope of drawing much of a retirement, but I don't think it matters anymore."

"You and Eli have been dreaming of this for a while. Soon it will be a reality."

"She wants us to draw plans for our cabin in the clouds. She'll have it dried in, and we can finish the interior if that's what we want, or the contractor can finish the entire project."

"Let them do all the work, and we can focus on making it home. If I know you two, there will be ample opportunity for you to build things."

Mark smirked. "That's what Eli said. I guess we have some thinking to do."

"Come to bed. You've got all day tomorrow and Sunday to plan. Get some rest. I know it's been a hectic week for you."

"Love you, honey." Mark kissed his wife.

"More. Goodnight and sweet dreams. Just don't knock me out of the bed building a log cabin in your sleep."

"I'll try not to," he promised.

†

Eli wasn't sure she had slept much at all, but when she heard someone moving around in the kitchen, she got up. A glance at the clock read seven, so she must have slept. She climbed from the bed and made her way to the kitchen. Mark was removing items from the refrigerator.

"Good morning."

"Did I wake you?"

"Nope, it was past time for me to get moving. I can't believe I slept this late."

"You ready for some tofu Shit on a Shingle?"

"SOS yes, but not that gawd awful tofu. It's almost criminal to make those boys eat it."

"They enjoy some of it though they won't admit that. I won't ruin a good batch of SOS though."

"What can I do?"

"Pour a cup of coffee and keep me company while I work my magic. In a bit, you can make the toast."

"That sounds easy enough."

Cruz heard her voice and started whining. "You can also let your daughter outside to pee."

Eli set her coffee cup on the counter and walked to the laundry room. She opened the door to the kennel. "Good morning, baby girl." Cruz raced her to the door and with a soft paw, hit the bell to communicate her need to go outside. "Off you go," Eli said and opened the door.

CHAPTER FOUR

Whit Brewer sat on her front porch to enjoy the crisp, North Carolina morning breeze. Her grandpa shortened her name, Whitney, when she came to live with her grandparents at eight-years old. "It's just too long for me to holler out," he'd tease her as she helped him around the farm. Whit seemed to fit her much better anyhow. It didn't take her grandparents long to realize how special she was at an early age. Not only was she brilliant, but Whit also had a way of sensing things she couldn't quite explain.

Her intelligence did not go unnoticed. Once tested at school, her classwork was accelerated and she graduated high school by age thirteen. Educators were amazed with her learning ability, and by the time she entered MIT, she was already into second-year studies. Barely eighteen, Whit was recruited as an analyst by several government agencies. Whit understood many of the assignments were black ops projects, but she enjoyed the challenge of coming up with solutions that their best hadn't even dreamed of. The agencies kept her on retainer and several times a year they would bring her in on an assignment. The rest of the time she kept her family homestead, and authored books on advanced physics and astronomy. She wasn't wealthy, but she had everything to meet her needs, plus some.

Whit enjoyed the fact she could grow, raise, or catch everything she needed for survival. Transforming the homestead to solar power had been a snap and, her first summer home from MIT, she had made the cabin and outbuildings self-sufficient for energy. She left her grandpa scratching his head in disbelief when she took a broken-down lawn mower and converted it to wood burned fuel. "Well I'll be damned," he kept repeating as she used kindling-sized wood and chips to fuel the previous gas burner.

Being so young in college and even in high school had left her feeling socially awkward. Most of the time, older students were embarrassed when someone so young was more intelligent than themselves. Whit was okay with being alone, and most times preferred to focus on her studies rather than the parties or ballgames her classmates attended.

After her grandparents had both passed away, she contemplated moving into town or a larger city. However, Whit felt comfortable being a recluse and had no desire to leave the one place she felt at home. She drove into town for supplies but didn't venture further unless called for a mission.

Whit reached down to stroke the head of Oscar, sitting beside her. The scruffy black tomcat looked at her through veiled eyelids exposing his bright green eyes. She heard an approaching motor and turned to look at the driveway a quarter of a mile down the mountain.

"I know we're not expecting visitors." She sat up straighter in the chair and watched a small red SUV pull to a stop. "Ah, the realtor."

Whit watched as the door opened and a petite woman climbed from the car and walked to the *For Sale* sign at the edge of the road. She grabbed the post and tugged it back and forth until the earth holding it in place gave way and freed it from the spot it had rested for almost two years. The woman carried the sign and placed it in the rear of her vehicle.

"It looks like we may be getting neighbors."

Her grandparents had sold a parcel of two-hundred acres when she was young. Once when she had asked why they sold it, her grandpa frowned and said, "we needed the money for your mom." Whit had never asked for further information. She knew the property had been in their family for hundreds of years, but the remaining half of the mountain was enough to meet their needs. The family who had purchased the property had built a cabin on the property. They lived there for six months before they realized the seclusion was more than they could take. For a few years after, they would sometimes visit on weekends, but those too faded and the property had remained uninhabited for almost five years.

"Maybe someone interesting will become our new neighbor," she told Oscar, who could care less. "I know you aren't impressed unless there is a treat or extra food," she teased the purring cat. "I guess time will tell. Are you ready for a hike to see if the blackberries are ripe yet?" He stretched. "I didn't think so, but you're welcome to join me. I noticed you were getting a little pudgy around the middle."

Whit stood and stepped off the front porch, surprised to see Oscar run to follow her. "Ha! I knew that would get you up and moving. Maybe our new neighbor will have a pretty little feline who might impress you." Oscar let out a meow and rushed ahead of her. "Slow your roll I need to get a basket from the barn."

†

"Strike three," the umpire bellowed. It was a beautiful day for baseball and Eli was torn between watching Brad's game and the enjoyment Mitch and Cruz were having in the area beyond left field. Mitch would hurl a tennis ball as far as he could, and Cruz would race after it, trot over to him, and drop the ball at his feet. It was hard to tell which of them was having more fun.

"Let's go, Brad, bring them in," Mark called to his son. With runners on second and third, a base hit should give his team the lead. Brad tapped his cleats to knock off any caked clay and took his position in the batter's box.

Eli watched as the pitcher tossed a fastball right down the center of the plate and her left foot swung out and kicked Mark. "Sorry, just a reflex."

"One that never gets old. I hope Brad won't pass on another pitch that sweet. Come on, Brad."

The next pitch was a duplicate of the first, and when Brad's bat made contact, the loud ping of aluminum bat announced a solid hit. The ball left the infield still climbing, and Mark grabbed her arm as they held their breath and watched it sail over the left field fence.

"Oh my God, his first home run," Mark called out then broke into laughter as Cruz raced after the ball. "I guess he'll get it for a souvenir after we wipe the slobber off."

The crowd cheered for Brad as he trotted around the bases. Cruz had made a dash after the ball and dropped it at Mitch's feet. Mitch picked it up, wiped it off and stuffed it in his pocket. "Way to go, Lil Bro," he yelled.

Brad was in full grin as he trotted around third and got a high five from his coach and made a solid landing on the home plate. He stopped on his way to the dugout and bowed. "That was for you Aunt Eli," he called out, and several heads turned to look at her.

One of the other fathers grinned at Eli. "I'll pay you ten bucks to show up at every game if he keeps swinging like that."

Eli smiled. "I'll come as often as I can," she promised. "Way to go Brad!"

In the final inning, Brad's team held the lead and Brad made a fantastic catch for the last out.

Mark treated everyone to burgers and ice cream after the game, and Eli got a good laugh when Cruz lapped at her ice cream and sneezed at the cold treat. She loved it though and ended up eating the cone Eli offered.

†

When they returned home, Mark told the boys to clean up and get dressed. Laura was taking them out to buy some spring clothes and to buy groceries for dinner. Eli sent her boss a quick email to let him know she needed the next week off and to give him an update. He was happy for her good fortune but sad he was losing a great employee. Eli assured him if he got in a bind, she'd be willing to help and, once hired, would train her replacement if needed.

When the rest of the family left, Mark joined her in the living room. "Ah, peace, and quiet, at last."

"You know you love those boys."

"It's not the boys," he scoffed. "So, what plans do we need to make?"

"I'll know more after going to Tallahassee next week, but I think I'm leaning toward a lump sum payout. I'm thinking I

31

can invest a good portion allowing for a steady income flow. I want to buy the property and supplies in cash and carve out enough for your second home."

"I think I built the cabin ten times in my sleep last night."

"A little excited?"

"That's an understatement."

"I'll bring you a check when I bring Mitch home. I'll layover here on my way to North Carolina to seal the deal on the property."

"Expect Mitch to ask you about spending this summer with you. He's already hinting that's what he wants to do."

"I'd love to have his company, and the rest of you as often as possible. I've got some plans in place, but I'll need his muscle to help reclaim and expand the garden site."

"Laura suggested last night that when I get vacation hours starting next month, I come and help over long weekends. She knows how I want to be there."

"How much longer before she can retire from the state?"

"Two years if they will still offer early outs to top managers. Not a moment too soon."

"That will get Brad into his senior year, won't it?"

"Yes, it will."

"What about Mitch? Does he want to further his education?"

"That changes from day to day. Sometimes he wants to go into mechanic school and the next he doesn't. I think after a summer working with you, he'll get a taste of real life and may reconsider school. Or, he may fall in love with working on the homestead."

"Only time will tell, but I promise to work him hard. He can fish for fresh trout, and we can eat what we grow or buy at the Farmer's Market until our crops mature."

"Man, I can't wait to get there."

"I hope to get a good start before you do. I want to plant some fruit and nut trees and get some berries in the ground to mature as soon as possible."

"I'll do my best to get there as often as I can this summer to help."

"No worries, Lil-Bro; it will all come together."

"Will you contact your financial planner to determine the best method to take your payout?"

"I emailed him this morning. I'll be getting a call from him Monday, after he's done some research."

"Do you plan to keep your home in Pensacola?"

"At least for now in case I need some beach time. I'll get the locks changed and security upgraded when I go home."

Mark was grinning until her phone began to ring. He looked down at the table the same time as Eli and saw Carol's picture pop onto the screen. "You going to answer it?"

Eli frowned as she shook her head. "Naw, I'll let it go to voicemail. I'm not ready to talk to her yet."

"I wouldn't blame you if you never spoke to her again, the way she betrayed you."

"I've given it some thought. Enough of that though, I need your opinion on something. I want a side by side, but I can't decide between a Gator or a Razor."

"What do you plan to use it for?"

"Utility vehicle, to get me to where your cabin will be and the top of the mountain."

"More need for power than speed?"

Eli nodded. "The Gator, right?"

"Razors are great for speed and fun, but the Gator will be a much better work vehicle. Better storage and pulling gears."

"A Gator it is then. I'll look up a dealer in North Carolina when I have a chance."

"I'll do it for you if you'd like."

"That would be great. Pick out what model, too, if you will, so I'll know what to order."

"Consider it done. I'll email it to you. I want to look for cabin floorplans and local builders. I don't think I'll have the time or patience to build it myself."

"We will have plenty of projects to work on together. I will wait until the summer to prepare for chickens. You can help me build the coops and laying houses."

Cruz had been resting beside her, but she started nudging Eli's hand with her muzzle. "I think someone wants to play, Mom."

"Do you think she'll do well in the mountains?"

"As long as she can be with you every day, she'll be fine."

"We'll be back in a few then. Come on, girl," Eli called as she stood and walked to the door.

†

Cruz ran ahead of her and located a tennis ball, trotted back to her, and dropped it at Eli's feet. Eli picked up the ball and threw it as far as she could and chuckled as Cruz launched to retrieve the ball. Eli realized how much she had missed the time spent with her pup. They were still playing when the door flew open, and Mitch came out.

"That was a quick trip. Did you get all set?"

"Yes, ma'am. I'll get my bag packed after dinner. What time are we leaving tomorrow?"

"After lunch. I've got some things to take care of in Pensacola, but I hope we can drive to Tallahassee on Tuesday and then spend some time in Destin."

Mitch tossed the ball for Cruz. "I am so ready to hit the beach."

"It will be fun. I'll try not to crimp your style with the ladies."

"Ha! I wish I had a style to crimp, but I enjoy looking."

"Never hurts to look," she answered with a wink.

Mark stepped outside. "Barbeque chicken good with y'all?"

"Heck yeah," they answered in unison.

Cruz was worn out and laid on the patio floor. "Well, that doesn't happen often," Mark said.

"She's had several good workouts today." Eli knelt beside her and stroked her head. "What can I help with?"

"Nothing yet. I'm going to fire up the grill. We should have a cold one and let the boys give us a fashion show of their new duds."

"We can do that," Mitch answered and returned inside.

"I'll go wash up and grab some beer. Living room?"

"That sounds good. I'll get the chicken ready to go on the grill and then join you for the show."

Eli returned inside where Laura was putting away groceries. "Let me clean up a bit, and I'll be back to help."

"I'm almost done so get ready for the fashion show. It will take the boys a few minutes to primp anyhow." Laura chuckled. "I swear sometimes they are worse than teen girls."

†

Eli stretched out on the loveseat and waited for the show to begin. Mark and Laura joined her with fresh beers and a glass of wine.

"They should be out in just a few minutes," Laura told them as she took her seat.

Bedroom doors opened, and Brad's phone started playing music as they made their way into the living room modeling the outfits they had purchased earlier. The campy antics of the boys had them laughing in no time, and when they had finished, Mark put the chicken on the grill. Eli joined him on the deck.

"I still can't get over how fast they are growing."

"I'm here with them every day and I can't believe it either." Mark placed the chicken on the grill. "It seems like we brought Mitch home from the hospital just yesterday, but look at him now. We stand eye to eye, and soon I'll be looking up at him."

"Must be the tofu. You've been blessed with two great boys."

"Yeah, most days they are keepers, but they can also be a handful to deal with sometimes."

"Well, Baby Brother, our parents said the same thing about us. We weren't always easy to handle, but they survived and so will you."

"I keep reminding myself of that. Have things started to sink in yet?"

Eli was peeling the label off the beer bottle. "Yeah, I think so. When I thought my world was crumbling around me, it turned into something new I have dreamed of for years. Without the recent events, I'd still be working in a job I love but a life I was beginning to struggle with."

Mark walked over and wrapped his arms around her. "I'm sorry for the pain you're going through, but I'm excited for all the changes coming. I can't wait to be there with you, so we can both share our dreams. I also hope you will find someone worthy of your love. I know she's out there just waiting to meet you."

"That's the last thing I'm thinking about right now. If a new love comes so be it, but I will never be that vulnerable again."

"Just don't let your recent experience prevent you from seeing something that could be beautiful."

Eli could feel the tears pooling in her eyes as she stepped away from Mark. "I'll do my best."

"You better, or I'll come to kick your butt."

†

Cruz pushed through the door onto the deck with Brad following her. "She still wants to play," he said as he found a frisbee and sent it sailing across the yard.

Eli clapped as Cruz jumped and caught the frisbee. "I'm so glad you learned how to throw a frisbee."

"Well, it's not a toy of my generation, so it has been challenging."

"Back in the day, us old folks could be entertained for hours with a rubber disc. But in fairness, it took your dad some time to master a good throw."

"That's right. For months Eli would whoop my ass at frisbee golf, until one day it just clicked. She still beat me all the time, but at least I made it challenging for her."

"Yes, you did. Those were some fun times. I may have to make a course in the mountains. See if we can rekindle the sport."

Brad threw the frisbee several times until Cruz's tongue hung out the side of her mouth.

"I think it's time for a break for Cruz. Brad, go ask your mom for a pan to put the chicken into please."

"Sure thing, Dad. C'mon, girl."

Cruz looked at Eli. "Go ahead, girl, and get something to drink."

She trotted inside behind Brad.

"No doubt she loves you most."

"I hope she'll be happy with me."

"I can almost guarantee it; she adores you. I never told you this, but after you left the first time, it was four days before she would eat. It took Laura's coaxing to get her to eat."

"I would have come to get her if you had. I love my little dog."

"I knew she would settle in eventually. She's been a challenge, but we love her too."

†

Eli, Mitch, and Mark stayed awake until midnight talking about plans for Eli's move to North Carolina. It was difficult to tell which of them was more excited about the future. Even Cruz curled beside her and listened to their conversation.

Mark watched Eli's hand stroke down Cruz's body as they talked. There was no doubt these two had a deep bond and he hoped Cruz would provide the companionship Eli would need as she adjusted to her new life. There were a lot of changes going on for his sister and, although most were positive, losing her best friend and her partner would potentially take its toll on her emotions.

Cruz interrupted their conversation when she yawned and rolled onto her back. "I think someone is telling us it's bedtime," Mark said. "You want to put her to bed for the night, Eli?"

"Sure, I'll let her out first. See you all in the morning," she answered, and opened the door for Cruz and the other dogs.

As Eli waited for the dogs, the cell phone in her pocket vibrated to prompt her she had a voicemail waiting for her. She had forgotten Carol had called earlier. She looked to see the dogs waiting for her at the door. "Okay, girls, it's time to call it a night." The two older dogs went to their beds, and Cruz trotted to her kennel.

"Goodnight, baby girl." Eli closed the latch and turned off lights on her way to the bathroom.

†

After slipping into her sleep shirt, Eli plugged her phone in to charge. She sat on the side of the bed and listened to the voicemail from Carol. Carol's attempts to apologize did not surprise her, but her next comments did. Carol said her picture was all over the television and social media as the latest lottery winner. Eli cursed herself for taking the selfie with Emily. Carol's congratulations followed, and then she said Sara had moved in with a co-worker. Carol said she had assumed Sara would live with her, but Sara was quick to inform her she had a better offer. "I guess we both got burned by her." Eli growled and placed the phone on the headboard.

"Karma is a bitch though," she whispered as she turned off the lamp.

CHAPTER FIVE

Mitch was awake, had showered and dressed when Eli walked into the kitchen the next morning. "Good morning, guys."

"Good morning, Aunt Eli. Do you want some coffee?"

"Sure, Mitch, two sugars and some creamer, please. What's your dad dreaming up for breakfast this morning?"

Mark turned around from the stove and grinned. "You are in for one of my most recent creations."

"Don't keep me guessing. What is it?"

"Shrimp and grits with Cajun cream sauce. I've added some scallops to the recipe too."

"Damn, that sounds sinful. You took out all the calories, too, right?"

"It's not all bad calorie wise. I cooked it for the staff at work last week, and the guys raved about it for days."

She looked over his shoulder to watch him sautéing the shrimp and scallops. "Maybe we should consider investing in a food truck. I think your cooking would be a hit in Asheville."

"It can always be an option. That's something you can look into when you have time. Check out the competition." Mark winked.

"I doubt there will be anyone with your talents, but it could be fun checking them out."

"I'll volunteer to serve as your guinea pig anytime, Dad. You've never cooked anything I didn't like. Except for some of the tofu recipes Mom asked you to try," he whispered.

Mark nodded. "I am not destined to be a tofu chef, and I'm just fine with that."

"Is there anything I can help with?"

"Nope, Sis, I've got this. Enjoy your coffee. You can also let your daughter inside." He nodded toward Cruz standing at the door."

Eli placed her coffee on the counter and walked to the door. "Good morning, baby girl." Cruz trotted through the door and sat at her feet. She bent down to stroke the dog's head.

"We treat them with buffalo rings on Sunday morning. Do you want me to get her one?"

"Sure, it would be great, Mitch."

"Don't forget the other two mutts. We don't want to start World War Three this morning," Mark warned.

Mitch disappeared into the pantry and returned with treats, as three eager recipients waited for him. "Here you go girls." He gave each one a chew ring. "They love those things," Mitch said as each dog took his offering and stretched out in the living room floor.

"Those should keep them busy until we can finish breakfast," Mark added. "Will you go make sure your brother is awake? He's got batting practice this afternoon."

"Yes, sir," Mitch answered and left the kitchen.

Mark looked at Eli. "He's been awake, dressed, and ready since six this morning. His bag is at the front door."

"I guess he's excited about a road trip." Eli took a sip of coffee. "Breakfast is smelling good."

"I amaze myself sometimes." He sat on a wooden stool as he stirred his cream sauce.

"I'm glad one of us learned to cook well. I do enough to get by, but I don't have your sense of adventure in creating new dishes."

"Maybe that's something else we can work on. Even if it might not turn out the best, I know two growing boys who will eat about anything."

"I can't wait to begin my schooling," Eli replied as Laura walked out of the bedroom into the kitchen.

"Do I need to worry about what I just heard? Who is teaching who and what?"

"Mark has promised to teach me to be more adventurous in the kitchen."

"I am not cleaning up after that. Mark is bad enough on his own." She groaned.

"Now, honey, you know you love my cooking."

"No doubt, but do you have to mess up every pot and pan in the kitchen?"

"It will be a price well paid to learn some new techniques."

Laura smiled at Eli. "Mark is a great cook and a good teacher."

"Thanks, honey. Will you pull down some bowls? Mitch is getting Brad up."

"I'm awake." Brad groaned as he walked into the kitchen.

"Always just in time for food," Mark teased his youngest.

"What can I say, Mitch taught me well."

"So well, you two get clean-up duty after we eat."

"No problem, Mom. Mitch said Dad was doing shrimp and grits. It makes it worth cleaning his mess."

"Hey, now, this is a masterpiece."

"It sure looks good, Dad," Mitch said as he handed him the bowls Laura took down from the cabinet.

Eli hugged Brad. "What time is batting practice?"

"We start at one, so I need to leave by half-past twelve."

"Do you have a game next Saturday?"

"Yes, ma'am, at eleven."

"Would you mind if Mitch and I duck out early today if we promise to make it back for your game?"

"Not at all. Even if you can't make it, it's okay for you to head out."

"Are you kidding me? I have ten dollars to make."

"What? He cocked his head at her comment, and Mark broke out laughing.

"After you hit the homer yesterday, Austin's dad promised her ten dollars for every game she comes to."

"Should I feel exploited?" He couldn't keep the grin off his face as he tried a fake pout.

Eli shrugged. "I ain't passing on a chance to make a ten spot."

"Well, it's not like you need it anymore, Aunt Eli."

"It's too easy to pass on, though." She ruffled his hair.

"I hope you do something with your bed head before you go," Laura said.

"I will calm it down, Mom. It was still wet when I went to bed last night."

Laura smiled at her youngest. "I can tell."

†

After a delicious breakfast, Mitch carried their bags out to the truck. "I guess it's time for us to hit the road."

Mark shook his head. "Don't let his excitement rush you."

"The sooner we get rolling, the faster we can make it to the beach." She grinned at her brother.

"That's true. Keep us posted on how things go this week, and let me know if there's anything you need me to do."

"Start spending some money getting the vehicles and tools ordered to get me up and running."

"You may regret giving me full reins to purchase what you need."

Eli picked up her phone. "Regrets, no. I know you'll only buy high quality where I may go with a less expensive option. For once in our lives, we don't have to worry about the cost of items."

"That may take a bit of getting used to, but I assure you I am up to the challenge, Big Sis."

"Have fun with it and make them work for your business."

"I can guarantee you that. There are too many companies out there who want our business."

"Amen to that."

Mitch returned from the truck. "All set."

"Let me say goodbye to Cruz, and I'll be ready."

Eli walked outside with Cruz. She knelt and hugged her neck. "I'll be here soon to get you for good. Try not to tear the house down before then. Love you, my little mutt." Cruz licked Eli's cheek and followed her inside.

Eli hugged Mark and Laura. Brad came racing into the room and wrapped his arms around her. "Have fun at your camp."

"I will. You two enjoy the beach."

"Oh, we will," Mitch promised.

"I'll walk out with you," Mark said as he opened the front door. He nodded toward Mitch walking ahead of them. "Make him earn this trip. Put him to work if you can."

"I have plans for our little beach bunny." Eli hugged Mark and climbed into the truck. "Let's roll."

†

As Eli waited at a light to enter the ramp to the interstate, she turned to Mitch. "Dig my laptop out of the bag behind my seat and grab a pen and notepad. I need you to research some stuff for me."

"Yes, ma'am," he answered, and started digging through the bag.

"You can plug the laptop in there." She pointed to a plug. "It should connect to the truck's Wi-Fi when you turn it on."

"Sweet! Can I get this truck when you buy a new one?"

"That's a possibility. Can you wait ten years?"

"There's no way you'll wait that long, Aunt Eli. You're as bad as Dad about trading vehicles."

"Well, this one's almost paid off, so we'll have to see what the new models look like."

"That's what I'm talking about! So, what do you need me to look for?"

"For starters, I need the contact information for security companies and pool maintenance services. I need to boost security at the house since I won't be staying there often. Sara took care of the pool, so I'll need a service for that."

"Sara is a real douche bag."

"Mitch, such language. Your mom would skin us both alive for talking like that."

"I know, Aunt Eli, but what she and Carol did was so wrong."

Eli looked at Mitch. "I guess your dad told you."

"Yeah, he did."

"I won't argue with you, but, because of her actions, I'm now a millionaire, and the last laugh is on her."

"Serves her right."

"Yep, she's such a douche bag."

"Do you think you and Carol will ever be friends again?"

"Maybe after the hurt fades a bit. I don't think I will ever trust Carol again, though. Why do you ask?"

"I know how much Carol loves your house. Maybe you might rent to her someday? I don't see you spending much time in Florida once you move."

"That may be an option down the road. I'll pay it off, make it as secure and maintenance free as possible." Eli took a quick peek at Mitch. He surprised her with how intuitive he had become. He was eager to please and tapping away on the keyboard.

Mitch started with the security companies, and Eli listened to the options and chose three services to contact. He scribbled down names and numbers. "I hope you can read my writing," he said with a sheepish grin.

"Don't have to. You can make the calls while I work on some other things. Do you think you can arrange some appointments?"

"Piece of cake. What else can I do to help things go smoothly?"

"I need to furnish the cabin. Can you research furniture distributors in the Asheville area? I want heavy wood furniture that will survive two teenage boys."

"What's the cabin like?"

"It's new. It's been a while since anyone lived in it. Three bedrooms and a fourth room I'll use as an office. The entire second floor is a loft with a spacious bedroom and a large bathroom. It has a private balcony which opens to the stream."

"I hope you're planning to use that often."

"I may start off downstairs, but you can bet my bed will be close enough to allow me to fall asleep to the sound of the stream."

"That sounds great."

"Your room will also be close to the stream. You could wake and catch your breakfast." Eli watched as his head whipped up.

"It would be awesome. I'm ready."

"You only have two months left in the school year, right?"

"Yes, ma'am. I hope I can take some exams early to cut a few days off."

"I'll be settled in by then. You playing football next year?"

"No, ma'am. I can stay until the first week in August."

"Time will go way too fast for both of us. We'll have time for some fun too. I promise I won't work you to death."

"Anything has got to be more enjoyable than mowing lawns in the Alabama heat. I know it gets warm in the mountains, but the afternoon rain and the breeze keep things cool instead of turning it into a steam bath."

"There are pools in the stream that will be nice to cool off in when it gets warm."

"Will you send me some pictures?"

"Oh, you can bet I will. I'll keep you posted on what I'm working on and what I find in the area."

"Dad says there are waterfalls close."

"I would guess at least a hundred within two hours. Is that something you'd like to check out?"

"Yes, ma'am. Dad showed us pictures of Sliding Rock and some waterfalls from when you two were kids. They were Polaroid shots, but they still had color."

Eli laughed. "I'm surprised they weren't chiseled in stone back in our day. Sliding Rock isn't far at all. I've got a new digital camera we can break in."

"That sounds like fun. What are your plans when you get there?"

"I need to inspect the outbuildings and shore up any weaknesses. There's a barn, and a couple other buildings, one I think is a laundry and outdoor shower, but I'm not sure it was ever finished." She looked over at her nephew. "You haven't seen the photos, have you?"

"You have photos? I can't believe you've been holding out on me."

"Click on my favorites in the top right-hand corner, and bring up the file named Heaven."

Mitch followed her instruction and immersed himself in studying the photos on the farm website. "I can see why you think this is heaven. I can't wait to see it for myself."

"What slide are you on?"

"Sixteen."

"I think number nineteen would make a perfect spot for your new home."

"There are two streams on the property?"

"Yes, one on each border. The one on the east, the one you're seeing, is the stronger, but both are stocked with native trout. What do you think of the view?"

"I bet it's beautiful, and you can see for miles."

"In every direction. The mist in the morning will make you feel you're in the clouds, especially in the fall."

Mitch continued the slideshow. "Snow? We have snow?"

His excitement startled Eli off the road. "Yes, there will be snow."

"This is getting better by the minute, Aunt Eli."

She smiled at him. "I'm glad you approve."

Mitch grew quiet as he completed the slideshow and looked over each photo. Eli was crossing the state line returning to Florida when he looked up from the laptop and spoke. "Can I ask you something?"

"Yes. What's up?"

"Can we skip the beach and go to North Carolina instead?"

"Whoa, Nelly. You should have warned me to pull over first." Eli pulled to a stop at a red light. "What about chasing hot chicks on the beach?"

"They can wait. I think I've gotten mountain fever."

"Well, it's your spring break. I don't mind going to the beach or the mountains."

He smiled, his braces flashing in the sunlight. "Let's go north then."

"I'll call first thing to see if we can schedule a meeting for early Wednesday in Tallahassee. If we can arrange for the security system and pool service by Tuesday, we can drive over Tuesday night."

"I'll call Dad tonight to let him know the change of plans."

"Are you sure this is what you want?"

Mitch smiled at her. "Yes, ma'am.

"Okay, then. I'll make reservations tonight."

"Do you want your new personal assistant to make them for you?"

"Why the heck not? Pull up my hotel website and reserve two rooms for Tuesday night in Tallahassee, and then rooms in Asheville through Saturday night."

Mitch followed her instruction and made the reservations. "See, I could be a great personal assistant."

Eli reached over and ruffled his hair. "You already are perfect. You ready for some sushi?"

"I'm always ready for sushi. I have to warn you, though, I'm hungry."

"Me, too, and do I need to remind you I'm a millionaire?"

"We may order two rolls then."

"Order whatever you can eat. I know you like the grilled salmon, so get it, too."

"A cold beer?" He grinned.

"I have to draw the line there, but we can get some O'Doul's for later."

Mitch shrugged. "It was worth a shot."

"Not one worth going to jail for though. You'll be legal soon enough."

"In less than a year now."

"Damn, you're getting old. What happened to my sweet little nephew?"

"You blinked, and he's all grown up."

"But I'm not ready for that." She turned on her signal to enter the parking lot of her favorite restaurant.

†

Whit filled her small basket with the first blackberries of the season. The winter was mild and spring had come early so there were a few ripe berries. As she started toward home, Oscar came trotting out from the shady spot he'd been napping in for an hour.

"So nice of you to join me."

The black cat blinked and stretched as he reached her side. Her footsteps startled a grasshopper to flight, and Oscar lunged after the insect. His attempt fell short, and he turned to look at Whit.

"I've been telling you that you need more exercise. You've grown fat and slow, my friend. Maybe we need a kitten to challenge you to be more active."

Oscar twitched his tail and trotted ahead of her.

"I knew that would get you fired up," she called. She plucked a berry from the basket and popped it into her mouth. "Not enough for jelly, but should be plenty for one of grandma's pie recipes, and maybe some pancakes tonight."

Many years had passed since her grandparents had been in her life, but there were days like today where the memory of fresh-picked berries brought them back to Whit. Her grandma would await her return whenever she went out foraging, and no matter how big or small her bounty was, gran would always act like it was the best haul ever. Whit would sometimes hear their words of encouragement float through the cabin. When she split wood for the woodburning stove, Whit thought she could smell the aroma of her grandpa's cherry pipe tobacco. As soon as she was big enough to split wood, he had given her the chore, and would sit on the steps and enjoy a pipe while he coached her skills.

She thought it was odd she had such vivid memories of them when she could barely remember what her mother looked like. Her mother had been absent most of her life, so she found it difficult to recall any memories of the woman who gave birth to her. There were photographs in albums kept by her grandma, but the smiling young woman did not resemble the last image Whit had of her mother. Whit was deep in thought when Oscar pounced out of the bushes, startling her and berries flew in every direction.

"Dammit, Oscar. Look what you made me do." Whit noted Oscar had jumped as high as she did and could not contain laughter as the hairs on his spine stood at attention. "Did you scare yourself too, smarty cat?" She knelt down and started retrieving the scattered berries. She couldn't help but pop a few of the sweet treats into her mouth.

"If I keep this up, there won't be a pie. I think I've already lost out on the pancakes," she scolded Oscar. She stood, and he trotted over to weave between her legs, loving against her. "Oh, no, sir, it's too late to smooth things over, but nice try." Whit took off at a brisk pace, causing him to run along beside her. She had to grin to herself, thinking the stealth attack was Oscar's revenge for threatening him with a kitten. "I believe I'll drive to town tomorrow and see about some kittens. It appears obvious one won't be enough to tackle the job."

Oscar raced ahead, leaping onto his favorite perch on the front porch. He stretched out in the sun when Whit climbed the steps and walked inside. She rinsed the berries and left them in a bowl of fresh water. Whit left the kitchen to return outside.

"I'm going down to the mailbox. I'll be right back."

Outsiders would think her odd for speaking to Oscar like he was human, but most of the time, he appeared to understand her better than most. She was glad she had rescued him from the dumpster at a local grocery store. More than once, his presence and companionship had proven invaluable.

Whit knew there was little chance of there being real mail in the box. The mail man put extra flyers in her mailbox to keep the spider webs from taking over. The farm was self-sufficient for utilities, the property paid off for years, and Whit didn't use credit cards, so there was little use for a mailbox. The walk was something she completed every day to maintain a routine, and get more exercise. She opened the box to find her bank statement and a grocery flyer with coupons. She closed the door and looked over at the neighboring mailbox. Would there soon be mail, she wondered? The *For Sale* sign was gone leaving an empty spot, and a quick glance found a heavy padlock still on the gate.

Whit walked up the drive, and her thoughts of a new neighbor turned to a mental review of her pantry. "Man, I hope I have all the ingredients for a blackberry pie. I've got my taste buds set on one now."

†

"Oh, my goodness, this was great food," Mitch declared as he pushed his plate away.

Together, they had devoured two large rolls of sushi, and he had ordered the salmon. Eli settled for hibachi vegetables and some fried rice. Mitch finished her rice when her appetite was satisfied. "Are you ready for a three-mile run?"

Eli watched Mitch's eyes grow wide. "Please tell me you're joking. There's no way I can run anywhere after that meal."

"I'll give you a break tonight, but I've got to get into shape to complete projects on the farm."

"Are you going to run? I feel bad if you're not because of me."

"I'm a big girl and don't mind running by myself. I'll take the night off and start tomorrow."

"I won't consume a ton of food. Or maybe we could run before we eat?"

"I've just started running again, so I may have trouble keeping up with a young buck."

"Ha! A tree sloth is more my speed. I'm gonna have to hoof it to hang with you."

"I can tell this will be fun."

Mitch shook his head. "I'm not sure I like your idea of fun."

Eli pulled into her driveway and hit the remote for the garage door. "Well, it's still standing."

"Did you have any doubt?"

"Naw, Mitch, but things are happening so fast, it makes the familiar comfortable when the future is so unknown."

"Unknown, maybe, but your future is wide open to make it anything you want it to be. If North Carolina isn't it, then you are free to go anywhere you wish, just let me make it clear, if it's Alaska or the Caribbean, I'm going too, no questions!"

"What if it's a little Podunk town in the middle of Kansas?"

Mitch grinned. "I'll stay in the mountains and see you at Christmas."

"I see how you are. Grab your bag, and let's get inside."

Eli was glad for Mitch's company. The house was quiet when they entered and felt so empty. Mitch must have thought so too.

"Alexa, play some disco."

"Shuffling disco songs," the AI answered.

"How'd you know I'd have Alexa?"

"Going senile? I gave her to you for Christmas two years ago, and you never regift."

"Okay, you got me there, but disco? Really?"

"Isn't it what old farts listen to when you need a pick me up?"

"I need to have a conversation with that father of yours about his parenting techniques. Disco's okay, but when you really wanna jam, it's got to be the Eagles. Alexa, play the Eagles."

"Shuffling songs by the Eagles."

"Take it Easy" started to play. "Now this's what I'm talking about." Eli swung her bag from side to side as she danced across the room to her bedroom. "You can have either of the guest rooms," she hollered to Mitch.

†

Eli tossed her small bag on the bed and pulled out her dirty clothes. She repacked the bag with one outfit and hygiene products for the trip to Tallahassee. She'd pack for the rest of the week later.

When she returned to the living room, Mitch was still in the guest bedroom, singing at the top of his lungs. She smiled at the fact someone his age even knew the lyrics, but he didn't miss a beat. Mark was teaching them right. Her laptop and his notes were on the kitchen counter. She turned the computer on and pulled up the first furniture website he had located. "Wow," she whispered when she opened the electronic catalog. Beautiful two-tone, log bed frames caught her attention. Matching dressers in the same colors made her first choices easy. She placed several items in the shopping cart to share with Mitch and moved on to the living room and dining room options.

"Amazing, they have everything I could dream of, including outdoor furniture for the decks and porches. Eli moved to the next site, but there was nothing which caught her attention. She looked up when Mitch entered the room. "Hey, come look at these."

"What ya got? Dad said to tell you he loves you more. I called him before it got too late. He goes to bed early."

"It happens when you get old, and you have to get up early for work. I can't wait until Mark can make a choice to get up at 0-dark-thirty because it's an option, not a necessity."

"I like your choices," Mitch said as he scrolled between items.

"What size bed?"

"A queen-size is plenty big for me," he answered.

"What type of mattress? You want to stick with the firm or go with something adjustable?"

"Adjustable would be nice."

"You are way too easy," she teased. "You good for more?"

"Yes, ma'am, what's next?"

"Go onto Amazon and start picking out sheets, towels, rugs, and anything else you would need to set up your room and bathroom."

"We need Mom for this. This is her forte."

"Let's put our selections in the shopping cart, and we can get her to approve or modify our orders."

"She'll love that. I don't know anyone else who loves to shop like her, unless it's your brother at one of the big box stores."

"I remember it took me four hours to get him out of an outdoors store once. He's worse than a kid in a candy shop."

Mitch pulled a bar stool next to Eli and began to scroll through the bed linens on Amazon. "So many choices."

"Pick out three or four patterns and place them in the cart." Eli glanced over at her phone to see the voice message light blinking.

Mitch looked at her. "It's been blinking like crazy since we got home. You going to check them?"

Eli placed the phone on speaker and pressed the voice mail button.

"You have six new messages," the automated voice announced. "First message." They listened to the first few messages from the local news channel and several financial managers wishing to offer their services. Then Carol's voice came through the speaker. "Hey Eli, I tried your cellphone several times and didn't get an answer. I hope I can see you soon and try to beg your forgiveness for my stupidity. Call me when you can. I miss my friend."

"Fat chance of that," Eli growled. The next message was Sara, and the second she began asking to come home, Eli hit the erase button.

"Will you ever speak to Carol again?"

"One day, but today is not the day."

"We all make mistakes. Don't you think Carol deserves a second chance? You've been friends forever."

Eli looked at Mitch. "Her betrayal was possibly the best thing in the world for me. I didn't see Sara was sucking the life out of me. I should give her a second chance for that, if for no other reason."

"I reckon that's why they say love is blind. It makes you see only what you want and not what's really there." Mitch grinned, and his braces sparkled in the kitchen light.

"Enough about my failed love life. How is yours? Are you seeing anyone special?" The pink flush rising to his cheeks did not go unnoticed. "What's her name?"

Mitch let out a deep sigh. "Sabrina. She's a senior at my school, but she doesn't know I exist."

"Well, I'm not high on relationship advice, but you need to talk with her, and get to know her if you're interested."

"I don't see the point. In a few months, Sabrina will graduate and leave for college next fall. Kelly goes to our church, and we've been friends for several years. I've been thinking about asking her to prom next year."

"So, go for it. I bet you'll look handsome in a tux. Just don't let your dad teach you to dance."

"Brad has been teaching me. He's a bratty younger brother, but he can dance, and the girls fight over him."

"Your dad was quite the lady's man in high school, but his dance moves weren't all that great."

"Did you go to your proms?"

"Heavens no. I was never interested, and the boys were too intimidated to even ask. Carol and a bunch of us had our own parties. No fancy dresses, no expensive dinners. Just a bonfire at the river and a few cases of beer."

"Sounds like a lot more fun."

"It was more our style. One of the girls brought a few joints, but of course, I didn't inhale."

Mitch grinned. "Of course not. Maybe I should just throw a party of my own."

"I think it's more important for boys to go to prom. I don't know why, but it seems more of a rite of passage for them."

"I may try once, just to see if your theory is correct."

"That's a smart decision."

Eli saw Mitch stifle a yawn and looked at her watch. "I can't believe it's after eleven already. You were awake early and we have a busy day tomorrow, so why don't we call it a night?"

"I won't argue with you. I'll see you in the morning. Love you."

"Love you more. Sleep well, Mitch."

"I will, Aunt Eli."

Eli shut down the computer and waited for Mitch to get settled in before she turned off the lights and walked into her bedroom. The empty bed called to her as she slipped into a nightshirt and between the crisp sheets.

CHAPTER SIX

Monday was busy, and by Tuesday morning, Eli's plans were in place. She had arranged a meeting for Wednesday morning in Tallahassee. Mitch packed their bags as Eli signed the contract with the pool service, and gave them keys and passwords to the security system. When she met him waiting at the truck, Eli tossed Mitch the keys. "You can drive."

"Sweet," Mitch said as he raced around to the driver's side and climbed in.

Eli pushed the remote to close the garage door, and pulled on her sunglasses as Mitch pulled out of the driveway. "Tallahassee, here we come."

"To the future," Mitch replied and pulled onto the road.

The meeting at the lottery office was more time consuming than she had hoped. It felt like forever had passed before she signed the last of the agreements and had the wire transfer arranged. It was two in the afternoon before she and Mitch escaped the capital city and were heading north.

"Are you okay with some fast food? I want to get to North Carolina before nightfall."

"Sure thing, Aunt Eli. A couple burgers will suit me just fine."

"We will dine like royalty tonight," she promised as she headed toward the interstate.

Once they made it through Atlanta, the traffic thinned out, and they made good time. Eli took over driving as they neared the mountains. The sun was creeping toward the horizon, but her heart was soaring. Her dreams were coming true, and she felt a weight lifting off her shoulders. She looked over at Mitch, who had been napping for the last hour. He was a great nephew and friend. Eli was thrilled he had asked to come with her and changed his mind from a beach trip to a mountain one. The change in elevation made her ears pop, and she looked over to see him stir.

"Welcome back, Sleeping Beauty."

"We must be close. My ears popped."

"Mine too. It shouldn't be much longer."

"Awesome," he said as he stretched. "Do you need a break?"

"Nope, I can wait until we arrive."

†

When she and Mitch crossed over into North Carolina, Eli rolled the windows down to breathe in the fresh air. "Home." She smiled at Mitch. They followed the GPS and found the hotel where they would spend the next few days.

After checking in, Eli climbed into the truck, she looked at Mitch. "You hungry?"

Mitch looked at her with a sheepish grin. "I'm a growing boy, I'm always hungry."

"Will a porterhouse and all the fixings fill you up?"

"I think it would be a good start."

"Let's grab some dinner, and we can crash. It's been a long day. I want to be at the bank early tomorrow to open an account before we meet Jenna for the closing tomorrow afternoon."

"Will we ride out to the property tomorrow?"

"Jenna promised the closing wouldn't take long. She'll take us out there afterward, and we can get started making plans for moving in."

"I can't wait to see this place."

"I think you will love it."

"No doubt."

Both she and Mitch ate their fill of steak, and when they left the restaurant, Eli was ready for a hot shower and a good night's sleep.

"I'll unlock the door adjoining our rooms in case you need something during the night," she told Mitch when he pulled her bag into the room.

"I'll do my best to keep the boogie man away."

"Okay, smarty pants. I may need you. Does that make you feel better?"

"Just holler, and I'll be there in a second."

"Do you want to sleep in tomorrow while I go to the bank?"

"No, ma'am, I want to do everything with you. Besides, you're carrying a large check, and you need a bodyguard."

"You have a good point there. I'll set the alarm for seven. That will give us plenty of time for breakfast before the bank opens."

"I can't even think of eating again." Mitch groaned as he opened the adjoining door. "It was a terrific meal, though, thank you."

"Thanks for coming with me. It has been nice having some time with you."

"It has been fun, and it's just beginning. I'm looking forward to seeing the new homeplace."

"Maybe we can spend a few nights there before we have to leave if Jenna got the utilities turned on, and we can get some of the furniture delivered."

"Do you want me to call them in the morning while you're in the bank?"

"What a great idea. I'll give you a credit card and the address in the morning." She reached for her nephew and wrapped him in a hug. "I love the way you think."

"Blame your brother. He taught me to think like that."

"Chalk one up for my baby brother then." She laughed. "Love you, Mitch."

"More." He grinned. "I'll see you in the morning."

†

Eli woke before the alarm the next morning, and she could hear the shower in Mitch's room. She wasn't the only one excited about the day. Her smile grew as she walked into the bathroom to prepare for her big day.

After dressing, she jotted down the address, her cell phone number, and took a credit card from her wallet. They could write the phone number and stock numbers on the laptop over breakfast. If they could deliver, Eli would buy a set of linens to get started from a local store.

The cook-to-order breakfast at the hotel was worth the price of the hotel. They feasted on eggs, breakfast meats, gravy, and biscuits as they wrote the stock numbers for the beds and other furnishings. She watched Mitch's smile grow as they wrote the numbers, and it made her wonder which of them was more excited.

When she finished her coffee, she checked the time. "The bank should open in a few minutes. Did you get enough to eat?"

"I'm stuffed to the gills and can't eat another bite."

As they left the breakfast area, she pointed to the front desk. "We've got a busy day today, so grab one of the to-go bags just in case you get the munchies."

Mitch took two bags and tucked the laptop under his arm. "All set."

Eli programmed the address to the bank into her navigation system and arrived ten minutes after they opened. "You good here?"

"Yes, ma'am, I'll get to work on our order."

"Come inside when you get done if you get warm. I hope this won't take long."

"I'll see you soon," he said, and Eli left the truck carrying a small shoulder bag.

Within minutes, Eli took a seat in an account specialist's cubical to open her account. When she handed the woman the check, her eyes grew wide at the large total.

"Excuse me for a minute."

When the woman returned, Eli was introduced to Martha Wilson, the bank president. "I am delighted to welcome you to town, and get whatever accounts you need arranged for you." She handed Eli her business card. "Please contact me if you have other needs. We offer a variety of accounts and financial plans for our customers."

"Thanks. After setting up the accounts this morning, I'll need a counter check to make a real estate purchase."

"Where will you be purchasing?"

"I've purchased a property called the Brewer Place."

"It is a beautiful property. I would love to have purchased that myself. It's a pleasure to meet you, Ms. Fortner, and I hope you will visit often."

"Thank you." Eli turned to the account manager. "Place half in a high-interest savings account and the other in checking. I need a counter check for this amount this morning," she added as she handed her a notepad with the price of her real estate transaction. "Some temporary checks, if possible?"

"If you'll give me a few minutes, I'll get these arranged for you. Would you like coffee or something else to drink?"

"No, thank you."

The woman began clicking away on her keyboard, and she stopped to ask if there would be a beneficiary or other person on the account.

"You can add my brother," Eli stated and gave the woman his information. "Can you also get me two thousand in cash for supplies?"

"No problem. In hundred-dollar bills or smaller?"

"You can make a couple hundred smaller bills. I hope to spend a night or two before I go to Florida to prepare for the move."

"We hope you will like our small town."

"I'm sure I will. I love this area."

The door to the bank opened, and Mitch walked inside. Eli caught his eye and waved him over. "This is my nephew and bodyguard, Mitch. Are we all set?"

"We hit the jackpot. The furniture will be delivered in the morning." He smiled a triumphant smile, flashing his braces.

"Great job." Eli gave him a high five.

The bank president returned carrying an envelope, and Mitch stood as she approached. "Hello, young man," she said, and then handed the package to Eli.

"This is my nephew, Mitch."

"Nice to meet you. We have a welcome package for all newcomers to town. It has a map and some phone numbers and locations of the critical areas you may need to visit. I hope this will come in handy."

Eli smiled and nodded. "Thank you. I'm sure it will."

The account manager handed Eli the check. "Let me go get your cash, and you will be set."

"That was painless," Eli said. "You want to take a quick spin around town before we go to Jenna's office?"

"Sure."

The woman returned and handed Eli the envelope.

"Thanks. Ready?"

"Waiting on you," Mitch replied.

Eli took out five, one-hundred-dollar bills and placed the envelope and check in her bag. She handed the bills to Mitch. "Put those in your wallet."

"What's that for?"

"In case I need to send you into town for something."

He grinned and tucked the bills into his wallet.

They drove around town, noting grocery and home supply store locations. They passed a John Deere dealership on the edge of town. "I wonder if your dad has placed our orders yet?"

"Only one way to find out?" Mitch took out his phone and dialed his dad and put him on speaker. "Hey Dad, Aunt Eli wants to know if you've placed her order yet with John Deere?"

"Oh, baby, have I placed her order," Mark answered. "You're about forty thousand dollars into John Deere. They offered some deals too good to be true."

"Dare I ask?"

"Two top-of-the-line Gators, and a nice mid-sized tractor with all the goodies. Plow, mower, push blade, even a dang auger. I couldn't resist."

"It sounds like you made a great deal. When will the order be ready?"

"Everything is in stock, and ready for delivery whenever you are."

"Do you have the order number? Mitch and I might want to do a little driving around the property."

"Sure, let me look it up, and I'll text it to you. How are things going?"

"Perfect so far. The bank account is open, Mitch ordered some furniture that is being delivered tomorrow, and we are about to head over to the closing."

"I am so excited for you, Sis. Are you going to stay on the property?"

"I hope so. I'd like to get familiar with the place."

"Okay, I just sent Mitch a text with the order number. Call me tonight and let me know how everything goes."

"Thanks, Mark," Eli said.

"Love you, Dad."

"Love y'all more. Have fun."

"Will do. I'll call you tonight." Mitch ended the call. He looked at Eli. "I guess I'm calling John Deere while you are closing?"

Eli turned on her blinker. "Nope, we are doing it now. We have time."

"Sweet," Mitch answered. "What are we going to get?"

"Might as well have them deliver it all. Gators first and then the tractor. We'll be putting them all to use soon."

Mitch was like a kid in a candy store, checking out all the fantastic equipment while Eli paid for the order and arranged for delivery. She finished and walked over to where he was sitting inside a model of the Gators she had just purchased. "Tomorrow will be very busy. Furniture, equipment, and some fun. Now, we have to roll."

Mitch climbed out and walked out with her. "Have I told you lately I love you, Aunt Eli?"

"It's been a few hours."

He grinned and hugged her. "I love you."

When he released her and stepped back, she answered, "Yes, but I love you more."

"Ha! No way, man."

"Let's roll. You can plug in the address for me."

†

They walked into Jenna's office, and she greeted them right away. "It's so good to meet you."

"Thanks, this is my nephew, Mitch."

"Nice to meet you, too," Jenna said as she offered him her hand.

Mitch shook it, and Eli noticed a slight blush. She would have to remember to ask him about it later.

"The selling agent is two minutes away, but come in and get settled. Can I get you two something to drink?"

"Water for me, please."

"I'll take a water, please, ma'am." Mitch held the door as they walked into a small conference room.

Jenna returned with three bottles of water. "Are you excited to move here?"

"I am beyond excited. Were you able to get the utilities turned on for me?"

"They are being activated this morning. There is only about a hundred signatures we will need," Jenna teased, pointing at the spread of papers on the table.

"Piece of cake." Eli opened the bottle and took a long drink. "Thanks for working this deal and at such a great price. I was prepared to pay the asking price if needed."

"I told you I'd work a great deal for you. You can spend the extra thirty thousand improving the property."

"We've already made a start on that this morning at the John Deere dealership."

"I hope they treated you well."

"Fantastic deal, too good to pass on," Eli answered.

"Here we go," Jenna said as she nodded toward the door. A man came in, and she made the introductions.

"Congratulations on a prime purchase, Ms. Fortner," he said as he shook her hand.

"Thank you, Mr. Jones. I've been looking at this property for quite some time."

"Let me assure you, Jenna got a steal for you on this piece of property. It's rare to find such a good plot at the price you got it for."

"She did an excellent job. I couldn't be happier."

"You ready to get started, Sam? We've got a new owner chomping at the bit to get moving."

"Yes, sorry. It looks like you have everything in order here. Let's do this."

Thirty minutes later, all the contracts were signed and copies made. With the check for the purchase transferred, Sam left the building.

Jenna looked at her watch. "Congratulations. May I buy you two lunch or do you want to go straight to the property?"

Eli looked at Mitch. "Are you hungry?"

"Yes, but I can wait if you want to go out to the property."

She turned to Jenna. "Let's eat. I've got the rest of my life to spend on the property."

"Excellent. I know the perfect spot, and it's on the way. I hope you like home cooking."

"Nothing better. Lead the way," Eli said with a smile.

The small diner was packed, but it didn't take long to get a table. "I promise you it's worth the wait," Jenna told them.

A hearty meal with portions Mitch had trouble finishing followed, and Eli decided this would be her go-to place to eat when she didn't feel like cooking.

"You weren't kidding. The food tasted terrific, and the prices weren't bad either," she told Jenna as they left the diner.

"I'm just sad they aren't open on Sundays. I'd eat here every day if I could. Are you ready to go home?"

"That sounds great."

Jenna handed Eli a set of keys. "The small one is to the lock on the gate. Maybe Mitch can open it for us when we arrive."

"I'm all over it," he replied and took the keys from Eli.

"We'll be right behind you. Let's go, Mitch."

When they climbed into the truck, Eli looked over at him. "I forgot to ask you something."

"What?"

"When you met Jenna earlier, you blushed. What was that all about?"

"Are you serious? If you hadn't noticed, she's beautiful, and she treated me like an adult, not a kid."

"You are a young adult. I still can't get over how grown you are. I still want to treat you like a kid."

"Aunts are allowed, but she was a total stranger. It made me feel good."

Eli chuckled. "You are such a goof, but I love you. What did you think about the food?"

"I was in heaven. I wanted a slice of the pie, but there was just no way. I'm thinking we may go there often." He grinned.

"At those prices, it's cheaper to bring you here than to cook for you." She turned the key to start the truck and pulled out behind Jenna's Jeep. She rolled down the windows, and the fragrance of sweet grasses from mowed hayfields filled the air.

"Doesn't that smell good?"

"It is the sweetest smelling grass I have ever smelled. Will we have a hayfield?"

"We can carve out some fields for hay. I haven't decided on animals yet, but we can always lease the fields or sell the hay ourselves." Her thoughts drifted back to scorching hot summers spent baling thousands of bales of hay needed to feed the family herds when they were growing up.

The property was thirty-five minutes out of town, and Eli concentrated on the winding road. "I bet this will be a fun drive in the winter."

"Stock up well, and you won't need to venture out often. This truck will handle anything you throw at it though."

When Jenna slowed and turned on her blinker, Eli felt her heart race. "Here we are, you can leave it open," she told Mitch as he left the truck to open the gate.

Eli pulled through the gate behind Jenna and stopped to retrieve Mitch. She followed the Jeep for several minutes until they crested the hill, and the cabin came into sight. Eli pressed the brake to take in the view.

"It looks so much bigger than the pictures."

"It's gorgeous. Look at the creek running beside the house. I bet it's got great fishing."

"Maybe we'll get a fishing rod so you can try it out," Eli suggested.

"I could handle that."

Eli moved forward and parked next to Jenna.

"Welcome home," Jenna said when Eli stepped out of the truck. "The porch light is on, so it means the power is on. Are you ready to go inside?"

"Heck yeah," she answered.

They walked toward the house and Mitch broke off to the right.

"I'll be right there," he said and walked down to the edge of the creek.

Eli nodded and walked to the front door. "Take your time."

†

Mitch could smell the crispness in the air as he made his way down to the water's edge. The creek was much larger than he imagined and the water flowed over several large river rocks, creating a soft rippling sound. "Man, this is heaven," Mitch spoke aloud. He looked toward the house and could see the deck off what Eli had described as the second-floor master bedroom. It ran the length of the house and was within a few feet of the creek. There was also a deck which was a wraparound extension from the front porch, with a sliding glass door leading into what he hoped was a bedroom. He could see Eli sitting in a comfortable chair sipping coffee as the morning came to life. "Beautiful."

Mitch noted he was standing in a small clearing and thought that, with a minimum of effort, he and Eli could build a small fire pit and add some chairs for a way to spend a quiet evening as the lightning bugs danced in the meadow across the stream. It took an effort, but Mitch tore himself away from the creek to walk inside the house.

Eli was standing in the middle of the cabin, taking in a panoramic view when Mitch entered. "Wow," was all that came out of his mouth. She turned to look at him.

"I take it you approve?"

"I'm wondering if Mom would let me finish high school here. This place is awesome, Aunt Eli."

"Don't go getting me in trouble with your mom already. You'll be surprised how fast the last year goes."

"I know. After spending the summer here with you, it will be hard to go home to Montgomery."

"I reckon it depends on just how hard I work you this summer."

"Bring it on. I'm already planning a fire pit and chairs down by the creek."

"That's the spirit. Come on, let's look at the rest of the cabin, and we can survey the outbuildings."

†

"You've got a great property here," Jenna said as they walked through the house. "The views up top are breathtaking, but you'll need a Gator to get there. There's a roughed in start to a roadbed, but it's not vehicle ready just yet. There is a possibility of easier access on the other side, but you'd need to put in a small bridge."

"So much possibility." Eli's eyes were already decorating the large rooms.

"If there is nothing else you need, I will head into town. I've got a potential new listing owner coming in this afternoon."

"Thank you for everything. This is a dream come true."

"Stop in before you head out of town if you can. Let me know if there is anything else I can do for you."

"Thanks, Jenna. We plan to take as much of this in as possible and head to the hotel tonight. Tomorrow and the next few days will be busy."

"Don't forget to have some fun. I'm not much of a fisherman, but I hear the creek is well stocked."

"I've already seen several in just a few minutes," Mitch chimed in.

Eli smiled at his excitement. She walked Jenna to the door and returned to the large kitchen. The previous owners had designed the kitchen and equipped it with double ovens, a large stainless grill, and other stainless appliances. Eli felt like she could eat for months on food that would fill the large freezer section. Her mind was whirling with items she would need to purchase to bring the kitchen to life. When they finished walking through the house, Mitch turned to face Eli.

"Are you still planning to use the upstairs area for yourself?"

"Yes, I think so. I didn't realize there was a deck on the first-floor master bedroom. Do you want to take this one?"

His face beamed, hearing her question. "I would love to if you don't change your mind."

"It's yours then. I can see you waking up and catching trout right off your deck." Eli chuckled.

"Maybe not right off the deck, but off the bank. There are several large rocks creating pools that are sure to hold some nice fish."

"We need to check out your theory soon. Are you ready to tour the outbuildings?"

"Yes, ma'am."

They walked out the front door and turned toward the rear of the property. At the bottom of the steps, Eli froze and tapped Mitch on the shoulder. He turned to look at her. "We have company," she whispered, and pointed across an open field. A doe and twin fawns were grazing on the tender grasses along the edge of the tree line. "I bet the western creek isn't too far away."

"This just keeps getting better and better." He grinned.

The first building they entered was the barn. It appeared older than the cabin but was in good shape. A hayloft looked like it was in good shape, too, and there were four small stalls, a storeroom, and an open space which would be big enough to store the tractor and Gators. A large sliding barn door covered the back entrance.

"This is perfect."

"Do you plan on having any animals?"

"I haven't decided yet, Mitch. It's good to have options. Let's go check out the other buildings."

The next building was smaller and closer to the cabin. It was a laundry room with a walk-in shower. The interior still needed to have sheetrock or some siding on three of the walls. Eli reached in and turned the shower faucet on, and water came tumbling out of the showerhead. Mitch turned the dryer on.

"Looks functional. The walls won't take much to finish. Does it seem odd the laundry room is out here instead of in the cabin?"

"Yes, but I think it will work fine. I like that there's a shower, too, so if we get messy working outside, we can shower and not track into the cabin."

"You make a good point. Do you want to use sheetrock or some wood siding in here?"

"I think wood planks would look great, and maybe add a small table and a chair or two to make it comfortable when doing laundry."

"You and I should be able to knock it out. Do you want to try for this week?"

"No, it can wait. I want the next few days for exploring, planning, and having some fun. I can work on purchasing supplies, tools, and other items while you finish out the school year."

"I hope these last two months go by fast."

"Don't rush, we will have plenty of things to keep us busy this summer, and for a long time after that."

"I know, I just can't wait to be here with you."

"I'm looking forward to it, too. Let's go check out the other building."

The third building was larger than the laundry and had at one time been a workshop. A worktable and bench lined one wall, and there were a few hand tools left behind.

"Your dad will love this," Eli said. "He's got enough woodworking tools to fill this place."

"Without a doubt," Mitch agreed. "We may need to buy a cot for him to sleep in when he gets working on a project."

"He can be a little obsessive, can't he?"

"Just a bit." He smiled.

"Why don't you grab a notepad and a pen from the truck and we can sit on the deck and make a list of items we need to purchase. You good for some shopping tonight?"

"I can handle that. You want your water out of the truck?"

"Yes, it would be nice. I'll meet you on the deck."

"I'll be right there," he said, and jogged toward the truck.

Eli walked inside her new home and flipped a switch to turn on large ceiling fans in the living area then walked through the door at the far side of the room to step onto the deck. Eli walked to the edge and sat, dangling her feet over the side. A cool breeze emanating off the water caressed her face, and the fragrance of blooming wildflowers welcomed her. "Home."

Mitch settled in beside her and handed her the notepad.

"You can make our list," she said.

"I can't promise you'll be able to read my writing, but I'll try to be neat."

"Deal. The first item, fishing gear. Fly rod or spinner?"

"A fly rod would work best."

"Okay, so make a list of the items you'll need to fish tomorrow."

Eli watched as Mitch added several items to the list, and when he appeared finished, she continued adding bed linens, some small kitchen appliances, pots, pans, dishes to get them started.

"We can do some grocery shopping after the equipment and beds arrive, or we can eat out until we move in. I'd suggest we check out the options in town until you can catch some fish for lunch or dinner."

"Sure, sounds great to me."

When they had a sizeable list made, Eli stood and stretched. "Are you ready for some retail therapy?"

"Yes, but I think we need to add a few chairs if we can find some we like," he suggested.

"I know we had some picked out at the furniture store, but I saw you looking at some today. How about we stop by there and add some to the order?"

"Perfect." He grinned.

"Let's lock up here and roll."

The afternoon was burning away as they drove through the gate, and Mitch hopped out to lock up behind them. It reminded Eli to have some extra keys cut for Mitch. That could wait until he arrived for the summer and had his own vehicle for transportation.

After stopping to add deck furniture to their order, Eli looked over at Mitch. "I don't know about you, but my lunch is long gone. What do you want to eat?"

"I don't care as long as there is a bunch of it," he answered.

"You want to go back to the diner? Maybe get some dessert this time?"

Mitch grinned. "We can work it off shopping afterward."

"I like the way you think."

After a hearty meal and two delicious slices of coconut cream pie, Mitch and Eli began their shopping adventure at the local big box store.

"You take a cart and start on your fishing equipment, and I'll start on the rest of the list."

"Okay, I'll find you shortly then."

"Hey, Mitch," she called after him. When he turned to her, she smiled. "Don't go the cheap route, get whatever you need and don't worry about the cost. We need to get you set up right. You might as well check into a fishing license, too. I don't know if you'll need one for fishing on private property, but check to find out. Do you remember the address?"

"Yes, ma'am, I've got it." He tapped his temple.

"Good, now go have some fun."

Eli stuffed the bottom of the cart full of pillows and selected two sets of sheets and light comforters. She was in the home appliance section when Mitch returned with a sizeable amount in his cart. He was wearing a sun blocking fishing hat.

"What do you think?" He pointed to his head.

"I like it."

"Good, I got one for you, too."

"Let's fill these carts and go get two more," she said as she pointed to a set of pots and pans. They filled their carts with dishes and small appliances before moving to the toiletries section. "Would you mind using the glassed-in shower upstairs for now until we can order some nice shower curtains?"

"Not a problem. I can use the one in the laundry room if needed."

"I don't think it's necessary unless you smell fishy," she teased. She grabbed a large bundle of toilet paper and paper towels. "We need to get some hygiene products and towels, too. You want to pick out your shampoo and soap? Any preference on bath sheet color?"

"Something manly," he said in his deepest voice.

She chuckled. "Pink it is then." Eli watched his laughter fade away, then selected a deep chocolate brown and hunter green set. "Manly enough?"

"Those will work fine."

"Let's take these carts to customer service and get a couple more. We need to pick out some garbage cans too."

Mitch followed her to the front of the store and got two more carts.

"I'll go get the garbage cans. Why don't you pick out the items to cook those fish you catch tomorrow, and I'll meet you over in grocery? Grab cases of water and sodas if you want some."

"Grab a coffee pot," Mitch said. "We forgot to put one on our list."

"Nice catch. I would have been a bear in the morning without coffee."

Eli picked a single-cup coffee maker and some garbage bags to go with the cans she had picked out. She chose a few items and was surprised by how her cart was filling by the time she made it to the grocery section. She picked out coffee, creamer, and sugar before locating Mitch.

"Do we want to get some deli meat, cheese, and bread for sandwiches? What type of chips do you like?"

"If you hadn't noticed already, I'll eat just about anything. I like those baked chips with turkey sandwiches."

"Okay, I'll get some deli ham and turkey. Swiss or American cheese or both?"

"Both. I'll grab some mayo and bread. Can we grab a gallon of milk and some cereal for breakfast? That should be easy."

"Go for it. How about some juice too? Apple?"

"Awesome. I'm getting hungry again just thinking about food."

"I think when I get back here, I'll find a feed store and get some deer corn, a feeder, and a salt lick for our four-legged friends."

"That would be great. I know you don't want any hunting on the property, but it would be fun watching the animals grow."

"I think there will be plenty of opportunities for your dad and you boys to hunt without being in our backyard. The National Forest is next to our property with about five thousand acres they open for hunting."

"That's good to know. I'll get the bread and condiments. Is there anything else?"

"Pick out some other snack foods, and I'll meet you at the registers when I finish in the deli."

They filled the rear of the truck and placed the cold foods in the refrigerators at the hotel for the night. Mitch smiled when he saw a six-pack of O'Doul's. "Are we celebrating tonight?"

"Put us a couple in the freezer section. I thought we'd have a brew before we call it a night."

Her phone began ringing. "Speaking of calls." She looked at her phone and saw it was Carol calling and let it go to voicemail. "Don't let me forget to call your dad."

"You got it. I'll hit the shower while the beer is chilling."

"Not a bad idea. I'll holler at you when I'm done, and we can crack one open and call home."

Eli grabbed a clean shirt and shorts to sleep in and walked into the bathroom. She turned on the shower and stripped out of her clothes. The water felt wonderful as it pelted down her body.

†

"You decent?" Eli asked Mitch.

"I've been waiting for you to appear for five minutes."

"Sometimes perfection takes a few more minutes," Eli said as she put her brush on the bedside table. "Crack us open and then call your dad."

Mitch took two cold bottles from the freezer and handed one to her. He picked up his phone and hit speed-dial for his dad.

"Hey, stranger," Mark answered. "What have you two been up to today?"

"Buying a slice of heaven and doing a lot of retail therapy, as Aunt Eli calls it."

"That sounds like fun. Do you like the property?"

"The place is phenomenal. I can't wait for y'all to see it. It's beyond fantastic."

Eli smiled at the way Mitch stretched out the word phenomenal.

"We spent the afternoon checking out the cabin and outbuildings, and they are better than I imagined."

"Sounds exciting. I'm happy for you, Sis."

"We have a large John Deere order and furniture coming tomorrow, so we'll be staying at the cabin for a few nights."

"Am I going to get my son back?" Mark chuckled.

"Yes, but I'm stealing him as soon as he gets out of school. We already have so many plans made."

"I think we'll all come for a long weekend when they get out of school."

"That will be great. I'm sure you will fall in love with the property. As soon as we get everything delivered and set up tomorrow, we're taking a ride on one of the new vehicles to see the rest of the property."

"Don't forget to take photos to share with your brother."

"We won't. I've got a digital with me, and if I can get internet access tomorrow night, we'll send you some. This place is fantastic. Better than I ever dreamed."

"It will only get better as you make it yours."

"Ours," she corrected him. "This place will always be ours."

"I just can't wait to get there, even if it is for a short time."

"Don't worry, Dad, we'll leave plenty of work for you to do."

"I'm sure you will. Eli, I hope you can get some work out of him."

"He's been a lot of help already. Definitely earning his keep."

"I'm proud of you, Son. You made a great decision to skip the beach."

"Yes, sir, I'm glad I did. I've had a blast with Aunt Eli. Tell Mom, and Brad, I said hello, and I love them."

"It sounds like you have a busy day tomorrow and you're an hour ahead of us, so get some rest. I love y'all and look forward to talking to you tomorrow night."

"Goodnight, Bro. Love y'all."

"Love y'all more. Have fun."

"Goodnight, Dad." Mitch ended the call. "He will love this place."

"I think so too. Here's to our new home," she said, and offered her bottle to Mitch.

"Home," he said and smiled. "I can't wait for tomorrow."

"Hit the sack, and I'm sure we'll both be awake early. We can grab breakfast and be at the property way before our deliveries begin."

†

The next morning, Eli found Mitch awake, dressed, and sitting on the bed, watching television when she finished dressing. "I'm not surprised you're awake and ready."

"Woke at five and couldn't get back to sleep so I snuck out for breakfast, too. Figured I could load the truck while you ate breakfast and got us checked out."

"You're not excited, are ya?"

"Maybe. Today will be fantastic."

"I think so, too. Let me pack my bag, and I'll be ready." She handed him the truck keys. "Do you want to get a luggage cart?"

"Naw, I've got this, so take your time with breakfast. The gravy is awesome this morning."

"Are seconds on your horizon?"

"That's always a possibility." He grinned and picked up his bag and several bags of groceries from his refrigerator. "I'll be back."

"You sure you don't want my help?"

"Nope, I can handle this. Piece of cake."

"I'm off to breakfast." Eli held the door open for him and finished packing her bag. She left it on the bed and left the room to get coffee and breakfast.

Mitch stepped outside into the crisp morning. "Man, I love this place." He opened the rear of the truck and placed the first load into the floorboard before jogging inside for more.

Eli poured a cup of coffee and surveyed the breakfast options. She ordered scrambled eggs, biscuits, gravy, and bacon to add to her juice and coffee.

Mitch waved as he passed the breakfast area, heading to the rooms. Eli nodded and sipped her coffee while she waited on her meal.

The cook delivered her food, and she gasped at the portions. "I'm not sure I can eat all of this."

"Mitch told me y'all have a busy day today, so you need a good breakfast."

"He did, did he?"

"Yes, he was my first customer this morning. We had a friendly chat until other guests started to arrive. He's a great young man."

"I'm blessed to have him for a nephew and friend."

"Trust me, he feels the same way about you. He adores you."

"The feeling is mutual."

"Enjoy your breakfast."

"Thanks."

Eli surprised herself by eating most of the food. She was getting a coffee refill when Mitch stepped into the breakfast area. "All done?"

"Yes, ma'am. I even double-checked to make sure I didn't leave anything in the room."

"Good job. Do you want anything else to eat?"

"I thought I may have another biscuit and gravy while you finish."

"Grab your food. You want some juice?"

"That would be great."

Eli listened to the banter between him and the cook. The bashful child had grown into a confident, polite young man. Mark and Laura had done a great job, and she was sure Brad would be just as enjoyable as he grew.

When he returned, he carried a plate brimming with biscuits covered with the hearty gravy. "I could get used to this."

"I'm glad your dad can make gravy. Mine always comes out lumpy."

"He's had a lot more practice than you, trying to keep us fed."

"You have a good point." She sipped her coffee as he devoured the biscuits.

They dropped the key cards at the front desk and took the receipt. When they stepped outside into the glorious morning, Eli turned to Mitch. "Wanna drive?"

"Absolutely," he answered, and opened the door for her before jogging around to climb in the driver's side.

"Home, James." She chuckled when he started the engine.

"Yes, Ms. Daisy," he shot back at her.

†

Mitch pulled onto the property after Eli opened the gate. She looked up the drive as she walked to the truck. The sun had risen, but the clouds hung low in the sky. The temperature was mild, but she was sure it would increase throughout the day. *What a beautiful morning.*

When she climbed in the truck, Mitch drove to the cabin. "Park over by the workshop, so we'll have plenty of room for deliveries."

"You got it, boss."

Eli turned to look at the load in the back seat. "On second thought, pull next to the porch. I forgot we had the truck loaded down."

"Yes, ma'am. I'll park it when we've finished unloading."

Working together they unloaded the truck, carrying the supplies inside.

"I swear I don't remember buying this much last night."

Mitch laughed. "We filled four carts as full as we could get them."

"Yeah, we did, didn't we?"

"Go park, and I'll start unloading the groceries."

She watched Mitch trot out to the truck. *Man, I wish I had his energy. I will start slow and build up my endurance if I'm going to survive here.* Eli opened the refrigerator and began loading it with groceries.

When Mitch returned, he asked, "Where do you want me to start?"

"Set your fishing gear on the porch, and then you can carry stuff to the bathrooms."

Mitch left the kitchen, and Eli could hear him whistling as he carried his fishing gear to the porch. When he returned, he took the hygiene supplies and linens to the bathroom. Mitch stocked all the bathrooms with toilet paper and placed towels and hygiene supplies in the upstairs bath. As he started down the stairs, Mitch looked out the front window to see a truck approaching. "We have a truck coming up the drive."

"Great, I bet it's the furniture," Eli said from the kitchen. "Let's go check it out."

Eli opened the front door and used the box of pots and pans to prop it open for the deliveries. Her assumption was correct as the truck was from the company delivering the bedroom furniture, couch, and the chairs and tables for the decks. She saw three large men climb from the cab of the truck.

The driver walked around the truck. "Good morning, ma'am. We have a load of furniture for you."

"Good morning. I'm glad you made it out so early."

"We try our best to beat the heat." He grinned. "Would you like to show me the bedrooms and how you want the beds and dressers arranged?"

"Sure, let's start downstairs. Mitch, have you decided how you want your room arranged?"

"Yes, ma'am. Do you want to follow me?"

Eli, Mitch, and the driver entered the cabin. "Wow, this is a great place."

"Thanks, we think so too," Eli answered.

After showing the man the two rooms, they walked outside where the other two men had unloaded the crates. "We'll carry the beds inside and assemble them there if that's okay with you?"

"That will be great. You can leave the deck furniture on the porch, and Mitch and I will arrange it later."

"I'll take care of it, Aunt Eli, if you want to finish arranging the kitchen," Mitch offered.

"You have a deal, young man." Eli returned to the kitchen.

"Is there anything I can help you unload?"

"We will never turn down the muscle of a young man," the driver replied. "I'm Jim, this is Pete, and the ugly one is Joe."

The younger man, Joe, turned to his partner. "When did you change your name?"

Pete snickered. "You know I got all the looks of this bunch."

Jim shook his head. "And I've got the brains and the keys to the truck. Less jawing and more work. We've got other jobs lined up for us." He shot a big grin to Mitch. "It's so hard to find good help these days."

As they began unloading cartons, Jim grabbed a bag of tools. "Bring the first bed and follow me."

Jim led them into Mitch's room and unpacked the frame sections of the bed. Pete placed a carton on the floor and looked out the glass door at the creek. "Man, what a view. I hope you like to fish. You've got a perfect spot."

"Two stocked creeks on the property. We will eat trout often." Mitch grinned.

"Welcome to a fisherman's paradise," Jim said. "Some of the best fishing in the state is in this area."

"I look forward to visiting as many of the good spots as possible this summer," Mitch said.

†

Eli heard the banter between the men and smiled as she loaded the dishwasher with new dishes and utensils and started the machine. She unboxed the coffee pot and small appliances, scattering them across the expanse of counter space. The cabin was taking shape as she made it her home.

When the deliverymen left, Mitch busied himself organizing the outside furniture while Eli made their beds. She tucked the comforter under one of Mitch's pillows and smiled. *It's beginning to feel like home.*

Mitch bolted into the cabin. "The John Deere delivery is coming up the driveway."

"Fantastic," she answered and followed him outside.

A semi-truck arrived, pulling an extended trailer loaded with equipment. Eli looked over to find a wide grin on Mitch's face. "Now the real fun can begin."

"No kidding." Mitch hopped from the bottom step, and they walked out to greet the driver.

Eli watched as a second man emerged from the cab of the truck and introduced himself as Alan Morris, the store owner. "I thought it would be great to get out of the office, visit our best new customer, and survey what other needs you might have," he told Eli.

Eli released the handshake. "We are starting from scratch, but this delivery will allow us to do some surveying of our own. I'll be moving in a week, and I'm sure I'll have another list of equipment we'll need."

"We carry Stihl and other popular brands in the store, so just let us know what you'll want. We offer excellent deals to keep our customers purchasing locally."

"I'm happy with your pricing so far, and I like to feed the local economy."

Mitch was inspecting the equipment as Eli and Alan were talking. Alan nodded toward him. "Is he your son?"

"My nephew and partner in crime. Mitch is my brother's oldest and will spend the summer with me until he finishes high school next year."

"Would you mind if we run him through the paces on operating the tractor and attachments? I think the Gators are self-explanatory."

"I'll listen, but I'm sure he'd enjoy learning to operate the different pieces. He's a quick learner, too."

"Let's get started so the two of you can have some fun."

"You'll get no argument from me," Eli responded and followed him to the end of the trailer.

"We've got everything fueled for you and brought extra fuel and supplies," Alan explained. The driver lowered the ramp and climbed up to drive the first Gator off the trailer.

Eli turned to Mitch. "Why don't you drive this one to the barn, and we'll use the second one after the delivery is complete?"

"Hang on a second, and we'll load the fuel cans and a case of oil onto the back," the driver suggested.

"You got it," Mitch said and began loading the supplies into the rear of the Gator.

The driver pulled the second Gator off.

"You can park it anywhere out of the way of the tractor," Eli said.

"Yes, ma'am," he answered and tipped his hat.

Alan asked, "What are your plans for the property?"

"I'm hoping my brother and his family will join me in a year or two. I want to build a second cabin farther up the mountain for them. We hope to do some organic farming and maybe raise some chickens for laying."

Alan nodded. "That will fit in well with the local market."

"I hope to get some fruit and nut trees planted this year and maybe bale some hay."

"When the Brewers owned the property, they grew some of the best hay in the area. I don't think it will take much to get some fields back in shape. The previous owners were city folk and didn't have a clue of the gold mine they were sitting on." He chuckled and shrugged his shoulders. "I don't know what they were expecting from mountain life."

Eli smiled at him. "I'm just thankful they were motivated to sell. I've been looking for a property like this for several years."

"You got a great piece here. A lot of good potential. You have enough acreage for just about anything you want. A stocked trout pond, orchards, or a small herd of cattle."

Mitch had returned from the barn. "I love the sound of having a trout pond."

"After the initial development, they aren't too much labor to maintain, and the local restaurants would purchase the fish without a doubt. There's a state fishery not too far who can help you build the pond and sell you fingerlings for starters."

The driver unloaded the tractor with the blade and mower already attached. Alan turned to Mitch. "Are you ready to learn how to operate this beast?"

Mitch looked at Eli. She nodded. "Heck yeah," he answered. "I mean, yes, sir," he corrected himself.

"There's just one other thing we need to get you started," Alan said. "I'll be right back."

They watched as Alan opened the passenger door and pulled out two green John Deere ball caps. He returned and handed one to Mitch. "Okay, now you're official. Let's get you on this tractor."

Mitch took the cap and adjusted it to fit his head. "Now we're talking." He grinned at Eli.

"Looks great on you," she replied. She adjusted her cap and put it on her head. "I guess I'd better get used to wearing hats."

"You just let me know when those start wearing out, and I'll keep you supplied," Alan promised.

The tractor was idling as the driver waited for Mitch to begin his instruction. Both he and Eli paid close attention as he walked Mitch through the gears, and how to operate the equipment.

Two hours later, Mitch was proficient in using the tractor and equipment. The auger and plow attachments were stored in the barn. Alan handed them both a business card. "Just let me know if you have questions or when you need other equipment."

"I'm sure I'll be seeing you again soon," Eli said as she shook his hand.

"Have some fun, and I look forward to seeing y'all often," Alan said and turned to walk to the truck. He stopped and turned to Mitch. "Let me know when you're ready to do some fishing, and I'll take you to some of my favorite spots."

"Yes, sir," Mitch replied with a big smile.

†

They watched the truck disappear down the drive. Mitch took the cap off and ran his hand through his dark hair. "You sure I can't finish high school here?"

"That would be fine with me, but I think your parents have other ideas. Just know you're welcome any time you want to visit."

"Thanks, Aunt Eli."

"You ready to have some fun?"

"I've been having fun all day. I'm ready to do some exploring, though."

"Let me grab my camera, and I'll be right there."

"Aunt Eli," he called after her. "Don't forget your gun. You need to get in the habit of taking it with you. You never know when you might need it."

"Point taken," Eli said, and continued into the cabin.

As Mitch drove the Gator on the roughed-in roadbed, they discussed areas where they would widen the path to allow larger vehicles. Mitch suggested buying a can of spray paint to mark the trees they would remove. A hundred yards farther up the path, the view opened into a large meadow.

Eli pointed to the left. "Let's go this way," she instructed.

The meadow looked like it had once been a hayfield. Relatively flat and a well-defined border of trees surrounded the grassy area. Eli noted a section of deeper green and pointed it out to Mitch. When they arrived, they found a bubbling spring. "That's a good sign," she said.

"It's not the only water in the area," Mitch said, as he pointed out the stream on the western edge of the property. It was more expansive and flowed faster than the one near the cabin.

"Take us closer."

Mitch pulled the Gator to a stop ten feet from the edge. "I bet it's filled with fish. See those natural pools?" He pointed to areas in both directions. "Trout would love those."

"I like the idea of having a trout pond for the local market. I'll contact the fishery and see what I can get arranged for a survey of the property. I bet there's more than one perfect spot here."

"I'll learn everything I can about raising them," Mitch said.

"Deal," Eli answered. "Let's go see what else we can find."

"Wait," Mitch said. He pointed toward the stream. "More deer," he whispered.

"I see them," Eli answered. "I thought I heard a turkey call earlier too."

"This just keeps getting better and better."

"Ready to roll?"

"Yes, ma'am."

As they continued up the mountain, Eli looked off to the right in one clearing, and she spotted a cabin in the distance. There was no one in sight, but it appeared inhabited. She tapped Mitch's arm and pointed across the mountain. "We have neighbors."

"They are tucked away there," he said. "Maybe we'll meet them soon."

"Maybe so," Eli answered. She didn't see any sign of a vehicle, but it could be in an outbuilding or on the other side of the cabin, out of view. "Let's go check out the building site where I'd like to build your cabin."

"Point the way," Mitch answered.

"Straight up the mountain." She grinned.

Mitch drove for another fifteen minutes before they reached another clearing, and Eli pointed for him to turn. "Drive over until we find the stream again."

The morning clouds had disappeared, and as they drove across the clearing, Eli could see for miles in every direction. "There." She pointed to another secluded clearing with rock outcroppings on one border.

Mitch pulled beside the outcroppings and turned off the motor. "This is beautiful," he said as he climbed out of the vehicle.

They had climbed to an elevation of thirty-nine hundred feet. The panoramic view was spectacular. "The fields look like a patchwork quilt," Mitch pointed out.

Eli nodded in agreement. The fields were a verdant green with crops, or a rich brown plowed and ready for planting. A crisp breeze blew across her face as she turned to look in all directions. "That's a refreshing breeze, too. I thought we could build the cabin, right there," she pointed to an area between the stream and outcroppings. She snapped more photos as Mitch walked the property.

He pointed and called out, "Another spring."

They walked over, and Eli snapped more shots. The spring was stronger than the previous ones they had encountered. Mitch bent down and cupped his hand to fill it with the cold water and brought it to his mouth.

"Cold and sweet," he said, "I'm going to grab my empty bottle. Do you want some too?"

"Please," she answered. Eli took some panoramic shots to send to Mark. She had described the build spot, but nothing could describe it better than photographs of the views he could look forward to waking to in the morning. A soft rumbling caught her attention as a jet streaked across the deep blue sky on its way to Asheville.

Mitch returned with empty water bottles and bent down to fill them with spring water. "Beautiful doesn't even begin to describe this spot. Dad is going to go nuts when he sees the pics."

Eli chuckled. "Yeah, I think he'll be calling us within minutes of seeing them. Can you imagine a cabin tucked away there?" she asked, pointing out the building site she imagined.

"It will be our little piece of heaven. I still can't believe all of this is true and I'm not in a coma dreaming all this."

Eli reached over and pinched him.

"Ouch," he cried out.

"Now do you believe you're not dreaming?"

"Yes, ma'am. That pinch was for real. I may be damaged."

"Come on, cupcake, we still haven't made it to the top yet."

"There's more?" he asked in disbelief.

"Yes, there's more."

They returned to the trail that changed to only a footpath. "Stop here, and we'll hike the rest of the way," she told him.

Mitch pulled to a stop. "How much farther?"

"I would guess a few hundred yards. Grab your water and follow me."

The climb was steep as the trees grew thicker. An immense forest swallowed them in shadows. Small critters skittered away from the sound of their footsteps. Mitch squinted, trying to get a glimpse of what they were. "Squirrels or rabbits, maybe even a chipmunk."

"Is that what I think it is?" he asked, pointing to a faded sign tacked to a tree.

Eli grinned at him. "It is. The Appalachian Trail runs across the top of the mountain. I think there's even an overnight shelter a quarter of a mile or so up the trail.

"That is so cool," he said. "Brad and I have talked about hiking it one day."

"You two young'ns go right ahead. I prefer my comfortable bed, hot showers, and a good meal."

"Aw, c'mon Aunt Eli, where's your sense of adventure? There are older folks than you who hike it every year. Some of them have hiked the trail multiple times."

"I'm proud of them, but I've got everything I need right here," she told him.

"How far are we from Springer mountain?"

"I'd guess at least a week or two depending on the speed of the hiker."

"Maybe we can do it in sections once Brad is out of school."

"That's not a bad idea. You could do a month each summer until you finish the entire trail."

"Maybe so." Mitch cocked his head. "Did you hear that?"

Eli remained silent for several seconds until she heard the call of a turkey. "I guess we have turkeys."

"I would say so. No telling what other critters we will find on the property. Should I try to call it in?"

"Sure, go for it." Eli watched the concentration on Mitch's face as he made a sound to lure the bird closer. She watched his eyes grow wide as the bird returned his call. "I think you got his attention."

"Yes, ma'am, and he sounds even closer." Mitch called again, and they remained still watching for signs of movement.

"Would you look at that," she whispered, and pointed to a spot fifty yards north of them where a majestic tom cautiously approached. "He's a big boy."

"Yes, he is. He'd make a good Thanksgiving meal."

Eli chuckled. "Do you always think in terms of food consumption?"

"Of course, Aunt Eli, I'm a growing boy."

Eli shook her head. She snapped a few photos, and they watched the turkey for several more minutes. "Are you ready to head to the top?"

"Yes, ma'am."

They walked to where they had parked the Gator and picked the trail heading north. The canopy of trees provided shade for the short hike to the top of the mountain. They saw several more AT signs posted, and when they reached the boundary of the property, they turned right. They followed the trail for about six hundred yards until they spotted a wooden sleeping shelter. Eli frowned when she saw several of the boards had pulled loose. "A hammer and a few nails would secure this place in no time. You up for it tomorrow?"

"Sure, or even today if you'd like."

"Nope, I want to see how good a fisherman my nephew is. What do you think, the creek at the cabin or the other one?"

"Let's try close to home. If I bomb out, we can always make a sandwich."

"It wouldn't hurt either of us to have one now, and then you can fish. Sound like a deal?"

"Sounds perfect to me. I never turn down an opportunity to fish...or eat."

"Let's go then. I think we've had a productive day. We can eat, and I'll check the internet connection to send your dad some photographs." Eli took one last look at the shelter, making a mental note of supplies they would need and then followed Mitch down the trail.

†

Whit had been in her observatory for hours when she heard the first rumble of traffic, and she turned her attention to the adjoining property to see the furniture truck making deliveries. She couldn't resist a peek at the activity and pulled out a pair of binoculars. Whit followed the movement as a young man and an older woman emerged from the cabin to meet the truck.

"Well hello new neighbors," she spoke to break the silence. She focused on the woman, who appeared to be in her

96

mid-forties. *Nice looking and quick to share a smile and laughter. I wonder who they are and if I should go meet them.* Whit watched the flurry of activity as cartons were removed from the truck and the woman disappeared inside. She turned to her computer, studying the charts on the screen.

Her focus was gone, and when the second truck arrived, thirty minutes after the furniture truck left, she stepped out on the balcony. "Wow, that's a load of equipment. Looks like the new neighbors plan to do some farming." She watched as the Gators and tractor were unloaded, and demonstrations on the tractor and attachments were completed. Oscar dozed in the sunlight, without a bit of interest in what was happening.

"Maybe the new neighbors will have kittens," she teased. Oscar opened an eye before yawning and turning away from her. She watched the activity for several minutes until her stomach protested. "I think it's time for some lunch. How about some tuna today, Oscar?" She watched as he stood and stretched. "Uh-huh, I thought it might get your attention. Let me shut down, and we'll head for home."

Whit turned off the computer system and locked the door behind them before climbing down the flight of steps. Oscar flew past her at the bottom and raced ahead. "I'm glad to see the mention of tuna motivates you to action." Down on the ground floor, she couldn't see what was happening next door, but she could hear the rumble of the tractor. She walked down to the small garden plot and selected a ripe tomato to go on her sandwich. "This should do."

The appearance of neighbors reminded Whit of the loneliness which crept in from time to time. *Could it be fun to have a close friend?* Through her entire childhood, she couldn't remember anyone she had called a friend. There were no sleepovers or slumber parties, no after-school events, no prom dates. She sighed as she bit into the sandwich. "Too bad, you don't like tomatoes. This year's crop is extra sweet," she told Oscar who was devouring the tuna she had put in his bowl. He didn't even bother to look at her. He was a great companion, but there were times she wished for someone to have an adult conversation with, and Oscar just wasn't up to the task. She looked at the deep red tomato sitting on the counter. *Maybe I should take a basket over to welcome my new neighbors. I've got more than I can eat, and I don't feel like canning them. It would give me a great excuse to visit.*

Whit made a second sandwich, poured a glass of tea, and walked to the front porch. Trees hid the view of the cabin and likewise her own, but she could still hear the buzz of activity across the creek. The rumble of the tractor had died down, and she could hear the purring of a smaller engine. An afternoon breeze was picking up, and she could see movement between the swaying limbs. *They must be heading up the mountain to investigate. I hope they are ready for some breathtaking views.* Once more, the mountain air fell silent except for the gentle whispering of the leaves.

†

Mitch pulled in front of the cabin. "I'll put the Gator in the barn if you'll fix some sandwiches."

"You got a deal. Two for you? Anything in particular?"

"Two will be great. Whatever you want, and maybe some chips."

"I'll meet you out on the porch in a few minutes," Eli said and stepped out of the Gator.

"Hey, do you want me to drive down and lock the gate?"

"Sure, go ahead. I doubt there's anything, but check the mail too."

"Yes, ma'am."

Eli watched Mitch make a U-turn and head down the drive. The smile on her face grew wide as she watched him disappear down the path. *I'm a lucky woman.* She entered the cabin and had to stop to marvel at the open floor plan. "Home." *This is the home I've longed for years to have. I wish I had a partner to share it with, but it just wasn't in the cards. I have Mark and his family, but that isn't the same as snuggling into bed with a lover every night.* She let out a deep sigh and walked to the refrigerator.

Eli was placing a stack of sandwich halves on a plate when her cell phone dinged. "Well, that answers one question. The internet is on." She looked at her phone to find an email from her boss, wanting to know if she would still be in the office on Monday. She chuckled and tapped a quick reply, confirming her presence. Damn, Monday was only three days away. Where did the time go? She and Mitch would have one more day on the mountain before they would drive back. It would be late when she arrived in Pensacola, but she wanted to spend every hour she could on the mountain.

Eli turned at the sound of Mitch's boots on the front porch and hollered out to him. "Come grab a couple bottles of water and a bag of chips, please."

"Be right there," he answered. "Wow, you must be hungry, too," he said when he saw the pile of sandwiches on the plate.

"The fresh air makes you hungry. Besides, it seems like forever since breakfast."

Mitch looked at his watch. "Well, it was about eight hours ago."

"No wonder I'm starving." She grinned. "We have internet. I think I'll pull out my laptop and shoot your dad some pics while you fish."

"He'll do monkey flips when he sees those."

"I think so too. I can't believe we only have two more days before we have to head south."

"At least you only have a week or two before you can return. I've got many more than that."

They carried the meal out onto the porch. "What do you want to do tomorrow? Besides fish?"

Mitch grinned. "You know me too well. I'd love to take some trout home. Rub it in a little, you know."

"Why don't you help me nail those few boards at the camp shelter and then you can spend the day fishing? I've got plenty of plans to make for future projects. Maybe we can build a fire ring down at the creek."

"There's enough small rocks at the corner of the field to at least get a start on a fire ring. We can plan it out tonight and build it in the morning before I fish."

Eli took a bite of sandwich and nodded. Her head was already whirling with ideas. After they built the fire pit, she could carry some of the chairs down from the porch. Maybe on the way from repairing the camp shelter, they could cut a few of the small downed trees for a campfire by the creek. *Yeah, sounds good.* A nice campfire by the water on their last night.

"Oh, hey, I almost forgot. When I put the Gator up, I climbed into the hayloft. You won't believe what I found."

"Tell me, I can't handle the suspense of guessing."

"You have a rather large stack of dried wood stored there. I'd say poplar, but I could be wrong. More than enough to finish the laundry room."

"Those are better than a treasure chest. It's a gold mine."

"Beautiful boards. You better use them before Dad sees them. I think there will be enough for some other projects too."

"Great find, Mitch. We may find other hidden gems on the property. You never know."

"Quite literally, I hope you realize. This area is full of sapphires and other gems. Up close to those rock formations would be a great spot for them."

"Maybe this summer, you and Brad can do some mining."

"That would be fun. Brad will love it here too."

"Does he play baseball in the summer?"

"No, they are done by Memorial Day. I don't think he wants to tie up all his summer vacation. He may do another camp or maybe a fall tournament."

"Are you sure you want to spend your summer here?"

"I'd rather be here than mowing the grass all summer."

"I plan on paying you for the hard work I'm going to put you through."

"It's not necessary as long as you feed me and I can fish."

"Trust me, you're going to earn every penny."

"Okay then, I won't argue with you." He popped the last bite of sandwich in his mouth. "Do you want me to carry this stuff inside?"

"Nope, you get to fishing. I got this. I'll grab the laptop and camera and move out on the deck so I can watch you fish."

Eli carried the empty plate inside. She picked up his empty water bottle. "Do you need a fresh bottle of water?"

"That would be great," he answered, looking up from the fly he was attaching to his line.

"Do you need anything else?"

"No, but thanks."

Eli straightened the kitchen and tossed a salad to eat with dinner. She was confident the Great White Fisherman would catch enough for their meal. She also placed a bundle of fresh asparagus in a marinade to grill with the fish. Eli took her camera and laptop out onto the deck and returned for water. Mitch had finished preparing to fish and was passing by as he approached the creek. "You got a hand for this?" she asked, holding out a bottle of water.

"Thanks, Aunt Eli."

"Go get them, tiger," she said as she handed him the cold water.

Eli settled in at the small table and turned on the computer, connecting it to the Wi-Fi. She looked up to watch Mitch begin his cast and marveled at the grace he displayed as he increased the length of his line until he reached the upper edge of a large pool. Eli took the camera and snapped several shots. She smiled at the pure joy on his face as he made the final cast, the fly drifting slowly to the surface of the water. Mitch had forgotten about his new fishing hat, but he was just as proud of his John Deere ball cap.

Eli waited for several minutes, watching him to see if a fish would strike. She was disappointed when the fly floated out of the pool, and he reeled it in to begin another cast but remembered fishing was a test of skill and patience. Mitch was at peace, and the smile on his face was priceless. She snapped off another shot, and he looked up to see her and waved.

Eli viewed the photo in the viewfinder and smiled. It was a great shot, one she would have enlarged and framed for her new home. It was great having Mitch with her, and she wondered how she would handle being alone. This place was a dream come true, but Eli had never been alone in her life. *Times are a-changing.*

Eli connected a cord from the camera to download the photos onto the laptop and waited for them to upload. She was staring at the computer when a cry of excitement from the creek broke the silence. Mitch had hooked a fish. She grabbed her camera and began taking photo's as he guided the fish toward him. When he bent down to remove the fish from the water, Eli was impressed with the size of the fish he held up to her. The fish was sixteen inches long, and the sunlight peeking through the trees glistened off the rainbow-colored skin as it dangled at the end of his line.

"Great catch," she said, as he shot her a grin and a thumbs-up before placing the fish in a bucket.

When the laptop finished loading, she disconnected the transfer cord and began reviewing the photographs. Her first email to Mark had images of Mitch on his first successful fishing adventure. She was sure he'd be proud and would be boasting in the office before he left work. She clicked on send and then sent several more emails with a dozen images each. Only a few minutes passed after she sent the first email before Mark started to respond. *That's my boy*, he said about the fishing shots. *I can tell he's having a great time. How about you?*

Eli answered him. Having a blast with Mitch. You're going to love it here.

Oh my God, the views are fantastic.

You must have just opened the folder at your home site. Yes, they are gorgeous. Pictures don't do them justice. Can't wait for you to see them in person.

Chomping at the bit here. I'll be there in three weeks for a long weekend if it's okay.

I should be settled in by then. Come anytime you're ready.

Don't I wish. I can't wait to share these with Laura and Brad.

Is he home yet?

Laura is gone to get him now.

Call us later then. We will be having a great trout dinner later.

I'm so jealous.

Eat your heart out. Eli didn't mention the idea Mitch had to bring a cooler of fish home for them, opting to leave it as a surprise.

Love ya, Mark wrote.

More, she answered with a smiley face.

She had finished writing when Mitch hollered out. "Got another one."

Eli walked to the edge of the deck and watched as he reeled in a native brown trout, just as big as the first. "He's a beauty," she called out to him as he lifted the fish to show her. "How many do we need for dinner?"

"I was thinking two each," he replied.

"Sounds great."

Eli leaned against the railing and watched him. It didn't take long for Mitch to land two more fish as impressive as the first.

"I'll get these cleaned," he said as he dropped the fourth fish in the bucket. "Do you want me to cook them?"

"You'd better if you want them to be edible. I tossed a salad and have some asparagus ready to roast or grill."

"This is perfect."

"Do you want me to start the grill to get it warmed up?"

"Not yet, I want to doctor them a bit after cleaning them."

"Very well. The kitchen is yours. I'm going to grab a cold beer and relax out here if you don't need me."

"I'm good. Sit back, and I'll let you know when dinner is ready. Do you want to eat out there?"

"Sure, why not? I'll come in and help you."

"No, ma'am, I've got this covered."

†

Eli took her beer and returned to the deck to scroll through the photos. Even though she was far from a professional photographer, she felt her attempts to highlight the beauty of the property had turned out well. The sun was fading as Eli leaned back in the chair and closed her eyes. The gentle rippling of the creek was relaxing, and she was looking forward to falling asleep to the sound in her first night in her new home. *It wouldn't take much to drift off right now.*

Eli startled awake when the door opened, and Mitch arrived carrying a fresh beer.

"Did you doze off?"

"I must have, the last thing I remember was closing my eyes and listening to the sound of the creek."

"It is peaceful out here," he replied and handed her the beer. "Dinner will be ready soon."

"Do you have time to join me for a beer?"

"I think so. The asparagus is in the oven, and the fish have about ten more minutes."

"Set the timer so we can check the food and grab a beer. We've both accomplished a lot and deserve to relax a bit."

Mitch grinned at her and disappeared inside. When he returned, he sat next to her. "I wish we had another week before I have to go home."

"It has been fun, hasn't it? Just think, we've just begun here."

"I just hope the summer doesn't pass so quickly." He took a drink from the beer.

"You don't have to wait until summer. Your dad is planning to bring the family for a long weekend in three weeks."

"Are you serious?"

"It's what he told me when I sent the pictures to him earlier."

"That's freakin' awesome. I was thinking about something while I was fishing and want your opinion."

"Go for it. Opinions are always free."

"Well, since I'm homeschooling this year, I set the pace of my classwork. If I worked hard for the next three weeks, I could knock off a large portion of my assignments. If I can convince Mom and Dad, would you mind if I finish the school year here?"

"What about your final exams?"

"All online." He grinned.

"I wouldn't have any trouble with that, but schoolwork would have to come before anything else. I won't have your mom going ballistic on both of us. What are your grades right now?"

"B's, and a C in math."

"Not bad. Can I make a suggestion?"

Mitch nodded.

"Show your parents you're serious by improving those grades in the next three weeks, so they can see how dedicated you are. How long would it take you to finish out your studies here?"

"If I can put a big dent in my assignments, maybe another two weeks. That would cut two weeks off for me."

"Sure, sounds doable to me. You want to talk to your parents about your idea on Sunday when you get home?"

"Yes, ma'am. I know you'll be eager to get to Florida, so I'll bring it up after you've left."

"I can stay to offer my support or a quick getaway vehicle if we need it," she teased.

"I've got this. We can always call you if Mom has questions."

The timer sounded, and Eli put her beer on the table.

"Sit tight, I've got this," Mitch said. "You want tea or another beer?"

"I think I'll switch to tea. You sure you don't need help?"

"Positive, but thanks. I'll flip the porch light on so we can see while we eat."

†

Whit woke from her nap and stretched on the bed before sitting up. Oscar was lounging on the end of the bed and looked at her. "Time for some food and then to get to work." She climbed from the bed and walked into the kitchen. The fresh tomatoes she had picked earlier were calling to her. She made two tomato sandwiches and poured some chips onto the plate. Whit placed a cup of dried cat food in Oscar's bowl. "I'm eating on the porch. Would you care to join me?"

He looked at her and meowed.

"Okay, I'll take your bowl out."

Whit found a small tray to place their dinner onto and poured a glass of water from the fridge. She flipped on the porch light and pushed the screen door open with her foot. Whit placed the tray on a small table and sat Oscar's bowl next to her chair. When she sat, she took a bite of a sandwich. The mayo leaked out from the corner of her mouth, and her tongue snaked out to pull it inside. "I have outdone myself," she told Oscar. "These are the best tomatoes I've ever grown."

Oscar, his face buried in the bowl, focused on his own meal, unconcerned with her enjoyment of the sandwich. A crisp evening breeze had blown in, the air filled with the fresh scent of night-blooming flowers. The dance of the lightning bugs across the meadow brought her attention to the cabin across the creek. Soft laughter floated across the breeze as her new neighbors enjoyed their dinner on the deck. Whit could see the glimmer of the light between the leaves swaying in the breeze. She continued her meal, watching for signs of movement.

107

†

Mitch took their empty plates into the kitchen. He insisted on cleaning the kitchen before taking a shower. Eli wasn't in an arguing mood and thanked him for a delicious meal. The cool breeze bathed her face, and the scent of flowers filled the air. She walked over to the railing and saw the soft yellow glow of lightning bugs floating through the dark night. Movement and a different light caught her attention through the trees. *That must be my neighbors. I won't have time to meet them until I return, but I will make it a point to be friendly.* Eli could hear Mitch moving around in the kitchen, and turned to walk inside, flipping off the light.

"This was a fantastic meal, Mitch."

"I'm happy you liked it, Aunt Eli. This was the first time I cooked them by myself."

"I couldn't tell it was your first. The fish was delicious and cooked to perfection. You can cook for me anytime."

Eli noticed a light blush rise to his cheeks. "Do you want to sleep in for a little while tomorrow?"

"Heck no…unless you do. There's time to sleep on the ride home. Way too many fun things to do to be sleeping half the day away."

"I don't know what it would be like to sleep late," Eli admitted.

"I pulled out the bacon to thaw. First one awake starts cooking it?"

"Agreed, unless it's before five o'clock. If you wake that early, close your eyes for another hour."

"Yes, ma'am. I'll run through the shower and hit the sack. Thanks for a great day."

"Thank you, and thanks again for a delicious meal. I think I'll relax on the deck until you're done showering. Tell me when you're off to bed, please."

"Will do."

†

Eli returned to her seat and stared out into the dark, moonless night. Through the canopy of trees, she could see a blanket of bright stars. *You don't see stars like this in any city.* Her neck grew stiff from staring at the sky, and when she lowered her gaze, she saw a flashlight beam making a trail up the mountain. *That's weird. Maybe my neighbor is a moonshiner or is growing her own stash of weed. Why would someone be hiking up the mountain this late in the day, except if they were hiding something? Why did I assume it's a her?* Eli watched the progress of the beam for several hundred yards before it disappeared, hidden behind the dense leaves bordering the creek bed. She waited for several minutes to see if the light would reappear, but time passed with no further view.

She sat and listened to the trickle of the water as it bounced across rocks traveling down the mountain and the whisper flowing through the leaves. *Was that my imagination or did I just hear a soft hello?* Regardless, what a beautiful sound. She felt the hairs on her arms standing as the breeze that had carried the scent of night blooms grew colder. *Will need to remember to bring a light jacket out next time.* A sound from inside the cabin grew louder, and Eli smiled as she heard Mitch singing in the shower.

"Good Lord, I hope this kid develops some skills, 'cause he sure won't make it in Nashville." She chuckled to herself. *I do love that kid.* Just as suddenly, the singing stopped, and she heard him turn off the shower. A few minutes later, he emerged wearing a pair of sleep pants and T-shirt, still towel drying his hair.

"Brrr...it has dropped a few degrees since we ate."

"Yes, it has. It may be a few more weeks before it stops dropping temperatures so drastically after dark."

"I packed a hoodie if you want it," Mitch offered.

"Thanks, but I'll take a shower and try out my new bed. I plan to leave the window cracked, but I bet I get up during the night to close it." She grinned at him. "The water can lull me to sleep tonight, though."

"It does have a peaceful sound to it, doesn't it?"

"Most definitely." She walked over and hugged Mitch. "Oh crap, I forgot your dad was supposed to call."

"Dang, I forgot to tell you, he called while I was cooking. Mom said he can't stop looking at the pictures you sent. He even told her she could order pizza, 'cause he wasn't cooking."

Eli laughed. "Your dad is smitten by this place."

"That is a huge understatement. I can imagine the smile on Dad's face when I hear the excitement in his voice."

Eli knew precisely what Mitch was talking about. She could hear it in Mark's voice whenever they spoke. "Thanks for a great day. Tomorrow will be just as fun. When we get done repairing the trail shelter, I'm going to run to town to buy a cooler. Is there anything you need?"

"A good filleting knife would be helpful."

"That's easy. You can fish while I'm gone."

"I've got no problem with that. Goodnight, Aunt Eli."

"Goodnight Mitch, see you in the morning."

She followed him inside and locked the door behind her.

"I locked the front already," Mitch called when he heard the click of the lock.

"Thanks." Eli climbed the stairs to her new bedroom, walked over to a window and opened it a few inches to allow the breeze to enter along with the sounds of the water. The angle of the view was slightly different from her bedroom, and the flicker of light caught her attention. Then it was gone. *Probably just my imagination or a reflection from a star.* Then she remembered there was no moon out tonight. *Maybe there is a moonshine still out there.* Eli chuckled and pulled out her sleep clothes, tossing them on the bed.

After showering, she dressed for bed and turned off the light. The room filled with fresh mountain scent and crisp air. Outside, she could hear crickets, their chorus broken from time to time by the loud calling of cicadas who roared above everything. Eli closed her eyes, intent on listening to the night and drifted to sleep.

†

The smell of frying bacon woke her the next morning. She stretched and sat up in the bed. From the appearance of the covers, she hadn't moved much during the night, and the window was still open. *I must have been more tired than I thought. All this fresh air.* Grinning, she climbed out of bed and slipped into her house shoes before walking to the kitchen.

Mitch looked up when he heard the shuffling of her feet as she climbed down the stairs. "Good morning, sunshine."

"Good morning. You have it smelling good in here."

"Your coffee is ready, just push the button. Bacon is almost done too. You need to cook the eggs though, mine turn out horrible."

"You're lucky, that's the one skill your grandmother taught me," she said as she turned on the coffee. "Fried or scrambled?"

"Fried would be great. I'll make the toast while you cook them."

111

Eli walked to the fridge and pulled out a carton of eggs. "Will three be enough?"

"Perfect," he said as he removed the pan from the heat.

Eli prepared her coffee and took a sip as she prepped a small frying pan for the eggs. "Hand me the butter, will ya?"

"You got it. Want some apple juice?"

"With breakfast, yeah. You can put the carton in the freezer to get it cold."

Mitch made the toast and poured the juice while Eli served the eggs. She carried the plates and her coffee over to the table.

"Let's eat."

After their meal, Eli cleared the table. "I'll get dressed and clean the kitchen. Will you head out to the shed and see if you can find a couple hammers and some nails?"

"You sure you don't want me to clean?"

"I've got this. You can wrap those last three slices of bacon in a piece of bread for your walk to the shed."

"No *problemo*," he said, grabbed a slice of bread and stuffed the bacon inside. "I'll get the tools, bring the Gator around, brush my teeth, and I'll be ready."

"See ya," Eli said. The sun had risen and was shining into her bedroom, setting the room alight with a golden glow. She freshened up in the bathroom and pulled on some worn jeans, T-shirt, and her favorite hiking boots. The kitchen only took a few minutes, and she was washing the last of the dishes when Mitch returned.

"I'll be right out," he said on his way past her.

"Almost done here."

Eli put the butter in the fridge and spied the lunchmeat. "We need to eat this for lunch, so it doesn't go to waste."

Mitch returned, and they walked outside together. "What a beautiful day. I can't wait to see this place in all four seasons. Do you think you'll have much snow?"

"I'm sure there will be several snowfalls, but it won't be like ski resort levels. Inches maybe, but not feet of snow."

"I'm betting this place will be gorgeous draped in a blanket of snow. Everything crisp and crunchy as you walk."

"You sound like you may have a bit of poet in you, Mitch, I like how you describe things."

"Just call em as I see em, ma'am." He grinned.

"Come on, you goof. Drive me to the top of the mountain."

"With pleasure," he answered, and climbed behind the wheel.

Eli sat beside him as he began the slow journey up the mountain. "Cruz will love it here."

"She's got acres to run wild. Will you get another dog for a companion?"

"I haven't decided yet. What do you think?"

"She may wear you out less if she has someone to play with."

"That is an excellent observation, one I will take into consideration. Do you plan on fishing the other creek today?"

"Naw, I just had such good luck at the cabin, I'll stick there unless they aren't biting."

"I'll prepare some sandwiches when I get home from town and join you if you haven't caught your fill."

"You ought to try your hand at fishing."

"Oh, I can fish. Fly fish, too, but I enjoy watching you catch them even more."

When they reached the end of the trail, Mitch pulled to a stop and took out a small toolbox with hammers and nails. They walked to the trailhead and on to the shelter. The air was still chilly beneath the canopy of green. There were no signs anyone had sheltered there during the night.

"I wonder how often hikers come through this way?"

Mitch placed the toolbox on the wooden sleeping platform. "It doesn't look like anyone has been here."

"I would think northbound hikers might show up soon," Eli said as she lifted the first board in place.

"Maybe so," he answered and pounded several nails to secure the board. "One down, four to go."

†

Whit jolted awake at the sound of pounding coming from the mountain top. Once again, she had fallen asleep in the lab and would be stiff and sore for hours before her muscles unkinked. "I wonder what the noise is, Oscar."

She picked up her binoculars and walked out to the deck surrounding the lab. When the banging resumed, she focused in on the sound and lifted her binoculars. She could see the trail shelter, and it looked as if her new neighbors were doing some repairs.

"Well, this is good to see. Which reminds me I need to pick a basket of tomatoes to bring to them as a welcoming gift."

Oscar looked at her with an expression that showed he was not impressed and swished his tail as he started down the stairs. His food bowl was at the cabin, and he would be starving to death by the time she filled it for him.

"Yes, I know, your food bowl is back at home. No, I refuse to bring one here. You know where to go for food. Heaven forbid you should catch a mouse or something wild."

Oscar's momentum got the better of him, and he ran-stumbled down the remaining steps. Whit laughed at his less than graceful descent, and then stopped. *I reckon I'd better not laugh until I'm on firm ground.*

†

Eli's head spun around at the sound of laughter. "Did you hear that?"

"Hear what? You imagining a Bigfoot encounter already, are ya?"

"No, I thought I heard a woman laughing."

Mitch looked at her with a perked eyebrow and shrugged. "I don't hear anything."

"I don't either." Eli frowned, confident she had heard the sound. "One more board and we're good to go." She held the loose end of the board for Mitch to secure. "I wonder what the regulations are for a fire pit here. Maybe it would make the spot more inviting, especially in the fall when the nights turn cold."

"I'll do some research for you when I get home. I would think it needs to be self-contained to keep the forest safe."

"Good point."

Mitch dropped the hammer in the toolbox. "Ready to roll?"

"Right behind you."

Whit untucked her T-shirt when she entered the garden and picked a dozen beautiful red tomatoes. Whit was sure she had a small basket to put them in and would deliver them after a hot shower and some breakfast. She entered her cabin and placed the tomatoes in the sink. She'd feed the ever-vocal Oscar, then rinse them before taking her shower. "Such a brat," she said while she opened a canister of food and filled his bowl.

Eli went inside for her truck keys and wallet while Mitch stored the tools and Gator. He was walking across the yard when she stepped outside. "Cooler, filleting knife, anything else?"

"Those should do it. Be safe."

"I will. Enjoy the fishing."

"I will."

"See ya."

Eli drove the truck down the drive and opened the gate. She pulled through and left it open until she returned. Eli lowered her shades and started toward town to the local "everything store" to purchase her supplies. She retraced the route she and Mitch had taken and slowed to a near halt when a sign caught her eye. *Humane Society.*

"It never hurts to look," she told herself and turned into the drive. "Still early, so hopefully they are open." She pulled into a parking lot with two cars and parked. Eli walked inside and was welcomed by a young woman.

"Good morning," the woman said with a cheerful smile. "I'm Erin, what can I help you with?"

"Hi, Erin, I'm Eli, and I'm new to the area, and thought I'd drop in to see what you have available for adoption."

"Welcome to the area. I hope you'll love it here."

"I do already."

"Is there something particular you are looking for?"

"Yes, there is. I'm looking for some barn cats and a companion for a two-year-old blue heeler who will be joining me soon. I'm partial to black cats, but they don't have to be black."

"Oh goody," Erin clapped her hands. "Do you know how hard it is to adopt black cats? People are so superstitious."

"I know, but every black cat that's ever owned me has had a unique personality."

Erin grinned at her pun. "That owned you. Ha, I like you already. Let me show you who we have in the habitat."

Eli was impressed at how well-kept the kennels and cat habitats were maintained. There were no odors, and the animals looked healthy but sad to be in a shelter. Erin hadn't been joking. There were a dozen young black cats in the habitat. "Do you alter and chip your animals?"

"Yes, our manager is also a local vet. Dr. Loren is great and will do everything she can to save an animal."

"That's what I like to hear."

Erin opened the door to the cat habitat, and they walked inside. A skinny black male approached Eli, and she bent down to pet him.

"This is Cajun," Erin said. "He's got a spicy little attitude sometimes."

"King of the habitat?"

"Most definitely and these are his siblings." She pointed out five other black cats.

"What about tuxedo over there?"

"He's Walter. He's been here since he was a kitten, but no one has ever adopted him."

The door to the habitat opened, and an attractive woman in scrubs walked in carrying a small kitten.

"Hello," she said with a smile. "Erin, Tomboy will be just fine," she said as she placed the kitten on the floor and he ran to pounce on one of the bigger kittens.

"Dr. Loren, this is Eli, she's new in town and is looking for some black cats and a companion for a blue heeler."

Eli's gaydar antenna started spinning as she watched the young vet give her the once over.

"Nice to meet you. As you can see, we are overrun with black cats."

"I love black cats. How do you think they will do as barn cats with acres to roam?"

"As long as they have some food and plenty of water to supplement what they catch on their own, they will be fine. How many are you looking for?"

"I was thinking six, but my numbers may be growing. Maybe a dozen?"

"That would be great. You have a large size property I take it."

"I bought the Brewer place, so plenty of room to roam. I'm heading to Florida tomorrow but will return in a week. Would you be able to alter and chip the ones I pick out?"

"As long as they are old enough. Tomboy is the only one in here who's too young."

"May I bring him in when he's old enough?"

"Absolutely."

"I want them all and Walter."

Dr. Loren looked at her in surprise. "Our fees are reasonable, but still not cheap. You sure you want them all?"

"Yes, Doc, and a list of whatever supplies I'll need for them to prepare for their arrival."

"Alrighty then. You're an angel for taking them. What kind of companion for your heeler were you thinking?"

"I'm not sure yet. Cruz is high energy, so I need someone to help wear her out every day until I decide if I'm going to raise any animals she can herd besides cats."

They all broke out laughing, but Dr. Loren stopped abruptly. She looked at Erin. "This is going to sound odd, but what about Molly?"

"Oh my gosh, it would be a match made in heaven. You have a barn, right?"

"Yes, a large one. Who is Molly?"

"You have to meet Molly," Dr. Loren said. "Then you can tell me if I'm crazy or not."

She led them from the cat habitat to the rear of the clinic and opened the door to a large run. A small baby goat rushed to them. Her black and gray body wiggled with excitement as Eli kneeled down to pet her and was welcomed with a lick to her cheek.

Dr. Loren smiled. "This is Molly. She's a pygmy goat, so she'll stay small. Won't get much bigger than she is now. A family bought her as a birthday gift for their young daughter, but they didn't have an environment to meet her needs. The Brewer place and another high energy animal would be perfect for her."

"I have never raised goats before."

"Not much to know. Food, water, shelter, and Molly will be good to go. We need to give her a good home. She needs much more space than we can give her here."

Molly took off, running around the room, bouncing off the platforms and toys they had given her.

Eli broke out laughing. "When I get home, may I bring Cruz for a play date to see how they get along?"

"That would be great. I don't want Molly going to a family who's going to fatten her up for a barbeque."

"Oh, hell no," Eli said.

"I'll even deliver the animals to you, to make sure you're set for everything and everyone," Dr. Loren offered.

"Deal," Eli said. She pulled out an American Express. "I guess you better start totaling my bill before I see someone else. Don't forget to add goat food to the list of supplies please."

Erin took the card and left the run.

Dr. Loren offered Eli her hand. "Thank you for helping us place some hard-to-adopt animals."

"You're welcome. My brother and his family will be joining me at some point down the road, so we can do more to help. I wish I could take them all."

"If you'll just help us with the black cat population that would be awesome."

"I'll take as many as you think I can support."

"I can do some house calls and provide some free healthcare if it will be an incentive."

"The house calls yes, but I can afford to pay. Running this place can't be cheap. I'd like you to be Cruz's vet, too, if you take new patients."

"I look forward to meeting her. When do you expect to be back in the area?"

"If all goes as planned, by next weekend. I could bring Cruz in for a play date Monday and arrange for the new family to arrive."

"That sounds perfect. I'll give you my card with my cell number. I do emergency calls twenty-four seven, and my wife sometimes tags along to assist."

"It's not a problem. You are both welcome anytime." What a smart way to confirm my guess she's a lesbian.

"Maybe once you're settled in, you can join us for a cookout."

"Sounds great, Doc. Thanks for the warm welcome."

They walked to the front where Erin was totaling the charges. "Dang, you might want to sit down first. With all the shots, chips, and altering fees, this is your total."

Eli looked at the invoice. She didn't flinch at the amount and added a two-hundred-dollar donation for food and supplies.

"That's not necessary, but thank you," Dr. Loren said.

"My pleasure. If I give you my email address, can you send me the list of supplies and where I can purchase them in town?"

"Everything you need you can get at Merrill's feed store, just outside of town. Open an account and they will deliver whatever you need."

"Thanks for the information. Erin, may I ask a question?"

"Sure thing." She smiled and cocked her head.

"My nephew Mitch is seventeen and will spend the summer with me, maybe more. Could I introduce you and maybe you can give him a tour of the town?"

"I'd be happy to." She grinned.

"Thanks. So, I'd better get on to my original adventure. I'll see you both soon."

"Thanks again," Dr. Loren said.

Erin waved, and Eli turned to leave.

†

Showered and dressed in her best pair of worn jeans, Whit filled a small basket with her fresh-picked tomatoes and emerged from her cabin. Oscar was asleep or feigning sleep in one of the rocking chairs and didn't offer to follow her on a journey. It had been years since she had visited the home of her closest neighbor. The previous owner had built a beautiful home, and Whit found it hard to believe anyone would want to leave such a peerless homestead. As she started across her yard, she hoped her new neighbors would stay this time.

Years ago, a large tree had fallen across the creek, making a natural bridge between the properties, saving her a much longer walk to cross over to the other homestead. A cool breeze graced the morning, and Whit could smell the aroma of trees and flowers in bloom. Birds sang as they perched in trees, watching her approach with a careful eye. Her steps fell quietly as she walked across the carpet of green grass, and her sudden appearance startled two chipmunks who skittered away into the bushes.

The fallen tree was three hundred yards above the new cabin and was still sturdy enough to allow her to cross. It had been a while since Whit had crossed over a log bridge, so she took her time placing her steps to prevent making an unplanned dip in the creek. She cradled her basket in her arms and crossed. Whit found the trail and followed it south to the cabin. A frown crossed her face when she didn't see the truck in the yard, and no signs of activity near the cabin. Prepared to step onto the porch to leave the basket, Whit heard a cry of excitement coming from the creek behind the cabin. She walked around the front of the cabin to locate the source of the sound. A young man was busy reeling in a fish, enjoying the well-fought victory. When he turned to place the fish in a bucket, he saw her.

"Hello," he called out. Whit realized he must have been startled. He had been concentrating on fishing and hadn't heard anyone drive up.

"Hello," she answered. "My name is Whit, and I live across the creek. I've got an abundance of tomatoes, so I thought I'd share them with you and come introduce myself." Whit held out the basket of tomatoes.

"Hi, I'm Mitch, and those look delicious. Did you grow them yourself?" He dropped the fish in the bucket and walked toward her, wiping his hands on a small towel.

"Yes, I did. I have a tendency to grow more than I can eat, and I've plenty of canned." She stepped forward to meet him and offered him the basket.

"Thanks, Aunt Eli and I both love homegrown tomatoes. Can I offer you something to drink?"

"That would be great if I'm not taking you away from your fishing."

"No worries, there's still plenty of daylight left. I'll give the fish a break for a little while. I've got bottled water, tea, or beer."

"A bottle of water would be great. Thanks."

"You want to have a seat down by the water?" He pointed out two chairs where they would eventually have a firepit down by the creek. "I'll be right back." He took the basket of tomatoes and disappeared inside the cabin.

Okay, that answers one question. The young man is her nephew, not her son or boyfriend. She walked down to the creek and sat. Very peaceful and a beautiful view of the water. She had always loved the rippling sound of the water cascading down the small falls made by the high rocks in the stream. Whit turned at the sound of footsteps as Mitch returned with two bottles of water.

†

Wow, she snuck up on me, but she is cute. The sprinkle of freckles across her cheeks reminded Mitch of Brad when he was smaller. They looked natural on her tanned skin, and her blond hair glowed in the sun. He reached forward to hand her a bottle and took a seat across from her. "I don't see a vehicle. How did you get here?"

Whit smiled. "I crossed the creek a few hundred yards up the mountain. A tree fell, providing a natural bridge about five years ago, making it much easier to cross the water. I'm sorry if I startled you."

"No problem. I just wasn't expecting to see anyone, other than Aunt Eli."

"Is she not here?"

"No, she went to town to get a few things. I'm catching a mess of fish to take home to Alabama with me tomorrow, for my family as a surprise."

"You're from Alabama?"

"Yes, ma'am, I am, but Eli is from Florida. She's taking me home tomorrow and making her move here next weekend."

"That's exciting news. I've been hoping for neighbors for years, and this is such a fantastic homestead. I grew up on this property as a kid and know just about every inch of the place."

"It is gorgeous here. Eli has plans to build a second cabin farther up the mountain for my parents, my brother and me. My dad, her brother and she have dreamed of living together here for years."

"My grandparents used to own this entire side of the mountain but sold this parcel years ago. It sat vacant for many years until some city folk bought it and built this cabin and the outbuildings. They didn't stay long and were rarely here. I guess the solitude was too much for them." She grinned and took a sip of the water. "This is an excellent spot for fishing, too, but it seems you've already figured that out."

His grin widened. "The fishing is fantastic. I caught a mess for dinner last night, and I'm taking some home to tease my dad and brother, Brad. I can't wait until I can come for the summer, maybe sooner if I can convince my parents to allow me to finish my school year here."

"Isn't it kind of late in the year to be changing schools?"

"I do my schoolwork on the internet, so I could finish out the year here," he explained.

Whit chuckled. "I forget how advanced the education system has become."

"Aunt Eli says it's come so far since her day when they used stone and chisels. She's not that old though."

"Technology has changed so much. Makes it easier to get an education and so much more."

Mitch's head spun around when he heard rustling in the bushes, and a black cat bounced into view. "Where on earth did you come from?" The cat approached confidently and rubbed against his legs.

"Mitch, meet Oscar. The laziest, but most loveable companion I've ever had. I think he must have been faking sleep when I decided to come over. He's a quite curious fellow and hates to be left out of anything."

"Hey, Oscar," he said and leaned over to pet the cat. "I hope you don't mind some company. I think Aunt Eli plans to rescue some barn cats, and Cruz will be coming to live with her here."

"Who is Cruz?"

"Her blue heeler pup. Eli's ex didn't like her, so we've been raising her. She's a great dog, just full of energy. She won't hurt other animals and loves cats, says they taste like chicken." He watched her face as his attempt at a joke hit home, and he started laughing.

Whit started to laugh. "You got me with that one."

"Sorry, I couldn't resist."

"It's a shame her ex didn't like Cruz."

"You'd have to know her ex. Sara's a bitch, excuse my language. She was jealous of the attention Eli gave Cruz. It broke Eli's heart to bring her to live with us. I think she wishes now she'd kept Cruz and booted Sara earlier."

Whit couldn't help but chuckle at the young man's honesty. "I can understand that. Animals are much more loyal than people."

"Do you and Oscar live alone?"

"Yes, my grandparents passed away a few years ago. I love this mountain and won't consider moving anywhere else."

"I can see why. I love this place."

"Have you found the cave yet?"

"Cave? What cave?"

"There's a small cave about three quarters of the way up on the eastern border along the creek. When you return, I'll take you there. It was a great place to hide out as a kid. The property has so many hidden secrets."

Mitch nodded. "Aunt Eli and I did some repairs on the trail shelter this morning. Do you see much traffic from the AT?"

"Sometimes a hiker will arrive, looking for help or better shelter. I don't open my home to strangers, but they can use the barn anytime."

"I think Aunt Eli may offer the outdoor laundry and shower building to some of the travelers. I'm not convinced it's a great idea until I get back, so she's not alone here."

"I've never had any issue, but you can't be too careful these days. I bet Eli would wait until you return to see if it is something your aunt wants to do. She could barter shelter and a hot meal for some work around the place." She smiled at him. "I've found most of the hikers don't want a handout and will help with whatever work needs doing."

"That's good to know. Aunt Eli has a lot of plans for this place."

"Like what?"

"She wants to install solar panels to power as much of the property as she can."

"Sweet. I made my place solar powered in my teens."

"Are you serious? How did you figure it out?"

"It's just something I knew how to do, don't ask me how though. With the purchase of the panels, battery, transfer switch and some young muscle, we could have this place self-sufficient in no time." She saw the smile on his face grow. "She would need to have some form of backup power for winter storms. A generator and a tank of propane would work."

"We could store it in the barn."

The ideas took form as his smile continued to grow.

"I'm hoping I can convince my parents to let me stay when we come to visit in three weeks. If I'm successful, could you help me set a system up for her?"

"I'd love too. I miss doing projects. I garden and do some work on the side, but I need a good challenge."

"We will be busy with lots of projects, at least through the summer."

They turned at the sound of Eli's truck coming up the drive. "I guess you will get to meet her today."

"Awesome."

Mitch stood and waited for Whit. They walked over to where Eli had pulled the truck to a stop.

†

Eli looked toward the stream and saw Mitch walking with a woman from the edge of the stream. "What the heck?" She looked for signs of another vehicle and saw none. *Who on earth can this be?* She turned off the engine and stepped out of the truck. The petite woman looked like a child next to Mitch, but she was drop-dead gorgeous. *Leave it to Mitch to sniff out the pretty women.* She had to restrain a laugh at her thought.

"Welcome home," Mitch called to her.

"Thanks," she answered, and then saw a black cat trailing behind them.

"These are our neighbors. Whit and Oscar," he said, pointing to the cat who had dashed passed them.

"Eli Fortner, and I take it you've already met my nephew, Mitch." She offered her hand to the woman.

Whit slipped her small hand into Eli's. "Whit Brewer, and my faithful companion, Oscar."

"Brewer? Was this place yours?"

"Not mine, but for many years, my grandparents owned the entire side of the mountain. They sold this parcel years ago."

When Eli realized she was still holding the woman's hand, she released it and smiled as she remembered her thoughts from the previous night. *She doesn't look like a*

127

moonshiner or a pot grower. "I'm happy I could buy this place. It's a dream come true."

"I'm glad you're enjoying the property. The family who built this cabin didn't stay for long. Such a waste."

"Yes, but it turned out perfect for me."

"You have a point."

"Whit brought us some homegrown tomatoes from her garden."

Eli watched a slight blush rise to the young woman's cheeks.

"Just a little welcome-to-the-neighborhood gift. I always overplant, so if you need some fresh vegetables, come and pick whatever you want."

"That's fabulous. I'm not sure I'll have time to plant a garden this summer." Eli pulled herself away from the gaze of Whit's green eyes, to look at Mitch. "Are you starved yet?"

"Not totally, but I could eat."

"Would you join us for some sandwiches?"

"I'd love to," Whit answered. "I'd like to see inside the cabin if you wouldn't mind. I watched them build it, but never saw the finished product."

Eli looked at Mitch. "You want to eat out on the deck?"

"I'll grab another chair while you make the sandwiches."

"How's the fishing going?"

"Good, I'll catch a few more after lunch."

"Let's get some lunch then. Follow me," Eli told Whit.

They entered the cabin, and Eli spied the basket of tomatoes sitting on the counter. "Those are beautiful," she said as she took one and lifted it to her nose. "Oh, my goodness. They smell so good. I'll start building some sandwiches if you want to have a look around."

"You need my help?"

"No, ma'am, I've got this."

Eli walked to the fridge and retrieved the mayonnaise and lunchmeat, placing them on the counter. As she began making the sandwiches, Whit wandered from room to room. *Whit is adorable. Too bad, she's so young. Can't be more than her late twenties at most.*

Whit walked from room to room, surveying the beautiful cabin. The final product was more delightful than she had imagined. The builders had spared no expense in developing the floor plan, optimizing the location of the stream and views of the lower valley. She climbed the stairs to find an empty loft next to a huge master bedroom and maybe even an office with great views. She walked to the window and looked out. Her home would be visible in the fall once the leaves fell. Now, it was hidden by a green canopy.

"This cabin is beautiful," she said as she began to descend the stairs from the loft. "I can't believe someone would build it just to abandon it."

Eli looked up at the sound of her voice, and she watched her travel down the stairs. "I know, but their loss is my gain. I fell in love with this place the first time I saw the photos."

"You can't ask for a more peaceful spot. Mitch seems to like it, too."

"He loves the opportunity to fish and explore. He and his brother Brad will have a blast living here."

"I've been here most of my life. When I went off to college, I couldn't wait to return."

"I can understand that. I'm looking forward to planting my permanent roots here."

"Mitch said he and his family will also live here."

"Yes, my brother Mark and I have always dreamed of having our own place. Circumstances changed, and I was able to retire early. He's still got a few years to go, but I'm trying my best to convince him to move as soon as he can."

"I bet it was fun growing up with a sibling. I am an only child and raised by my grandparents."

"Siblings can be fun or a pain in the ass. I got lucky with Mark. He's a good friend, and I adore his boys and wife."

"Are they planning to build here?"

"I've already picked out a spot higher up the mountain near the western boundary and rock formations, which I think will be a great spot."

"Sounds perfect. Great views and Mitch will be near the even bigger stream."

Eli smiled and nodded her head. "Close enough for comfort, but enough distance to offer them privacy."

Mitch entered the kitchen as she was placing the last stack of sandwiches on the plate. "We're all set on the deck. I'll carry those out if you want to grab a drink and some napkins." Mitch washed his hands and turned to Eli.

"Do you want some chips?"

"I can never pass on chips." He grinned and picked up the plate.

"I'll grab a bag and another plate."

Whit looked at Eli. "Is there anything I can do?"

"Grab some napkins off the counter."

"Simple enough."

"Oh, and grab the salt and pepper shakers, too. I didn't season the tomato sandwiches yet."

As they settled around the small table to enjoy lunch, Eli turned to Whit. "Mitch asked me this morning how much snow we can expect."

Whit turned to Mitch. "This place is beautiful when it snows. The most I can ever remember getting at once was about eight inches, but that was rare. Most snowfalls are around three to five inches." She paused. "The streams don't freeze, but there will be ice, and the branches will be covered in snow and ice."

"I can't wait to see this place in the winter." He took a large bite from a tomato sandwich. "These are to die for. Do all vegetables grow well here?"

"Most of them, yes. Grandfather used to have a garden plot just across your front yard. He'd use the water from the creek to irrigate his plants."

"That's good to know. I want to put a garden in, and it sounds like the perfect spot."

"There shouldn't be too many rocks that have come to the surface, and with a few more modern additions, we should be able to rig a water pumping system for you."

Mitch saw the surprised look on Eli's face. "Whit is a mechanical genius. She's agreed to help me install solar panels if you still want to do that."

"Is that right?"

"She converted her grandparents' cabin, now her cabin, when she was a teenager."

Eli's right brow shot up in disbelief. How long have these two been chatting? They seem to have shared quite a bit of information.

"I'd love to go solar and install a backup generator in case we have extended winter storms."

"We've got one in the plans, too. You provide the finances, and we'll do the rest."

Eli could hear the excitement in his voice. "What else have you two conspired on since I've been gone?"

"That's pretty much it," Mitch admitted.

Whit came to his rescue. "He says you have great plans for the property."

"Plenty of ideas. I'll work on tilling the garden plot, planting some trees and berry bushes, finishing the laundry building, and widening the trail on the mountain until he returns. I need young muscle." She looked at Mitch and saw him smiling.

"Muscle I got. It's the planning I'm short on," he admitted.

"I've got planning covered. Once your dad visits and approves the building site, I'll start looking for a contractor for your home."

Whit chimed in. "There are several reputable builders in the area I can recommend."

"That would be great. I'm thinking access from the other side of the stream farther up the mountain. I want this trail to stay open but small. I don't cherish the thought of large vehicles passing through my yard every day, so I'll need a bridge across the stream."

"It shouldn't be any problem at all. As long as your brother has a four-wheeled drive vehicle, he can make it to the building site with no problem."

Mitch chuckled. "We got that covered. Dad and I have trucks, and Mom has an SUV."

Eli nodded. "If clearance is an issue, she can always park down here and use a Gator to go the rest of the way."

Oscar jumped onto the railing of the deck and dropped to the floor. "Oscar, you were not invited," Whit chided the friendly cat.

Eli smiled. "He's more than welcome. I hope he won't mind some company. I stopped in at the local shelter and put in a hefty order."

"Really, Aunt Eli? What did you pick out?"

"You won't believe me?"

"Try me."

"You know black cats are my favorite, right? Well, they have an overabundance, so we're adopting a dozen of all ages. They will be brought up to date on shots, chipped, and altered while I'm gone."

"You must have met Dr. Loren then," Whit stated. "I take Oscar to see her."

"I did, and she will deliver all the animals when I make it home."

"What about a playmate for Cruz?"

"That's the part you won't believe, Mitch. They have a baby pygmy goat named Molly, who has as much energy as Cruz. She's adorable, and I'm going to take Cruz on a playdate to see how they get along."

"A baby goat?" he cried out. "They are so danged cute."

"I think Cruz may have met her match with Molly. We can prepare a stall for her to sleep in, and she can roam with us during the day."

"Oh my gosh, sounds perfect."

"Like a match made in heaven, and I haven't met either of them. Mitch is right, though, they are cute and playful."

"A family bought her as a birthday present for their daughter without thinking about the space she would need. She should be perfect here with all the space to run and play."

"I look forward to meeting your four-legged family, and your two-legged one, too." Whit grinned.

"I'll be taking Mitch home to Alabama tomorrow and return to Florida to prepare for my move. I hope to return no later than next Sunday, so please drop in to meet Cruz. She's a mess, but I love her."

"She'll love it here and living with you again. Cruz whines for an hour every time you leave."

"Just one more time then, and we'll be together," Eli answered. "I'll never leave her again."

133

Whit could see the adoration Eli had for the dog all over her face. "I look forward to meeting Cruz and spending more time getting to know her. I reckon I'll head home and leave you two to prepare for your trip. I'll drop by next Monday after you've settled in. Thanks for lunch."

"Thanks for the fantastic tomatoes."

"Any time. Please come over and pick whatever you'd like. I overplanted this year."

"How did you get here? I didn't see a vehicle?"

"About three hundred yards upstream, there's a tree that created a natural bridge between our properties. A much shorter walk than going all the way around. Do you expect any mail? I can check it for you while you're gone."

"That would be great. Shouldn't be much mail, but it will give me an excuse to come over and check out your garden."

Whit laughed. "You don't need an excuse. Drop by any time."

"Would you mind showing us where the bridge is?" Mitch asked.

"Sure, no problem. Come on, my lazy cat," Whit called to Oscar who had found a sunny spot to nap in. He lifted his head at the sound of his name and stretched as he stood and meandered toward her. Whit turned to look at Eli. "I've been threatening to go get some kittens for months to keep him company, but now I won't have to. You hear this Oscar, kittens and lots of them." She chuckled as he dashed past her to the front door. "See, he can move fast, but usually only associated with meals though."

They all laughed as he slid to a stop and waited for the door to open. Eli and Mitch walked out with Whit and followed the trail up the mountain until she showed them the overgrown path to the bridge.

"I'll clear this out a bit when I get back," Mitch promised.

"No worries," Eli said. "I plan on doing some trimming along the trail anyhow, so I'll take care of this."

When they reached the log, Oscar scampered ahead. Whit stopped and turned toward them. "Have a safe trip, and I'll see you when you get home."

"Thanks again," Eli said, and they watched her turn to cross the bridge.

As they started down the trail home, Mitch bumped into Eli's shoulder. "That was interesting."

"What do you mean?"

"Well in case you didn't notice, Whit is pretty darn cute and blushed almost every time you spoke to her."

"Are you kidding me?"

"Aunt Eli, I swear sometimes you can be so obtuse."

"Obtuse? Where did you hear such a big word?" she teased.

"Hey, I know a few of them, but seriously, I think she's into you."

"Mitch Fortner, she's way too young for me. She's not much older than you."

"Age means nothing as long as they are consenting adults. If you like what you see, go for it."

"I am so going to have a conversation with your dad," she teased. They fell silent as she contemplated her nephew's words. *He was right about some things, she is cute as a button.*

When they arrived at the cabin, she tossed him the truck keys. "Go get your cooler and filleting knife out before you return to fishing. Do you want me to clean what you've already caught?"

"No, ma'am, I'll do them all at once. I'll grab the chair and bring it down if you want to break out a cold one and watch the Great White Fisherman at work."

"That sounds like the perfect way to spend an afternoon. What do you want for dinner?"

"Those sandwiches were delicious, and we still need to finish the lunchmeat so how about another round of sandwiches?"

"Fine by me," she answered and walked into the cabin to grab a cold beer. She grabbed a second to share with Mitch. He was almost of legal age, and she'd much prefer he drink in a safe environment than out somewhere else. No matter how much he was growing, he was still a young man. "Here, I think you deserve one of these."

Mitch smiled as he took the beer from her. "Just don't tell Mom."

"I wouldn't dare," she answered, and sat in the chair, stretching her legs out toward the water.

†

Whit returned home and spent some time in her garden, surveying her vegetables. "I think it's time for some fresh corn and a nice salad," she told Oscar, who was weaving through the stalks. She picked several ears and walked to the house to get a pail for the other vegetables. After filling the container, she went to the kitchen to prep them for dinner.

As she sat at her small table, Whit found her thoughts drifting across the stream. Her time spent chatting with Mitch revealed a wealth of information about him and his aunt. Whit had plenty of intelligence, but her experience in the realm of sexuality fell far short for her age. There had been a brief encounter with a fellow student at MIT, but the woman wasn't looking for a permanent relationship and ended the affair after two months. Whit felt guilty for not being devastated by the news, but she realized her life was full without the demands a relationship would make on her. Today, seeing Eli, Whit wondered if her theory was still valid. Something about her had a magnetic effect that made her want to get closer. The warmth in Eli's dark eyes drew her in like a moth to a flame. They reminded her of dark cocoa, sweet and comforting. She was almost sure the look would change dramatically when Eli's ire was sparked, and the dark eyes would fill with dangerous emotion. She hoped she would never be the recipient of that glare.

Whit felt the warmth and strength in Eli's hand as she held on after their greeting. There was a low buzzing of electricity which passed through their touch, and she was sure Eli felt it, too, causing her to release her hand. It was all too soon for Whit's liking. She felt a deep attraction to the woman that she couldn't fathom, but it was definitely there.

Mitch seemed quite the character. He had a quick wit for someone his age, but she could also tell he held several passions in his life. Fishing was an obvious one, but his adoration of his aunt was refreshing. Happy to spend time with her even if it meant long hours of work. He didn't seem to be someone who would shy away from commitments. Whit was looking forward to working with him on their solar project and would begin designing a system before his return.

As she peeled and chopped her vegetables, she found her muscles aching from the broad smile on her face. She was excited to have new neighbors and was looking forward to getting to know them better. Whit placed her salad in the refrigerator to chill and turned on her computer.

Her curiosity stoked, she completed an internet search for information regarding Eli. She was disappointed to find there was so little information beyond necessary demographic facts. Whit was surprised to discover she was forty-four. She did not look her age. People often told her she didn't look her age either, because of her petite stature, but the sixteen-year difference in their ages wouldn't deter her at all. Whit had never fit in with her age group as a child, and had blended well with an older crowd. Her quick advancement in her education through her undergraduate and doctorate work had always placed her in groups with more mature students. At first, her fellow students questioned her abilities, since she was such a young age, but once they learned of her work, they never doubted her intelligence.

Whit entered her private server and watched the video feed she had recorded the previous night. Something in deep space seemed off, but she could not determine just yet what it was. Tonight, she would search the area for further clues. Something in her gut just didn't feel right, and she wanted to find the answers, if possible. She uploaded the file and sent it to one of her fellow scientists with a note to inquire about his potential theory of what seemed to be emerging. She ran a query through the NASA dedicated site she had access to but did not see any evidence of an anomaly. "Interesting," she whispered as she closed down the link.

†

Eli relaxed in her seat, watching as Mitch reeled in several more trout. The breeze had picked up, cooling the air coming off the water, and if she looked at the right spot, she could glimpse the cabin across the stream. *I hadn't expected to find I have such a beautiful neighbor, but it is a welcome surprise.* She was deep in thought replaying the encounter with Whit when Mitch hollered out.

"Earth to Eli."

Eli startled when he called her name, and she looked over to find him smiling at her, his rod in one hand and a bucket of fish in another.

"There you are." He grinned. "I thought I'd lost you for a minute. What were you thinking about so hard?"

"Just relaxing and enjoying this beautiful day. Are you done fishing?"

"Yes, ma'am. I've got enough for a great meal when I get home. I will take these out by the barn to clean them. Do you want me to bring you a fresh beer?"

"You sure you don't need my help?"

"No, ma'am. I can handle this. I think I'll store my fishing gear out there if that's okay with you."

"That's a good idea. You go ahead. I'll wait until you finish and we'll have a beer together. I was thinking about building a campfire tonight, but I think we should wait until we get a pit built."

"That dog will hunt," he said. "I'll see you in a bit."

Eli smiled at his comment. Despite being raised in the city, Mitch was a pure country boy at heart. She had grown accustomed to his presence and worried she would miss him when he went back home. She sighed at the thought. *At least I'll have Cruz and a brand new four-legged family to keep me company. Plenty of projects to get started on. I'll stay so busy I won't have time to dwell on his absence. There's always a cute neighbor to get to know better if I need some human companionship.* She chuckled to herself. "You, old cougar." After the recent demise of her relationship with Sara, Eli reminded herself to choose more wisely if she began a new relationship. She wasn't sure she was ready for that, especially with someone as young as Whit, but damn, she was attractive.

The breeze flowing through the trees caught her attention, and she swore she heard Whit's voice whispering *Welcome*. Surely, she just had an audible hallucination. There was no way she could hear a voice from that distance, especially a whisper. The incident wasn't the first time, and it left her questioning what was going on. Eli knew that sound traveled well across bodies of water, if the temperatures were moderate, but a whisper seemed impossible. She was pondering the enigma when the sounds of Mitch's boots thumped on the porch.

He popped his head out the door. "I'll place the fish in bags and put them in the fridge. I need to clean up a bit and then I'll grab beers. Is that okay?"

"Yes, it's wonderful. I'm enjoying this nice breeze and the sound of the stream."

"Well alrighty then." He chuckled and disappeared into the cabin.

Moments later, Eli heard a rustling noise at the edge of the stream and looked up to find a doe and twin fawns approaching from the far side of the stream for a drink. She crept to the door and motioned for Mitch to come outside. The slight click of the door opening caught the doe's attention, but she did not bolt away. Eli and Mitch approached the railing to watch the small family quench their thirst.

When they had their fill of the sweet water, the doe led the fawns into the meadow.

"That was neat," Mitch whispered.

"Yeah, it was. I want to get a salt lick or a deer block to put upstream a bit. It's nice to see the wildlife from our deck."

"Pretty cool," Mitch answered.

The breeze blew across the deck, and Eli caught a whiff of Mitch. She wrinkled her nose. "Ewww, you smell fishy."

"I know. I'm headed to the shower now."

"Good." Eli chuckled and watched him go.

†

After sharing the last of the sandwiches, Eli cleared the kitchen. "I'll pack my bag so we can roll out of here early in the morning."

"I've got my bag packed already, so I'll be ready. What time do you plan to leave?"

"I figure we can get ready and have some breakfast by six, if we get to bed early tonight."

"No problem. I'm bushed. It's been great being here with you."

"I know, I'll miss the heck out of you while you're gone."

"I keep praying Mom and Dad will let me stay when we come to visit."

"Buckle down on your schoolwork, so they'll know you're serious. I think if you can show your parents you're committed to finishing early, they will let you stay."

"I sure hope so. Can we stop somewhere in town for ice for the fish? I don't want to deplete your supply here."

"No problem. I spotted a few machines when I was in town today."

"I'll see you in the morning then." He walked over and hugged her. "Goodnight, Aunt Eli. Love you."

"Love you more. Sleep well."

†

Eli didn't have much to pack when she realized she would only bring it home in a week. She placed her laptop and a few items together, and clothes for the trip home, before showering and climbing into bed. Her window remained open and filled the room with the scent of the mountain and the crisp temperature. She sighed in contentment as her body relaxed in her comfortable bed. *This is home.* The chorus of crickets lulled her to sleep.

CHAPTER SEVEN

The next morning, they were on the road early as planned. Mitch started the day talkative, but as they drew closer to Montgomery, he grew quiet. She looked over to find him staring out the window. "You okay? You got quiet on me all of a sudden."

"I already miss the mountain." He looked at her, and she could see tears pooling in his eyes.

"It won't be long before you can come back. I will miss you, too. I've enjoyed this week."

"The best spring break I've ever had," he said as he swiped his hand across his eyes.

Eli's heart ached for Mitch. She knew he loved the mountain as much as she did. She would do her best to convince Mark to let him stay when they visited. Eli was sure she could monitor him to complete the rest of his schoolwork.

Eli looked down at her gas gauge. She didn't need gas yet, but it was a convenient excuse to make a stop. "I'll take the next exit to get gas and stretch our legs. You want to drive the rest of the way home?"

"Sure." He perked up in his seat.

Eli smiled and turned on her blinker. "I've got the munchies. Do you want something to snack on?"

"Do I have to remind you I'm a growing boy? I never turn down food."

"I reckon I forget." She pulled into the island for gas and handed him a card. "Fill us and meet me inside the store."

"Yes, ma'am," he replied and bounded out of the truck.

Eli walked to the store to peruse the aisles. *I need a Mountain Dew to give me some caffeine.* She plucked out a large bottle and a bottle of water. She was studying the candy selection when Mitch joined her.

"I want one of everything." He chuckled.

"I'm going sweet and salty," she answered as she picked out a payday, and then some peanut butter cups.

Eli climbed in to the passenger side and opened the glove compartment. She took out a set of keys and handed them to Mitch.

"What are those?"

"Your keys to our new home. When you return, you can get into the property, the cabin, and the barn."

"Thanks, Aunt Eli." He tucked the keys into his pocket and started the truck.

Once on the road, the miles to Montgomery flew by. When Mitch pulled into the drive at his home, he stopped and turned to Eli. "Thanks for a great week."

"We will have many more to come, I promise. I'll grab your bag if you want to carry the cooler inside."

"Works for me," he answered, and handed her the keys.

Brad and Cruz met them at the door. "Cruz knew you were here," he said and reached for Mitch's bag. "What you got in the cooler, Bro?"

"You'll just have to wait and see."

Mark walked to the door. "Hey, you two. Welcome back. Did you have a great trip?"

"Best spring break ever," Mitch replied. "Wait until you see what I brought home."

"Put the cooler on the table and show me. I'm dying with curiosity now." Mark moved the placemats from the table, and Mitch lowered the cooler.

Laura walked into the room. "I thought I heard you two. Hey, Son," she said and kissed him on the cheek. "What have you got here?"

Mitch opened the lid. "I brought home a mess of fresh trout for dinner."

Eli looked at Mark. "He caught and cleaned every one of them by himself and wanted to surprise y'all." She could see Mitch's face beaming with pride.

"The fishing was insane. I could almost cast from the deck, and there's an even bigger stream where our cabin will be built."

"If your mom and dad approve of the spot," Eli reminded him.

"Are you kidding me? They will freaking love it. Brad, you will be in heaven there."

"It sounds incredible," Brad admitted. "I hope you left some fish for me."

"There are plenty of spots to fish around the area, but I doubt we will ever need to go off the property."

Mark looked at Eli. "Are you sure you brought back my son? I haven't seen him this excited in years."

"I love the place, Dad. It was my best spring break ever."

Mark grinned at Eli. "He's got the bug, too, huh?"

She looked up from where she was kneeling with Cruz. "Oh yeah, big time. The place is better than I could have dreamed, and has so much potential."

"We have a mechanical genius for a neighbor, and she's going to teach me how to install a solar power system."

"You've already met the neighbors? Y'all have been busy."

"Wait to you hear about Aunt Eli's plans for a playmate for Cruz."

"Do tell, what animal do you plan to torture?"

"The local animal shelter has a baby pygmy goat, named Molly. I think she will give Cruz a run for her money."

Mark broke out laughing. "That's incredible, but I think you're right. If they get along, they will have all that property to play."

"I plan to stop by Saturday to pick her up, if that's okay?"

"We'll miss the little terror, but I know she'll be happier with you."

"I hope so. I've missed Cruz so much. I should have never given in to Sara. That's one mistake I'll never make again."

"We live, and we learn," Laura chimed in.

"Yes, we do," Mark agreed. "Can you stay for supper?"

"I need to get on the road. This week will be crazy busy as I get ready to move and close out some projects for work. Enjoy those fish. He was excited to bring them home to you."

"My mouth is watering already."

"He cooked some one night for our dinner and did a fantastic job. Best fish I've had in a long time."

"You want to cook tonight?" Mark asked Mitch.

"Sure, if you'll make Grandpa's hush puppies and some garlic grits."

Mark smiled at his son. "That's too good of a deal to pass on."

"I hate to drop him and run, but daylight's a-wasting." Eli took Cruz's face in her hands. "I will be here for you soon." She kissed her nose and looked at Mark. "Will you walk out with me?"

"Sure. I'll be right back."

"I'll see you next weekend, thanks again for all your help, Mitch. Love y'all."

"See you soon, Aunt Eli."

Mark walked out to the truck with her. "Is everything okay?"

"It couldn't be more perfect. I wanted to give you a heads up on something. Mitch had a fantastic time and was a joy to have around. He wants to double down on his schoolwork and hopes to convince you and Laura to allow him to stay when y'all visit in a few weeks." She paused for a breath. "The internet is functional, and I will make sure he finishes his assignments before I work his tail off every day, if you let him stay."

"You sure you are okay with that? He can be a real slug about doing his schoolwork."

"Being in the mountains will be motivation enough for him, I think. He was the happiest I've ever seen him there. If he can get ahead on his assignments like he plans, I'd like for you to consider his request." She shuffled her feet for a second. "Mitch had tears in his eyes when we left this morning."

"I'll talk it over with Laura. She'll be the hard sell, but if he can get ahead, I think he deserves a chance."

"I do too. Thanks for considering it."

"Thank you for allowing him to go with you this week. Mitch seems so much different since he left."

"Mitch's a great worker, and there are so many challenging projects to tackle. He won't have time to dwell on life."

"Let's see how he does this week and when he plans to spring it on us. I appreciate the heads up. This way, I can break the ice with Laura."

"I hear ya, Baby Bro. Love you guys."

"Love you, too. Text me when you make it home. I miss you already."

She hugged him and opened the truck door. "See you soon."

"Be careful."

Eli backed out of the drive and turned south for the final leg of the day's journey. It was still early afternoon, and she would make it home well before sunset. Traffic was light, and she found her thoughts drifting to North Carolina.

Eli pulled into her drive and triggered the remote to open her garage door. The house was quiet when she entered, and it didn't feel much like home. *I guess I just need to work through the bad memories. This is still my home, just not the one I want to live at for now. I can always return when I need a beach fix.*

She tossed her bag on the bed and looked around her room. There's little I will take away from here. It feels good to start fresh in the mountains. Maybe some clothes and a few belongings. I can always come back if I need something I've left behind.

She remembered her promise to text Mark when she made it home, so she picked up her phone. *Made it.*

Great news. You're missing a great fish dinner. Mitch did an excellent job.

I never had a doubt. Mitch is a good kid. Enjoy dinner, and I'll talk to you soon. Love ya!

Love you too.

147

Eli walked to the living room where she had left the boxes she had bought to store Sara's belongings and assembled the last six. She was sure they would hold everything she needed to take to North Carolina. She filled the first box with a variety of boots, shoes, and a drawer of socks dumped out of her chest of drawers.

Inspecting her closet, Eli looked at all the business attire she had amassed during her working years. "I won't need much of this after this week." She decided on six outfits which she could wear during a variety of events. "I'll donate the rest of you on my next trip home."

Loading a box of jeans and T-shirts brought back some forgotten memories. Trips to concerts, vacations, and her favorite sports teams flooded her with emotions. Most collected with Carol and Sara. She sealed the box and carried it to the garage to load into her truck later in the week. Warmer clothes and jackets were next. She didn't have much in the way of winter-weight clothing, so she would have to make some purchases in North Carolina. Sweatshirts and pants filled a box with a few light-weight jackets thrown on top.

Eli's stomach growled to protest that she hadn't eaten a meal since breakfast, and her travel snacks had long burned off. She opened her refrigerator and saw nothing which appealed to her, so she ordered from her favorite pizza company. The light for her answering machine was blinking, and she pushed the button to play. Most were sales pitches by financial firms and another message from Carol. She sat down at her table and created a list of items she would pack for the move as she waited for the pizza to arrive. *What should I do about Carol?*

When she left at the end of the week, Eli didn't have plans to return for a while. If she wanted to meet with Carol, it would have to be in the next few days. She used her phone and sent Carol a text. *Not ready to forgive you yet, but willing to hear you out. Dinner Wednesday?* Eli debated for several seconds whether to send the text. "What the hell, I guess a lifetime of friendship is worth an hour of my time." She hit send.

Eli walked from room to room and put together a small box of photos and other items she planned to take to the cabin. For a moment, she felt melancholy about leaving this part of her life behind. Eli had experienced so much in Pensacola and had established an excellent career, but she felt overjoyed by the prospects awaiting her in North Carolina. Eli had paid her dues, and by a stroke of luck realized her dreams several years earlier than expected. Eli refused to waste her energy dwelling on what once was; instead, she'd focus on all the possibilities ahead.

Her doorbell rang, and she could see a pizza delivery woman standing at the front door. She took a twenty from her wallet and opened the door.

"Your pizza, ma'am." The young woman shuffled as she handed the box to Eli. "Hey, aren't you the lady who won the lottery? Congratulations."

"Thanks," Eli responded and handed her the twenty for the pizza and a tip. "Keep the change," she added with a wink. "Maybe go buy a lottery ticket."

"I may just do that. Have a great night."

"You too," Eli responded and stepped inside. The garlic butter smell assaulted her nose, and her mouth began to water. "Only ten thousand calories," she said as she kicked the door closed behind her. Eli heard a thud and turned to see the door had not closed. She saw a booted foot in the doorway and spun in time to see Sara standing in the stoop.

"What do you think you're doing here?"

"I thought I'd drop by and we could have a chat. I am so sorry about what happened."

149

Sara took a step toward Eli.

"No, that's not about to happen. Stop right there. You no longer live here, and you are not welcome. You have only seconds before I call the police."

Sara smiled. "You won't do that."

"Do you want to find out?" Eli glared at her.

"Why do you have to be such a bitch?"

"Strange question coming from you." Eli took a step toward the door and grabbed the handle. "Don't ever set foot on this property. I doubt the hospital administration would like it if one of their employees had a restraining order against them."

"You wouldn't." Sara sneered.

"Oh, yes, I would." Eli slammed the door and leaned against it waiting until she heard angry footsteps stomp away before looking at the video camera. She panned the camera and watched Sara climb into her car and listened to the screeching of tires as she pulled away. "I won't miss that." She set the deadbolt and the alarm.

Eli placed the pizza on the bar in the kitchen and pulled out a beer. "Might as well add some extra calories." She chuckled. In the commotion with Sara, she hadn't heard the text from Carol arrive. Her phone pinged again to alert her. Eli picked up the phone to read the message.

Perfect, when, and where?

Our usual sushi spot, five o'clock and you're buying.

Absolutely. Thanks. See you then.

The flavor of the meats and cheeses exploded in her mouth, and she enjoyed three slices before deciding to save the rest for the next day. She was one of those odd people who enjoyed cold pizza for leftovers. Most of the time, she never even bothered to reheat. "I like what I like," she said as she closed the box and placed it in the refrigerator. She drained the bottle of beer and tossed it in the waste can.

Eli walked to her bedroom and moved the empty boxes to the end of the bed. "I'll fill you later this week." She rinsed off in the shower and dressed in nightclothes. *A few days in the office, and I'll be heading north again, to my new home.* She stretched out on her bed and listened to the soft whirring of the fan. *I have no clue what I'll say to Carol or what to expect from her.* Eli drifted off to sleep, too tired to worry about those scenarios in her head.

Eli walked into her boss' office and met with a round of applause from her co-workers. They had all gathered to share their congratulations and their envy for her winning the lottery. Eli was surprised by their excitement for her, and she realized she would miss them. She'd worked with most of them for twenty years.

Once the office thinned out, she and her boss got down to business. He introduced a young woman named Tracy, who would take over her position. She seemed competent and confident she could handle the role. After a two-hour meeting to bring them up to speed on several open projects, Eli shook her boss' hand.

"Thanks for all you've done for me over the years."

"You've been a great employee and friend. I hate to see you go, but you deserve to have all your dreams come true. Just keep your phone handy in case I need you to answer some questions."

Eli smiled. "I will. I'm heading to North Carolina soon, but call if you need me. I won't leave you hanging. Thanks for letting me go on this short notice."

"Not by my choice. I'd never let you go if I could keep you."

"Thanks, Chuck. That means a lot."

"Good luck and drop by when you come into town."

"I will." Eli left his office and stopped by personnel to sign her discharge paperwork and to give out forwarding address information. It was early afternoon when she left the office and walked to her truck with tears filling her eyes. *Another chapter done. A new one beginning.* Eli wasn't ready to go home, so she took a long drive down the beach and pulled over to watch the waves breaking onto the shore. The sugar-white sand of the beach was dotted with beach-goers, and a few children played in the surf. This would always be home, but a new home and new adventures awaited her.

When she returned home, she filled the remaining boxes and turned on her laptop. She had sent Laura an email asking her to choose items she and Mitch had put in her shopping cart and to add anything else she thought Eli would need in her new home. Laura had emailed her and told her to not freak when she saw the items left in her cart, but they would all fit in well within her new home. Eli looked at the list and approved of Laura's choices. She was about to hit order when she realized she wouldn't be there to accept the shipments. Eli made a mental note to order them on her way to North Carolina. Eli would have plenty of boxes for her new feline family to play in.

Deciding on leftover pizza, she turned on the oven to reheat it. Eli looked through her messages and saw Mitch had sent her a text. Eli smiled when she read his short message.

Broke the plan to Mom and Dad last night. Not an outright 'no,' but 'we'll see.'

That's good news. Now the rest is up to you. Get to work on those school assignments.

Eli could see the movement on the screen, indicating he was writing a response. She popped the pizza in the oven and waited.

I sat up late last night and have been working on them today. I'm caught up and starting on assignments to get ahead of schedule. Trying to pull that C to a B this week.

You can do it. I'm proud of you.

Thanks, Aunt Eli. Let me get to work. Love you!

Love you too. See you soon.

Eli was excited Mitch was working hard on his assignments. She wrote a text to Mark and sent it. *Mitch told me he didn't get an outright no. Seems excited and working hard.*

It was several minutes before Mark responded. She had just taken her first bite of the steaming pizza when her phone pinged.

I don't know what you did with my son, but thank you. I've never seen him this motivated. He didn't work this hard to get his truck.

He fell in love with the property and the potential it has for fun projects for a young man. You and Laura have done well raising him. You should be proud.

More so every day. How's everything in Pensacola?

Going well. Finished work today. Got boxes packed. Meeting Carol for dinner Wednesday. May start back earlier than planned.

I'm glad to hear you're meeting Carol. Come anytime you're ready. Heading to a meeting. Love ya!

Love you too.

†

Eli finished eating and returned to her laptop. She opened a new Word document and began to make a list of the tasks she wanted to work on when she returned. She spent an hour writing them down and then went back to prioritize them. Preparing for the new family was paramount. She checked her email and found a list of items to purchase from Erin and Doc Loren. She looked at the website for Merrill's Feed store and arranged an online account. They didn't provide a weekend delivery service, so she placed her order for delivery on

Monday. Eli continued to make a list until her eyes started to feel heavy. There was one more item she wanted to search for and went to her standby Amazon to begin her search.

"Bingo," she spoke aloud when she found an in-ground fire pit with a snuff-it lid which would allow her to choke out the fire and protect the area from embers. It had a lift-out container to allow for the removal of ashes. "Perfect," she said, and added the item to her shopping cart. If it worked well at the creek, she would purchase another for the trail shelter on the AT.

Satisfied with her progress, Eli retired for the evening and dreamed of a young woman, with a sprinkling of freckles across her face, and green eyes that sparkled when she looked into them.

"Whit," she whispered in her dreams.

†

Whit sat in the lab trying to focus on work, but her mind continued to drift away from the heavens to think about her handsome new neighbor. She'd been gone for two days, and Whit wished for the weekend when she could expect Eli to return. Maybe she would cook a vegetable meal from her garden that she could share with Eli when she came home. She was sure Eli would be tired from the long drive and wouldn't feel like cooking a hot meal. *Yes, that's what I'll do.* She took out a notepad and started making a list.

154

CHAPTER EIGHT

Wednesday arrived, and Eli was awake early. She decided to go for a run and then relax until it was time to meet Carol. Eli still wasn't sure what to say to her old friend, but Carol deserved a chance to explain her actions. The more she thought about the events of the last week, Eli felt like she should thank Carol for her part in changing her life. Her luck and life had changed for the better since arriving home early to find Carol and Sara in bed together. If she hadn't stormed out to go for a run and bought the lottery ticket, her life might have stayed the same. Or worse, she could have been miserable and forced to work longer before she could retire and follow her dream.

She laced her shoes and grabbed a bottle of water to take on her run. The sun was up, and a beautiful day was blossoming. The humidity was low, but she soon worked her body into a sweat. *Might as well get used to sweating. I've got a lot of physical work planned and will be doing a lot more sweating before it gets done.* Just the thought of North Carolina put a smile on her face. When she slowed to a stop and drank her water, she watched the traffic leaving her neighborhood as people began their commute to work. *Soon, all I'll do is walk outside the cabin to do my job. No more commuting or lonely nights spent in hotels.*

Eli started walking home to cool down and added a stop to a big box store to purchase a few tools to complete her projects. A shovel, chainsaw, and hatchet would get her started. She could get other supplies once she returned. Eli was excited about putting in the fire pit and having it installed and stocked for Mitch's return. There were plenty of downed trees, and smaller trees she planned to take down, to open the trail to the top of the mountain. Eli would purchase a small firewood rack for the pit and a larger one for the cabin. As she cut the trees into sections, she could use the Gator to haul them down and sort them into the racks for future use. Getting excited about her plans, Eli walked fast, eager to return home to a shower. She planned to spend the rest of the morning making her purchases and packing the remaining boxes in the rear of her truck. Tomorrow, Eli would drive to Montgomery and then drive to North Carolina on Saturday morning. She wanted to arrive early so Cruz could burn off some energy after the long ride and be able to settle into her new home. They would spend Sunday exploring and then go for the playdate with Molly on Monday.

†

Eli returned from shopping and loaded the boxes into the rear of the truck. She had stopped by the post office to place a forwarding order for her mail and couldn't think of anything else she needed to do, so she decided for a short nap before preparing to meet Carol for dinner. She had just stretched out for her rest when she heard her phone ping with a text message.

Four more assignments completed this morning, and I now have all B's.

That's excellent news. How many more will you get done this week?

I'm hoping for at least five more.

I'm coming tomorrow, but will wait if it will interrupt your flow.

Really? I'll work even harder if you're here. I'll even make you lunch if you get here in time tomorrow.

I'll treat you and Brad to lunch if you get a lot done between now and then.

Deal. Getting back to work. Love ya!

More.

Eli set her alarm and snuggled into her pillows.

†

Carol paced her apartment, nervous as a cat. Relieved that Eli had answered her attempts to communicate, Carol had no idea what she could say to make things right between them again. They were both been used by Sara. Carol realized too late she had been a fool to jeopardize their friendship for someone so shallow. Eli would eventually forgive her, but she doubted she would ever regain her trust or respect.

She showered and dressed for dinner. She took a ride to the beach before meeting Eli. Maybe the water would calm her nerves and bring her peace before she faced the friend she had betrayed.

†

Eli turned off the alarm and stretched before climbing out of bed. She stripped out of her clothes, placing a load in the washer before streaking to the bathroom. Alexa was playing the Eagles, and the hot shower was invigorating. She was singing along with Glenn Frey as he belted out the lyrics to "Take it Easy." *I need to pack Alexa.* Eli slipped into a pair of jeans and an Eagles T-shirt. *Might as well stay in a good mood. No matter what happens tonight, I'll be on my way home tomorrow.*

As she drove across town to the restaurant, Eli let her thoughts take a trip down memory lane. She and Carol had experienced and survived so much during their long-term friendship. Happiness and heartbreaks, deaths, and births. Eli was disappointed in Carol, but she was sure she had done things she had been forgiven for. Destroying their friendship should not be the last act of Sara's departure. Carol was too significant in her life to let that happen. Eli pulled into the parking lot and saw Carol pacing near the front door. She parked and walked to the restaurant.

Carol looked at her as she approached and offered her a nervous smile. Eli returned her smile and raised her arms for a hug when she walked to Carol. The shocked look on Carol's face made Eli chuckle.

She whispered to Carol, "Don't get me wrong, I'm still mad at you, but I won't let Sara take you from me."

"I deserve that for being such a fool. I am so sorry Eli, I never meant for things to turn out like this. I don't deserve your forgiveness."

Eli released her and shrugged. "I don't think it turned out too bad. I'm now a millionaire about to embark on my dream journey of owning a piece of heaven in North Carolina and bringing Cruz home where she belongs."

"You make some valid points. I'm sorry I hurt you."

"It was the best hurt I've ever felt. I should have recognized long ago that Sara and I weren't forever. You helped me see that clearly."

"Still, I betrayed your trust and our friendship."

"Yes, you did and it will take some time before I can trust you again. I know how manipulative Sara can be and I think she played both of us. She's always been selfish, it's her needs first before she considers anyone else's."

"I should have been strong enough to not allow my own urges to win out. Yes, she's a master manipulator, but I lost sight of our friendship. We've been through too much together for me to betray you. I saw an article in the paper this morning which was interesting."

"Do tell," Eli said.

"I saw that Sara was arrested for driving under the influence last night. The mug shot in the arrest section was not complimentary."

"I guess karma is a bitch. She dropped by last night wanting to talk her way back in and I threatened to call the cops on her for trespassing. She needs new tires with the way she pulled out of my street. I'm sure my threat wouldn't have damaged her career as much as an arrest. I don't wish her bad things, but what goes around comes around."

"Hope I don't get karma like that, even though I deserve it."

Eli could see the tears in Carol's eyes. "We all have speed bumps in our lives from time to time. I've driven past it and so should you. You can start by buying me dinner."

Carol sighed and smiled. "You got it. You can fill me in on all the happenings in your life."

"C'mon then, I'm hungry." Eli pulled the door open for her friend to enter.

Once they ordered their sushi and meals, Eli told Carol how she had gone to the beach for a run after she found them together. "Stopping at the store for a drink was the start of my future. I didn't realize what happened for a day or so." Eli took a drink of the water. "When I found out I had won, I knew what I would do, and within hours, I had contacted my realtor in North Carolina to make the deal for me."

"I know you've dreamed of owning property there for years. I'm happy it has come to fruition."

"I've drooled over one piece of property for months, even if it was not within my price range, but winning the lottery changed all that. The place is gorgeous, and I can't wait for you to see it."

Carol's smile spread across her face. "I'd like that. Maybe I'll make a road trip once the school year ends."

"It would be great. Mitch is spending the summer with me, helping with projects. I'm sure Mark and the rest of the family will be up often, too. I've already picked out a spot for their cabin."

"I bet Mark is on cloud nine."

"I keep teasing him with photos, and it's driving him crazy. Mitch spent his spring break there with me last week and fell in love. He's got two beautiful streams to fish from and acres to roam."

The waitress brought their sushi rolls to the table.

"I can't wait to see Cruz with so much room to run and play."

"I know how much you miss her."

"No more. I'm driving to Mark's tomorrow, and will head home on Saturday."

"I love the smile on your face when you talk of Cruz and North Carolina. I will miss you, but I know that's where you are meant to be."

Eli nodded as she bit into a piece of sushi. "It feels like home. I'll still keep my place here in case I need a beach fix, but my heart lies in the mountain. I thought it from the first time I set foot on the property, and the mountain whispers to me to soothe my soul."

"Wow, that sounds deep." Carol smiled. "I think you have found what you have longed to have for years."

"I have. It just feels so right. You want to come by the house for a beer?" Eli asked as Carol paid the check.

"Yes, it would be great. I don't know how long it will be before I see you again."

"I'll see you at the house then," Eli said and walked to her truck. She took a deep breath. "I'm glad we set that straight," she said as she reached down to start her engine.

Eli pulled into the garage and waited for Carol to arrive. When they walked into the house, Eli took two beers from the refrigerator. She handed one to Carol.

"Cheers," she said and tipped her bottle toward her friend.

"Cheers."

They walked into the living room and sat on the couch. "You said you planned on keeping this place. Would you consider allowing me to rent it?"

Eli broke out laughing and saw the confusion on Carol's face.

"What is so funny?"

"Mitch made the same suggestion. He thought you might want to live here."

Carol smiled. "Smart boy. My apartment lease is up in September. I'd love to rent this place from you. I'd leave your room as is, and you could come any time you want."

"We can talk about it when you come for a visit. It makes sense for someone to get some use out of this place. It's been a great home." Eli stood and walked to the kitchen. When she returned, she handed Carol her keys. "In case you need to get in here for some reason. I've got a pool service coming by, lawn care, and the security system has been updated. The code is our college graduation date."

Carol took the set of keys and looked at the photo. "Those were some great times, weren't they?"

"Yeah, they were. College life was a blast, and then we landed in the real world."

Carol grinned. "I think we turned out pretty good."

"We did." She turned in her seat to look at Carol. "Who's going to keep you out of trouble when I'm gone?"

"Lord knows I need to find someone who's trustworthy," Carol answered. "I will miss you. Since we've become friends, we've never been far apart from one another."

"I know. Come for a visit whenever you can. My door is always open. You may like it there and find a spot for yourself."

"You never know. I've still got a few years until I can retire. Keep an eye out for a spot you'd think I'd like."

"Will do," Eli answered and took a long drink of her beer.

"What time do you plan on leaving tomorrow?"

"As soon as my feet hit the ground. I can't wait to start this adventure."

"Promise me you'll keep in touch and let me know how things are going."

"I will, and we even have internet in the hills. I'll send you some photographs of the stuff we'll be working on."

"That sounds like fun. I'll head out so you can get some sleep. I love you, my friend."

Eli stood with Carol, and she hugged her. "I love you too. Try to stay out of trouble. I'll call you soon."

Carol held the keys and then tucked them in her pocket. "Thanks for tonight. I don't deserve forgiveness, but I'm glad you have found your happiness."

"Lord knows I've made plenty of mistakes. I can't let this ruin a friendship we've shared for so long."

They walked to the door together. "I'll call you soon. Be safe driving home."

"See you soon, Eli." Carol turned and walked to her car.

Eli watched her pull out of the driveway, then locked the door and set the alarm. She dumped the empty bottles in the garbage and walked through the house. Eli loved this home but knew it was time to move on with her life. She prepared for bed and slipped into a deep sleep.

†

Eli woke before the alarm, showered, and was ready to hit the road before the sun came up. She made a final walk-through of her home and felt a twinge of sadness for leaving it behind.

"Too much to look forward to ahead. Shake it off," she told herself, set the alarm, and locked the door to her past. She walked to her truck to start her brand-new life.

An hour after starting her journey, Eli pulled into the Smokehouse restaurant for breakfast. The cathead biscuits, farm-fresh eggs, and sausage breakfast were plentiful, and when she finished eating, she approached the counter to pay. When her eyes landed on the homemade cinnamon raisin biscuits, Eli bought a dozen to take to Mark and the boys who loved them. She topped off her tank and returned to the highway.

Mark and Laura would be at work, and Brad still in school when she arrived. Mitch should be awake and completing schoolwork. She'd take him to get Brad and then lunch if he'd made good progress on his assignments.

There was no rush for her to make it to Montgomery, so Eli exited from the interstate to take some back roads. She rolled her windows down and let the refreshing morning breeze blow through the truck. Eli had always been in a rush to get to her destination. She realized it had been many years since she'd driven through the small towns and countryside of south Alabama. Eli slowed when the city limit sign came to view, and a bright yellow school bus pulled in front of her as they stopped at a traffic light. She looked to her left to find three older gentlemen sitting on chairs outside a general store. They looked at her and smiled. She returned their warm smiles and waved as she pulled away from the light. The bus turned on the blinker and pulled into the drive of the combination elementary, middle, and high school campus. The memory of attending a small-town school system, much like this one, brought a smile to her face. She and Mark had been taught by one of the same teachers their father had as a child. That memory brought a twinge of sadness to Eli. Her father, a well-educated man, had succumbed to Alzheimer's disease after the affliction had destroyed his beautiful handwriting and sharp mind. She remembered how painful it was to see his decline year after year, until his brain went to sleep, and his body failed to recover.

The smell of fresh-cut hay brought her back from the painful memory. Just ahead she saw the faded, red, baling machine being pulled by a Massey Ferguson, looking worn by the summer sun. As children, they had spent many summers baling hay in the intense Florida sun. It was hot, physically demanding work, but were some of her most fond memories growing up.

The ping of her phone announcing a text drew her attention. She pulled off the road and looked at the message from Mitch.

On your way yet?

Sure am. Will be there in an hour.

Sweet. I've got three more assignments done. I'll have another by the time you get here. You want me to make lunch?

Naw, I promised to take you and Brad to lunch.

Just me. Brad has an afterschool activity today, so I won't get him until four. We can grab some ice cream after we get him.

Sounds good. What do you want for lunch?

How about some wings?

Perfect. See you soon.

Drive safe.

Will do. Love ya.

When Eli pulled onto the road, she soon found herself behind a line of traffic. She could see a John Deere tractor at the head of the line. With a shallow ditch running on both sides of the road, the farmer could not pull over to let the traffic pass, so Eli bided her time until a driveway came into view and the driver pulled off the road. She watched as traffic flew by and at least one driver blew his horn and shouted as they passed the farmer.

"Must be a city slicker." She chuckled and waved at the farmer as she passed the idling tractor. He smiled and returned her wave.

The sweet aroma of fresh-cut hay and the rich smell of the turned earth filled the truck. Soon these pleasures would be a part of her everyday life, and the heat and odors of big cities would be left behind.

Eli pulled into the drive at Mark's and reached over to get the bag of cinnamon raisin biscuits. She heard the door open, and Cruz and Mitch rushed out to meet her.

"What me to grab your bag?"

"Sure, the back is unlocked," she said as she knelt down for waves of kisses from Cruz. "Hey, baby girl. I missed you, too." She laughed and kissed the dog on the top of her head. "How's the schoolwork coming?"

"Really good," Mitch answered. "One more down and another almost half done."

"Fantastic news," she said as she held the door open for him. "I'll take the dogs outside and see if I can wear Cruz down a bit while you finish your assignment. Will you start another one before we go to lunch?"

"No, but I need to complete a test. If I do well, it will bring a 'B' to an 'A' so cross your fingers."

"Are you prepared for it?"

"Yes, ma'am, I'm sure I can do it."

"I'm extremely proud of you. You've made a great deal of progress since you've come home."

"I've got a goal to work towards." He grinned. "If I can finish early, I can work with you full-time. I'd much rather do that than sit in front of a computer all day."

"You keep this pace, and you might be close to finishing when y'all come visit."

"That's what I'm hoping for."

"See what you can accomplish when you put your mind to it? I know your dad is also proud of you."

Mitch chuckled. "Even Mom said she was amazed by the amount of work I've finished. She even checked with my teacher to make sure I was doing everything right."

"It sounds very positive, and if you keep it up, I bet you'll be staying on with me when they leave to come home."

"I sure hope so. I'll put your bag in my room and get to work. You know where everything is, so make yourself at home."

"Thanks. Oh, I brought biscuits from the Smokehouse," she said, and placed the bag on the counter.

"Cinnamon raisin?"

"Of course. You want me to pull out one for you?"

"Those are my favorites. Yes, please. I'll be right back."

Eli pulled down a plate and took out a giant biscuit and licked the stickiness from her fingers. "Damn, those are sweet," she said, and handed him the plate.

Mitch hugged her. "Thanks. I'm so glad you're here."

"Eat and get to work. I'll be out in the yard when you're done."

Eli opened the door and let the dogs outside. Cruz rushed ahead of Riley and searched until she found a tennis ball. She trotted to Eli and dropped the ball at her feet. Eli picked up the ball and waited for Cruz to sit and then sent the ball sailing across the yard. She laughed as Cruz flew after the ball and jumped to catch it on the second bounce. "Good catch," Eli called out, and Cruz rushed to her with the ball. She dropped the ball and sat in front of Eli. Eli reached down and patted her head and praised her performance. Cruz kept looking at the ball, unimpressed by the praise and urging Eli to throw it again.

"I know, just hush and throw the ball." She picked up the ball and threw it across the yard. She spotted a chair and took a seat while Cruz retrieved the ball.

They continued to play until Cruz's sides heaved as she tried to catch her breath. "Time for a break," Eli told her. "Go get a drink."

Cruz followed her command and went to get a drink of water. She lapped at the water with the same vigor she chased down the ball, and then trotted to Eli and placed her head in her lap.

"You're such a good girl," she praised Cruz. "I can't wait for you to see our new home." Cruz's chocolate brown eyes looked at her with such adoration. "I will never leave you behind again, I promise."

The sun felt good on her skin, and a slight breeze had come up. With the neighborhood gone to work or school, the air was filled with bird song and the noise of distant traffic. She watched a squirrel hop onto the top of the fence, grabbing Riley's attention. She took off after the squirrel, but her slow, plodding gait didn't worry the squirrel one bit.

Eli turned at the sound of the door opening as Mitch entered the yard. He saw Riley plodding after the squirrel. "What on earth is the big goof doing?"

"Hunting squirrels." Eli chuckled.

"Well, I think the squirrel population is safe then."

"Yeah, I'd have to agree with you. Did you finish your work?"

"Yes, ma'am, and my test."

"How do you feel about the test?"

"Pretty good. It was much easier than I thought. I'll get my results later today."

"See what happens when you apply yourself?"

"I know. I should have been working this hard all along."

"At least you're working hard now. That's what counts. You hungry yet?"

"Silly question. How about some wings before we have to go get Brad?"

"That sounds fine. Let's put the dogs up and roll."

Mitch directed her to a local wing spot, and when they walked in, she wasn't sure if he liked it for the wings or the scantily clad waitresses. They sat at a table, and Mitch's eyes were spinning in his head, trying to watch all the women bouncing around filling orders.

"What do you recommend?"

"I like the jerk wings and the honey mustard," he answered, as a cute blonde waitress approached.

She returned Mitch's smile. "My name is Lindsey, and I'll be your server today. What can I get you two started off with to drink?"

"I'll have sweet tea," Eli answered.

"Me too," Mitch replied.

"I'll be right back with your drinks," Lindsey said and returned to the counter.

Mitch's eyes never left her until Eli cleared her throat.

"So, I'm going for the jerk. What about you?"

"I'll do the honey mustard so you can try them," he answered.

"That's a good plan. You want any appetizers? You like fried pickles?"

"Love them. Let's get an order when Lindsey comes back."

"So you can watch her again?"

His face turned red. "Yes'm that'll do."

"Did it just get hot in here or what? Your face got red."

"You are so funny."

"I know, a laugh a minute. You order for us when Lindsey returns, okay?"

"Sure thing, Aunt Elizabeth."

"Oh, Elizabeth. I think I hit a hot button."

"You're such a smart ass sometimes."

"Yep, and proud of it, but I'll try my best not to embarrass you in front of Lindsey."

"Thanks. Lindsey's on the way with drinks."

Eli put her hand to her mouth and motioned to lock her lips. Mitch's face broke out in a grin.

"Here we go. Two sweet teas. Are you ready to order?"

"Yes, we'd like an order of fried pickles to start. Then a dozen jerk and a dozen honey mustard."

"Do you both want fries with that?"

Mitch looked at Eli, who nodded with a grin. "Yes, that will work."

Lindsey took the order and walked to the kitchen.

"Isn't there a country song for that?"

"For what?"

"Do you want fries with that?" Eli answered.

"Did you get too much sun sitting outside, or are you just going senile?"

"It's true though, just look it up if you don't believe me. Tim McGraw, I believe."

"Yes, yes, I know. No need to look it up."

Eli let him enjoy his ogling in peace for the rest of the meal. She had to admit, the food was good, even though she doubted Mitch chose this place for the food. *He's a teenage boy. Gotta remember that.*

When Lindsey brought the check, Eli reached for it. "I've got this," Mitch said and opened his wallet and pulled out several bills.

"How much do you have left?"

"All but this." He grinned as he placed the bills on the table, leaving a generous tip for Lindsey.

"Good boy," she said, and they stood to leave. She looked at her watch. "We have an hour before we pick Brad up. Do you want to do some shopping, or are you suffering from eye strain?"

Mitch pulled his sunglasses down. "I can always do some shopping. I'd like to look for some new flies to use on the trout."

Eli tossed him the keys. "Take us there."

"Your wish is my command," he said, and bent forward in a servant's gesture.

†

When they arrived at the outdoor shop, Mitch walked into the fishing department while Eli browsed through the clothing section. The store was having a massive sale on cargo shorts, and she wanted several pairs. Eli had a plethora of running and dress shorts, but nothing that would be as functional for working around the homesite. She decided on several more pairs and went in search of a cart and to find Mitch.

When she found him kneeling in an aisle looking at flies, she realized just how much he had grown. Even kneeling, he was almost as tall as her. "Hey, they've got a great sale on cargo shorts. Do you need some to work in?"

"I've got a few, but I could use more."

"Come over to the clothing department when you finish here, and you can pick some out. Are you having any luck with finding flies?"

"Several," he answered, holding bags of fishing lures.

"Get what you need, and I'll see you in a few."

"Yes, ma'am," he answered and returned to his search.

Eli entered the shoe department to check out work boots. She found a pair of light-weight ankle-high boots and a sturdy pair of rubber galoshes for wet jobs. Eli selected her size and tossed in a few pairs of boot socks. She returned to the clothing department to wait for Mitch and found he was already looking at the shorts.

"At this price get ten pairs, since they're on sale for buy one get one free."

"Sweet," he answered and started loading them into the cart.

"Do you need some T-shirts to work in? They've got Dri-fit shirts on sale too."

"Those would be nice this summer."

"Let's get a bunch, and I'll put them in your room."

They selected a dozen shirts each. Mitch's phone pinged. He pulled it out to find a text from Brad. "Brad says he's ready for me to pick him up."

"Text him and tell him we'll be on our way soon."

They passed through check-out, and Mitch loaded the bags in the truck. "You want me to drive?"

"Sure, since you know where we're going."

Brad had forgotten about her coming, so he was excited to see her red truck pull in front of his school. He was more surprised to find Mitch driving. "I hope your insurance is paid up. I'd hate for Mitch to ruin my future truck," he teased as he climbed in the back seat.

"He's done well driving me around today. You up for some ice cream?"

"Oh, heck yeah, I'm starving."

"Do you need food, then ice cream?"

"If we go to Dairy Queen, I'll get a hamburger. Coach ran us to death today."

"Better get a move on before he expires on us, Mitch."

†

Mark and Laura had made it home from work when Eli and the boys returned. "I sure hope you didn't spoil your appetites," Mark said. "I've got orange juice chicken marinating in the fridge."

"I'm sure these two will be hungry again in thirty minutes," Eli said with a chuckle.

"It will be hours before it's ready, but we have tofu they can snack on." Mark grinned at his wife. "I'm sure your mom will fix you some."

Mitch shrugged. "Thanks, Dad, but I'll wait for the chicken. What else are we having?"

Laura wrinkled her nose at Brad. "I'll toss a nice salad, and once your brother gets the boy funk off of him in the shower, he can help me wrap some asparagus spears in bacon for roasting."

Brad stuck his tongue out at Laura's comment. "Yum. Will you also roast some corn on the grill, Dad?"

"I think that could happen, but now you better go hit the shower. You do stink." Mark laughed.

Eli looked at Laura. "What can I help with?"

"You can assist your brother when he starts to cook."

"Simple enough. I love the selections you approved for the cabin. I'll order them tomorrow so I can be at home when they arrive."

Mark opened the refrigerator. "When are you leaving?"

"I want to head out early Saturday so we can still have daylight to roam a bit before we retire. I'm sure Cruz will be ready to play after the ride."

"Probably so, she's not the most patient rider," Mark agreed.

She looked at Mitch. "Dang, I forgot to pick up some new toys and supplies while we were out today."

"That's okay, we can go out tomorrow afternoon before we get Brad."

"I'd recommend a case of tennis balls and a couple new frisbees. She's worn out every one she's got now," Brad chimed in.

"Why are you still in my kitchen and not in the shower?" Laura asked.

"I'm going," Brad said, and skulked out of the kitchen.

Laura turned her attention to Mitch. "How did you do on your assignments today?"

"Really well. Which reminds me, I need to check to see if my test score posted yet. I'll be right back."

Laura smiled at Eli. "He's been working hard since he came home. I don't know what you promised him, but it's working."

"No promises. It was Mitch's idea to see if he could stay and finish his last assignments in North Carolina. At the pace he's going, I'd think he wouldn't have much left after y'all visit."

"You sure you can tolerate that much Mitch?" Mark looked at her. "He can be a handful."

"If not, I know how to bring him home. I love the kid, and we get along well. I promise to work him hard and make him earn his keep."

Laura picked a head of lettuce to unwrap. "Just don't spoil him too bad."

Eli feigned hurt by holding her hands to her chest. "I would never dream of it."

"Yeah, right." Laura chuckled. "If it keeps him this motivated, keep doing what you're doing, please."

Mitch walked into the kitchen, holding a piece of paper. "You might want to sit down for this," he told his mom before handing her the document.

Laura leaned against the counter. "98! Mitch, that's wonderful. The best test grade you've had all year."

"Keep reading. My grades are down at the bottom."

"Two A's and three B's, I'm proud of you, Son." She held her arms out and hugged him close. She looked at Mark and nodded.

"I guess you'd better plan what you want to take to North Carolina for the summer," Mark told his son.

"Really? Can I go now?" he pleaded.

"Not now, Eli needs some time to settle in, but you keep up the good work, and you can stay when we go for a visit. If Eli hasn't changed her mind."

Eli smiled. "Are you kidding, I'll have a list of projects a mile long by then. School first, then we work in the afternoons. Deal?"

"Deal," Mitch answered, and grabbed her in a bear hug.

"Okay, don't squeeze me to death. I'm excited to have you come, too."

CHAPTER NINE

Mitch was the first to greet Eli Saturday morning when she walked out of the bedroom.

"Good morning. I've got Cruz's crate, her bed, and a few of her old toys already in the truck. When you're done with your bag, I'll pack it too."

"Are you ready for me to leave?" she teased.

"No way, but I know you're eager to get to the mountain. Wish I could go."

"I know, but you'll be there soon. I'm proud of you. Where's Cruz?"

"I fed her, and now she's outside. We played for a little bit, too."

"My goodness, what time did you get up?"

"About an hour ago."

The door to the master bedroom opened, and Mark walked out. "I thought I heard you two. Will you stay for breakfast?"

"I'd love to, but I'm itching to hit the road. I'll hit a drive-through if I get hungry."

"I can understand. Laura is almost awake, but I can't guarantee Brad is coherent."

"I'll sneak in and tell him goodbye. He'll be asleep before I leave the room."

"Mitch, will you grab Cruz's leash and get her ready?"

"Sure, Dad."

"You want a coffee or something cold to go?" Mitch opened the refrigerator.

"A bottle of water will do me fine. I can't wait for y'all to come visit."

"We may arrive in the middle of the night. I wanna leave as soon as possible."

"Just call to let me know when you're coming. Mitch has a key to the gate, but I'll be waiting for you."

Laura entered the kitchen. "I love you, Sis, but I'm going back to bed. It's way too early to be bright-eyed and bushy-tailed on a Saturday morning."

"Give me a hug and get in the bed then," Eli said as she walked to her. "See y'all soon."

"We may get some mysterious bug and call in sick a day early," she said. "I don't think anyone will be productive on Friday anyhow."

"The more time you can spend, the better. Thanks for taking care of Cruz and me."

"Anytime." She turned to Mark. "I'll see you in about two hours."

"Okay, I'll try to be quiet," he promised.

"I'll be right back." Eli entered Brad's room and shook him. "Brad, I'm leaving. I love you and will see you soon."

"Love you more, Aunt Eli," he said without opening his eyes.

Eli chuckled and left his room. She heard a soft snore as she pulled the door closed.

Mitch and Cruz came rushing inside. "She's all set. Do you want me to harness her in for you?"

"Yes, go ahead, and I'll grab my bag."

Mark handed her the water. "I'll get your bag."

"Let's go then," she told Mitch.

Mitch opened the passenger side of the truck, and Cruz jumped in. He clicked in her harness, then kissed her head. "You be a good girl, and I'll see you soon."

"She will miss you."

"Naw, she will have so much fun getting to be with you again that me and Brad will be a distant memory."

"She won't forget you."

Mark came out with her bag. "Back seat or truck bed?"

"You can just toss it on the seat. Thanks, Bro."

"Welcome." He hugged her tight. "Have fun, and we'll see you soon. Call to let us know you made it home."

"Will do." She hugged Mitch. "Keep going on those assignments, and the time will pass quickly."

"I'll keep you posted. Would you mind if I call?"

"Anytime you want. I'll send you some pics, too."

"Awesome. Be careful and tell the fish, I'll be back soon. Whit, too." He winked.

"You're so bad," she said, and punched him in the shoulder.

"Why do I think there's a story behind that exchange?" Mark asked.

"Mitch can fill you in since he's all-knowing. I'm gone," she said, and climbed in behind the wheel. "Love y'all."

Eli backed out of the drive and turned to Cruz. "Let's go home, baby girl."

Cruz licked her hand and settled into her seat.

†

The traffic was light as she pulled onto the interstate, heading north. The sun was breaking through the trees as mile after mile slipped away. She could feel the smile growing on her face as she talked to Cruz, telling her all about their new home.

After pulling into a rest area for a break, Cruz laid down and yawned. Eli turned on the radio, and within minutes, Cruz was napping. Eli was glad they had made it through Atlanta before the traffic picked up. The rest of the trip would be smooth sailing. When she pulled into a drive-through lane at a hamburger spot, Cruz lifted her head.

"Yeah, you get one too, but it won't be a habit for you to eat fast food." She paid for her purchase and returned to the highway to look for a picnic spot. A few minutes down the road, she spotted a scenic lookout which had a few benches. She pulled in, located a parking spot, and grabbed the bag of burgers, her water, and a bowl for Cruz. Eli unhooked the harness and took the leash in hand. "Let's eat," she said, and Cruz jumped out of the truck.

Eli placed the items on the bench and walked Cruz to a grassy patch to relieve her bladder. When they returned to take a seat, Eli looped the leash around her ankle while Cruz sat waiting for her burger. Eli placed the bowl on the ground and reached for her burger. She bit into the burger and gazed out at the mountains.

"It won't be long before we're home," she told Cruz who had devoured her burger and was looking at Eli's last bite. "Okay, you win," Eli said and gave her the chunk of burger and poured a small amount of water into the empty bowl.

"Drink up, and we'll walk a bit before the last leg of our drive."

Cruz lapped at the water while Eli finished the bottle. She gathered her trash and took the leash in hand. "Let's go girl." Eli dropped the garbage in a can and walked Cruz down a path. A soft breeze brushed across her face as Cruz explored the scents on the trail. "You need to find a potty spot so we can get on the road." After a few minutes, Cruz finished her business and Eli picked it up with a plastic bag and dumped it in a barrel. "Good girl. Let's hit the road."

When she pulled onto the highway, Eli rolled the windows down. Cruz stuck her head out the window and enjoyed the crisp air before settling in beside Eli for the rest of the drive.

Just under an hour later, Eli pulled into her drive and opened the gate. After pulling onto the property, she checked the mailbox to find it empty. They drove up the drive, allowing Cruz to look out the window at the thick forest of trees.

"We are at home, baby girl," Eli said as she crested the hill in front of her home. Parking close to the cabin, Eli pulled her bag from the seat before walking around to open the door. Cruz's entire body was wiggling with excitement as Eli opened the door and removed the leash and harness.

"Let's go," she said, and Cruz jumped out of the truck and started running. Eli placed her bag on the front porch and returned to the back seat. She opened a shopping bag holding a frisbee and waited for Cruz to return.

Cruz ran with her nose to the ground, taking in all the new scents with enthusiasm. She circled the barn and the other outbuildings before returning to the cabin. When she saw the frisbee in Eli's hand, her nub of a tail began wagging. "Are you ready to play?"

Cruz sat down, waiting for Eli to throw the frisbee. Eli smiled and let the frisbee sail and watched Cruz chase after it, catching it before it hit the ground. "Good catch," she hollered out. Cruz trotted to her and dropped the toy at her feet. "That's a good girl," Eli praised, picked up the frisbee and let it fly. Cruz ran faster this time and jumped high in the air, catching the frisbee as it started toward the ground. Her speed and leap got her off balance, and when she landed, Cruz got her feet tangled and flopped to the ground. Eli broke out laughing, and Cruz stood still holding the frisbee in her jaws. They played for almost twenty minutes before Eli made her take a break.

"Let's get you some water, and you can explore while I unload the truck."

Eli opened the tailgate and picked out bags holding Cruz's food and water bowls. She unlocked the cabin door and placed the empty containers on the counter. Then she went out to retrieve her suitcase and pulled it inside. "How about some ice water?" She picked a bowl, filling it with ice and cold water from the refrigerator. She placed it beside the front door and left Cruz to drink while she started unloading.

†

Whit had stepped outside just as she saw the red truck pull through the gate. She walked to the garden and began picking fresh vegetables. It wasn't long before she heard Eli's laughter and Whit walked to the end of the row and peeked through the branches. She could see Eli, and watched as she threw a frisbee for a beautiful, blue-coated dog. "Aww, isn't that sweet," she spoke aloud as she watched Eli kneel and hug the dog.

"I'm glad you came home early," she whispered.

†

180

Eli felt a breeze blow across her neck and heard a whisper too low to make out. She looked toward Whit's cabin but didn't see any sign of movement. *Today is our day. Tomorrow we will go next door to visit.*

When Eli had unloaded the truck, she walked out and sat on the porch steps. Cruz had wandered outside and was busy exploring. When she heard Eli's boots on the wooden floor, she rushed to her owner.

"Come over here pretty girl," Eli called, patting the step next to her, and Cruz climbed up beside her.

"You like our new home?" Cruz licked her hand and ducked her head under Eli's arm. Eli draped it across the dog's body and pulled her close. "I sure have missed you. I promise nothing will come between us again." Cruz laid her head down in her lap, and Eli's hand stroked down her body. Her dog's thick fur was soft and warm on her palm. She enjoyed the time with just the two of them as they looked across their front yard. "Do you want to go for a ride?"

Cruz's ears perked, and she jumped down the steps. "Let me go to the bathroom and grab the keys." Eli walked into the downstairs bath, and Cruz was hot on her trail. "I won't leave you." She chuckled and washed her hands, then grabbed a fresh bottle of water. She plucked the keys off the counter. "Let's ride."

They walked out to the barn, and Cruz sniffed the ground as Eli pulled out one of the Gators.

"Hop in," she called and patted the seat beside her. Cruz jumped into the seat. "Hold on, it gets bumpy," she warned as she sent the Gator forward up the trail toward the top of the mountain. Cruz's head swiveled from left to right as they ascended the trail and Eli pulled into the field where Mark's family cabin would sit. She slowed to a stop and stepped out of the Gator, walking toward the stream. Cruz's ears heard the rushing water, and she ran ahead of Eli. Other than the Gulf,

181

Eli realized Cruz had never seen a stream or river. She observed Cruz as she stepped onto the rocks at the bank of the stream and dipped her muzzle into the running water. She took a tentative drink and looked at Eli.

"Tastes good, doesn't it?"

†

Whit listened as the rumble of the Gator's engine disappeared into the mountain. *They must be exploring. I bet they are both on cloud nine to be together again.* She had filled her basket and walked into her cabin. "I think I'll bake an apple pie," she said as she placed the basket on the table and walked to her pantry to pick two jars of apples she had canned from last season. "These will do just fine." She smiled as she planned a nice lunch for tomorrow to welcome Eli and Cruz home. She had plenty of fresh vegetables and would fry some chicken to complete the meal. Whit whistled to herself as she pulled out the ingredients to make her apple pie and then went to work.

†

Eli watched Cruz play in the shallow water and pulled her phone out to take a video of her. She let the camera roll for about thirty seconds, then sent the file to Mitch. She dialed Mark's number to let them know she and Cruz had arrived.

"Hello. Yes, we made it home just fine. I just sent Mitch a video of Cruz playing in the stream in your front yard."

Eli could hear Mitch laughing in the background. "Tell her not to scare off the fish," he shouted across the room.

"Yes, I heard him. Tell Mitch there is plenty of fish for both of you."

She listened to Mark and Mitch for several seconds. "We've been exploring. She's having a blast if you can't tell."

182

She heard Cruz run through the water as she left the stream and took off after a rabbit. "Oh, my goodness she's chasing a rabbit." Eli watched the rabbit disappear into a thicket, and Cruz paced in frustration when she couldn't find a way in. Eli laughed and told Mark, "Rabbit one, Cruz zero."

Eli could hear Mitch laughing. "She wouldn't know what to do with it if she caught it."

"Sure, she would, she'd take it to her mama to throw it again." Mark chuckled.

"That wouldn't surprise me," Eli replied. "We're going to see what else we can find. I'll call y'all tomorrow."

She walked to the Gator and drove to the thicket where Cruz still paced. "C'mon girl," she called, and Cruz ran in front of the Gator. "Okay, you can run for a while." She pulled onto the trail and drove to the end of the path. Cruz sat at the footpath to wait on her. "You want to make it to the top?" Her ears perked, and she stood to walk beside Eli.

Eli walked to the edge of her property and then turned right to check the trail shelter. The boards were still in place, and she noticed boot prints in the soft soil. "So, the hikers have arrived," she told Cruz, who sniffed around the shelter. Eli noticed small paw prints next to the footprints. "They must have a fur baby with them, too." There was no sign or sound of anyone nearby, so they must have stopped for a rest and moved on the next day. Eli had never gone farther down the trail than the shelter, and her legs needed a stretch from the drive.

"You want to walk a bit of the trail?"

Cruz jumped to her feet, always ready for action. She trotted ahead of Eli as they followed the trail for several hundred yards until Eli spotted something curious through the trees. Eli moved off the trail a bit and walked south. She reckoned she was still on the border of Whit's property. A large tree had a treehouse built into it.

"That's interesting. I wonder what it is for?" The tree had a staircase up to the building. "Too high for a moonshine still and not big enough to grow much pot," she told Cruz, who just looked at her. "I'll ask Whit what it's for."

They walked farther down the trail until they heard a woman's laughter. Eli froze, startled by the sound until it came again, just above the path. Cruz had alerted to the noise and was looking deep into the woods. "Should we investigate?"

Cruz looked at her, then to the woods. Her hackles were not standing on end, so she wasn't anxious about the sound. She stepped forward, her nose to the ground and started to pick her way through the brush.

"I guess that's my answer."

Eli followed Cruz until she heard splashing water. A few more steps ahead and the brush opened into a small clearing. A woman sat on a nearby boulder, watching her canine companion romp in a small pool. The woman had a long greying braid running down her back that swung from side to side as she laughed at the dog's antics. She had not seen or heard their approach. When the dog, a medium sized, brown, and black shepherd mix spotted Cruz, she let out a soft woof, and the woman turned her head.

"Oh, hello," she said. "I didn't hear you come up."

The dog resumed playing, and Cruz whimpered with excitement. "Go ahead, but play nice."

Cruz rushed into the pool and began splashing water.

"I hope I didn't startle you. I'm Eli and that's Cruz. We were just out for a walk when we heard you laughing."

"Hi, Eli. I'm Margret, and that's Andi. Let me move my pack, and you can join me. It's such a beautiful day."

Eli waited until she moved the large pack and then took a seat on the boulder. Eli nodded toward the backpack. "Are you a northbound hiker?"

184

"Yes, Andi and I have made it this far from Springer Mountain. I've got a few more weeks of hiking time, and then we'll head home to Florida."

"What part of Florida? I just moved here from Pensacola."

"I live in Ocala. Land of the racing horses."

"I grew up not too far from there in Lake County."

"I've done all the trails in Florida, so I thought I'd set my sights on the AT."

Eli watched Cruz and Andi playing in the water. "That must feel good to them."

"I was thinking about taking a quick bath, but the water is chilly."

"It stays cold even through the summer months. Do you plan to stay at the shelter tonight or are you moving on?"

"The shelter looks like as good a place to stop as any. It's always nice to find one to have a roof over our heads."

"Could I interest you in a hot shower and something to eat in exchange for helping me with a chore?"

"What did you have in mind?"

"I have an outbuilding with a shower and laundry room, but the interior walls are not finished. When my nephew was here with me for a few days, we found some beautiful wood boards in the hayloft, but I failed to have him assist me with getting them down." She kicked a rock with her foot. "I want to start on the project soon. Would you let me hand them down to you in exchange for a shower and a meal? I'm just getting home today, so I haven't grocery shopped yet, but I can chase something up."

"A hot shower would feel good. We're used to eating on the trail so it wouldn't have to be anything fancy."

"If the bread is still fresh, I can whip out some grilled cheese or tomato sandwiches. My neighbor grows the sweetest tomatoes I've ever eaten."

"I'll take a grilled cheese with a slice of tomato on it any day," Margret answered. "You have a deal. There's plenty of daylight left to get done and make it to the shelter before dark."

"Let's do this then." Eli stood and called to Cruz. "Shake it off, baby girl."

"She's a beautiful pup. Is she a blue heeler?"

"Yes, a miniature, but she doesn't feel like it when she plops in my lap."

"Andi's a rescue. I don't know what all she's got in her, but she's a great companion, and doesn't mind hiking."

"That sounds like a perfect match. Let's go. I parked my Gator at the edge of my property, so you can have a ride down the mountain. I'll bring you back if it gets too late."

Eli placed Margret's backpack in the Gator and started to turn around. "Let's go home Cruz," she called out, and the two dogs trotted ahead of the four-wheeler. "Hang on, it gets a little bumpy."

"This is such a beautiful area," Margret said as she surveyed the property.

"A little piece of heaven for me. My brother and his family will join me here in a few years."

"Are you all by yourself?"

"Just Cruz and I for now. My oldest nephew, Mitch, will be here this summer working with me."

"That will be nice."

"He loves to fish, and both sides of the property have nice trout streams. He's already caught a few, and they were mighty tasty."

Eli rolled up to the cabin and parked in front of the barn. "Are you hungry, or do you want to help me with the boards first?"

"Let's get your boards down, and I can help you carry them."

"If we can get them down, I'll carry them tomorrow. No worries." She pointed to the laundry room. "It's not far. I'll measure and cut them, so having them down from the loft will help."

"Lead the way then."

Eli walked through the barn door and climbed into the hayloft. She took the tarp off the boards and then lowered one end down to Margret. "These aren't too heavy, are they?" she asked as she let go of her end of the board.

"Goodness no. I grew up carrying bags of horse feed and bales of hay."

"Alright then, you can stack them right below the loft. Thanks for your help."

"No problem."

Cruz and Andi were playing outside when Eli and Margret emerged from the barn. "Thanks for all your help."

"That was a low price to pay for a hot shower and a good meal."

"Quite a bargain for me, too. You saved me a lot of steps up and down the ladder."

"A win-win situation all around then," Margret responded.

"If you'll give me a minute, I'll go into the house for some linens. Mitch has already stocked hygiene supplies in the shower. Feel free to use the laundry equipment, too, if you'd like. All the supplies are in the cabinet."

"Thanks, I've got some clothes which could use some soap and water."

"I'll be right back then." As Eli started toward the cabin, the dogs were lapping water from the bowl. "Would you like something to drink? I've got bottled water, a few beers, and some sweet tea."

"A glass of tea would taste great. I'll start some laundry while I'm waiting."

"Sounds good. I'll be right out."

Eli walked into the spare bathroom and picked out linens for her guest. She walked into the kitchen and poured a large glass of sweet tea. Eli surveyed the contents of the refrigerator and also found a package of ham still fresh.

"That will add to the sandwiches." She took the butter from the fridge to allow it to soften.

When she walked into the laundry room, Margret was loading clothes into the washer. Eli placed the linens on the folding table and sat the tea beside them. "Would you mind some ham to go on the sandwiches?"

"I never pass on protein. That would be great."

"It's about Cruz's dinner time. Can Andi have a bit of kibble with her new friend?"

"I'm sure she would enjoy it. I'm getting kind of low on her supplies."

"No worries, we can get you stocked up. Is there anything you need?"

"No, I snack on trail mix, and fresh berries when we can find them."

"I'll raid the pantry and see what else we can fit into your pack."

"Thanks for your generosity, Eli."

"My pleasure," she answered and left the building.

†

Margret watched Eli leave and stripped out of her clothing, tossing them in the washer. She then turned on the shower and pulled out some clean clothes to wear. She hadn't planned on being able to wash clothes, so a bit of laundry and a hot shower were a luxury she wouldn't see again until the end of her hike. Margret picked up the linens and walked to the steamy shower. The water felt divine as it cascaded down her skin, and the hygiene products were high-end, which smelled terrific as she shampooed her hair and bathed her body. *I'll be the best smelling hiker on the trail. At least for a day or two.*

†

Eli returned to the cabin and filled two bowls with dog food and carried them onto the porch. "Eat up, girls," she said as she placed the protein-packed meal on the floor.

Both dogs began eating right away, and Eli noted the enthusiasm Andi showed for the meal. She filled a gallon-sized zip-lock bag of dog food and plucked out a couple bags of dog treats. She would restock this week, and she was sure Cruz wouldn't mind sharing with her friend.

After washing her hands, she started pulling out ingredients for the humans' meal. She opened a bottle of beer and started preparing the sandwiches to grill. Eli also found a bag of unopened chips that would go well with the sandwiches. There were a few cans of mixed nuts she could send along with Margret. She made a mental note to start a shopping list soon and would stock up on some extra non-perishable items in case she had future trail visitors. *Maybe Margret would give me some ideas for foods to store which are convenient and not too heavy to pack.*

Her eyes landed on a couple cans of Vienna sausage. Mitch loved those disgusting little things, but she would replace them if Margret wanted to pack them along. She chuckled at the thought of Mitch fishing out the tubular masses of god knew what and eating them with cheese and peanut butter crackers. To make it worse, he liked them cold out of the refrigerator, with the jelly chilly and clinging to the pieces. She and Mark had eaten their fair share of them in the hayfields growing up as kids, but she swore she'd never consume them again unless desperate.

†

Margret pulled herself away from the hot water and dried off, slipping into clean clothes which felt good against her cleaned skin. She brushed out her hair and smiled when the fragrance of the shampoo lingered in her hair as she returned it to a braid. The washer had stopped while Margret was showering. She placed the load into the dryer, brushed her teeth, and stepped outside into a beautiful late spring afternoon.

The dogs were sprawled about the porch, dozing as their meals began to digest. Andi lifted her head as Margret stepped onto the porch and knocked on the door frame. Inside she could see Eli toiling away at the counter.

"Come on in," Eli called. She turned to see Margret enter with the empty tea glass. "Would you like a refill, or something else?"

"Another glass of tea would suit me just fine."

†

"Have a seat at the bar, and I'll get you a refill." Eli turned toward the refrigerator. "I found some mixed nuts and some Vienna sausage in the pantry if you'd like to take them along. Some dog food and treats for Andi too. Can you give me an idea of some items to have on hand for hikers if I get any other visitors?"

"Nuts are always a good option, trail mix, too. Those small packs of crackers and cookies are like heaven at the end of a long day of hiking. Tea bags and packets of instant coffee and zip-lock bags. It makes it easier to store and pack items."

"I'll grab bags for you, and you can pour those nuts into one of them and have a few extras." She walked to the pantry and pulled out several bags. "Anything else?"

Margret chuckled. "Toilet paper is always a hot commodity."

"That's not a problem. I keep a large supply at all times. "How many rolls can you carry?"

She watched Margret filling the bags with nuts. "Two will be just fine. Thank you for your generosity."

"If you don't like the Vienna sausage, my feelings won't be hurt if you give them to Andi. Mitch loves those things, but he eats them cold with the jelly congealed around them."

"I like them, but Andi will enjoy a share of them, too."

"Good. I'll replace the cans in the pantry when Mitch returns."

"It sounds like the two of you are close."

"He's my brother's oldest of two sons. Mitch has had some issues with schooling, but I guess we all aren't cut out for traditional education. He's a great kid and a hard worker, and I will enjoy having him around. Mitch also loves to fish, so this is like a piece of heaven for him, too."

Eli began cooking the sandwiches on the grill top. The smell of the melting cheese and the honey-cured ham filled the air, and the sweetness of the tomatoes added to the aroma. "I've got some chips to go with the sandwiches."

"That sounds perfect. You know if you are serious about other hikers stopping here to barter, you could keep some frozen left-overs like chicken and dumplings, chili, or something like it that's filling that you could pop in a microwave for a hot meal."

"Those are great ideas, and I think I can handle most of those. I make a mean meatloaf, too."

"Any of those with some instant potatoes and maybe a vegetable would taste like a king's feast to a hungry hiker.

There are long stretches you aren't near a town to go in for a decent meal."

"I could make some burger patties, too. Those are quick and easy."

"You start serving burgers, and the hikers will make this a favorite stop."

"How would I draw them in?"

"Word of mouth on the trail spreads fast, and you could make a note to leave in the trail shelter of your offer of work for food and a hot shower. I'll advertise for you on my journey. Be careful though, not all hikers are good people, and I'd keep alcohol out of the deal."

"That makes good sense. I'd appreciate your word of mouth to anyone you meet that you think would benefit from some TLC. I'll wait to post a notice until Mitch gets here."

"A wise decision. There are a lot more women on the trail now in pairs or threesomes. Also, some great men, but you have to be cautious, and I wouldn't offer an overnight stay for anyone, including me."

"I was thinking about the barn, but you're right. Thank you for your advice."

"You've been nothing but generous to Andi and me. I think we both needed a break. The trail is a grand adventure, but that shower was to die for. Clean clothes will be a blessing, too."

Eli served two sandwiches apiece onto plates and opened the bag of chips. She watched as Margret's eyes grew wide.

"If I eat all that, I might not make it to the shelter. It looks and smells delicious though."

"What you can't eat, you can take with you for a midnight snack or breakfast in the morning."

"That's a great idea. It would be a good breakfast."

"I have enough ham left for another, so if you can eat both, go for it."

Eli poured out some chips and passed her the bag. "You can take those for leftovers, too."

"I don't want to clean you out."

"I've got to grocery shop soon anyhow. Eat all you can."

Margret finished one sandwich and chips. She placed the other sandwich in her zip lock bag.

"You sure you don't want another?"

"No, this will make a great breakfast. Thank you so much for your kindness."

"My pleasure. If you want to check your clothes, I'll pick up here and take you and Andi to the top."

"Can I help you clean?"

"No, ma'am, I've got this."

Margret picked up her bags of supplies and walked out to the laundry. Eli cleaned the kitchen and then walked to the bathroom for two rolls of toilet paper before exiting the cabin.

Margret had shouldered her pack and was emerging from the laundry room. She grinned when she saw the toilet paper in Eli's hand. "Oh my gosh, I almost forgot about that." She tucked the rolls into her pack."

Eli stored Margret's pack in the rear of the four-wheeler, and they started up the mountain. The dogs trotted along beside them as they bounced over the rough terrain.

"I'm going to have to smooth this out a bit." She chuckled.

"You've got such a beautiful place. I wouldn't change much of the environment."

"I don't plan to, but I need to get around the property in a hurry if necessary, so clearing this path a bit will help. I'd like to keep my teeth from jarring out of my head, too."

Eli hit a rather large bump, and Margret reached for the grab bar. "There is that," Margret agreed.

When they reached the top, Eli slowed to a stop. "It's been nice having you visit." She reached into her pocket and pulled out a business card. "The phone number is good. Give me a call when you've ended your journey, to let me know you made it home."

"I will," Margret said and stepped out of the Gator. "I've enjoyed spending the day with you and Cruz. Thanks for the extra supplies, too."

"My pleasure. Have a safe and pleasant trip."

"Thanks again for everything. I'll call when I make it home."

†

Eli watched as Margret and Andi made their way down the path. Cruz started to follow until Eli called her. "Time for us to go home, baby girl," she said and patted the seat beside her. Cruz jumped into the vehicle, and they returned to the barn.

Eli spotted the pile of lumber she and Margret had brought down from the loft. There was still daylight left, so she planned out the interior walls of the laundry room. She walked into the cabin for a notepad and pen. Eli measured the walls to get the proper length and walked to the woodshop to gather a saw, a square, hammer, and nails. She spotted a garden rake in the corner and smiled. "That will do just fine." She took the tools to the laundry building and got her measurements, the square, and saw to carry to the barn.

"I need to remember to get some sawhorses," she told Cruz, who trotted along beside her. "I reckon I can use the bed of the Gator for now."

Eli placed the first board over the bed of the Gator and measured out her length and then checked it before using the square to draw her cutting line. The saw came to life in her hand as she trimmed the first board for her wall. Cruz sat in front of her watching, and when the scrap fell, she rushed over

194

to smell it. "Smells good, doesn't it? It will make some good kindling for the fire pit."

Eli carried the first board inside. "Dang, I knew I forgot something." She walked to the workshop and found a small level. "This should do." She used the garden rake to steady the first board as she leveled and nailed one end and then the other. "A few more nails and we'll have our first wallboard up, Cruz." As soon as she heard her name, Cruz jumped, ready to go wherever Eli was going. "Let's get another board."

†

Whit was sitting on her front porch sipping coffee when she heard the whine of a skill saw. *I wonder what she's up to?* She had listened to the Gator motor earlier and could have sworn she heard two dogs barking. *I wonder if Eli brought a friend along for Cruz?*

She checked her watch. "We have a couple hours of daylight left, Oscar. Should we go pay Eli a visit and invite her to lunch?"

Oscar stretched and followed Whit inside to get a flashlight. "I know you see well at night, but I don't cherish a dip in the stream." Flashlight in hand, Whit started across her property. She made it over the log bridge and waited for Oscar to follow, making it look easy. "Show off," she declared as he raced ahead of her.

Whit could hear hammering ahead, and a few moments later, she saw Eli emerge from the clearing ahead, followed by a dark-colored dog. *That must be Cruz.* She raised her hand when Eli looked at the trail to see her approach.

"Howdy, neighbor. Welcome home. I heard a skill saw, so I thought I'd come over to see what you were up to."

195

"Thanks, Whit. I'm glad to be home. I thought I'd start on a project while there was some daylight left. I'm putting up the interior walls of the laundry room."

"You need an extra set of hands?"

"I've been using a garden rake to prop the boards on, but an assistant would be much better. The rake doesn't talk much."

"You may think I talk too much," Whit said with a laugh. "Is this Cruz?"

"Yes, it is. The one and only." Eli saw a confused look on Whit's face. "What is something wrong? You have a funny look on your face."

"I could have sworn I heard two dogs barking earlier."

"You did. We had visitors off the trail today. Cruz and I did a bit of exploring along the trail and heard laughter and splashing, so we decided to investigate."

"Must have been one of the spring-fed pools above my property."

"Yes, that would be about right. So, anyway, we investigated and found a lovely woman laughing at her canine companion, Andi, as she played in the pool. We struck up a conversation, and we bartered a little bit of labor for a hot shower and a meal for them both."

"So, I did hear two dogs playing."

"Yes, Andi and Cruz got along well. I just took them to the trailhead a little while ago."

"You know you can always call on me if you need some help until Mitch comes back," Whit offered.

"I hadn't planned on starting anything until tomorrow, but I had some energy to burn off. I appreciate your offer and your assistance. I just need to cut the next board, and we'll be ready to go."

Oscar and Cruz were circling, sniffing at one another. Cruz hadn't experienced many cats, so Oscar would be a good test for the tribe being delivered next week. They laughed as Cruz stuck her butt in the air and knelt in front of Oscar wanting to play.

"That's a good sign," Eli said. "I was curious about how she would react to other animals besides dogs."

"She's beautiful. Does she enjoy all the space to roam?"

"We haven't covered everything yet, but she seems to enjoy it so far. Found the western stream and enjoyed the cool water and chased after a few critters."

Whit watched as Eli meticulously measured and then remeasured the board before cutting. When Eli looked up to find her watching, she smiled.

Whit smiled. "Measure twice, cut once. My grandpa taught me that."

"Let's go get this one on the wall. I think three more boards should have the longer side done."

"This is beautiful wood. Where did you get it?"

"Mitch found it under a tarp in the hayloft. I needed someone to help bring them down, so Margret, the lady from the trail, helped me out. I handed them down to her, and she stacked."

Eli picked up the board, and they walked to the laundry building. "While Margret took a shower and started a load of laundry, I fed the dogs and made some grilled ham and cheese sandwiches with the last of your tomatoes added in. They were delicious if I say so myself."

"Before I forget, I wanted to invite you over for lunch tomorrow. I've got a bunch of fresh vegetables from the garden, and I'd thought I'd fry some chicken."

"You've got my mouth watering already."

"There's a bunch of tomatoes ready for picking, so bring a basket, and we can fill you up."

"You have so got a deal."

†

Eli raised the board and leveled it before putting a nail in each end. She was preparing to nail the remainder of the board to the studs when she dropped the nail. Eli and Whit both bent over at the same time and bumped into one another. Eli grabbed Whit by the shoulder to steady her, and they ended up in a close embrace.

"Whoa, that was almost a disaster," Eli said, still holding Whit. *Damn I am so tempted to lean in and kiss her. Holy shit where did that thought come from?*

"Isn't it the assistant's job to step and fetch it?" Whit chuckled.

"Could be dangerous with a hammer in my hand." Eli released her and stepped away. "Are you okay?" *I need to put some space between us right now.*

"Of course I am, silly. I'm not fragile, I'm a country girl as strong and agile as they come."

Eli broke out laughing. "That's a good one."

Whit was mesmerized by the way Eli's eyes sparkled when she laughed. It was a perfect look for her, one she hoped to see more often. *For a moment, I thought she might kiss me.* The idea sent butterflies stirring in her stomach. *There is no doubt I'm attracted to her.*

"Are all the boards the same length?" I need to think of something besides those beautiful lips brushing against mine.

"Remarkably so. The builder had an excellent eye for detail, and the building is square so far."

"Do you want to cut the other boards and I'll help you carry them over? Maybe we could finish the room before it gets dark."

"It would be great to have the first project done. You sure you don't mind helping?"

Whit brushed a strand of hair from her face and tucked it behind her ear. "I enjoy building things, remember?"

"How could I forget? Mitch has already asked me if I've ordered the solar panel system yet. I think he was disappointed I hadn't. He wants it to be his first project."

"That will be fun. How's Mitch doing on his schoolwork?"

"He's been going at it like a maniac since he got home. He's already ahead of his schedule and pulled his only grade of C to a B. I'm so proud of his hard work."

"It's great what the right form of motivation can do. Mitch's excited to come live with you."

"He's a great kid, even if I am a biased aunt. He's socially awkward with kids of his own age, but he does well with adults. I think it's a self-esteem issue." She let out a soft sigh. "He's always been larger than most of his classmates, but he got teased a lot for his size, and he's not the quickest thinker in the world. The kid has a heart of gold, though, and will work hard when he's motivated." She smiled. "Mark asked me if I brought the right kid home when we got to Alabama. He sensed a change in him, and Mitch has worked hard on his schoolwork. Before it was like pulling hen's teeth to get him to buckle down."

"Now that's one I haven't heard in a while. My gran used to say that."

†

Eli watched the smile fade from Whit's face. She felt the sadness wash over her as she mentioned her grandparents.

"I love all the old country sayings. People today don't have a clue of the way old timers used to talk.

Straightforward, to the point without a bunch of sugar coatings. People think a fur piece is a mink coat."

The comment brought the smile to Whit's face. Eli felt relieved to see it return. She sensed Whit had struggled with a great deal of sadness in her short life, but today was not the day for deep conversation. Eli measured and cut the last two boards, and they carried them to the laundry building. She measured the lengths of the next wall and working together, they finished the remaining two walls. Eli gathered her tools to take to the workshop, and when they stepped outside, they realized night had fallen. She looked at Whit. "I didn't think we were in there so long."

"Me either, but you can scratch one project off your list." Whit ran her hand across her cheek.

"Thanks for your help. It made the project easier with you here."

"You're welcome. It was fun working with you."

"I haven't grocery shopped yet, but there is a frozen pizza and cold beers if you'd like to join me for dinner. It's not gourmet, but it'll fill our stomachs. I don't reckon we get pizza deliveries out here."

"Heaven's no, but yeah, I could eat a slice or two as long as there are no anchovies."

"Oh, hell no. Don't want to waste a good pizza."

"I don't have cat food yet, but I believe there's a can of tuna left for Oscar."

"He'll be over at your house all the time for tuna. He loves it."

"Let me close the barn, and I can get cooking."

Eli took the can of tuna from the pantry and placed it on the counter. "You want to dish dinner up for Oscar while I feed Cruz? There's a small food bowl in the cabinet by the sink," she pointed out. Eli portioned out some kibble for Cruz and placed it in her bowl and started the oven. "Would you care for a beer?"

"I haven't had one in a while, but sure, why not?"

"I have alcohol free if you'd rather have an O'Doul's."

Whit shook her head. "Naw, hit me with the real stuff."

Eli pulled out two beers and handed one to Whit. "Do you want a glass?"

"This is good," Whit answered and took a tentative sip.

The expression on Whit's face made her think Whit didn't drink often. She took the pizza from the freezer and placed it on the pan. "I make these from scratch, but I don't have the ingredients yet."

"I love a good homemade pizza. Do you make your own dough?"

"The only way to go."

"So, what's next on your list of projects?"

Eli took a barstool across from Whit. "I have some orders from Amazon which should start arriving tomorrow. One is an in-ground firepit I want to put down by the stream, with chairs. I was thinking I would start digging the hole since I have the dimensions." She looked at Whit. "I plan to use the scraps from our boards today to cut into kindling."

"I could do that while you dig. Then I'll start lunch."

"I can handle it if you want to sleep in."

"What's that? I haven't slept past six in years. I'll even toss in some ham biscuits for breakfast if you make the coffee."

"Ma'am, you have yourself a deal." The oven chirped to let Eli know it had pre-heated. She stood and placed the pan in the oven. "Pizza is on the way."

The two of them finished the entire pizza. "I didn't realize how hungry I was," Eli said as she fed Cruz the last piece of crust.

"You'll find the fresh air and exercise affects your appetite. With everything you have planned, you won't have to worry about it changing your waistline either. You burn off the calories as fast as you eat them."

"I'm looking forward to fresh vegetables."

"Maybe we can work on grandpa's old garden plot down by the western stream. It shouldn't be too hard to turn with your tractor. I can help with removing any rocks which may get turned up. You could use them around your fire pit area."

"That's a great idea. Maybe make a small rock wall and enclose the firepit with smaller rocks. I've noticed a small pile of rocks already in the field. Overgrown with grass, but I can use the Gator to bring them over tomorrow while you make lunch."

"Sounds like a good plan." Whit stood and picked up her plate. "I'd better be going. We've got a busy day planned for tomorrow."

"Leave the plate. I'll clean later. Do you want me to walk you to the bridge?"

"It's not necessary, but I'd enjoy the company."

"Oh, before I forget again." Eli reached into the drawer and pulled out an old business card and handed it to Whit. The address is not current, but the cell number is good. Call me if you ever need anything."

"Let me scribble down my number as well for you." Eli gave her the notepad and placed her number under a refrigerator magnet. "There, all set. Just let me grab a flashlight."

†

As they walked up the path toward the bridge, they were close enough their hands brushed together as they moved. The touches, however brief sent vibrations through Eli's body.

When they reached the bridge, Whit turned on her flashlight. "Thanks again for all of your help tonight."

"It was my pleasure. Thanks for dinner and good company. I'll see you for breakfast at about eight?"

"I'll be awake earlier if you want to come over. I'm usually up and dressed by seven."

"I'll see you then." Whit started to turn toward the bridge and then spun around to face Eli and stood on her tiptoes to plant a kiss on her cheek. "Sweet dreams."

Whit could feel her face burning with a blush as she rushed to the log and began the journey across. *Why on earth did I do that? I must be some kind of blithering idiot.* She stepped to avoid taking a dip and was ecstatic to hear Eli call out to her in a cheerful voice. "You too! Be safe."

†

Eli was shocked by Whit's sudden turn and the sweet kiss to her cheek. She had not expected Whit's action, but she could not deny the smile growing on her face or the racing of her heart. Eli waited until Whit and Oscar made it across the log and disappeared into the darkness.

"Let's go home, Cruz." The dog danced around her as she walked to the barn. There was no hope of falling asleep, so Eli began carrying the scraps of wood to a stump she would use as a chopping block. In the morning, she would cut it into kindling. For a moment, she considered starting the project tonight, but afraid in her excitement, she might lose concentration and cut off a finger. Eli stacked the wood beside the stump and returned inside to clean the kitchen. Being around Whit gave her the energy she hadn't experienced since her early twenties, and Eli realized just how much she liked the feeling.

She plucked her final beer from the fridge and walked out onto the deck. The full moon had risen and was casting a beautiful glow across the water. "What a beautiful night," she whispered into the breeze.

Eli was surprised when the wind blew, and the leaves on the trees seemed to answer her.

"Yes, it is," floated to her ears.

Surely, it's just my imagination. Can the mountains really whisper? She contemplated the thought as she enjoyed her beer. "Definitely need to go shopping soon." Eli returned inside, dropped her bottle in the garbage, and headed for the shower. Cruz was close on her heels and plopped down on her bed, exhausted from all the activity. Eli had set her crate in the corner to give her the option if she felt she needed the comfort, but she was glad Cruz slept on the open bed. The cabin didn't offer many opportunities for a dog going through the terrible-two puppy stage she was still experiencing, so as long as she didn't become destructive, she would have free roam. Eli showered and slipped naked between the sheets. She drifted on the soft moonlight and fresh breeze into her dreams.

CHAPTER TEN

Cruz's whining the next morning woke Eli before the sun was up.

"Do you need to go potty?" Cruz rushed through the bedroom door. "I've got to grab a robe," Eli called out as she crept out of bed. She slipped the robe over her shoulders and tied it while making her way downstairs. She opened the front door, and Cruz rushed out into the grass. "Had to go bad, huh?" Eli asked as she ran her hand through her hair. Cruz circled the yard, looking for the tennis ball she had left the day before. Eli spotted it on the porch railing and picked it up. "Looking for this?" she asked, holding the yellow ball. Cruz stopped in stride and sat, "Good girl," Eli praised and threw the ball across the yard. She climbed down and sat on the top step and waited for Cruz to return. They played fetch until Eli's urge to pee kicked in.

"My turn to go now," she said as she followed Cruz into the house. Eli used the downstairs bathroom and walked into the kitchen to brew a cup of coffee. She sat at the counter and started writing her shopping list. The only deliveries Eli expected today were the packages from Amazon. Hopefully, they would arrive early and she could grocery shop after having lunch with Whit. She sipped on her coffee as the grocery list grew.

After her first cup, Eli went upstairs to dress for the day. She chose some old jeans, a T-shirt, and work boots. Digging a hole was never fun in sneakers. She walked out to the workshop to retrieve her shovel, tape measure, and the hatchet for chopping kindling. After placing them by the stump, she donned work gloves and walked to the barn for the Gator. She stopped at the workshop to get the garden rake just in case she needed it. Cruz trotted along beside her as she drove to the spot where the rocks laid. Looking over the pile, Eli realized there were more there than she had thought. She began placing the rocks into the bed of the Gator until she had a load. Eli climbed behind the steering wheel and drove to the stream. She backed to within a foot of the water and began laying down rocks to establish a base for her wall. Even in the chilly morning air, Eli could feel the perspiration trickling down her spine and smiled. *I'll be stiff as hell tomorrow, but it feels good to be working on my property.*

†

Whit was also awake early. She had showered and dressed while the oven was pre-heating. She pulled out some frozen biscuits to pop in the oven while she fried some ham steaks. Whit hadn't thought to ask Eli if she wanted yellow mustard or jelly for her biscuits, so she packed both in her basket. Whit liked her blackberry jelly on biscuits, but also mustard.

Whit was almost giddy with excitement to spend another day with Eli. She had returned home last night and slept like a rock. Tonight though, she would need to do some work. She slipped two plastic knives and some napkins in her basket. Oscar had made short work of his breakfast and sat staring at her for a handout.

"You devil, you always know I cook a small piece for you." She took the portion she had cut into small bits for him and placed them in his bowl. The timer went off, and she put the bread in a bowl and covered it with foil to help hold in the heat. She cut the ham steaks into portions and dropped them into a plastic container then snapped the lid. "I think I may have over-estimated the biscuits," she told Oscar. "I have no idea why I cooked a dozen. Oh well, Eli could snack on them between projects."

She let out a soft laugh and picked up the basket, then turned to the refrigerator for a stick of butter. Just in case. She walked to the log bridge and crossed, her feet falling into place as she nearly skipped across the bridge. As she approached, she could hear the low rumbling of the Gator's motor. *Someone is already busy at work.* She smiled when she saw Eli backing the vehicle into place by the stream, loaded down with a pile of rocks. She could see the wall Eli was building and the shape of the barrier emerging.

Cruz spotted them first, and let out a soft woof.

†

Eli was making her third trip to the water when Cruz let out a woof to let her know Oscar and Whit were approaching. She pulled the Gator into place and stepped out to greet her visitors.

"Good morning."

Whit surveyed the growing wall and whistled. "You must have been moving at the crack of dawn. It's looking good. Do you want to finish the load or take a break?"

"I think I'll take a break. Yeah, someone, I won't name which four-legged critter, needed to go to the bathroom about five-thirty." She laughed as Cruz came rushing over and sniffed at Whit's basket.

"Don't fret, I brought you one, too," Whit told her. "Oscar's already had his breakfast."

Eli pulled off her gloves and tossed them in the passenger seat of the vehicle. "Those smell terrific. Let's go inside, and I'll start some coffee."

"I wasn't sure what you like on your biscuits besides ham, so I brought yellow mustard, blackberry jelly, and butter."

"All three will work fine, especially if it's homemade jelly."

"Yes, from last season's berries. There are a few ripe early, but we're still almost two months from the peak season."

"I love fresh berries. I can't wait to plant my own." Eli went to the coffee pot and began making coffee. She pulled down a second mug for Whit. "I have some fine china in the pantry," she said, opening a stack of small paper plates. "We can have the real ones if you prefer."

"Those are just fine. Do you plan to start a compost bin?"

"Once I study on them a bit."

"They are easy to make and maintain. The nutrients enrich the soil and will help your plants grow strong. I can make you a list of the items to put in your bin unless you want to research them yourself."

"I'll take all the help I can get."

"I'll make a list for you today and show you how I have mine set up."

"Thanks." Eli watched Whit bring out the bowl of biscuits. "Were you hungry this morning? That's a huge pile of biscuits."

"I must have been, but you can snack on them later. Just don't ruin your appetite for lunch."

"That doesn't seem to be a problem here. I'm almost always ready to eat."

"What do you want to try first then? Jelly, mustard, or butter?"

"Jelly, please. I can't tell you how long it's been since I've had homemade jelly with the person who made it."

"No pressure there," Whit said as she split open a biscuit and placed jelly on both halves before placing a slice of ham on it.

"What do you take in your coffee? I have sugar, milk and some French vanilla creamer."

"A little bit of sugar and some French vanilla, please."

"Just like mine." Eli poured a cup of coffee and began brewing a second. She carried the mug over to Whit. "Here, you are, ma'am."

"Smells good."

"Not like those biscuits." She picked one off the plate and took a big bite. Her eyes grew wide as she chewed and swallowed. "Oh, my goodness, these are fantastic. Keep them coming. I see why you baked a dozen now."

Whit smiled with pride from Eli's praise. "Do you want to try the mustard and butter?"

"Just the mustard, but I don't see how it could beat this jelly."

Eli walked over to prepare her coffee, still munching on the biscuit. "This ham is so sweet."

"Honey ham steaks. They are delicious, aren't they?"

"Most definitely," Eli said and popped the last bite in her mouth as she carried her mug to the bar.

Eli devoured four biscuits, two each with jelly and mustard. "I still like your jelly the best."

"I'll leave what's left in the jar and send you home with another later today. I've got plenty to hold me over."

"I'd better stop now, or there won't be any more work done today. The biscuits hit the spot."

"There are a few leftovers even after I give one to Cruz." Whit smiled as she broke a biscuit and ham into smaller bites.

"Lawdy, she's gonna get spoiled."

"Gonna? Don't you think she already is?"

"Okay, maybe just a little."

"I'll put the condiments in the refrigerator if you want to put the biscuits and ham in your microwave. Then I'll be ready to chop some kindling."

"Sounds good. Thanks for a great breakfast. I'm going to the grocery store later, so my treat next time. I can whip up a mean omelet."

"Would you mind if I went with you to pick out a few things?"

"No, I'd love the company."

Whit pulled up a chair next to the stump and began chopping the sections of boards into smaller pieces. Whit would pause to watch Eli. She had measured out her spot and started digging. Whit could see the tiny trails of perspiration rolling down her face and arms as she toiled, lost in concentration. *Damn if she's not handsome even when she's sweaty.* She pulled her eyes away from Eli to resume her task.

Eli had stopped for a break for a sip of water when she heard a truck approaching the drive. She looked to see a mail truck plodding along and pull to a stop in her yard.

"Ms. Fortner, I presume," the older gentleman said.

"Yes, that's me."

"I have a bunch of boxes for you. If you sign, I'll start unloading."

"I'll give you a hand and a warning, this is just the start of them."

"That's fantastic news. I love coming out here. I used to play out here as a kid. Hey Whit, how are you?"

"Fine, Mr. Harvey, you're looking great."

"You're not too bad yourself, young lady," he said and added a wink to Eli. "Welcome to the neighborhood."

"Thanks, Mr. Harvey." After they finished carrying the boxes to the front porch, Eli asked, "Can I get you some cold water and maybe a leftover ham biscuit?"

"The water would be great, but the missus filled me full of bacon and eggs this morning."

"I'll be right back." Eli disappeared into the house and returned with a cold bottle of water.

"Thanks, muchly. I'll leave you younglings to your chores. See you again soon."

"Nice to meet you, Mr. Harvey."

"You too, Ms. Fortner. Bye, Whit."

"Bye, Mr. Harvey."

They watched him turn around and disappear down the drive.

"He and my Grandpa were best friends growing up. He could tell you some wild stories of the adventures they had as children. I don't know if you noticed the limp, but he lost his left leg in World War Two."

"He seems like he could be quite the character."

"Oh, for sure he is. He loves sweets, so sometimes I leave him some cookies or a candy bar in the mailbox. He's our regular carrier too."

"I will add some goodies to my grocery list. I see you're just about done with the kindling."

"Yes, I am. How are you coming with the hole? Find any chinamen yet?"

"Nope, but I swear I got a whiff of fried rice once or twice."

Whit chuckled. "Is there a bucket or a box I can put this into for now?"

"Yes, there's an empty five-gallon bucket in the workshop. Hang on, and I'll get it."

"Finish digging, I'll find it. You don't have any skeletons out there, do ya?"

"Nope, fresh out today." Eli opened the carton with the firepit inside and carried it to the hole. She saw Whit was stepping out of the workshop with the bucket. "Hey, grab me a Phillips head screwdriver if you would, please."

"You got it."

Eli eased the metal drum out of the box and tried it in the hole. "Just a few more inches." She pulled the drum out and resumed digging.

Whit put the kindling in the bucket and took the screwdriver to Eli. "Here you go."

"Thanks, I've got to screw on the lid, then I think we will be good to go."

Whit watched Eli work and how at ease she was with tools. "You're good with your hands."

Eli's head whipped up, and she grinned at Whit. "I'm very good with my hands." Eli couldn't resist the comment.

"I meant with tools, silly woman."

Eli couldn't help but notice the blush that rose to Whit's cheeks. *Why do I find it impossible to not flirt with her?*

"I'm good with tools too, especially power tools." *Damn, there it goes again.*

Whit's blush deepened, but she rose to the challenge. "Maybe you can give me a demonstration sometime."

Eli nearly choked on her heart which had risen into her throat. "Maybe so," she said and resumed installing the lid without looking at Whit. Eli felt her face grow warm with a blush. She lifted the drum and settled it into the hole. "There, all set."

"It fits perfectly," Whit, said as she walked over to examine the pit. "Will you try it out before Mitch and the family arrive?"

"That depends."

"On what?" Whit asked.

"Do you like s'mores?"

"Do bears shit in the woods?"

Eli burst out laughing. "What if I grill some steaks tomorrow night and we can make s'mores for dessert?"

"Sounds delicious. It's a date."

Eli returned her smile and put her shovel in the back of the Gator. "I was thinking. Would it be better to build a mold around the wall, and pour some concrete mix in it to help hold the rocks together?"

"It wouldn't be a bad idea. I've got a hoe and a wheelbarrow." Whit examined the length of the wall. "If you buy four bags of concrete, that should be plenty, with enough left over to pour a pad under your firepit."

"I hadn't thought about a pad."

"Only an inch in the bottom wouldn't hurt. You won't even need to dig it deeper."

"Can we still use it tomorrow night?"

"Sure, it will dry fast, in a couple hours. Pour it first, and you'll be set. I've got some pieces of plywood which should work for a mold."

"After lunch, I'll bring Cruz home and crate her while we go to town. I can pick them up when we get home from the store. There's plenty of two by fours to use for supports."

"I love it when a plan comes together. I'll head home and start working on lunch unless you need me for anything else."

"What time do you want me over?"

"Give me until one if that's not too late."

"I'll work another hour and get cleaned up. See you then."

"Sounds great. C'mon Oscar," she called to the cat sleeping in one of the porch chairs. He stretched and bounded down the steps.

Eli put her gloves on and resumed building her wall. *One more good load ought to do it.* She could see real progress, but gaps that couldn't be filled with the odd-shaped rocks were present. Adding concrete to solidify them was a great idea. She looked up to catch a glimpse of Whit as she crossed onto her property. *I think I'm in trouble with this one so close by, but I enjoy her company and conversation. She doesn't shy away from hard work either. I can't have imagined Sara ever getting her hands dirty.* "Oh, girl, push the thought right back where it came from," she told herself.

She finished emptying the rocks and then drove for another load. There was still a substantial amount of stones in a pile. She loaded what she thought would finish out her project and drove to the stream. A half-hour later, she placed the last rock in the wall and stood back to look at her handy work. "Not bad if I say so myself. Will it do, Cruz?"

Cruz cocked her head and let out a soft woof.

"I'll take that as a yes."

Eli picked up all her tools and returned them to the workshop. She parked the Gator in the barn and walked to the cabin. Eli took a long drink of water and went upstairs to shower. She decided on a new pair of cargo shorts and a

Southern Girl T-shirt. S*hould do well with a pair of loafers. Let her know I can clean up nicely.*

†

Eli shook her head at the thoughts running through her brain as she stripped down and took a shower, complete with leg and pit shaving. When she dried off, she added a touch of cologne. *Why do I feel like a teenager?* She checked the time and realized she needed to get a move on, or she would be late.

"You're lucky, Cruz, you didn't have to shower or shave. I will need to think about giving you a bath soon. I bet you'd do just fine in the walk-in shower."

She dressed and slipped into her loafers. She spotted Whit's basket still on the counter. "Guess I'd better return this, so she can refill it soon. Let's go, girl," she called, and Cruz trotted to the door.

The path from the end of the bridge took them beside Whit's garden plot. Eli was impressed by the size and the variety of vegetables. "Nice," she said as she reached the end of the garden and started across the yard.

†

Whit had gone into the shower when she returned home. Dressed in her newest jeans and a tank top, Whit went into the kitchen to get to work. She had sliced fresh tomatoes and onions the night before and had a nice cucumber salad chilling. Whit had the green beans in the pressure cooker and had the stovetop full of corn on the cob, sautéed squash, and onion, and the chicken was frying away. All she needed to do was whip up the cornbread. Whit blended the ingredients, and then grinned. She wanted to give her lunch date the full experience. She walked to the pantry to find a bag of

215

cracklin's, crushed them to smaller pieces, and poured half the bag into the mix. *I hope she doesn't have any allergies, but it's too late to take the cracklin's out now. I guess I need to ask her about allergies. I'd hate to put her into shock.*

She placed the cornbread into the oven and turned the chicken. Whit looked at the clock. "Shit, I'm running behind." She set the table and checked to make sure the tea was cooling. She placed a container of butter on the table along with salt and pepper. Whit was pouring the squash into a serving dish when she looked out the window to see Eli approaching.

"Damn, she looks good." She admired the long, tanned legs and the perfect fit of the shorts. "She's killing me." Whit concentrated on pouring the hot food into the serving bowls and made it to the table without tripping.

Eli stepped onto the porch and knocked.

"Come in." She heard the invitation from inside.

Eli opened the door and entered a room filled with succulent aromas. "I think my senses have died and gone to heaven," she announced. "Lunch smells great."

"I forgot to ask you if you had any food allergies earlier. Do you?"

"I'm allergic to stopping when there's good food around, but other than that, no."

"Come on in. You can have a seat at the table. The rest will be ready in a minute."

"Is there anything I can do to help?"

"Grab the cucumber salad and sliced tomatoes and onions out of the fridge. You can pour us some tea, too. Sorry, I'm running behind schedule."

Eli laughed. "I promise I won't die of starvation anytime soon. Relax and take your time." She took the two dishes to the table and placed them in the center.

Whit used tongs for fishing four ears of corn out of the boiling water into a bowl. She handed the bowl to Eli. "You can slather these with butter while they're hot."

"Yes, ma'am," Eli replied and buttered the corn. "Did you grow everything in the impressive garden of yours?"

"I sure did. Everything but the chicken is grown on this land." She pulled the chicken out of the pan and placed it on a tray to dry. The timer chose the exact moment to signal the cornbread was done. "Dang, I need three more sets of hands."

Eli reached over and turned off the timer. "What's in the oven that needs to come out?"

"Cornbread. There's an oven mitt in the drawer." She nodded to a drawer next to the stove.

Eli opened the oven and removed the skillet filled with cornbread. "In cast iron like my dad used to make." She smiled and placed the skillet on a trivet to cool. "This plate for the cornbread?" she asked, pointing to a large round plate.

"Yes, please. I'm almost done here."

Eli placed the plate over the top of the skillet and flipped the skillet, releasing the cornbread onto the plate.

"You did that well. I often leave a small section stuck to the pan."

"Lots and lots of practice," Eli said. "Oh, my goodness, did you make cracklin' cornbread? I haven't had that in years."

"I like to add a little spice to my cornbread. It goes great with all the fresh vegetables."

"I can't wait to dig into all this goodness."

"Go ahead and get started. I'll bring the chicken over in a second."

"Want me to butter you a slice of this cornbread?"

Whit smiled at her. "Yes, that would be great."

217

Thirty minutes later, Eli pushed her plate away from her. "I can't eat another bite."

"Too bad, there's fresh-baked apple pie for dessert."

"Damn, now you're telling me this. That's cruel."

"Why don't we go out to the garden and pick some vegetables for you to take home. Maybe you can make some room for pie."

"You want me to help you clear the table first?"

"No, I'll do that. Take the basket, and I'll join you in a few minutes. Pick whatever you want."

"Oh, dear lord, can you put me in your wheelbarrow and roll me out?"

"Come on, lazy bones." Whit took her hand and pulled her out of her chair. She picked up the basket and pointed to the door.

"Yes, ma'am, I'm going," Eli grumbled. "C'mon, Cruz, we've been banished from the house." Eli could hear Whit's laughter as they walked through the door.

†

Eli walked into the garden plot and was amazed by the rows of vegetable growing and the lack of weeds. *She must spend a lot of time here.* Eli recognized the corn Whit had served as a strain called sweet sixteen, with kernels that were a mixture of white and yellow corn. Some of the most delicious she'd ever eaten. Eli pulled off several ears for the basket. Sweet yellow and red peppers weighed heavily on the bushes, and she plucked two of each color. The next row was okra, one of her favorite vegetables. She pulled out her pocketknife and began cutting the small pods from the stalks.

"Damn," she called out. "I love this stuff, but it makes me itch. Well worth a little discomfort to have some fried, I reckon."

"Hey, where are you?" Whit called out.

"Between the corn and the okra," she answered.

Whit joined her and noticed the red marks on her arms from scratching. "You want me to cut it?"

Eli noticed Whit had put on a long-sleeved shirt. "Yeah, if you wouldn't mind. The stuff tears me up."

"That's why I need long sleeves. I react the same way, but damn, it's good eatin'."

"Yeah, it is. One of my favorites. Mom never had to worry about storing any of that leftover when she fried it in buttermilk and cornmeal."

"I just stew it on top of a pot of green beans, but fried sounds good."

Eli made a face at the mention of stewed okra. "Too slimy for me."

"It's an acquired taste," Whit replied.

They cut more okra and walked down the row.

"You have asparagus? Those would be great roasted with our steaks."

"Let's cut some then." Whit started cutting the slender stalks and handing them to Eli. "How do you plan to cook them?"

"I roast them in the oven with bacon wrapped around them. A little salt and pepper and a drizzle of olive oil."

"That's making my mouth water," Whit replied.

"Tastes good, and good for you. I may roast some of these peppers, too, to go with the steak."

"They are delightful this year. I can cut the yellow ones into rings, and snack on them raw."

Eli walked beside Whit. "You have an impressive garden. I hope one day, mine will be as good."

"Have faith, it will be. It will take a few seasons to bring your soil to its peak, but you'll get there. Grandpa used to grow some fantastic food from that spot."

"What do you think I still have time to grow this season?"

"Anything you see here. We had an early spring, so I jumped on planting early. Summer hasn't even arrived yet."

"Maybe I should jump on my tractor and start plowing. I guess I need to put some fencing in to keep the wildlife from eating my plants."

"That won't be difficult to do. Some fenceposts and some hog wire should do the trick. I've got an old gate in the barn you can have."

"The tractor came with an auger, so digging fencepost holes will be a breeze."

Whit could see the excitement on Eli's face. She knew she was eager to start turning the earth for her garden. "Do you trust me to do your shopping?"

"What? Yeah, why not?"

"I could pick up your groceries if you wanted to start on the garden plot this afternoon."

"No, I wouldn't ask you to do that, but if you could help me measure the plot out maybe you could create a list of materials I'd need. You're good at that. I could call in an order and have them delivered with the animal feed tomorrow."

"Sure, I can do that. If we get home in time, I can start mixing the concrete for your retaining wall while you play farmer."

"Sounds great. Should we go measure now? My basket is almost full already."

"Let's put a few of the tomatoes in there, too, in case you want another sandwich. I'll send you home with leftovers, or you can just come and eat with me."

"It would be easier to come here, wouldn't it?"

"Yes, but that's up to you."

"Go grab your grocery list," Eli replied.

After crossing from her property, Whit took the basket of vegetables into the house and placed them on the counter. She spotted Eli's list and stuck it in her pocket, while Eli retrieved a measuring wheel and a can of spray paint from the workshop.

"That's a handy device," Whit, said as she met Eli in the field.

"The former owner left a few tools behind. I'm glad this was one of them. It will get good use here. How far away from the stream should I start?"

"Fifteen feet should be plenty."

Eli walked off fifteen feet and sprayed the ground with orange paint to mark her first spot. Then she turned right to mark off two hundred feet and painted another place. A turn to the left and two hundred more feet defined the southern boundary of her plot and the second left, and then the last spot was marked.

"That will be a nice-sized garden. It will keep you busy this summer. While you're riding the tractor, you need to give some thought to what you want to grow, so we can get seeds or plants later this week." As they walked to the truck, Whit added, "A small tiller would come in handy too. You can borrow mine if you're not ready to purchase one yet."

"I'd appreciate it if you could make me a list of garden tools I need."

"That's not a problem. I'll knock it out for you tonight."

"Thanks. Let me put Cruz in her kennel and grab my list and keys, and I'll be ready."

"I picked up your list already."

"I'll be right back then."

Whit sat on the steps as she waited for Eli to return. Oscar weaved between her legs. "I'm going to town. You can stay here or head home."

Oscar answered her by climbing the steps and jumping into a chair.

"Alrighty then, enjoy your nap."

Eli returned with her keys and unlocked the truck. "Ready to roll?"

"Yes, ma'am," Whit answered, and walked to the passenger side and climbed in. "Do you have a pen?"

"In the console," Eli answered. She watched as Whit got the pen and started scribbling on the back of her shopping list. By the time they made it to the supercenter, Whit had a sizeable list. "Any of that we can buy here?"

"If you want to start your grocery shopping, I'll pick up the things on my list and see what of the gardening supplies we can get here."

"Deal," Eli said as she located a parking spot. They both grabbed carts out of the corral as they entered the store. "I'll see you in a few."

Eli watched Whit walk away, one hand holding the cart and another on the shopping list. She pulled her eyes away and opened her notepad. *Might as well start on aisle one.* She was happy she didn't have to go through the produce area. Whit had enough vegetables growing to feed them both for weeks.

An hour later, they met in the meat department, where Eli was examining steaks. "Those should do well," she spoke to herself.

"Those look delicious." Whit was standing beside her when Eli looked up.

Eli looked at her full cart. "Almost done?"

"Yes, ma'am, I've got a huge cart waiting for you in customer service. I got your concrete and some stakes to use on the wall. They were cheap, so no need to make some from scraps."

"Great idea. I think I'm all set," Eli answered as she placed several packs of steak in her cart.

A young man from the garden center loaded the rear of Eli's truck with supplies while they placed the groceries inside the vehicle. "Thanks," Eli said to him, and trotted around to the driver's side.

"Stop at your place first?" she asked when she climbed inside.

"Yes, please. I can put away my groceries, and we can get the plywood and my wheelbarrow."

"Didn't I just buy one?"

"You did, but it needs to be put together. Mine's already good to go. You can put yours together later."

"Makes sense. Do you need anything else from town?"

"Yeah, I do," Whit said and pointed to an ice cream place. "An ice cream cone."

"That's good. My treat, though," Eli insisted.

"You don't have to twist my arm. Pull into the drive-thru."

They ordered two cones and were on the road in no time. Eli licked the mound of soft serve as she drove, and Whit couldn't keep her eyes off her. *Maybe this wasn't such a good idea.* She could feel the heat rising up her neck and pulled her eyes away to open the AC vent.

"Are you hot?"

"Just don't want my treat to melt too fast." She smiled at Eli and concentrated on her ice cream.

When Eli pulled into Whit's driveway, she noticed a few ruts had formed from water erosion. "You know, my tractor has a blade attachment. I could barter your help for smoothing out your drive for you."

"Good deal," Whit answered as she took the last bite of the cone into her mouth.

Eli pulled to a stop close to Whit's home, and they carried her groceries inside and put them away. Then Whit led her to the barn, and they picked up several sheets of plywood and placed them over her wheelbarrow. Whit grabbed a hoe and turned to Eli.

"Do you have a garden hose?"

"Yes, it's hanging in the workshop."

"Good, I don't have to carry water to mix the concrete then."

When they arrived, Eli carried in a load and went upstairs to release Cruz from her kennel. "Good girl," she praised as they rushed down the stairs.

After putting the groceries away and the supplies on the porch, Eli pulled on her John Deere cap.

"That looks good on you," Whit told her. "I've never seen you in a cap before."

"I'm hoping it will help to keep the sun out of my eyes. Do you need my help?"

"No, I've got this. Get to plowing." Whit grinned.

†

Eli opened the door of the barn and took the keys for the tractor from the hook. She was glad she had paid attention when Mitch got tutored on driving the tractor and on installing the different attachments. Eli climbed onto the tractor and backed it into position to snap the connectors to the plow attachment into place. She used the lever to raise the plow attachment and put the tractor in gear. *Just like riding a bike. Once you learn, you never forget.*

"Oops, maybe a bit too quick to brag," she said after she popped the clutch too early and the tractor lurched ahead. "One step at a time."

Whit was working on securing the plywood form as she drove by on her way to the field. She shot her hand up in a wave, and Eli sent her a thumbs-up sign.

"Be careful," she heard Whit call out to her.

Eli tipped her cap and opened the throttle. When she reached her first marker, she slowed to a stop. "It's now or never," she said as she lowered the plow and then let her foot off the brake. She watched the plow dig into the earth churning black clods of soil. "I've got a lot of work to do here before I'll be planting anything," she reminded herself. Eli would need to make several passes over the plot in a variety of directions to turn the soil and loosen the grass that had grown over it for who knew how many years. She could feel her face breaking out in a grin as she made her first pass. Eli guided the tractor in an arc to make another pass and saw the depth of her first attempt. *Wow, looks perfect.*

Eli was excited at how rich the soil looked. She continued to plow until she had the entire plot covered with a first pass and then changed directions, breaking the dirt into smaller clods. *This will need a lot of raking to remove the grass and roots.* Eli was excited by the smell of the fertile soil. The sun was fading as she finished a second pass, called it a night, and went to check on Whit.

†

Whit had mixed the first bag of concrete and removed the firepit from its resting place. She poured two inches of concrete into the hole and smoothed it flat with a small piece of board. It didn't take her long to fill the first level of the form, ensuring the gaps between the rocks were filled with the stabilizing medium. Whit had installed the top level of the support and was mixing the last two bags of concrete when she heard the tractor approaching. She looked up and saw Eli smiling at her. *I could get used to the sight.* A strand of hair had fallen in her face as she bent over the wheelbarrow, and she pushed it away with the back of her hand. Eli signaled she was taking the tractor to the barn and turned away.

Whit added more water and continued to mix the concrete with the hoe. She had worked up a sweat and would welcome a refreshing shower. When she was satisfied with the texture, she added the mix to the form, concentrating on filling all the gaps and creating a smooth top surface. She did not hear Eli approach.

"Can you take a water break and I'll help you finish?" Eli was standing beside her, holding a cold bottle of water.

"Yeah, that sounds good. I'm almost at the end, so it won't take us long to finish." She took the bottle of water and took a long drink. "That tastes so good."

"Refreshing, isn't it?" Eli took a bandana from her pocket and used the water to wet it. She stepped in front of Whit and used the wet cloth to wipe the concrete mix from her cheek.

"I thought I'd better get it off before it started burning."

"Thanks, I think it already had. My face felt hot."

"Still red, but not bad. Thanks for all your hard work."

"Don't thank me until we take the form off to see if it worked."

"I'm sure it will turn out just fine. You don't seem to be a person to do something less than perfect."

"Oh my, I can see you're going to be good for my ego, but yeah, you're right, I don't do things half-assed. If I choose to do something, it has to be done right."

"I don't know about you, but I think it's quitting time after we finish here."

"I agree. I'm looking forward to a shower and an early night. It's been a productive, but tiring day. You're still welcome to come over for leftovers, though."

"Why don't we save them for lunch tomorrow? I have supplies coming in the morning, and Cruz has a play date tomorrow afternoon."

"That is a good idea. You have supplies for a sandwich or something, right?"

"Yes, I do. I promise I won't go to bed hungry. Let's finish this, and I'll give you a ride home."

"I won't argue with you. I'm bushed. I think Oscar abandoned me an hour ago."

"Let me start shoveling then, and you can pack the remaining gaps."

Once they finished, Eli cleaned the tools and placed them in the wheelbarrow. "I'll take these to your barn when we get to your place." She loaded them into the rear of the truck while Whit went inside to wash her hands.

Eli drove her home, and Whit went made a plate for Eli while she placed the tools in the barn. She met her at the truck with the plate covered in foil. "I can't stand the thought of you eating a cold sandwich after such a long day."

"Thank you. I'll take your cooking over a sandwich any day." She took the plate and bent down to kiss Whit on the lips. "Thanks for being such a good friend."

"My, pleasure," Whit said. She could feel the heat rising up her neck, and she was glad darkness had fallen. She wanted nothing more than to deepen a kiss with Eli, but she sensed the time wasn't right for either of them. Lord knows what she smelled like at the moment.

"See you tomorrow?"

"I'm sure I'll head over at some point. Would you mind if I go on the playdate?"

"The more, the merrier, and you can meet the rest of the future family."

"Have a great night, Eli."

"You, too, Whit."

†

Eli and Cruz rode home, and Cruz rushed to find a tennis ball. Eli placed the plate of food on the railing. "Okay, but just a few minutes. I need to shower and eat." She hurled the tennis ball across the yard and sat on the steps. Cruz raced after it and dropped the ball in her hand. "Good girl." Ten minutes later, the dog's heavy breathing prompted Eli to end the session. "It's time for the ball to go night-night." She placed the ball on the railing and picked up her food. "Let's go."

Eli placed the food on the counter and climbed the stairs to shower. The water cascading down her body felt terrific, her muscles relaxing as she bathed. Eli reviewed her day and was pleased with the progress made on her projects. She dried and slipped a T-shirt and boxers on before going downstairs. Eli placed food in Cruz's bowl, put her own plate of food in the microwave, and looked at her phone. She noticed she had missed a call from Mitch. Eli pressed the button to return his call, and placed the phone on speaker, as she set the microwave to warm her food.

"Hey, Aunt Eli," he answered.

"Sorry I missed your call. I must have been on the tractor when you called."

"Cool, what were you doing today?"

"I worked on a couple of small projects and then decided to start working on a garden plot."

"Oh, wow, that sounds like fun. How'd you do on the tractor?"

"Fine, once I got the hang of it again. I've finished two passes to turn the soil, but there's still a long way to go before I can plant anything. Maybe I'll have something in the ground by the time y'all arrive."

"You've got some shipments coming in tomorrow, don't you?"

"Yeah, some stuff came in today, but the animal feed and more furniture arrive tomorrow. Cruz and I'll go on her playdate tomorrow afternoon, and if all goes well, the fur babies will be delivered the next day."

"You have to send me some video."

"I will. How's it coming along with school?"

"I'm knocking assignments out left and right. I shouldn't have much left by the time I come up."

"That sounds great. I'm proud of you. Whit sends a hello, too. She cooked lunch for us today out of her garden." The timer on the microwave pinged to announce her food had warmed.

"Is that your dinner?"

"Yeah, she sent a plate of leftovers home with me tonight. She went grocery shopping with me this afternoon and helped with a few projects."

"Tell her I said hello, please. Is Cruz enjoying herself?"

"She's having a blast. I'm glad to have her here for some company."

"Go eat your dinner before it gets cold. Thanks for calling. I'll try calling tomorrow night again."

"Okay, if I miss you, I'll call you when I get settled. Love you. Hugs and love to everyone. Proud of you, Mitch."

"Thanks, Aunt Eli. Love you, too. Goodnight."

Eli poured a glass of tea and removed her dinner from the microwave. She covered the corn and cornbread with butter and settled in to eat. The food tasted even better as leftovers. Whit had loaded the plate well, and Eli struggled to finish, but she did. After washing the dishes, she took her tea and opened the door. "The last call for the evening," Eli told Cruz who rushed outside. She watched her disappear in the dark and sat in one of the porch chairs. The smell of the turned soil floated across the breeze, making Eli smile. "A great day of work," she spoke aloud. "I'm sure I'm going to feel it tomorrow."

The call of an owl broke the silence, and she listened to it for several minutes until her eyes began to feel heavy. "Let's go baby girl," she called to Cruz.

†

Whit heated a small plate of food to eat before she showered. Her arms and legs ached from the hard work. She had forgotten how demanding it was to mix concrete. *The shower will relax me, and I won't be too sore tomorrow.* Oscar had already retired for the evening, so after she ate, she showered and fell into bed.

CHAPTER ELEVEN

Eli woke rested and with minor soreness the next morning. She opened the door for Cruz and left it open. There was a cool breeze, and Eli opened the sliding door to the deck to welcome the freshness inside. She turned the oven to pre-heat and placed three ham biscuits in a pan to warm, while she opened a pack of steaks and put them in a container to marinate. Eli shucked the corn they had picked from Whit's garden, and washed and sliced the okra and peppers. She placed the vegetables into the refrigerator for later and returned upstairs to dress. When the biscuits were warm, Eli spooned blackberry jelly onto them and grabbed her coffee from the machine. She walked onto the deck and placed her food on the table.

The sun was painting the mountain with glorious color. Eli took a bite of biscuit and groaned at the explosion of tastes in her mouth. She decided to allow the sun to dry out the turned earth before she resumed plowing. Eli would use her measuring wheel and paint to map out the fence allowing an additional ten feet to give her plenty of room to move a tiller about. Once she finished plowing and installed the fence, she would have to use a small rototiller to continue to cultivate the soil. She would mark out the location of the posts and then also set up a spot close by for her compost bin. Whit had assured her the grass they raked from the plot would be good to start the foundation of the bin.

Eli was walking toward the workshop when a truck pulled into her drive. She waved to the driver and motioned him to pull in front of the barn. The two delivery men went to work unloading bags of feed and straw for the stables. They unloaded the extra chairs, and Eli directed them to place them near the firepit. The last items were the fence posts and corner posts she would use on the garden and compost bin. Several rolls of hog wire and staples were included.

"You can unload those down there," Eli said, pointing at the freshly plowed plot.

They drove the truck closer and emptied the rest of her supplies. She watched them depart and walked to the house. Cruz trotted the edge of the field, her nose to the ground following the scent of a critter that had passed through overnight. Eli whistled to her, and they entered the barn. The men had delivered a salt lick and mineral block for the deer. She placed them in the rear of the Gator and drove from the barn with Cruz sitting beside her.

When they reached the clearing she had picked out for Mark's cabin, she drove to the stream and parked. She placed the blocks about ten feet apart. "I hope they find them here. If not, we'll move them to a different place."

As they drove home, they saw Whit on the path ahead of them. She turned at the sound of Eli's approach and stuck out her thumb.

"Hey, lady, want a ride?"

Cruz jumped out and ran ahead as Whit slid into the seat. "Hey," she said as she settled in place.

"How are you feeling today?

Whit shrugged. "Sore, but not as bad as I thought."

"Me too. That shower and bed sure felt good last night."

"Amen. I barely remember laying my head on my pillow. I slept until seven this morning."

"You don't have the four-legged alarm clock I do. I like it that way though. The early mornings here are so beautiful."

"Yes, they are. Lovely and crisp mornings and evenings. It never gets terribly hot, although we do have heat, it just doesn't last long."

"I need to store the feed and straw before we go into town. It won't take long."

"I'll help. Did you order bins?"

"Yes, ma'am, one for cat food and another for goat food."

"You're confident they will hit it off today?"

"Cruz and Molly are both so high energy, it seems like a match made in heaven."

"I think you're right. You want me to spread some straw in a stall and set out the feeders?"

"Yes, I'll store the feed if you'll do that."

"Can we take the plywood down, too, before we go to see if the retaining wall is stable?"

"I can handle the barn if you want to start on that. The tools are in the workshop. I think there's a small pry bar hanging above the table. It and a hammer should make it easy."

"I can do that."

Eli pulled to a stop in front of the barn. She walked inside to start work as Whit headed for the workshop. Eli took a bale of the straw and opened the first stall. She used her pocketknife to cut the string and began to scatter the straw across the floor. Then she hung the automatic feeder and water system. She opened the first feed bin and emptied a bag of food for Molly. The second bag she placed on top. After opening the second bin, Eli filled it with cat food. There was also a small trough she placed just outside the barn to fill with fresh water. Eli was excited to have the rest of her fur family delivered the next day. She parked the Gator in the barn and looked for Cruz. She walked out and found that Cruz had followed Whit down to the stream and sat watching her pry the plywood away from the rock wall.

"Wow, what a great looking wall."

Whit took a step toward her. "It did turn out sturdy. We make a good team," she said and high-fived Eli.

"Yeah, we do. Hey, I want to pick up three more sheets of plywood to make the compost bin. I've already got the spot marked out and have posts but not wood."

"Easy peasy," Whit said. "Do you plan to make a three-sided bin? What about a lid?"

"Do I need a lid and four sides?"

"Not necessarily, but you may need a lid and a fourth side, especially before winter."

"Should we make it complete from the onset?"

"I'd get the materials. Once you get the compost started, you can put the lid and front on to help heat it."

"You're my expert so just let me know what we need."

"Three more sheets and two sets of hinges. No big deal."

Eli stacked the boards and stakes in a pile. "Do you want me to drop these by your place?"

"I don't think I need them for anything. Can you store it in the barn or workshop?"

"Sure, no problem. Thanks!" Eli picked up the pile of boards and carried them to the barn. Cruz trotted along beside her. "Ready to go meet your family?"

Eli opened the door, and Cruz jumped in the seat. Eli opened the door for Whit and walked around to enter the truck. "Should we stop off for supplies first?"

"Naw, we should have plenty of time afterward. I'll give Jimmy a call and have him pull the order together for us. Anything else you need?"

"A nail apron, I think, will make hanging the wire a lot easier."

"Good suggestion. I'll add it to the list." Eli listened as Whit placed the order and explained she was helping her new neighbor get started on some projects. After a few minutes of chit chat, Whit ended the call.

"All set. Jimmy will have them waiting for us at the front of the store this afternoon."

"Thanks," Eli said and concentrated on the winding road. "You hungry?"

"A little but not bad."

"Could you eat a burger?"

"Yes, I believe I could."

A few minutes later, Eli pulled into a drive-thru and ordered three burgers, one with just meat and cheese for Cruz. Earlier, Eli had spotted a picnic table next to the river on one of her trips to town. She pulled onto the roadside and grabbed Cruz's leash and water bowl.

"Let's eat," she said to Cruz, who jumped out of the truck.

Eli took Cruz's burger and broke it into small bites as Whit poured her a bowl of water. Cruz sat, waiting for her special treat. Eli set the bowl in front of her and smiled. "Take it slow," she warned.

Eli looked at Whit. "She must have been from a large litter and had to compete for food. Sometimes she eats so fast, she gets choked."

After finishing their burgers, Whit collected the trash and placed it in the garbage while Eli walked Cruz to let her potty. When they had loaded into the truck, Eli said, "I have to admit I'm excited and a little nervous about Cruz meeting the new family. I'm not sure how she and the cats will get along."

"She does well with Oscar," Whit reminded her.

"No offense, but Oscar isn't going to run from her. Kittens might. I don't want her to get used to chasing them."

"Let her wear herself out playing with Molly first, then see if you can take her into the cat habitat to lie down and let them ease into a visit."

"How'd you get so smart?" Eli teased. "That's exactly what we'll do."

"If you sit down on the floor with her, I'm sure all the animals will feel safe and approach."

Eli smiled as she pulled into the drive of the shelter. She opened the door and clicked the leash onto Cruz's collar. "Let's go baby girl." She allowed Cruz to sniff all the different scents on the ground and find a spot to pee before they entered the building.

Erin was working at the front desk and looked up to see them enter. "Welcome back. Oh, isn't she beautiful?" She turned to Cruz, "Come here, baby girl."

Erin walked around to kneel to Cruz. "You are so pretty. I hope you and Molly become good friends today."

Cruz licked the young woman's face. "Such a sweetheart. How are you? Hey, Whit, I didn't recognize you for a second. It's been a while."

"Yes, it has Erin. I keep threatening Oscar I'll come and get a kitten to keep him on his toes, but just haven't made it in."

"Well, unfortunately, we have many to choose from so if you see someone you like we can add it to the crew we're delivering to Eli tomorrow." She looked at Eli. "Did your supplies get delivered?"

"Yes, ma'am they did, and we're all set for the new arrivals."

The hall door opened, and Dr. Loren came through. "Hey there," she called out. "Ready for a playdate?" She knelt down in front of Cruz. "What a cutie. Welcome back, Eli, and hello, Doc, it's been a while. How have you been?"

"Well, thanks. Helping Eli and Cruz get settled in next door."

Dr. Loren looked at Eli. "You couldn't ask for a better neighbor. Are we all set to meet the family?"

"Whit had an excellent idea to allow Cruz and Molly to meet first, to enable her to burn off some energy before she meets her feline family."

"That is smart. Are we ready?"

"Let's do this," Eli said and walked beside Whit as they followed the vet and Erin down the hall. "Should I leave her on her leash at first?"

"Play it by ear. You know Cruz's temperament best. When you think she's ready, cut her loose."

When they reached the door to Molly's enclosure, Eli knelt down and hugged Cruz. "Play nice," she said. Cruz whined with the excitement she felt coming from Eli.

The door, and Eli and Cruz walked inside. Molly saw them enter right away and rushed over to them and skidded to a stop a few feet away. Cruz looked at Eli, and she knelt down beside her companion. "Cruz, this is Molly."

Cruz quivered with excitement as the small goat took a tentative step forward, and then another until they were nose to nose. Molly licked Cruz's muzzle, then bent forward with her butt up in the air. Cruz mimicked her behavior. A universal sign of *I'm ready to play*. Eli removed the leash and sat on the ground.

Molly stood and took two hops toward Cruz then dashed away. Cruz was quick to follow, and when Molly skidded to a halt at the end of the enclosure, she spun around to rush Cruz. Cruz sidestepped the oncoming goat and then pivoted to resume the chase. Molly jumped over the small barrel and toys in her playpen, and Cruz followed in hot pursuit.

Everyone watching broke out in laughter as Molly jumped over Cruz, and they ran in circles around the enclosure. Eli stepped out of the area to join the others. "I think we've made a match."

Dr. Loren stopped chuckling. "I'd say so. Look at them go. Just watching them is wearing me out."

When they were both winded, Molly led Cruz over to the water dish for a drink, and then they plopped down next to each other to catch their breath.

"I guess I won't need to order a case of tennis balls just yet," Eli said.

"Oh, I'm sure Cruz will still want special attention from you," Dr. Loren said. "Don't think you're getting off that easy."

"My throwing arm is getting plenty of workout from chores around the place," Eli assured her. "They seem to be getting along well. Do you think we should try for the cats?"

"No time like the present," Dr. Loren said.

Eli stepped inside and called to Cruz. She snapped her leash on, and Cruz turned to look at Molly and then to Eli. "Don't worry, she's coming home tomorrow, and you can play all you want. There are others I want you to meet."

They walked down the hall and Erin opened the door to the cat habitat. Eli saw black cats everywhere in the room as she led Cruz inside.

"I know you feel way outnumbered, but they are friendly." She sat down on the floor and had Cruz lay down beside her. They waited for a few minutes. Cajun was the first to approach. He sniffed Cruz and enjoyed a moment of scratching from Eli before the others approached. Walter came next, followed by Tomboy, who scrambled into Eli's lap. "Good girl Cruz," Eli praised as Walter laid down beside Cruz and they were nose to nose. Eli ran her hand down Cruz's back, and that was all the invitation Tomboy needed to play. He pounced on her hand, and Cruz startled but continued to lie beside Eli as the small kitten climbed down her back.

"Good girl, Cruz," Eli repeated. She unclipped the leash and left the room. There were a few hisses, but Cruz backed off and went to the next cat to greet them.

"You've got a great pup there," Dr. Loren said. "You sure you're ready for this crew?"

"The feeders are set, and there's a bed of fresh straw in Molly's stall. I don't know what else we can do to prepare."

"Is it okay to deliver them after lunch tomorrow?" Dr. Loren asked.

"That will be fine," Eli answered. "I've gotten some deliveries, so I can place the boxes in the barn for them to play in."

"Hey, we can use those plywood scraps to build some perches too," Whit added. "I can do those while you finish plowing the garden plot and dig the holes for the posts."

Dr. Loren's brow shot up. "Oh my, you have been busy. You hit the ground running, didn't you?"

"Yeah, I have so much I want to do," Eli answered.

"Just don't forget to stop and have some fun once in a while," Dr. Loren encouraged.

"I won't, but this has been fun. I know what you mean, though, about pacing and not burning myself out. I have a great neighbor to keep an eye on me, who won't hesitate to let me know when I'm doing too much."

Dr. Loren grinned at Whit. "Good job, Doc."

Whit shrugged. "Hey, I try, what can I say."

Cruz walked over to the door, and Eli opened it then clipped on her leash. "Are you ready for a nap now?" she teased.

"She's had a busy afternoon," Erin said. She looked at Whit. "Did you see anybody you liked?"

"I think so." Whit looked at Eli. "Could I talk you out of Walter? He seems older and pretty laid back."

"He's been here for quite some time," Erin said. "Walter gets along with the younger cats, but he may do better with Oscar."

"Consider him yours then," Eli said.

"Thanks, he sure is a cutie."

"You're welcome. I'm not sure what Oscar will think though."

"Oh, he'll be put out for a day or two, but I think he'll enjoy the company. He seems to enjoy hanging around your place with Cruz."

Eli laughed. "Ha! That may change tomorrow once we have the invasion of the kittens."

"You could be right, but I doubt it," Whit answered.

"Okay, I think we're all set then. You two ready to head out?"

Whit nodded. "Yeah, we'd better go before we find someone else to adopt."

Cruz whined as they walked past Molly. "You'll get to play all you want tomorrow." Cruz looked at Eli and smiled her doggy smile and trotted ahead.

"I swear she just smiled at you," Erin said.

"She does sometimes when she's thrilled," Eli answered.

"We'll see you about one tomorrow," Dr. Loren said as they walked out.

"Sounds great, we'll be waiting."

Whit held the door open for Cruz and Eli. "That went well."

"Better than I imagined." Eli loaded Cruz into the truck, and they stopped to pick up their supplies before heading home. Cruz curled into a ball and fell asleep on the ride home.

"What project do you want to start first?" Whit asked as Eli slowed to pull in her driveway.

"I'd like to make one more pass with the plow to break the clods and let them dry in the afternoon sun. After that, it should be easier to rake the grass and roots out of it."

"Would you mind if I worked on the perches for the barn cats?"

"Not at all. You should be able to find any tool you need in the workshop."

Whit nodded. "If you'll pull over to where you want the compost bin, I'll help you unload the wood."

Eli pulled the truck to a stop, and Cruz bounced up in the seat. "Welcome home, sleepyhead," Eli teased. She opened the door, and Cruz jumped down.

They unloaded the truck and Eli helped Whit carry the tools to the barn. "You sure you don't need my help?"

"No, farmer girl, I've got this. Go put on your cap and get to plowing."

Eli smiled and opened the barn before climbing into the cab of the tractor. She plucked her John Deere cap off the gear shift, pulling it down over her eyes, and started the tractor. She had forgotten the tractor came equipped with a radio, and reached down to turn it on, scrolling until she found a country station. *Now we're all set.* She drove the tractor to the garden and engaged the plow. The sun had begun to dry the earth she had turned yesterday, and she was sure by tomorrow she could start the long task of raking out the plot. Plowing was the simple part. She would make the final pass and then swap out the plow for the auger to begin digging her post holes. If she got that much done by the end of the day, she would feel she had accomplished a lot. *One row down and many more to go.* Eli made the turn to start another pass and sang along with the radio.

†

Cruz had followed Eli out to the garden, but became bored and decided to find out what Whit was making in the barn. She walked to the front of the barn and sat watching Whit as she measured and cut the wood.

Whit looked up to find Cruz watching her. "Hey, Cruz. Not too exciting watching Mom plow, is it? You can keep me company while I make perches for your new brothers and sisters."

Whit planned and measured out the sections of the board she wanted to cut and used the spare two-by-fours for supports. When she had the first perch hung, she stepped away to examine her handwork. "Not a bad first attempt," she told Cruz.

Cruz wiggled her body at the attention and stepped forward to lick Whit's hand.

"You did excellently today," she told the excited pup. "Your mom is proud of you."

Cruz spun around in circles, making Whit laugh. "I know you love her, and I think I'm falling for her, too." *Where on earth did that come from?* "I reckon I should get to work and stop thinking crazy thoughts."

Whit was finishing the third perch when she heard the approaching tractor. She looked up to watch Eli drive the tractor into the barn and disengage the plow. She pulled the tractor into position and hopped down to attach the auger.

"You're handy with the tractor," Whit called out.

"I think I'm getting the hang of it. I'll need your help to guide me to the holes. Let's take a break first." Eli walked through the barn and surveyed the perches Whit had installed. "I'm not the only one handy with tools. Those look great."

"Thanks. I think the cats will like them."

"You know, I had the craziest thought when I was plowing."

Whit cocked her head to the side. "Dare I ask?"

"I was thinking about a playground slide. I'm sure the cats will find a way into the hayloft, and I thought a slide would be an easy way for them to come down safely."

Whit broke out laughing. "Oh, my word, that's genius, and I think it would work."

Eli took off her cap and ran her fingers through her damp hair. "You want some water?"

"Yes, it sounds good about now. I'm at a good stopping place."

"I see you have a supervisor," Eli said, indicating Cruz sitting at the front of the barn.

"She thought plowing was too boring to watch, so she's been keeping me company."

"It was boring, but it's looking good."

"Have you decided on what you want to plant yet?"

"Oh yeah, a little bit of everything. I thought I could plant some beans in with the corn. Maybe a few rows of zipper peas. Some okra and tomatoes. Squash, cucumbers, and the list goes on and on. I was thinking about some blueberry bushes along the outside of the fence. What do you think about that?"

"I love your ideas. Didn't you also mention some fruit and nut trees and blackberries?"

"Yeah, I've got a lot of work to do, huh?"

"Yes, but in just over a week, you will have a strapping young man to help."

243

Eli's face lit in a smile. "That's right."

"You can focus on getting the garden ready for planting, and I'll get your water system flowing. We can order the seeds and plants you'll need so after your brother and his family leaves, you can focus on planting."

Eli nodded. "You sure you have time for all this?"

"I love a good challenge. Besides, I'm procrastinating on writing my next book."

"I didn't know you are a writer. That's neat. What do you write?"

"Don't get all excited. I write college textbooks."

"You know, I couldn't help noticing Dr. Loren calling you Doc. It's more than a nickname, isn't it?"

"I was a child genius. I graduated high school by thirteen and had my Ph.D. in Astrophysics from M.I.T. by eighteen."

Eli watched a blush rise to her face. "Wow, I knew you were smart, but damn, girl. Should I be calling you Dr. Brewer?"

"Please don't. Just call me Whit. It's just a title." She knew her words had come out a bit too harshly when she saw Eli recoil. "I'm sorry that came out too strong. People put too much weight on titles. I was born with gifts, and I use them."

"No problem. I just know it isn't easy to advance so quickly in high school period, much less an institution like M.I.T. It's an accomplishment to be proud of, and I bet your grandparents were delighted."

"Oh, they were. I was the talk of the town for years, but now I'm just Whit, and I like it like that."

Eli could sense that she had hit a hot button, so she let the conversation slide. She realized how little she knew about her new friend, and getting her to reveal anything about her life would take patience. "Let me go get the water. Do you want anything else?"

"No, thanks." Whit watched Eli walked away and could kick herself for reacting like she had. She had taken her share of bullying and teasing for being such a smart person, but Eli was only being kind, not condescending like her classmates had been.

"Take a chill pill, girl," she told herself as she left the barn and met Eli at the cabin steps.

Eli held out a bottle of water. "Here you go."

"Thanks," Whit replied and took a long drink before sitting down on the steps. "That's so refreshing."

"Not as good as the water here, but it'll do in a bind. I'll keep some of the bottles and fill them from the tap. I don't think I've ever tasted such good water before."

"The springs are icy and almost sweet during certain times of the year. It's as if Mother Nature knows when we need a pick me up."

"That's a unique way of thinking about it, but I agree with you. Once I get the hang of the auger, I don't think it will take more than an hour to dig the holes. After those, we're done for the day, if you want to go home and freshen up while I start on dinner."

Whit smiled and lifted her arm. "Do I smell bad or something? I can stay and help with dinner unless I offend your sense of smell."

"No, no, not at all, but I confess I do have an ulterior motive. I never got to try your pie yesterday."

Whit laughed. "We did forget all about it, didn't we?"

"Yeah, until I was in the shower last night and I remembered it. I thought, damn, all the good food, but no pie."

"I'll go home for it when we're done and take a quick shower while I'm there."

"You don't have to. I like you just the way you are."

"I'll go get the pie and check on Oscar. I haven't seen him since we got back from town."

"Maybe he smelled the cat scent on Cruz." Eli couldn't help but chuckle. "Do you think he'll get along with Walter okay?"

"I think so. Walter seems pretty laid back too."

Eli glanced at her watch. "Do you think we have enough daylight left to dig holes?"

"I think so if we get moving and get a rhythm going. Go get your tractor. Do you want to start at the compost area?"

"As good a place as any, I reckon. I'll see you in a few."

Eli sat her water on the step and walked to the barn as Whit and Cruz made their way to the site of the compost bin.

"It's just four holes. You can get this right," Eli said as she put the tractor in gear. "The others will be a piece of cake after those first few."

Whit found the four spots Eli had painted, and when she arrived with the tractor, Whit guided her to place the auger bit over the first spot. "Give it a go," she said.

Eli held her breath as she began working levers to place the tip of the auger against the bare ground and another to start the rotation. She released her breath when the bit hungrily chewed into the earth. Eli realized she had failed to do one thing. Intending to dig the holes three feet to give them a solid foundation, Eli forgot to measure the depth of the auger. She pulled the lever to stop the rotation and lifted the auger from the hole. "Damn, I forgot one thing," she growled as she jumped down from the tractor.

"To measure the depth of the auger. I just thought about it, too. How deep do you want to go?"

"Three feet. Let me grab my measuring tape and paint." Eli stormed off into the workshop.

Eli returned with the tape and paint. She opened the tape measure and found she was only three inches short. Eli marked the correct distance with a spot of color on both sides. "Once we get it right, we can go by the dirt on the auger." She laughed.

"That's true," Whit answered. "Knock 'em out, girl."

Eli grinned and dropped the tape and paint into a storage basket in the tractor and finished the first hole.

"Perfect," Whit hollered when she reached the correct depth. "On to the next?"

Eli pulled forward to the front corner and drilled the next hole. "We got this," she said and shot Whit a grin. Within minutes they had dug the four holes for the bin. Eli pulled the tractor to the perimeter of the garden plot. "You want to give it a whirl?"

"Heaven's no, you got a groove going. Let's keep it that way."

Working together, they drilled the holes for all of the posts and still had daylight left.

"Done," Eli called out when the last hole was dug. "C'mon up and I'll give you a ride to the barn."

Whit was laughing as she climbed onto the tractor and sat on Eli's knee. "Yeehaw let's go home!" she cried out.

Eli chuckled and put the tractor in gear. She leaned forward to steer the tractor, pressing her body into Whit's. Eli could feel the warmth of her skin through the thin fabric of her shirt and the smell of shampoo still lingering in her hair. The ride to the barn was all too short for Eli's liking. She felt the absence of Whit's weight when she pulled the tractor pulled to a stop and Whit jumped off. She shook her head and steered the tractor into the rear of the barn.

When she walked over to the porch, Whit was unpackaging the wheelbarrow. "What are you doing?"

"Scavenging boxes for the cats," she replied with a grin. "You can attach the handles and the wheels while I go home for the pie. I brought your electric screwdriver, so it shouldn't take long."

"No rest for the weary." Eli chuckled as she sat on the steps and picked up the directions. She turned the paper around in several positions, looking at the diagrams. "Do you reckon they intentionally make this as confusing as they can?"

"It can't be too hard. A few screws and bolts here and there," Whit said.

Eli grinned at her. "I'm on it. Go get the pie. I need something sweet before I cook dinner."

"It'll ruin your appetite."

"No, it won't, I'm starving."

"Okay, I'll be right back. You want some ice cream or cheese to go with it?"

"While they both sound lovely, I just want pie, and lots of it."

"I'm gone already. Cruz, do you want to come so she doesn't start snacking on you?" Whit heard Eli's laughter and her command to Cruz.

"Go ahead, just be careful on the bridge," she warned. Cruz ran to catch Whit.

Eli concentrated on the assembly project and was cruising right along when she heard laughter and looked up to see Cruz and Whit approaching. It only took a few more seconds to understand why Whit was laughing. Cruz was soaking wet as she rushed to her. "What happened?"

"Little miss smarty pants thought she'd be clever and take a short cut. Instead of taking the bridge, she plunged right into the stream. I have to admit, she's a good swimmer."

"And now a wet dog. I have a mind to take you to the laundry room and give you a shower."

"Then you will both be wet."

"You have a point. Cruz will dry off soon enough. You will get a bath soon, though."

Cruz sat down in front of her and gave her the best doggy smile she could muster.

"I guess I forgot to tell you she loves playing in the water."

"That's okay, it just scared me for a minute until I saw her swimming and having fun." Whit stepped onto the cabin steps. "You've almost got it whipped. Do you want me to heat you a slice of this pie?"

"That would be awesome. Let me get this wheel on, and we should be good to go."

Whit cut a large piece of pie and placed it in the microwave to warm it. The heat brought the brown sugar and cinnamon aromas wafting out the vent. Whit's stomach grumbled. "I know it smells good. I think I'll have a slice too." She cut a second slice and was popping it in the microwave when Eli entered. "All done?"

"Assembled, and it made it to the barn without anything falling off, so we'll call it good. Damn, that smells wonderful."

"Settle on a chair, and I'll bring it. I'm joining you. What do you want to drink?"

"Some sweet tea," Eli answered and took a bite. "Oh my, this is good."

Whit poured two glasses of sweet tea and took her slice of pie from the microwave to join Eli. "Glad you like it. I enjoy baking."

"Which is good to know. I think I'll plant several apple trees just for your pie baking practice."

"Bring it on," Whit challenged. "I'll bake them as long as you'll eat them. I end up freezing at least half when I bake pies. I have a slice or two, then I want something else."

"You, my friend, have a deal. I may plant an orchard." Eli grinned. "You know, Mark and I have tossed around the idea of selling organic vegetables at the Farmer's Market. I bet your fruit pies would go over well there, too."

"That's true. I'm not sure I want to do that much baking, though." Whit shrugged. "Who knows."

"Not a problem. It was just an idea tossed out. You'll find Mark and I do that often."

"What's he like?" Whit asked.

"A bigger, more teddy bear version of Mitch, with less hair. He's got a heart of gold, and would give you the shirt off his back if he likes you."

"It sounds like the two of you are close."

"My best friend and confidant," Eli admitted. "We've both had our share of rough spots, but we've always been there for one another. I can't wait for you to meet him and the rest of my family." She smiled at a thought. "If Brad doesn't have you in stitches, no one can make you laugh. He's such a clown but can turn on the charm in an instant. I feel sorry for the girls at his school. A personality totally different from Mitch, but they complement each other well. Most of the time, anyhow."

"I can't wait to meet them and hear all the stories about you growing up. It sounds like Mark would have the dish on you."

"Ha! I'm an open book, but he can tell stories of the trouble we got into as kids. That's for sure."

Eli finished her slice of pie. "Are you ready to start dinner?"

"Yes, what can I do to help?"

"There's a head of lettuce in the refrigerator. You could toss us a nice salad and use some of the cheese and veggies from your garden. I hope you like honey mustard or ranch."

"This is your lucky day. I like both."

"I'll get the veggies ready to go on the grill, and start on the steaks." Eli walked over to start one of the ovens and put a pot of water on to boil. She pulled out the asparagus, wrapped them in bacon, seasoned them with salt and pepper, and drizzled olive oil over them before popping them in the oven. She turned the second oven on broil, then placed the pepper rings on the grill with more olive oil.

Whit watched her while she whipped up the salad. "I didn't see a grill. Are you going to use the flat top there to cook the steaks?"

"No, ma'am, I'll do the peppers and corn there. I broil my steaks in the oven. Much faster and so much better for you. Mark is the king of the Big Green Egg, though, so you'll get your fill of grilled meats. Ain't nothing that man can't cook. His OJ chicken is to die for."

"Sounds interesting. I'll look forward to tasting it." Whit finished the salad and put it in the fridge to chill, then sat on a barstool to watch Eli work.

"How do you like your steak cooked?"

"I prefer it not mooing, but I don't want it well done. Medium to medium rare, I guess."

"I will make your taste buds explode," Eli promised.

Whit chuckled. "I'm ready for that." She watched as Eli pulled the steaks from the refrigerator and dredged them through the marinate one last time before placing them in a broiling pan. "Good grief, they even smell good raw."

"You want to set the table? We can use real plates tonight." Eli spread some olive oil on the flat top and took the corn from the boiling water and placed it in the oil. She turned and opened the refrigerator and pulled out a container of ground parmesan cheese. Eli flipped the grilling peppers and checked on the asparagus.

"Looking good," she announced as she peered through the oven door. "You can pour us some tea, or whatever you'd like to drink."

The timer sounded, and Eli flipped the steaks and turned the corn. The kernels were just starting to brown. She opened the parmesan cheese and sprinkled the cheese, turning each one until coated.

"That's something I've never had before," Whit said as she watched Eli.

"I could be wrong, but I think you will like this meal."

"Wrong, I'm going to love it. My mouth is watering already."

"Hand me a plate for the peppers and corn, please. You can pull down one of the long serving dishes for the asparagus, too, please."

Whit lined up the empty dishes and watched Eli fill them with vegetables, then placed them on the table.

"You can bring our dinner plates over. The steaks will be done in just a few."

Whit watched Eli remove the steaks from the pan and spread butter over the top of them.

"Let me get this pan rinsed, and we'll be good to go," she said and handed the plates to Whit.

†

"It was a fantastic meal. I must admit, that was the best steak I've ever eaten," Whit praised as she reached for her tea glass.

"I'm glad you enjoyed it. What did you think of the corn?"

"It was spectacular. I like your sense of adventure with food. I would have never thought to try that."

"It's just as good with some dry ranch dressing mix," Eli replied. "Do you want a cup of coffee while our dinner digests?"

"Yes, that sounds good. Do you also want to try out the fire pit tonight?"

"Of course, that's our dessert." Eli was grinning. "I'll go start the fire if you'll brew us a cup."

"Sounds great to me."

Eli left the cabin, and Whit began making the coffee and picking up the dishes.

Eli used some of the kindling Whit had chopped and a few small logs to start a fire in the pit. She watched the flames as they began to lick around the dried wood and the fire came to life. She placed two chairs around the fire pit and waited to ensure the logs had ignited before walking inside. There was a cool breeze kicking up, and the night-time symphony of insects had begun. The moon had yet to rise, and she could see fireflies floating across the stream, dancing through the tall meadow grasses.

This will feel good if the temperature keeps dropping. Eli placed a few more sections of small logs next to the pit in case she needed them and walked to the cabin.

†

Whit had cleaned the kitchen while she was waiting on the coffee. She was loading the dishes in the dishwasher when Eli returned.

"You didn't have to do that. I was coming to clean my mess."

"It's the least I could do for such a fantastic meal. Besides, you weren't messy at all. I have no clue how to clean the flat top, so I'll leave that for you."

"It's simple, but it has to cool first. I'll take care of it later." Eli pulled out several long forks to use in toasting the marshmallows over the fire. She added large puffy marshmallows, graham crackers and chocolate bars to the tray she had set up. "I think that's it. Are you ready?"

"Oh, yes, ma'am, I haven't had s'more's in ages. You grab the tray, and I'll bring the coffee."

They settled around the fire pit, and Eli placed the tray on a small table between them. "What a beautiful night."

Whit glanced at the stars. "The sky is so clear. You can see so many stars that are sometimes not always visible to the human eye."

"You know, I've meant to ask you something," Eli said. "I noticed one of your big trees has some sort of treehouse in it."

Whit chuckled. "My lab and office space. I have a state-of-the-art telescope and other equipment I use for my research."

"Oh," Eli said. "One of the first nights Mitch and I spent here, I saw a flashlight beam headed up the mountain. I'll admit I did some speculation whether you were growing pot or making moonshine, but the lab's not big enough for either."

Whit broke out laughing. "You are hilarious. I guess it would seem odd to see someone heading into the mountain late at night, but that's when the stars are most visible. Like tonight. No light pollution coming from artificial lighting, and minimal cloud cover." She was still chuckling when she said, "I could take you with me one night and show you around the galaxy."

Eli's head whipped toward Whit. "I'd love to. I used to look forward to the field trips to the planetariums when I was a kid."

"Well, I can show you my personal planetarium."

"That's awesome. I'll look forward to it."

"Moonshine and pot, really, Eli?"

"Hey, I didn't know, and I hadn't met you yet, so my imagination kind of got the best of me." She felt her face warm with a blush. "I should have kept that admission to myself."

"Heaven's no, but I think it's hilarious." She nodded her head. "I can understand your imagination going in that direction. I haven't thought about adding any pot to my garden, though."

Eli placed a marshmallow on the end of the toasting fork and handed it to Whit. "You first, while I get your crackers and chocolate ready."

"Oh, goody," Whit said and placed the fork over the flame. "I like mine toasty," she said as the sugary treat burst into flame. She brought it to her mouth, blew out the fire, and placed it on top of the chocolate.

Eli used the second graham cracker to squeeze the marshmallow off of the fork. "Here you go, my friend. Eat up." Eli watched Whit's eye light up as she bit into the sticky goodness.

"Just as good as I remember," Whit said, popping the last bite into her mouth. "Your turn," she said and handed the fork with a fresh marshmallow on it to Eli.

"I'm more of a soft melted person myself," she said as she placed the fork over the fire. She noticed Cruz sitting next to her watching her as she licked her muzzle. "Do you like marshmallows, baby girl?"

Whit fished one out of the bag and handed it to Eli. "I know she shouldn't have chocolate, but try this."

Eli offered the squishy treat to Cruz, who took it from her palm. She chewed and chewed the sweet treat and then sneezed. "Okay, so maybe not the best choice for sharp teeth." Eli laughed.

"She had to try it though, to find out," Whit replied.

"Yeah, she did." Eli pulled her fork from the fire and placed it between the graham crackers Whit was holding. Whit handed her the s'more, and Eli took a bite, the chocolate oozing out the sides. "Oh, my goodness, I forgot how good these are."

Whit stabbed another marshmallow. "How long has it been?"

Eli thought for a few seconds. "Wow, a camping trip with the boys about eight years ago."

"It was past time then," Whit said as she set her marshmallow on fire. "I even like just the marshmallows by themselves."

Eli watched as she popped the hot treat in her mouth then started waving when she realized how hot it was. She grabbed Whit's tea glass and handed it to her. "Careful."

Eli made another treat and then sat in her chair for a break. "I'd say the firepit is a success."

"It burns well, doesn't it?" Whit sat down beside Eli, who was staring into the fire.

"Yeah, it does. I can tell this will be a favorite spot."

The conversation fell silent for a few minutes. The wind picked up, and rain began pouring down on them, not a gentle sprinkle, but a massive droplet rainstorm. Eli looked at Whit, who was just as shocked by the sudden change in weather. Eli laughed and started grabbing the S'mores ingredients and closed the lid on the firepit. "Grab our drinks, and let's make a dash for the porch."

Whit grabbed their glasses, tea, and coffee sloshing as she spun toward the cabin and started jogging. Cruz, excited by the activity, danced around the women as they rushed toward the cabin. She barked, and they laughed as the rain soaked their clothes.

Eli was the first to reach the porch. She turned to Whit. "Where on earth did that come from?"

"I didn't think it was supposed to rain until later tonight," Whit answered as the rain flowed down her face.

"I wasn't expecting a downpour like this," Eli said as Whit turned and watched the rain running down the roofline.

"Me either. I don't know about you, but I'm soaked." Whit grinned at Eli to see she was just as wet.

Cruz was standing beside them and shook the water from her coat. Eli laughed. "Thanks, baby girl, just what we needed, more water." Cruz barked at her, and Eli picked up her ball. "Think that was funny, huh? Let's play!"

Eli let the ball fly and then ran out into the yard into the rain. Cruz raced after the ball and caught it, but when she tried to put on the brakes to stop, her feet slid on the wet grass, and she went tumbling. Eli was still laughing when Cruz regained her footing and came rushing toward her and jumped into Eli's arms, and they both dropped to the ground in a puddle of water. Cruz licked Eli's face, and she laughed uncontrollably.

"Y'all are crazy," Whit said from the safety of the porch. She couldn't help but laugh at the pair, now entirely soaked.

"I have to admit, it was fun." Eli took a step onto the porch. "I haven't played in the rain since I was a kid." *I should pick her up and carry her out in the rain.* Eli was contemplating the idea when the night was lit by a bolt of lightning and an ear-shattering crack of thunder. Cruz nearly bowled her over as she leaped onto the porch, sliding with a thud into Whit, who barely kept her balance. Eli's quick reaction to throw out an arm to steady her prevented Whit from falling.

Whit took a step forward, slipped on the wet porch, and landed in Eli's arms.

Eli caught her and held her close. She could feel Whit's warm breath on her face as she laughed. Eli leaned forward and pressed her lips to Whit's. She could taste the sweetness

257

of the chocolate, and when her lips parted, Eli took the kiss to another level.

Whit's hand moved to the back of Eli's head, pulling her forward to deepen the kiss, and moaned as their tongues began a sensual dance. When Eli broke the kiss, they were breathless and looking into one another's eyes.

"I don't know where that came from either, but I enjoyed it," Whit said as she relaxed in Eli's arms.

"I did, too," Eli admitted. She kissed her again, a sweet kiss of exploration.

Not to be outdone by her humans, Cruz stepped close and showered them both with kisses, causing them to break out in laughter again.

"I love you, baby girl, but Whit's a better kisser," Eli teased, and Cruz replied with a loud bark of protest.

Once the laughter faded, Eli could feel Whit shiver. She smiled. "We'd better get out of these wet clothes and get warm." She helped Whit to her feet. "I don't have a shower curtain in place downstairs, so you'll need to shower upstairs in my bathroom. There are fresh towels under the sink, and I'll dry off and put some dry clothes for you on the bed. I'll make us some coffee while you rinse off."

Whit nodded and allowed Eli to lead her into the house.

"Holler if you need anything."

Eli watched Whit start upstairs and then stop and turn to her. "You could join me."

"Thanks. I don't think we are ready for that move yet."

Whit smiled. "It didn't hurt to ask." She continued up the staircase.

Eli shook her head and walked into the downstairs bath. Mitch's robe was hanging behind the door, so she stripped out of her soaked clothes and dried her body. She slipped into the oversized garment and tied the belt around her waist. Eli ran her fingers through her hair to smooth it down. *Yeah, I could have joined Whit in the shower, but we've just started getting to know one another.* A shower would have led to sex, and Eli wasn't ready to plunge headlong into another relationship just yet.

✝

Whit entered the bathroom. What was I thinking? Obviously, I wasn't thinking. I just assumed Eli is into me. But the kiss. What that felt like was real, or else I've gone insane. The look she gave me after the kiss could not be denied. She is interested. I've just got to be patient and not pressure her into something Eli isn't ready for yet. She must still feel the sting of betrayal from her ex and best friend.

Whit removed her wet clothes and draped them over the shower door, then reached inside to start the water. She opened the cabinet and pulled out a clean towel and washcloth. Whit stepped into the shower and allowed the hot water to cascade down her body. She reached for a bottle of shampoo and lathered her hair. The smell of the shampoo filled her nostrils, reminding her of Eli, so she pushed the images out of her head and rinsed her hair. She was bathing her body when another flash of lightning lit up the room, and the power flickered off.

"Oh, shit."

✝

Eli was using a towel to dry Cruz when the lightning flashed. She grabbed a flashlight when the lights went out and started up the stairs. Eli pulled out a pair of sweatpants and a T-shirt, placing them on the bed with a flashlight she had on her nightstand, then stopped outside of the master bath. "I reckon you know the power is out. I placed a flashlight and some dry clothes on the bed for you."

259

"Thanks, Eli."

Eli smiled to herself and grabbed a pair of sleep pants and a T-shirt and walked down the stairs. She slipped into the clothes and placed the robe in the bathroom. *No power, no coffee. I can start a fire, though, to help us warm up.*

She had already laid a fire in the fireplace, so she just needed to start the kindling. The wood had been drying for days so it caught fire, and flames began to lick up the sides of the logs. Eli sat in front of the fire and enjoyed the growing warmth. Cruz walked over to her and laid down, placing her head in Eli's lap.

"Good girl," Eli praised as she began stroking down Cruz's back.

The warmth of the fire on her back and the softness of Cruz's dried coat relaxed Eli, and she felt her eyes closing until she heard a step as Whit started down the steps. The rain was still pelting on the roof as Whit descended the steps and walked toward them.

"That fire is beautiful. Mind if I join y'all?"

"Please do. It feels great. Sorry, no power, no coffee." Eli scooted closer to Cruz to make room for Whit.

"No problem. The shower felt great, and this fire is warm," Whit said as she sat close to them.

"The rain doesn't sound like it will be letting up soon. Would you mind spending the night here? I can drive you home if you prefer," Eli offered.

"I don't have a problem crashing on your couch. There's no need for us to get drenched again."

"I'm sure Mitch wouldn't mind you sleeping in his bed." *I'd love to have you in mine, but I don't trust myself with you.*

Well damn, I was hoping she would offer to share her bed with me. Whit smiled at Eli. "That's good. I'll let you cook me breakfast, and then I'll head home. I will make the supply list for your power system, so you don't have to worry about being out of power again."

"I'll place the order as soon as you have everything you need on the list. Do these pop-up showers happen often?"

"Not as a rule," Whit replied. "They generally accompany severe weather systems like tornadic activity."

Eli grabbed her phone and looked up the weather. "Doesn't look like anything severe, but it appears we will have a few more hours of rain according to the radar images."

Cruz stood and stretched before walking to her bed and plopping down.

Eli watched her pup move in a circle in her bed. "The fire is getting warm. Do you want to move to the couch?"

"It is toasty." Whit stood and offered a hand to Eli, then they walked to the couch.

"About earlier," Eli started.

"It's okay. I was wrong to ask you to join me in the shower," Whit said.

"No, it wasn't wrong. The timing just isn't right yet. We are getting to know each other. I don't want to rush into anything," Eli explained. "Being betrayed by my ex has left me a bit gun shy."

"I can understand," Whit said and lowered her head.

Eli reached over and lifted Whit's face and looked her in the eyes. "I am very interested in you, but I need some time. I'd be lying if I said I didn't worry about the age difference, but you seem older than your age."

"I'm not sure how to take that," Whit said.

"As a compliment," Eli assured her. She brushed a strand of Whit's hair away from her face and tucked it behind her ear. "You're beautiful and intelligent. My attraction to you scares me a bit. I'm not a love-at-first-sight type of person."

"So, now you say I'm scary?" Whit replied.

"Stop it, silly woman. Quit twisting my words. I'm trying to have a serious conversation with you."

Whit chuckled. "I'm sorry. I wish you'd relax. I understand the timing isn't right, and I assure you I will wait as long as you need. I can't, however, promise you I will be patient. That's not one of my better qualities."

"I appreciate your honesty." Eli moved closer. "It's too early to turn in, so tell me about you."

†

A log collapsing in the fireplace startled them awake. Eli had her arm draped around Whit, and they had fallen asleep on the couch. She looked into Whit's sleepy eyes. "I uh, guess we fell asleep." She grinned.

"I can remember being toasty warm and comfortable." Whit looked at her.

Eli leaned down and kissed her. "Are you ready to stretch out in a bed?"

Whit looked down at her watch. "It's almost three."

"Too early to be awake. C'mon," Eli said and offered Whit her hand and led her toward the stairs.

"I thought Mitch's room was downstairs."

"It is, but you're coming upstairs with me."

Whit arched an eyebrow.

"To snuggle." Eli chuckled. "We've got a busy day tomorrow."

"Yes, we do." Whit followed Eli up the stairs and snuggled in beside her. She fell asleep with Eli's arm, draped protectively around her.

CHAPTER TWELVE

Eli woke several hours later and crept from the bed. She and Cruz walked outside into a beautiful sunrise. The rain had stopped during the night, and the temperature was cool, but not cold. Cruz relieved her bladder and raced to Eli. "We can play later. I promised a lovely woman breakfast." She chuckled. "Let's go get you fed first."

Eli left the door open and walked into the kitchen to begin cooking. During the night, the power had returned, and the clocks on the stove and microwave flashed, waiting to be reset. She checked her phone for the correct time and entered it on both devices.

"I think a nice steak and cheese omelet will do nicely, don't you, Cruz?"

Cruz licked her lips at the mention of steak. She watched as Eli opened the refrigerator to pull out the ingredients she needed. After placing them on the counter, Eli prepared a cup of coffee and set the coffee maker for Whit when she arrived. Eli began chopping the leftover steak into small pieces, adding bits of veggies to the mix. *Might as well toss in the kitchen sink.*

✝

Whit's eyes popped open, and she was disoriented until she realized she was sleeping in Eli's bed. She rolled onto her side to find she was alone. Whit couldn't resist hugging Eli's pillow to her face to breathe in her scent. She could hear sounds of movement coming from downstairs, and once she had stretched and given a final yawn, she left the bed to walk to the bathroom. A glimpse in the mirror gave her a shock when she saw how disheveled her hair had become. She dampened her hair and prayed it would calm down and not scare everyone in the house.

✝

Cruz saw her as she started down the stairs, and Eli turned to see Whit.

"Good morning. I was trying to be quiet, but you know how that goes. I'm sorry if I woke you."

"You didn't. My bladder needed some relief. What are you creating?"

"I thought I'd make us an omelet with the leftover steak."

"Oh, yummy. What can I do to help?"

"Nothing just yet. Make yourself a cup of coffee. Later you can pour us some juice."

Whit prepared her coffee and then sat at the bar to watch Eli cook. She cracked and whipped eight eggs, then poured in the steak and other ingredients.

"That will taste fantastic," Whit said.

264

"Yes, it will. Do you like salsa, guacamole, or sour cream on your omelets?"

"Yes, to all," Whit answered. "Do I need to get them out of the refrigerator and put them on the table?"

Eli turned around to look at her. "Yes, please. I'll drop the toast in a minute if you get the condiments out."

"On my way," Whit replied.

†

After consuming the monster omelet, Whit and Eli carried their coffee onto the deck.

"What plans do you have for this morning? Dr. Loren won't be here until around one, right?"

"Yes. The rain last night has left the garden too wet to do much there, so I'll work on setting the fence posts and building the compost bin. What about you?"

"I need to go feed Oscar and do a few things around the cabin today. I want to put your supply list together for your solar system. I don't know if they will have the supplies in stock or if they'll need to order."

"I'll put in an order as soon as you have the list ready. Thank you."

"I'd love to have everything we need to make it for Mitch's first project when he gets here."

"He will love it. He's so excited to see how it works."

"I should have some tomatoes ready. Do you want some for sandwiches today? I thought I'd pick a basket for Dr. Loren, too."

"That sounds delicious," Eli answered. "I hope the slide gets delivered this morning, so we can attach it to the loft."

"The cats will love it," Whit said as she drained her cup. "I'm heading out now. Thanks for the great breakfast. I'll see you in a couple hours."

"You're welcome. Thanks for all of your help. Hand me your cup, and I'll take it inside."

Whit handed Eli her cup and then stood on her tiptoes to kiss her. "See ya." She spun on her heel and hopped off the porch steps. Cruz followed her to the edge of the path, then rushed home.

"You can go," Eli told her, but she trotted back. "Time to get dressed for work and get at it," Eli said with a chuckle.

Eli climbed the stairs and smiled when she saw Whit's clothes hanging over the shower door. They brought the memory of last night rushing to her. Eli smiled at the thought of snuggling into Whit. She bathed her face and brushed her teeth before dressing in shorts, a T-shirt, and her work boots.

"Time to get to work," she said and jogged down the stairs.

Eli started with the compost bin and was amazed at how the project came together. She even improvised on her design and cut notches in two boards to allow the lid to prop open when she was putting items for compost inside. "That will save me a few goose eggs on my head," Eli told Cruz. When she had finished the design, she stepped back to look at her handiwork. "I think, with a coat of paint, we can call it done."

The sun and the temperature were rising in the sky as Eli began setting the fenceposts for the garden plot. After completing one side, Eli and Cruz walked down to the stream. Eli sat on a boulder while Cruz lapped at the pooling water, splashing in the current as she chased a leaf or minnow. "Don't scare off Mitch's fish." Eli saw some older pipes which ran along the bank, and she wondered if those were remnants of the irrigation system Whit's grandfather used to water his garden. *When I get the hog wire installed, I can plant the trees and berry bushes, which reminds me, I need to place an order.*

Eli finished her water and began setting posts again. Cruz darted past, alerted to Whit's return.

"You've made a lot of progress this morning. The compost bin looks great."

"I thought a coat of paint would be nice, and we'd call it done."

"That could be a quick and easy Mitch project after the wood cures a bit," Whit suggested.

"It will come out in a camo pattern knowing Mitch."

"It will blend in well that way." Whit chuckled. "Where can I help?"

"Grab a pair of gloves from the workshop, and you can drop the posts in the holes we dug yesterday. The water has seeped into the ground and didn't mess up our holes."

"I'll be right back. Do you want me to fill your water bottle while I'm there?"

Eli smiled at Whit. "Yes, please, it would be great."

When all the side posts were set, Eli decided they would take a rest and eat some lunch. "We've made good progress this morning. I know the afternoon will be shot as the new family gets settled into their new home. Maybe I can finish the last few posts later today."

"You need to remember to pace yourself and take breaks. We can hang the fence wire tomorrow. I'll need you to drive over to pick up the gate, though."

"That's no problem. I want to order the trees and berry bushes today, too."

"Which reminds me," Whit said as she fished out a list from her overall pocket. "The solar system supply list. I can call both orders in if you'll write down the trees and bushes you want."

They sat on a boulder down by the stream, sipping on water as Eli finished the list, adding the trees and berry bushes.

"There, that should do it." She handed the list to Whit, and they began walking.

As they approached the cabin, a delivery truck from Merrill's started up the drive. Eli looked at Whit. "Here comes the slide." She grinned.

Eli waved the driver over toward the barn. Whit followed them and greeted the young man. "Hey, Evan, I haven't seen you in a while. How are you?"

"Good thanks, Whit. I'm home for spring break from college and thought I'd help Dad out a bit with deliveries."

"How's it going at Western?"

"Not bad, I've got one more year before I go out in the real world."

"I'm sorry, Eli, this is Evan Merrill."

"Nice to meet you, ma'am. You've got me curious why you want a playground slide out here."

"You won't believe this. Eli has adopted a slew of cats from Dr. Loren for barn cats, and she's sure they will find their way into the hayloft. She came up with the slide as an easy way for them to come down from the loft."

"That is genius," he said. "Do you need some help attaching it? I don't have another delivery until later."

"I'd love some help. Can you have some lunch with us? We've got fresh tomatoes from Whit's garden."

"Oh, heck yeah. That sounds fantastic. Let's get this unloaded and attached."

Whit watched them unload. "I'll start on some sandwiches if you don't need my help."

"Thanks, this shouldn't take long at all."

Eli and Evan carried the slide into the barn and placed it in the position where she wanted it. "That will work," Eli said as the slide butted right to the bottom of the loft.

"If you have a drill, I'll climb the ladder to the loft and attach the slide," Evan offered. "It's only a few bolts, and the kit comes with a socket that will fit any standard drill."

"I'll be right back then," Eli said, and walked to the workshop for the drill and an extra battery pack. She handed the tool to Evan, and he scurried up the ladder.

"I can't believe how perfect it fits. It's level too," Evan said as he sank the first bolt into the loft base. "One down, three to go." He grinned down at Eli. When he finished, he sat down on the edge of the loft and took a test ride down the slide. "Yes'm, it works just fine. The cats will love it."

"Thanks for your help, Evan."

"No problem. That was easy. Are you here by yourself?"

"My nephew will be here soon through the end of the summer. His family will build a home farther up the mountain one day."

"I'll be home for the summer, so if you need help with any big projects, I'd like to work for you."

"Do you know anyone with a hay baler?" Eli asked.

"Dad's got everything you need for baling hay."

"I've got fields I'd like to cut for hay this summer. Let me know when you get home from school. I don't know if I'll sell it or save it. I haven't decided on animals yet, except for cats and a miniature goat."

"A goat? Those are so damn cute."

"A playmate for Cruz. Her name is Molly, and she's being adopted today, too."

"That is great. I hate to see the animals at the shelter. It makes me want to bring them all home."

"I tried my best, but stopped at a dozen black cats," Eli told him.

"It's ridiculous how people are so superstitious about black cats. Every one I've ever met has the neatest personality."

269

"That's why I love them so much. Black cats are unique."

"Your pup won't chase them?" he asked.

"She might at first, but I'm hoping Molly will wear her out playing, so she doesn't have the energy to herd cats."

Evan's laughter filled the air. "Heelers are super energetic."

"Yes, but I wouldn't trade her for anything."

"I think she feels the same way. She's right beside you every step you take."

Cruz looked at Eli with her soft brown eyes. "That's my girl. You ready to eat?" Eli asked Evan.

"Yes, ma'am."

When they entered the cabin, they found that Whit had made a pile of sandwiches, and they were sitting on the table with plates and a bag of chips. "What do y'all want to drink?"

"Sweet tea for me, please," Eli answered.

"That's good for me, too," Evan said.

Whit poured three glasses of tea and brought them over to the table. "Evan, can I send an order with you?"

"Sure can. If we have it in stock, I can bring it out to you. What do you need?"

Whit pulled out the list she and Eli had worked on together and handed it to the young man.

Evan let out a low whistle. "Wow, quite a list. The only thing I know for sure that we won't have is the generator, but Dad has the contact for a local Generac dealer. They are, by far, the best brand." He studied the rest of the list. "The trees and bushes shouldn't be a problem. I'm not sure if we have all the solar panels in stock, but I'll check and order them when I get to the store."

"I've already got an account set up at the store, so you can charge the items," Eli instructed him.

"You will be busy for a while," he said. "I can deliver and plant the trees and bushes later this week if you'd like some help. I could use the money, and I'm not afraid of hard work."

"You have a deal, young man," Eli said. "I've got a tractor with an auger attachment you can use if it will make it easier."

"It won't be wide enough for what we will be planting, but you can use it to start holes, so I'll know where you want things to go."

"I can do that with no problem. I've gotten lots of practice with the post holes." Eli let out a soft chuckle.

When they finished eating, Evan picked up the list. "May I call you to confirm what we have in stock and what needs to be ordered, and to set a day and time to plant?"

"Absolutely," Eli answered and gave him her cell number.

"Thanks for lunch. I'll call later today. Good to see you, Whit."

"Thanks, Evan. We'll see more of you soon," Whit answered.

Whit placed the last of the sandwiches on Eli's plate. "I know you wanted to do your own planting, so thanks for letting Evan do the work for you. He's a good kid."

"Hey, any young person who's willing to do hard work to help get through college is good in my books. Too many kids expect everything to be paid for, and don't realize the value of their education because they didn't have to work hard for it."

Whit tossed the paper plates in the trash. "That's true. I'm sure you will be right there with him, helping." She smiled.

"Hey, can't I use those to start my compost pile?"

Whit took them out of the trash. "You sure can. I don't know what I was thinking. Shred them, and we can toss them in. When you rake the grass in the garden plot it can also go in there."

"I need you to make a list," Eli said. "Or print me off a list of items if it's easier."

Cruz walked to the door and whined. She had heard the drone of the diesel engine before either woman were alerted them to Dr. Loren's truck coming up the drive.

"I think my family has just arrived," Eli said and walked out into the yard.

Erin was in the passenger seat of Dr. Loren's truck and climbed out as soon as the engine turned off. Cruz rushed to greet her, covering her face with kisses as she knelt next to her.

"Somebody is excited," Erin said between giggles.

"Several somebodies," Eli said. "Wait until you see what we've got set up in the barn. Hey, Dr. Loren," Eli said as the vet walked around to the side of the truck.

"We have some distressed babies ready to get out of the carriers," Dr. Loren said. "If y'all will help me, we can let them escape and start exploring their new home." She looked at Whit and grinned. "Walter's asleep in the rear seat."

They unloaded six large animal carriers and let the cats loose to explore. The crate Molly was in was too large to remove with her inside. "Stand back, and I'll let Molly out next," Dr. Loren warned.

Cruz could smell Molly in the truck, but had not seen her yet. She paid little attention to the cats as they were released, preferring to sit at the end of the truck to wait for her friend.

As soon as Dr. Loren opened the crate, Molly leaped out onto the ground and rushed to Cruz. They stood nose to nose for several seconds before Cruz took off running toward the garden plot, with Molly in hot pursuit.

Dr. Loren smiled as she watched them play. "I think it's safe to say those two have bonded well."

"Me too," Eli said as she reached into the truck and handed Walter out to Whit. He started purring the minute she cuddled him in her arms.

Eli looked around and saw black cats everywhere and smiled. "Come check this out," she told Erin as they started toward the barn. Eli opened the door, and Erin broke out laughing.

"That's a fantastic idea," she said. "Dr. Loren, she put up a slide for the cats to come down from the hayloft."

"A what?" Dr. Loren asked.

"A playground slide, it works for humans, too." Whit grinned.

Dr. Loren examined the feeders and automatic watering systems Eli had put in place. "These cats will be so spoiled." She rattled one feeder, and several of the cats came rushing in to start eating. "Y'all did an excellent job setting up a stall for Molly, too. She will be comfortable here. You know I just had a thought." She grinned at Eli. "You could put a short rope or leash on the stall latch. As smart as Cruz is, you could teach her to come let Molly out in the morning to play."

Eli nodded and chuckled. "That is too funny. I was thinking the same thing earlier."

"She'd catch on in no time," Whit said.

Eli turned when she heard Cruz barking. "That could be problematic," she said and pointed to Molly on top of the new compost bin. "Thank goodness the lid was closed."

"Why don't we build them an obstacle course where they can run and play?" Whit suggested.

Dr. Loren looked around. "You got some rocks you could make a mound out of, and I'm sure we could get some used tires to partially bury so they can race through those."

"Maybe even a large plastic barrel, we could cut the ends off to make a tunnel for them." Eli grinned.

"Now that will be fun. You want some help?" Dr. Loren asked.

"Sure, this could be fun, and maybe others could come out and play," Eli answered.

"I'll volunteer to draw something up," Erin said. "Maybe Evan can help us out with some of the supplies."

"Evan as in Evan Merrill?" Whit asked.

"Yes, we've been dating for a year. Evan's home for spring break right now."

Eli smiled. "He just left here thirty minutes ago. You just missed him. He helped me secure the slide, and he'll do some planting for me later this week."

Dr. Loren looked at her young assistant. "Why don't you draw up a course and create a supply list. Once we know what we need, we can all pitch in and build it. Does that sound like a plan?"

"Sounds fantastic to me. Let me know how much we need for supplies, and I'll drop it by the clinic."

"You got it." Erin grinned at Eli.

"Whit built some perches in the barn for the cats, but if you can create some designs which might interest them, toss those in, too, please."

Erin rubbed her hands together. "I love a challenge."

"Do you have questions?" Dr. Loren asked.

"No, I think it's just a matter of getting settled in," Eli answered.

"You have my number if you need anything."

"Programmed in my speed dial," Eli assured her. "Call me when you've got our design worked out," she said to Erin.

"I will. Have fun with the new family. Bye, Tomboy," she called out to the kitten pouncing on a larger cat.

Eli and Whit watched them leave and then walked to the front steps. They took a seat and watched all the activity around them. Cruz and Molly were weaving in and out of the fenceposts they had planted earlier. Cajun had claimed residence on the porch railing and was overseeing his kingdom from above. Several of the older kittens had made it into the barn to eat and had discovered Whit's perches. Walter, who had yet to leave Whit's arms, was still purring as she rubbed under his neck.

"Where's Oscar?" Eli asked. "With all these black cats, it's hard to tell who is who."

"He's the one on the stone wall giving me the stink eye for loving on Walter," Whit said with a nod toward the fire pit. "He's the only one with a collar and an attitude."

Eli reached over to scratch between Walter's ears. "He has quite a motor. I don't understand why he was never adopted. He's a handsome cat."

"He was just waiting for us," Whit said.

"I reckon so. I think I'll set a few more of the posts before the afternoon gets away. Would you like to join me at the diner in town tonight for supper? I didn't pull anything out to cook."

"I think we both deserve a break. I'll take Walter home and get him settled and take a shower. Do you want to drive over and pick me up later? We can put the gate for the garden in the back of the truck."

"I won't be late. As soon as I get a call from Evan, I'll start rounding everyone up for the evening, then I'll shower and come get you."

"See you soon. Aww crap, I forgot to give Dr. Loren tomatoes."

"We can eat those tomorrow. I'm certain we'll be seeing Dr. Loren again this week."

"Don't forget to drink. It's hotter than you think out here."

"Yes, Mom," Eli teased. "I will."

Eli pulled the gloves from her pocket and walked to the garden. Tomboy pounced beside her as she walked. Cruz and

Molly had worn themselves out. Eli called Cruz and walked to the stream so she could get a drink of water, and Molly followed her example. "Good girls."

Cruz and Molly curled up in the shade as Eli began working. Tomboy sat on the pile of rocks, watching her as she packed dirt into the hole. She used a piece of a broomstick to tamp the soil in the hole to make it sturdy.

Evan called to report they were one panel shy of filling the order, but he would deliver it in two days. He told Eli the trees and bushes could be delivered as early as tomorrow afternoon. "Dad said I could stay and start planting if you're ready."

"I'll be ready. I'll scc you tomorrow. Thanks, Evan. Oh, Erin will be calling you to enlist your help in building an obstacle course."

"She called ten minutes ago, all excited. I'm more than happy to help, and Dad may have some stuff around here he's eager to get rid of that may be perfect."

"Sounds great. See you tomorrow."

"Goodbye, Eli."

Eli slipped the phone in her pocket. "Only one more post to set, and I'll call it a night."

Tomboy continued to watch her, and when she finished, he trotted over to her and started rubbing against her legs. She reached down to pick him up. "Are you claiming me?" she asked and planted a kiss on his nose. She cuddled him in her arms as she walked to the barn.

Cruz and Molly trotted along after them, and after placing Tomboy on a perch, Eli walked into the stall and sat on the fresh straw. Cruz and Molly followed her inside. Molly went to the food bowl while Cruz took a drink.

"It's time for the rest of us to get settled in," Eli told Cruz as she stood and walked to the stall door. She stopped to pet Molly. "I'll see you later."

Eli flipped a switch to turn on soft light. She thought both Molly and the cats might adjust better if there was a low light left on. The goat trotted to the gate and stuck her nose out. Cruz licked it and turned to Eli.

"She'll be alright. We'll check on her later."

When they walked to the cabin, Eli left the door open and filled Cruz's bowls with food and clean water. "Time for me to hit the shower," she told Cruz, who had her face buried in her food bowl. Eli pulled out some clean clothes and started the shower. She ran her hand down her leg and decided it was time for a shave. "Alexa, play the Eagles," she called out as she stripped out of her clothes.

Eli had finished showering and was drying when she looked into the bedroom to find a black ball of fur curled on her bed. I guess I need to make some decisions about leaving the door open now the family has grown. The last thing I need is Molly and her energetic self in the middle of my bed. Eli chuckled at her thoughts as she wrapped the towel around her body. As she approached the bed, Tomboy raised his head and blinked his bright green eyes at her. "You're making yourself at home, aren't you?" He blinked again. Eli sat on the end of the bed. "You know a mama shouldn't choose a favorite, but you sure are making it difficult." She reached over to stroke his fur which felt much more like a rabbit's, and he began to purr. "Turning the charm up a notch." She chuckled and scratched under his chin. "What will all the other kittens think?"

Tomboy stretched and reached for her hand.

"I can tell you're not worried what the others will think. Let's play this by ear and see how things go. Cruz may have something to say about you on the bed, though. Even she doesn't sleep here."

Eli finished dressing and went downstairs. Tomboy followed her, and they walked out to the barn together. Cruz was sitting outside Molly's stall and whined when Eli walked up. "No time like the present," she said. Eli searched and found a short piece of rope and tied it onto the handle of Molly's stall. "Come, Cruz," she instructed and offered the end of the line with a large knot tied in it to the dog. Cruz bit the knot and with a gentle nudge from Eli backed up, sliding the handle of the stall to the open position.

"Good girl, Cruz. Let's try it again." Eli took the rope and pushed the handle to close the gate. "Open it," she said and pointed to the knot. Cruz grabbed the rope and pulled the gate open. "Good girl. Get Molly." Cruz ran inside the open gate to greet her friend.

"You want to go play for a bit?" The word "play" was all the invitation they needed. Cruz rushed out of the stall with Molly right behind her. Tomboy jumped out of the way to keep from getting bowled over, causing Eli to laugh. She watched the two disappear into the open field and turned toward the barn. Black cats of all sizes were hanging out everywhere. She refilled the feeder and counted heads. "Yep, all present and accounted." Several pairs of bright eyes watched her from the loft, and Eli wondered if they'd tried the slide yet. *Tomorrow when I'm dressed for work, I'll demonstrate.*

Chapter Thirteen

When they returned from dinner, Eli pulled the truck into Whit's yard. The bumpy drive reminded her she needed to come over and do some blade work to smooth it out.

"Thanks for a great dinner." Whit smiled. "Are you ready to pick up the gate?"

"Sure," Eli answered and turned the truck off.

After loading the gate in the truck, Eli shuffled her feet a bit. "It's turned out to be a beautiful night."

"Yes, it has. Great for stargazing. Do you have time to walk to the lab with me?"

"Absolutely," Eli answered.

"Let me check on the boys and grab a flashlight."

Eli sat on the steps as she gazed at the cloudless sky. The stars glimmered brightly against the deep black sky, and the early evening breeze was filled with the scent of many blooms. Eli smiled when she heard the call of the owl she had heard on previous nights, then stopped to worry about the safety of the cats. *Surely there are enough mice and other critters to feed a hungry owl.* She was lost in thought when Whit emerged.

"All set?" she asked.

"Yes, ma'am. You don't think the owl will come after the cats, do you? I just heard one calling."

"I don't think so. There should be much easier prey for owls to eat. Cats are agile and will stick close to the barn."

"I hope so. How's Walter adjusting?"

Whit smiled. "Like he's been here all along. Oscar's even warming to him a bit. At least he's stopped hissing at him."

"Well, that's a start. Tomboy seems to think he should be a housecat. I left the front door open, and he was curled on my bed when I got out of the shower."

"That should be interesting. Does Cruz seem to be okay with him?"

"So far, so good. I don't know if Tomboy will come inside tonight when I get home, though. He was hanging with his homies in the barn when I left."

"You have to admit, he is a cutie."

"No doubt. Not sure cute enough to sleep on my bed, though."

"I dunno, you let me sleep there," Whit teased.

"You are infinitely cuter and don't shed. Or do you?" Eli teased back.

"Not that I'm aware of. Tomboy will make a nice footwarmer this winter, though."

"I'll take it under advisement."

"Let's go make some moonshine," Whit said and turned on the flashlight. "I have to laugh every time I think you thought I was making shine or growing weed."

Eli shrugged. "What can I say, I have an active imagination."

"Yes, you do. I hope you're ready for a climb."

"I think these old bones can manage. What got you so interested in astronomy?" The two women continued to walk up the mountain.

"Several things. When I was young, I saw the Brown Mountain lights more than once."

"What is that?"

"It's a mysterious phenomenon which has occurred over the Brown Mountain range since the early 1900s. People have seen lights hovering over the mountains that no one has yet to explain."

"Like a UFO?"

"That's one possibility." Whit chuckled. "It even had its own plug on television during an episode of the "X Files." Other shows such as "Ancient Aliens" have also reported on the lights but to no avail. They're still a mystery."

"Very interesting."

"At one point, the government claimed they were only lights from vehicles or even an old railroad line. That was ruled out when there was a great flood which made the area unpassable for a period, and the lights were still seen."

"Being the skeptic I am, that would have been my first thought. So, you've seen them yourself?"

"Four times, to be exact. They all seem to occur in the fall to early December."

"What were they like? I can't claim to ever have seen anything like that."

"Bright white lights that glowed then faded. They would hover over the hilltops and then, in a split second, disappear from view."

They reached the majestic oak and started to climb the steps. "You aren't playing with me, are you?"

"No, I'm dead serious. Songs were written about them, one claiming the lights to be 'Ghost Lights,' of a slave carrying a lantern in search of his master."

They reached the top of the stairs, and Whit entered an access code on the door panel. Eli thought it seemed odd to have such security until Whit opened the door to her lab. The small area was filled with computers and other electronic equipment, and a rather large telescope lens which Eli hadn't noticed during the climb.

"Wow," Eli remarked as her eyes scanned the room. "Definitely not a moonshine still."

"I'm sorry I only have one chair, but let me check on something, and then I'll give you the grand tour of the universe like none you've ever seen." She pointed to a small daybed. "You can have a seat there if you'd like."

Eli nodded and walked over to the small bed and took a seat. Her eyes scanned the room, amazed by the size of the interior and the equipment filling every counter space. "Do you spend a lot of time here?"

"Sometimes I do. I get caught up in my work, and before I realize it, the sun is on its way. I broke down and brought a day bed, so if it's late when I finish, I just crash here."

Eli watched her manipulate dials, fine-tuning the focus of the telescope until Whit reached the area she was searching for. She wrote several notes, releasing a soft sigh as she scribbled.

"Is there something, in particular, you're looking for?"

Whit turned to look at Eli. "There's a dark spot way beyond the planets I've been watching for a few days now. I know it's not another planet, but I haven't figured out the enigma yet. Do you want to see?"

"Sure," Eli answered, and walked over to the chair Whit vacated.

Whit bent over her shoulder. "Let your eyes relax for a moment and then focus on the far right of the view. There's something there that's not a shadow, but I haven't been able to determine what it is yet."

Eli stared into the lens, and the shadow came in to view. "I think I see what you're talking about. Sort of an oval-shaped dark area?"

"Yes, that's it," Whit said. "I've talked with colleagues at other agencies, but they haven't found it yet. I'm glad you can see it, so I know I'm not crazy." Whit fell silent after the comment.

Eli felt her move away and turned to look at her. "Are you okay?"

"Yes, and no," she answered. "There is another reason I'm so interested in the stars, but I'm hesitant to share it with you. I'm afraid you will think I'm crazy."

Eli spun around in the chair. "I don't know what that could be until you tell me, but doubt it will make me feel any different about you."

"I'm not so sure," Whit said, and Eli could see a moistness in her eyes.

Eli walked over and sat on the bed beside her. "Tell me, and trust me."

Whit nodded and took a deep breath. "You know I was raised by my grandparents. They were my mother's parents, and they took me in when my mother needed to be hospitalized when I was about eight."

Eli thought it had been strange she never talked about her parents, but it wasn't a deal breaker. Eli waited for her to continue.

"When my mother was in her senior year of high school, she became pregnant with me. Grandpa was furious and demanded to know who the father was so he could make the young man step up to the plate, you know, be a father to his child. My mother told him she had been walking through the woods near the top of the mountain one afternoon and she met a stranger. She described him as the most handsome man she had ever seen, with deep green eyes. Mom never mentioned a name but claimed he took her into a beautiful crystal cave on the top of the mountain where they made love for hours." Whit took a deep breath and let it out slowly. "My mother claimed he was not from this world, and came to give her a star child, filled with special gifts. When he walked her home that night, he kissed her, and she never saw him again."

Eli looked into Whit's green eyes. "So, you never knew who he was?"

"No, but my mother was adamant about him being from another world, and searched for him for years, roaming the top of the mountain, hoping he'd come back for her. She was so obsessed with her story my grandparents broke down and sought a mental evaluation for her. She'd stopped eating, and would wander the woods for days without sleeping. and failed to care for me as a child."

"What happened to her?"

"She was diagnosed with a string of mental illnesses, and even though prescribed medications, she wouldn't take them. When Grandpa found her nearly frozen to death in the snow one night, he decided she wasn't safe from harming herself or me and had her committed."

"I'm sorry if it hurts to talk about her," Eli said, and placed a comforting hand on Whit's shoulder.

"I look at pictures in photo albums my gran kept, but I don't recognize the vibrant young woman in those. All I can remember of her is the unkempt hair and fragile body of a tragically ill woman who kept telling me 'he's coming back for us'."

She looked into Eli's eyes and forced a smile. "I was so terrified of her manic behavior that Grandpa never took me again to visit. Two years later, she committed suicide."

"How did that happen in a hospital?"

"She wasn't swallowing her meds, and she'd saved enough of them to overdose. She left a note saying her star man had come to her in her dreams and was coming to take her home."

Eli pulled Whit into her arms and held her as the tears flooded down her face. "I'm so sorry it happened," was all she could think to say.

When her tears subsided, Whit wiped her face. "I want you to know I am different."

"Of course you are," Eli answered.

"No, I am different. I think there was a grain of truth to Mom's story."

"What makes you think so?"

"I tested at the genius level, way beyond what was normal when I was six. I have other gifts too. I feel things when I'm around other people, like their emotions, sadness, grief, pain, and I feel what they feel."

"That alone is not unheard of," Eli said.

"When I was at MIT, one of my classmates was studying DNA, and one night she tested mine. When the results came back, her professor demanded to know where the sample came from. The DNA sample wasn't entirely human as we know it."

"She never gave you up, did she?"

"No, thank god. She convinced him it was a prank, and even though she got in major trouble for her actions, she never told anyone."

"Nothing you've told me tonight makes me think or feel differently about you."

"You're not worried I'll go screaming into the night, raving like a lunatic, or change into some lizard-like creature who'll eat all your kittens?"

"Now I think you've seen too much sci-fi on tv. What happened to your mother was tragic, but I don't think you'll become either of those. Is that why you study the stars?"

"In some ways, yes, but I'm drawn to the skies in a way I cannot explain."

"All I see in you is a beautiful, caring, and intelligent woman. Yes, you may be different for a reason. Maybe you'll discover something great that will help all mankind, but if not, I'll still love you."

Whit pulled out of Eli's arms. "What did you just say?"

"That you're beautiful, caring, and intelligent."

"No, way past that. You said, 'I'll still love you'."

Eli smiled. "I do love you. You've found a place in my heart I didn't even know still existed. You accept me for me, not what I can give you."

"Don't freak out on me, but I feel pain and sorrow from you along with joy and happiness."

"My ex and my best friend were having an affair. I came home early from a business trip and found them in bed together. I was hurt, more so by my friend than my lover, but it led to a great change in my life."

"How so?"

"When I fled my home that night to keep from murdering them, I went for a run on the beach. I ended up buying a winning lottery ticket which allowed me to become your new neighbor."

"You're kidding me, right?" Whit chuckled.

"Nope, I'd been drooling over this property for months, but it was out of my price range. Then I became a millionaire and the realtor was the second call I made. Mark was the first."

"That's karma at its finest."

"Mark and I have dreamed of a place here for years. Now, those dreams are coming true."

"I am thrilled to have you as a neighbor and hopefully something more," Whit said with a smile.

"Definitely something more," Eli answered and leaned forward to kiss Whit. "I worried about the age difference, but you know what? I don't give a damn anymore. I just want to be happy, and being around you makes me happy."

"Do you still want me to show you the universe?"

"Yes, but not tonight. I have a little dog who is doing the pee-pee dance about now. Tomorrow night maybe?"

"That's a date. Maybe your cute neighbor will invite you over for spaghetti."

"Dinner sounds wonderful. I'll start the holes, so when Evan gets here, we can begin planting. I may also see if he wants to help me hang the hog wire around the garden."

"If not, I can help you."

"Are you going down or staying for a bit?"

"I think I'll get some work done. Take the flashlight. I have another here."

"I'll see you tomorrow then," Eli said. She kissed Whit goodnight and climbed down the stairs. "What a beautiful night," she said as she walked down the mountain.

"Yes, it is. Goodnight, my love."

Eli wheeled around and saw Whit through the window. She smiled and returned to her truck.

†

Cruz didn't waste any time emptying her bladder. Then she found a ball and rushed to where Eli was sitting on the steps. Eli tossed the ball into the darkness and then felt Tomboy rubbing against her legs. "You snuck up on me.

287

Where did you come from?" Eli reached down to scratch the kitten as Cruz searched frantically for the ball. *I need to get some of the light-up rubber ones if we will be playing fetch at night.* Cruz located the ball and trotted to her.

"I'll get some to make it easier to see at night. We'd better call it a night for now. We have a busy day tomorrow." Eli placed the ball on the railing and walked to the door. Both Cruz and Tomboy trotted beside her. She looked down at Cruz. "What do you think? Should we let him stay inside?" Cruz licked the kitten on the top of the head. "I'll take that as a yes." She entered and locked the door behind her.

She slipped out of her clothes into a nightshirt as Tomboy waited on the bed. "Okay, this is only a trial basis. If you're not a good boy, it's out to the barn for you." Cruz curled in a ball at the foot of the bed once Eli climbed under the sheets. Tomboy waited until she got settled and then stretched out along her hip, just in reach of Eli's loving hand.

"Such a charmer. Just like someone else I know."

†

Eli stretched and looked at the clock. Five in the morning, but she felt rested and ready to go. By the time she got dressed, had breakfast, and tended to the animals, the sun should be up.

When she stepped outside, the crispness of the air surprised her. Eli contemplated going inside for a light jacket then decided the activity would warm her.

"Go get Molly," she told Cruz, who bolted ahead of her into the barn. A few seconds later, the dog and goat came barreling out. "Whoa, slow your roll," she cried out as Molly almost bowled her over.

"It's time to feed up everyone," Eli said as she stepped inside the barn. Cajun raised his head and looked at her with sleepy green eyes. "Chow time, everybody," she announced as she placed a scoop of food into the cat feeder.

Eli added a scoop of feed to Molly's bin and a flake of hay. After counting heads and satisfied that all the cats were present, she walked back and threw open the door. Eli climbed into the tractor and turned the key to start the engine. Several cats fled from the noise, but they would grow accustomed to the sounds soon enough. The auger was still on the tractor, so she would begin digging the holes for the trees and bushes they would be planting. She pulled her John Deere cap off the shifter and plopped it on her head.

Eli had an image of where she wanted things planted in her mind, and she would start with the blackberry and blueberry bushes along each side of the garden. She began digging the holes to mark the locations and soon had one side finished. Eli watched Cruz and Molly chasing one another as she worked, and a smile covered her face. *I think the apple and peach trees will go well down here and the nut trees in the next clearing.* Once done with the holes on the far side of the garden plot for berries, she took a break.

Eli walked to the cabin and made a cup of coffee to go into a thermal coffee cup, then stepped onto the porch. She sat down on the steps just as her phone pinged with a message.

Good morning, Aunt Eli.

Good morning, Mitch, what you doing up this early?

Trying to finish a few projects, then I'll start packing.

Just a few more days, and you'll be here.

I know, I can't wait.

You mind packing a blow-up mattress for your brother to sleep on? Unless you're willing to share your bed.

Heck no. Brad snores too much. I'll pack the mattress for him.

Thanks, I haven't gotten around to deciding on a bed for the loft space yet. There's a king-sized bed in the back master for your mom and dad.

Cool. How's it going there?

Good so far. The animals have arrived, and I've been working on the garden plot.

How do Cruz and Molly get along?

Perfectly. Cruz has already learned how to open the gate for Molly to come out and play.

Really? That's neat. What about your cute neighbor?

We've been spending a lot of time together. You're right, she's fun to be around. She's been a great help here. Today the solar panel system will be delivered. She wants it to be your first big project once your parents and Brad go home.

Why do we have to wait?

Because it's time to have some fun. The rest of the family hasn't been here yet, remember? I'm sure you boys will want to do some fishing. Do I need to get a couple extra fly rods?

Might not hurt.

Okay, I'll get them before you arrive. You have enough flies and other supplies?

Yes, ma'am. What I sent with you should be plenty.

Okay, get back to work. Ping me later. Love you.

More. Mitch replied and added a smiley face.

Eli looked down at her watch. It was a little past seven, and she was sure Merrill's would be open. She dialed the number and smiled when Evan answered the phone.

"I need to add a few items to the delivery if you have them. I need two fly rods and a big green egg grill, cover, and pellets if you have them." Eli listened as he checked the stock and confirmed availability. "Great. Thanks. I'll see you later today. Goodbye."

Coffee in hand, Eli strolled out to the tractor. Molly and Cruz were taking a break near the compost bin. "Y'all go easy today," she called to them.

†

Whit heard the drone of the tractor, and then it stopped. She was about to walk over when she heard it start again. *I'll let her work for a little longer, then I'll take over some fresh apple turnovers for a snack.*

Walter and Oscar were winding around her legs, ready for breakfast. "I know you two think you're starved since you can see the bottom of your food bowls." She poured fresh dry food in each of their bowls and made a cup of coffee. She made sure she had all the ingredients for spaghetti and a nice tossed salad.

†

Eli made quick work of the holes to be dug near the garden and drove the tractor up the mountain to what would be a hayfield later in the summer. She bored the holes for the nut trees and then headed to the barn. She was busy swapping the auger for the blade attachment when Cruz barked. Eli looked up and saw Whit walking down the trail. It couldn't be possible, but Whit seemed prettier every time Eli saw her.

"Good morning," she called out.

"Good morning. You're up bright and early."

Eli spotted the basket in Whit's hand. "You too."

Whit lifted the basket. "I had a notion some apple turnovers would be a good morning treat."

"That sounds great. Why don't you go inside and start some coffee? I'll come in just a minute."

"You got it." Whit smiled and walked to the cabin.

291

Eli finished attaching the blade and drove the tractor to the front of the cabin. She parked and went inside.

Whit had just made the second cup of coffee. She reached into the basket and pulled out a turnover. "Still warm."

Eli took a bite and moaned. The sugary sweetness and crunch of the apple slices filled her mouth with a rush of pleasure. "Damn, these are good. What a pleasant surprise. I think I worked my cereal off an hour ago."

"I think you're finding out how important it is to start off with something hearty in your stomach. Even though you don't feel you're working that hard, you're still burning calories."

"Lesson noted, ma'am," Eli said and took another bite. A soft moan filled the kitchen.

"You keep making those sounds, and I'll let you eat them all," Whit replied.

"They are just so good," Eli raved. "I'm so glad I'm planting apple trees."

"What do you plan on working on next?"

"I've got the pilot holes dug, so I thought I'd do some work on your driveway."

"Are you afraid my little car may get lost in one of the ruts?"

"I think I can smooth it out for you. It will also allow me to practice using the blade."

"You can practice any time you want. Is there anything I can do to help?"

"Not that I can think of right away." Eli leaned against the counter as she munched on a second turnover. "On second thought, can you draw the location of the berry bushes and trees for Evan in case he gets here before I return? That way, Evan can start planting."

"Still want the fruit trees here and the nut trees up top?"

"Yes, ma'am. The berries on either side of the garden, too." Eli walked to the refrigerator and removed a bottle of water. "Maybe you can whip up something for lunch?"

Whit smiled. "I'm sure I can find something to feed us."

"I'll see you soon," Eli said and kissed her before leaving the house.

Cruz ran to meet her. "You need to stay with Whit. I'll be home soon," she promised as she climbed into the cab of the tractor and started down the driveway.

†

The grading of Whit's driveway went smoother than she had anticipated, and Eli was rather pleased with her efforts. The ruts that had jarred her teeth were gone, and a level path replaced them. Eli noted areas where the rainwater had created the grooves and began thinking of a design to alleviate the washouts. A few well-placed cuts would redirect the water flow and prevent any damage to the drive. *It's the least I can do for all she's done for me.*

Eli had seen the delivery truck pass by a half-hour earlier, but she was determined to finish working on Whit's drive. Now done, she was eager to get some trees and bushes planted. She lifted the blade and drove for home.

As the tractor crested the hill, she could see Evan and Whit planting berry bushes. She turned the tractor to head to the garden plot intent on pitching in with the planting.

Whit heard the rumble of the tractor and saw the smile on Eli's face as she drove toward them. Eli stopped the tractor and was climbing out of the cab when her foot got caught on a pedal, and she fell forward on her way out. Whit cringed as she saw Eli's head strike against the metal frame of the cab, and she fell to the ground.

"Eli," she screamed and ran as fast as she could to the tractor. Eli was out cold, and the gash above her right eye was pouring blood.

Evan heard her scream and raced to the tractor. "What happened?"

"She tripped climbing out of the cab and hit her head on the frame." Whit looked at him and felt the panic threatening to take over. "Should we call 911?"

"No, not yet, take the bottle and fill it with some cold creek water and let's see if we can revive her." He pulled off his T-shirt and folded it several times before pressing it against the cut on her head. "Get it wet and wipe her face. It won't hurt to pour some of it on her face."

Whit took the bandana he offered and raced back.

"There's so much blood." Whit cringed at the sight but did as he instructed.

"Head wounds always bleed because there's little muscle to protect the scalp and so many blood vessels." He lifted his shirt and found the bleeding had slowed.

Whit poured the cold water across her face and bathed her cheeks with the wet bandana. She felt relieved when she saw Eli's eyes flutter and then open.

Eli lunged, trying to sit up.

"Hold your horses, Grace," Evan told her. "You have a nasty little cut above your eye, and you need to relax so it will stop bleeding."

"How long was I out?" Eli asked with a groggy voice.

"Maybe a little over two minutes," Evan replied. "You need some stitches and to get checked for a concussion."

"I'll be alright," Eli insisted.

"You sure will after I take you to the hospital," Whit said. "No arguing."

"Yes, ma'am," Eli answered, too tired to argue.

"If you stay with her, I'll go get her truck and will take her to the emergency room to get checked out," Whit told Evan.

"Do you want me to go with you?" he asked.

"If you can help me get her into the truck, I can handle it from there. Stay and get some planting done. If we're not home before you leave, please put Cruz in her crate in the room at the top of the stairs."

Cruz heard her name and rushed over to Eli. She licked her hand and sat beside her. She whined as she smelled the blood.

"I'm okay, baby girl. I'll be home later. You be good for Evan," Eli told her.

"I'll be right back," Whit said and raced across to the cabin to grab the truck keys.

Evan dabbed at her wound. "You will be okay. A few stitches and a whopper of a headache for a few days, but you'll survive."

Whit returned in Eli's truck and raced to them. "I've wanted to get behind the wheel of this monster," she told Eli. "I'll be careful with her, I promise."

"Help me get her on her feet," Evan said. "Can you hold the shirt in place? Be sure to keep the pressure on it."

Eli placed her hand on the makeshift pressure bandage.

Evan wrapped his arms around her waist and helped her to her feet. "Let's get her into the truck," Evan said, and they began walking to the passenger side. He helped Eli into the seat and fastened her seat belt and closed the door. Evan knelt down to hold onto Cruz's collar. She was whining, and he feared she'd chase after the truck. "Call me to let me know how she's doing," he told Whit.

"I will," Whit said and put the truck in gear. "Let's get you fixed up," she said as she pulled onto the drive.

†

Three stitches, one CAT scan, and a booming headache later, Eli was discharged from the emergency room with a diagnosis of a mild concussion. Eli groaned when the ER doctor told her she had to restrict her activities between the bed and the couch for the next seven days.

Whit knew that would be the hardest part of Eli's recovery. Keeping a proud and active woman on the sidelines for seven days would be almost impossible, but she would try her best. Maybe once Mark and his family arrived, she would have some back-up for keeping her calm and rested.

Whit assisted Eli into the truck seat and snapped her seat belt on. Eli placed the bottle of analgesics in the cup holder and reached to feel the bandage above her eye.

"Yeah, you look like you lost a round or two in a boxing ring, but it will fade, and if you follow instructions, you'll be on your feet in no time."

"I've got too much to do to be lying around all day," Eli growled.

"Don't get grumpy on me. You heard what the doctor said. Too much jarring movement can worsen the concussion, and you'll be back in the ER to be admitted," Whit warned.

Eli's head slumped forward. "I'm sorry, I just hate feeling helpless."

"I'll be around to be your arms and legs. In a couple more days, Mark and the family will be here, and I'm sure Mitch will wait on you like you were a Princess."

"Yes, he will." She smiled then grimaced. "Ouch, that hurt," she complained.

"You'll be tender until the cut heals. I know it's impossible for you to not smile or laugh around Mitch, so just be prepared."

"I need to move downstairs to Mitch's room. I don't think I can handle stairs right now."

"I'll take care of that when we get home. I'll grab your pillows and some clothes to bring downstairs."

"I'm sorry. I need you to stay with me until Mark gets here. The doctor said someone should monitor me. I could call and see if Mitch could come sooner."

"Nonsense, it will give us time to get to know each other better. I don't mind at all. I can go home to check on my boys, but they may just come over and join the fun."

"I don't like pulling you away from your work for several days."

"This is the age of laptop computers. I will bring one over and work while you are napping. The doctor said you'll nap over the next couple of days, so no big deal."

"Thank you."

"Are you hungry?"

"Yes, but the thought of eating right now makes me nauseous. I'll try to eat some soup or something later. I've got some in the pantry."

"You like tomato soup and grilled cheese sandwiches?" Whit asked.

"Love them," Eli said. "They might taste good later, but please don't wait on me to eat."

"I promise I won't starve. I'll get you comfy on the couch for a bit and run over to my place to feed the boys and grab some clothes."

"Can you reach over the visor for my sunglasses? The sun is killing me."

Whit handed Eli a pair of sunglasses. "You'll be sensitive to light and other things for a few days. It's a good thing you don't watch a lot of television or play video games."

"Amen to that," Eli said, and placed the dark glasses over her eyes.

†

When they returned to the cabin, Evan was sitting on the steps with Cruz. It was evident they had been playing fetch the way Cruz's tongue was hanging out the side of her mouth.

Eli watched as he jumped up and trotted over to the truck and opened the door for her.

"How are you feeling?"

"Like I got hit by a Mack truck, but the doctor says I'll live. You didn't have to wait until we got back."

"I just finished a little while ago, and Cruz wanted to play after I put Molly in her stall. I got everything planted, but we'll need to work out an irrigation system."

"You planted everything?" Eli asked.

"Yes, ma'am. Everything is in the ground. You digging the pilot holes made it so much easier. I hope you didn't mind me using a Gator to haul the trees to the field."

"Heavens no. I just can't believe you got everything planted. You're amazing. It would have taken me a day or two, at least."

"Naw, it wasn't that bad. I placed the planter buckets by your compost bin in case you wanted to use them." Evan held out his hand to help Eli out of the truck as Whit walked around. "Let me help you."

"Thanks, Evan."

Whit smiled at him. "She's got a mild concussion and has to take it slow for a week. Three stitches to her noggin, too."

"You're lucky nothing was broken. That was a hard fall you took." Evan placed her hand inside his elbow.

Eli took a step toward the cabin. "I think I've learned my lesson. I have to be more careful where I put my feet and not get in a rush."

"I can understand your excitement, but Rome wasn't built in a day, remember," Evan teased.

"I know, I just wanted to have some things done before Mark and his family arrived."

"I'll do whatever else you need. Just make me a list. It's not busy at the store." Evan smiled at her.

Whit nodded in agreement. "If he needs any help, I'll be here too, and you can supervise from the front porch. I know I won't be able to contain you inside."

"I can start in the morning by setting up your Big Green Egg. I placed it over on the end of the porch for now."

"I'll make a list of supplies needed to install the irrigation systems, and we can work on those tomorrow, too," Whit said.

Evan guided her up the steps and into the cabin. "Couch or bed?" he asked.

"Couch for now, please," Eli answered.

Eli sat down, and Evan turned to Whit. "I'll jot down my email address. If you send me the list of supplies, I'll bring them out in the morning."

Whit's face lit up. "Great idea. Run it past your dad to see if I left anything out and add whatever he recommends." She smiled at Eli and then turned to Evan. "Would you mind staying for just a few more minutes while I run over to my place?"

"Not at all. I'll write my email address for you too."

"I'll be back soon."

"You're taking the truck, right?" Eli asked.

Whit chuckled. "I could get spoiled driving her. I won't be long, though."

†

Whit drove to her cabin to throw some clothes and hygiene stuff in a bag and grabbed her laptop on the way out to the truck. When she returned inside, she fed Oscar and Walter and made sure they had fresh water. "I'll be spending the next few days next door, but I'll come over to check on you." She petted each one and then drove to Eli's.

†

"I can't believe you planted all the bushes and trees today," Eli said as Evan took a seat beside her.

"I've had tons of practice working with Dad all these years. It was a beautiful day to be working outside too."

Eli reached into her pocket for her wallet and pulled out three one-hundred-dollar bills. She offered them to Evan, and he hesitated in taking the money.

"You know that's twice what that job was worth," he told her.

"Maybe to you, but I think it's a bargain. I believe in rewarding hard work. Some people would have taken days to do that amount of work. I appreciate all you've done so far."

"I've enjoyed it, and I look forward to seeing what Whit has in mind for an irrigation system. She's a whiz with all things mechanical."

Eli felt her face ache when she smiled, but it was worth it. "She is brilliant and creative."

"She's the smartest person to come out of our little town."

"What are you studying at Western?"

"Business management so one day I can take over the store from Dad when he retires. I've grown up in the business,

300

but he insists I go to college and get a business degree. I haven't learned near as much in three years as I have in my life with him."

"Sometimes, it's more of a goal for parents to see their children achieve a college degree. It's also about socialization and growing up, too, so don't forget to have some fun. Life changes dramatically once you graduate."

"I know. Mom's already hinting at marriage and grandkids." He smiled.

"You and Erin are dating, right?"

"Yes, ma'am. She's very special to me."

"Do you think she's the one you'll marry?"

"That's possible." He grinned. "Erin finishes high school this year. She doesn't want to go to college, but Dr. Loren is sending her off to vet tech school in the fall."

Evan looked out the door and saw Whit pulling into the yard. "I believe your watchdog has returned." He chuckled. "I don't envy her the job. It won't be easy, making you rest."

"I'll try to be as compliant as I can, but I'll admit I'm not a good patient."

"When will your family be here?"

"Sometime Friday morning," Eli answered.

"Just make me a list of anything you want to have done before they get here, and I'll take care of things."

"Thanks, Evan. I'll see you tomorrow."

He stood to leave and stopped at the door. "Oh, I hung the two fly rods in the barn with the other."

"Perfect," Eli responded.

Evan held the door open for Whit. "Do you need help?"

"Nope, I've got this, Evan. Thanks, I'll shoot you an email tonight."

"I'll see you tomorrow. Call me if you need anything tonight."

"I will. Thanks."

Whit placed her laptop bag on the counter and carried the bag into Mitch's room. "How are you feeling?" she asked as she walked into the living room.

Eli's head snapped up, and she cried out from the sudden movement. "Damn, that hurt. I must have been nodding off."

"Do you want to stretch out on the couch, or change into sleep clothes and crash on the bed?"

"I think I'll stick to the couch for now. I hope you don't mind me crashing out on you."

"Absolutely not. If you're asleep, I don't have to worry about you doing stuff you're not supposed to be doing." Whit chuckled. "I'll bring some sleep clothes down if you want to change."

"Thanks, it would be more comfortable."

"Do you need another pill?" Whit asked.

"No. I'm okay, I just moved too suddenly."

Whit climbed the stairs and brought down several options for sleep clothes. She brought Eli into the bedroom and sat her on the bed. "Let's get these work boots off you first."

Eli allowed Whit to undress her and assist with putting on a T-shirt and loose-fitting shorts. "This feels better already."

Whit grabbed a pillow off the bed and carried it to the couch. Just as she got Eli settled, her cell phone pinged with a message from Mitch.

You have time to talk?

Whit read the message to her. "It would be easier to talk than try to text. Do you want me to dial for you?"

"Yes, please," Eli answered.

Whit punched the speed dial for Mitch and handed Eli the phone. Then she walked to the counter and set her laptop on the kitchen table, giving Eli some privacy. She turned on her computer and began making the list of supplies for Evan.

When she heard Eli end the call, she walked into the living room. "Everything okay?"

"Yes, he was just asking about some of the things he wanted to bring to make sure it was okay."

"Did you tell him about your injury?"

"No, I don't want him or Mark worrying. They can tease me all they want when they get here on Friday."

"I'm sure they will be excited to see you and know that you're okay. Then the teasing might set in." Whit laughed. "You ready to lie down for a bit? Need something to drink first?"

"No, I'm good. Just tired."

"Do you want a blanket or anything to cover you?"

"I don't think so. What are you working on?"

"Drawing up the supply list for the irrigation systems we will need so I can email it to Evan." She brushed the hair from Eli's face. "I'll let you sleep for a few hours, then we can see if you're ready to eat."

"Sounds good. Make yourself at home."

"Will do. Get some rest. I'll be here if you need me." Whit smiled as Cruz stretched out in front of the couch, and Tomboy snuggled into Eli's arms. Her hand stroked down his side until she drifted off to sleep.

†

Whit finished creating the list and sent it off to Evan. She took out a legal pad and drew out the design of the system she would put into place at the garden spot and the hayfield where the nut trees were planted. She glanced up to see Eli resting, her hand holding Tomboy in place as he snoozed with her. Whit checked her email to find Evan had already opened the supply list, and then she shut down the system to relax for a while before starting dinner.

Cruz lifted her head as Whit walked past the couch to sit in the recliner. As soon as Whit was settled, Cruz lowered her head and resumed her nap. The quiet teased Whit, and she soon found her head nodding. It had been a long day emotionally instead of physically. She was terrified when she saw Eli fall from the tractor, blood already rushing down her face. Whit felt her heart plummet into her stomach when she reached Eli to find her unconscious. That was never a good thing. It was a huge relief when the doctor said it was a very mild concussion. Whit heeded his warning that Eli needed to rest and not worsen her condition by doing things she shouldn't. That reminded Whit that she needed to place the bloodied clothes she had on in the laundry before the blood stains set into the fabric. Whit walked into the bedroom to retrieve the clothing and slipped out the front door. She stepped outside and smiled when she found Oscar and Walter sitting on the porch.

"Did y'all get lonely?" Oscar blinked his green eyes at her. "I'll be right back," she said and walked out to the laundry room.

After treating the bloodstains, Whit put the clothes in the washer and started the cycle. She walked out to the barn to make sure the animals had food and water, then to the cabin and sat on the front porch. Oscar and Walter approached her for petting. She looked out across the field toward the garden as the sun was slipping below the trees. *We can work on getting the fence up around the garden after we get the irrigation system in place.* She added the task to her mental list of things to accomplish before Friday. *Two days should be plenty, with a young man helping.* Her stomach growled, and she returned inside to start dinner. She hoped Eli would have an appetite and be able to put something in her stomach before going to bed.

304

Whit walked inside and crept into the kitchen and opened the pantry door to find two cans of tomato soup. She opened them and poured the contents into a pot to warm while she began building the grilled cheese sandwiches.

Whit had four sandwiches ready to cook. She turned the burner on under the soup and went to check on Eli. She sat down on the edge of the couch and touched Eli's arm. "Hey, sleepyhead, it's time to wake up."

Eli's eyes popped open, and she braved a smile as Tomboy stretched and caressed her chin with his paw.

"Neither of them has left you since you laid down," Whit said. "Cruz is right here." She pointed at the floor.

"My babies," Eli said.

"I think they love you." Whit grinned. "Are you up to grilled cheese sandwiches and tomato soup?"

"I'll try. Let me sit up for a few minutes, okay?"

"Take whatever time you need. I haven't started cooking the sandwiches yet. Do you want me to wait?"

"No, I'll be steady by the time they are ready."

"Wait for me to come to assist you, please. You don't need a fall tonight."

"Yes, ma'am. I promise I won't be making any sudden movements."

"You need a drink and a pill?"

"A glass of tea would be great, but I want something on my stomach before I take a pill."

"I think that's a wise decision. I'll bring you a glass."

"Thanks," Eli said and reached down to stroke Cruz's head. "Mama's protectors."

†

305

Eli ate the soup, and most of one sandwich before her stomach began to protest. "The meal was delicious, but I think I need to lie down."

Whit stood and offered her hand. "Come then, and let's get you into bed."

Eli allowed Whit to tuck her into bed. "Will you join me in a bit?" she asked.

"I'll clean the kitchen and finish a few things and join you. Do you need something for nausea?"

"Not a bad idea."

"I'll be right back then." Whit poured another glass of tea and took a pill from the bottle. "Here you go." She handed the tablet and drink to Eli. She left a light on in the bathroom and turned off the bedside lamp. "Call out if you need anything."

"Whit," Eli spoke.

"Yes, Eli."

"I need something," she said. "A kiss." She smiled and regretted doing so as the pain raced through her.

Whit sat on the edge of the bed and leaned down to plant a sweet kiss on Eli's lips. "Try to rest."

"I will," Eli answered.

Whit cleared the kitchen and sat at the table to finish making the list she had started. The irrigation system and fencing around the garden would take the better part of the next two days. Whit would use the chainsaw to cut some of the fallen trees to use in the firepit if time allowed. If she couldn't get to it before the family arrived, she'd enlist Mitch and Brad's help. She was sure they'd jump on the opportunity to help.

Whit locked the front door once Cruz had come in for the night, and made her way to the bedroom. She changed into her sleep pants and shirt, then brushed her teeth. She pulled the bathroom door behind her leaving only a sliver of light to illuminate the bedroom. Cruz was curled on her bed, and

Tomboy stretched out beside Eli. Whit eased onto the bed and lay on her side, watching Eli sleep. She wanted to reach out and touch Eli, but she feared to wake her from a healing sleep. Instead, she observed the gentle rise and fall of Eli's chest as her breath left her body with a soft purring noise. She was smiling as Eli's eyes fluttered and then opened.

"Hey," Eli whispered.

"Hi. I hope I didn't wake you. I was trying to be quiet."

"You were. My body felt you come to bed, and you aren't close enough." She raised her left arm. "Will you snuggle me?"

Whit allowed her body to answer as she moved close to Eli and placed her head on Eli's shoulder. Whit's hand rested on Eli's stomach. "I can feel your heartbeat," she whispered.

"There, that feels better. Thank you," Eli said.

"My pleasure. How are you feeling?"

"Exhausted, but my nausea has passed. I think I'll live now you're here to protect me." She bent forward and kissed the top of Whit's head.

"I'm not going anywhere, so go to sleep," Whit said as she snuggled in closer.

CHAPTER FOURTEEN

Whit was cooking bacon when Eli walked into the kitchen and hugged her from behind. "Good morning," she said as her lips caressed Whit's neck. She felt Whit shiver and hugged her close. "Are you cold?"

"Heaven's no. I think my temperature just rose about ten degrees when you wrapped me in your arms."

"Smells good. I'm hungry this morning. Will you fry some eggs and make some toast to go with the bacon?"

"I'll fix you anything you want."

"Are you ready for more coffee?" Eli asked as she pulled a mug down from the cabinet.

"I will be after you get yours prepared," Whit answered.

Cruz came trotting in from outside.

"Have you eaten already?"

"She was hungry, too. Finished her bowl of kibble, but I promised her some bacon and eggs."

Eli knelt and hugged Cruz who licked her face. "You're getting so spoiled."

"It's not like she could get more spoiled but she's a good companion. She only left your side to eat and go potty."

Eli poured her coffee and then made a fresh cup for Whit. "Is there anything you'll let me help with?"

"You can pull down some plates and set the table for us. Just don't get in a hurry or try to move too fast. I'll have the eggs and toast ready in a minute. If you sit at the table, you can butter the toast."

"Yes, ma'am," Eli answered and set the table. When the toast popped up, Whit carried the slices over to her and dropped two more in the toaster.

"Does Cruz have a preference for how she likes her eggs?"

"She'll eat them any way you want to fix them. It would be easiest to scramble them with some cheese and bacon. It can wait until we're done eating. She won't starve."

"Cruz may see that differently." Whit chuckled as she slid two fried eggs onto Eli's plate and grabbed the toast. "Go ahead, and I'll join you in just a few minutes."

"I can wait."

"Please eat while it's hot," Whit replied.

"Yes, ma'am." Eli used her fork to mash her eggs and began eating. She realized she didn't have juice and stood to retrieve two glasses. "Do you want some apple juice?"

"That sounds good. Do I need to do some grocery shopping before the family arrives?"

"Would be a good idea. I can work on a list today, and if you feel up to it later, we can eat at the diner and then grocery shop."

"Oh, now you're talking. I think Evan and I can get the irrigation set, and the fence and gate built around the garden in the next two days. Maybe while you're making a list, you can add anything else you'd like him to do before they arrive." Whit sat down to eat with Eli.

"It will be huge if you get that done," Eli answered. "The only other thing I'd like to get done is a small stack of firewood for the fire pit. If it doesn't happen, Mark and the boys can do it."

"I think we can get a small stack easy from the fallen trees, and then Mitch and Mark can add to it if they want."

†

When Evan arrived, he and Whit began working on the irrigation system in the upper field as Eli sat on the porch, adding to her list. She couldn't ride in the Gator on the rough trail, but there was nothing said about her walking. Cruz cocked her head to the side when Eli stood and placed her notepad in the chair. She descended the steps and took a few steps toward the path up the mountain. Eli had never paid attention to how uneven the trail was until a jarring step made her head pound. She stopped, and even the dark sunglasses she was wearing couldn't block the pain from the movement and bright sunlight.

"The hell with this," she said. Defeated, she turned and walked to the cabin. Eli left her notepad on the porch and walked in to stretch out on the couch. She opened the bottle of pain pills and downed one with a long drink of water.

Whit smiled at Evan when she turned the faucet and a stream of water filled the irrigation system. "One down and one to go." She pushed buttons to set the timer on the system and walked toward Evan.

"It amazes me how easy you make things look," Evan praised. "I thought I knew a bunch about plumbing, but you create magic."

"It's not difficult if you work with Mother Nature and gravity. Work with what she gives you, and don't force things." She walked over to the Gator. "I want to check on Eli before we start on the system for the garden. Are you getting hungry?"

"Naw, I'm good. I had a huge breakfast."

"We can take a break for some sandwiches when you're ready," Whit said as she climbed in behind the wheel.

When they reached the cabin, Whit stepped out of the Gator. "Start unloading the pipes, and I'll walk over after checking on Eli."

"You got it," Evan said as he slid over to the driver's seat. "Take your time."

Evan drove away, and Whit frowned when she saw Eli's notepad on the porch. She stepped inside and saw Eli stretched out on the couch her arm draped over her eyes. She thought Eli was napping and turned to walk outside.

"I'm awake," Eli said.

Whit turned around and walked over to her. "Are you feeling bad?"

Eli removed her arm and squinted at Whit. "Feeling stupid is more like it."

"What happened?"

"I thought I'd be smart and walk up to check on you and Evan. A few steps on the uneven trail taught me it was not my brightest decision. I took a pain pill and stretched out here."

Whit took a seat on the edge of the couch. "I can't leave you unsupervised at all, can I?"

"Yes, you can. I promise I have learned my lesson. I'll crash here until you return, and we can make sandwiches together for lunch. How are things going?"

"Great. We finished at the top and are ready to work on the garden system."

"I feel so useless." Eli groaned.

311

Whit stroked down Eli's face. "Right now, you need to concentrate on feeling better. Your family will be here in two days, and I know you won't rest like you should."

"I won't have any choice once they get here. Mitch is worse than Mark. He won't let me do anything when he finds out what happened. I will never live down my less than graceful behavior."

"I don't know Mitch well, but I bet he wouldn't tease you if he didn't love you and worry about you."

"That's true. Mitch comes by it honestly. I promise I won't get off the couch unless I have to pee." Eli grinned at Whit. "One more thing."

"Anything," Whit answered.

"A kiss."

Whit leaned down and kissed Eli. "I will return for more of those soon. I promise."

"I'll hold you to it. Now go before I change my mind and hobble out to the garden."

"Don't even think of it," Whit warned. "I'm gone."

Eli watched her leave and closed her eyes, slipping off to a restful sleep.

Tomboy had followed Whit into the house, and when she left, he jumped onto the couch and snuggled into Eli. Cruz was curled in a ball on the floor, guarding her master as she slept.

†

"How's she feeling?" Evan asked when Whit returned?

"She's resting now. She thought she'd be smart and walk to check on us, but a few steps onto the uneven ground taught her otherwise."

312

"Eli doesn't appear to be someone to comply with bed rest orders." He grinned as he connected two sections of pipe.

Whit was connecting the pump to a connector. "You hit that nail on the head. She hates not being out here helping."

"If we bust our tails today, we should be able to finish the irrigation systems and maybe fencing the garden. At least get some of it before we run out of light."

"Even if we need a few hours tomorrow morning, we can still cut and haul some firewood and call it a day by lunch tomorrow," Whit replied. "I know she wants enough for a few campfires, so it won't take long at all."

†

After a short lunch break for sandwiches, Whit and Evan began working on the fence around the garden plot and ran out of daylight before they could hang the gate. "That will only take a few minutes in the morning, and then we can gather wood. You've worked hard today, Evan. Thank you."

"I've learned a lot from you these past few days." He grinned at her. "I hope once I graduate and get a place of my own, you will help me make it as self-sufficient as possible."

"I'd love to," Whit said as she walked him to the truck. "Have a great night, and I'll see you in the morning."

Whit made rounds through the barn to make sure Molly and the cats had food and water before returning to the cabin. She had to admit keeping up with Evan had been exhausting, but they had accomplished a great deal.

As she stepped onto the porch, she could smell spaghetti sauce on the stove. Whit stepped inside to see Eli in the kitchen. "Something smells delicious."

"I thought I'd make some spaghetti for dinner. It should be ready in a few minutes. You have time for a shower or you can just sit and relax for a bit."

313

"I'll run through a quick shower then. Be right back," Whit said as she stood on her tiptoes to kiss Eli.

†

Whit insisted on cleaning the kitchen after dinner while Eli stretched out on the couch. When she finished, she placed Eli's head in her lap as they watched the end of a ballgame. They were both struggling to keep their eyes open, so Whit suggested they retire for the evening and led Eli into the bedroom.

"Do you need a pain pill?" she asked before climbing into the bed.

"No, I think I'm good. I just need you to snuggle into." Eli smiled.

"I'm on my way," Whit replied and climbed into the bed.

Eli snuggled into her and pulled the covers over them, and it wasn't long before they both drifted off, their bodies entwined.

CHAPTER FIFTEEN

A crack of thunder woke them just after five the next morning. Whit picked up her phone to check the time and the weather. "It looks like this rain will be here most of the day," she reported.

"Why don't you text Evan then and take the day off? Tell him he can come out tomorrow and meet the family. Maybe he and Mitch can bring in the firewood."

"That sounds like an excellent plan." Whit sent Evan a text he answered right away. She smiled and returned the phone to the table. "All set for tomorrow."

Eli snuggled into Whit's body. Her hand slipped beneath Whit's shirt, making contact with her warm skin. "You are nice and toasty," she whispered.

"Your touch feels nice," Whit answered, as Eli's hand caressed her stomach.

"Should I continue?"

"Yes, please," Whit answered.

Eli took great pleasure in exploring Whit's body with her touch, sharing sweet kisses which grew more passionate as their bodies pressed together. Eli broke the kiss and whispered against Whit's cheek. "I need to be naked with you."

"Oh, yes, please, Eli," Whit responded.

Eli lifted the shirt over Whit's body then removed her own before sliding out of her shorts, then pushing Whit's down her legs, tossing them into a growing pile of clothes. She draped her right leg over Whit as their bodies melted into one another. Eli looked into Whit's eyes. "I want you," she whispered.

Whit nodded, unable to speak of the growing desire rushing through her veins as Eli cupped a breast in her hand.

Eli ran her thumb over Whit's nipple, feeling it harden beneath her touch as her chest swelled with a deep breath. She captured Whit's moan in her mouth as her finger and thumb rolled the nipple between them. Eli kissed down Whit's chin to her right breast, her tongue snaking out to tease her nipple as her hand continued to caress the left. She heard a gasp as her mouth covered Whit's breast and felt her hand move to the back of her head, pressing her mouth down. Eli moved to lie between Whit's legs and felt the heat emanating from her core against her stomach, and the flow of Whit's pleasure coating her skin. The scent of her desire fueled Eli as she ached to feel Whit's excitement blossom into orgasm.

Whit's body reeled with pleasure as Eli's warm mouth captured her breast. When their bodies came together, she felt a shiver of anticipation flow through her. Eli's teeth grazing her nipple was too much to bear, and she was thankful Eli began to suckle her sensitive flesh. Her limited experience did little to prepare her for the ache of need which ran through her as her hips began to undulate against Eli's body.

Eli sensed Whit's growing need and raised up on her hands to move her mound on top of Whit's. Their bodies created a sensual rhythm as she leaned in to kiss Whit deeply. The wetness growing between them increased as Whit's legs locked around Eli's and her hips thrust into Whit's. She could feel the hunger in Whit's kiss as her tongue danced in her mouth. Whit's hands clutched her ass as she thrust to meet Eli. She broke the kiss gasping for air as she groaned, her body slipping over the edge into blissful orgasm. Her body shook with spasms beneath Eli, who also came in a burst of passion.

Eli moved down to taste the rush of pleasure escaping Whit's body. The swirling of her tongue between Whit's lips extended her orgasm. When Eli's tongue entered her, she cried out as a second climax erupted, coating Eli's face with moisture. Eli drank from her body until Whit's hands clutched at the sheets. Eli planted soft kisses up to Whit's face. The taste of their passion swirled in their mouths as Whit's right hand slipped between them and entered Eli's wetness. Eli's hips thrust into Whit as she rode her fingers into a wave of orgasm and collapsed on top of Whit.

When she could speak, Eli lifted her head and looked into Whit's sparkling eyes. "That felt so good," she whispered.

Whit smiled. "Was worth waiting for even though some days it was torture." Whit withdrew her fingers, and Eli rolled onto the bed beside her.

Cruz whimpered at the front door, begging to go outside. Eli laughed and started to climb out of bed.

"I'll let her out," Whit said and kissed her before leaving the bed. She opened the front door, and Cruz flew outside to relieve her bladder, then rushed in from the rain.

Whit climbed into bed. "I left the door cracked in case she needs to go out."

"Smart move," Eli replied as she pulled Whit down on top of her. "I don't plan on leaving this bed just yet," she said as her hands caressed Whit's back.

"That's good to hear. I'm nowhere near done with you," Whit whispered in her ear, then she sucked her earlobe deep into her mouth.

Hours later, after feasting on each other, Whit curled up next to Eli and placed her head on her shoulder. The rain continued to fall, but the growling of Eli's stomach was loud.

"Are you ready for some breakfast?" Whit asked with a grin.

"I'm starving," Eli replied. "I think we've both worked up an appetite."

"Lie still for a bit, and I'll get breakfast started," Whit told her, then nibbled on her nipple.

"You keep doing that, and I'll have you for breakfast," Eli warned with a grin.

"You can have seconds after breakfast and a shower," Whit said as she climbed from the bed and stretched.

†

After a shower, they returned to bed. "I'm glad it rained. I think this is exactly what we needed to do today," Eli said as she ran her fingers through Whit's damp hair.

"I agree. We've been working hard ever since you arrived. It was a much-needed break for both of us, and it was a heavenly morning."

"No regrets, then?" Eli asked.

"None. I knew we should be together, and I'd wait as long as necessary for you to realize it too."

"Maybe I just needed a good knock to my head to wake me up," Eli teased.

"Maybe so. Speaking of which, how are you feeling?"

"Never better. It's starting to itch, so I guess it's healing."

"Do you want to keep the bandage off today and let it air? It may help with the itching."

"Not a bad idea." Eli reached and removed the bandage. "How does it look?"

"No redness, and it appears to be healing well. It should only be a week until we can remove the stitches."

"I still don't think I'll be doing much bending or running for a while."

"No, you still need to take it easy. We've got a good jump on projects, so you need to relax and enjoy time with Mark."

"Oh crap, speaking of which, we never grocery shopped."

"You owe me dinner at the diner, too," Whit reminded her. "Do you want to shop while it's raining and then grab some dinner to bring back here?"

"That's not a bad idea. Maybe a couple pies, too, if they have some. The coconut cream is to die for. Should we call to place an order for pies, just in case?"

"Sure, that's not a bad idea. I'll get dressed and go feed animals. You can dress and call while I'm in the barn. I need to drop by and check on my boys, too."

"Sounds wonderful to me. Thank you," Eli said.

"For what?"

"For coming into my life when I needed you most."

"That goes both ways. I've never been so happy in my life."

"Ditto," Eli said and kissed Whit. "We better get out of this bed, or we'll spend the rest of the day here."

"I wouldn't mind, but we need to get the groceries in. There's always tonight." Whit smiled and wiggled her eyebrows.

†

"I'm glad we ate dinner before grocery shopping," Eli said. "I can't imagine how many more groceries we would have come out with if we had gone in hungry. Two carts full should feed even the hungriest of boys." She placed the last of the bags on the kitchen counter.

"You, couch, rest, now," Whit instructed with a dramatic motion toward the couch.

"Yes, boss," Eli responded. "I need a kiss first to hold me over."

"Fine with me. There will be more after I have these groceries stored."

Eli wrapped her arms around her and kissed Whit, and for a short time, the groceries were forgotten. Breathless, Whit broke the kiss and pointed.

"Consider me gone," Eli said. She released Whit and walked to the couch and stretched out. Cruz trotted to her with a ball in her mouth and whined. "I know it's been a few days."

"I'll be outside with Cruz for a few minutes," she said to Whit.

"Wait, you don't need to be bending and throwing a ball," she reminded Eli.

"I won't have to," Eli replied and opened a cabinet next to the door and pulled out a Nerf dog gun. She picked an extra tennis ball, placed it in the barrel and slid a lever back to load the ball.

"Looks like fun, but please at least sit on the steps," Whit requested.

"I will, and I'll leave the door open so you will hear me if I call out to you. Let's go," Eli told Cruz.

Whit stored the groceries then joined Eli and Cruz on the porch. Cruz was sitting in front of Eli, her tongue hanging from the side of her mouth. The sun sank toward the horizon as Whit sat beside Eli.

"Go get Molly," Eli said, and Cruz trotted to the barn. Moments later, she and Molly came flying out of the door, racing across the open field.

Whit placed her arm around Eli's waist and laid her head on her shoulder. "This will be a beautiful sunset."

"Yes, it is," Eli answered and kissed the top of Whit's head.

They sat in a comfortable silence as they watched Cruz and Molly play together until they were both panting for air. With a contented sigh, Eli looked at Whit. "I think it's time to feed everyone and call it a night."

"I can do that. Go inside and rest."

"I want to go with you and check on the cats. I don't feel like I've spent much time with them since they arrived."

"Okay," Whit said and stood. She offered Eli her hand, and they walked to the barn together.

Just as they stepped into the barn, Cajun came sliding down the slide. Eli broke out laughing. "He would be the first to learn how to use the slide." She knelt down and scratched under his chin. "Are you keeping everyone in line?" His loud purr was his answer as he leaned into her hand.

Molly trotted into her stall and waited for Whit to place fresh food and hay in her bin. The cats started a chorus of meows when they heard the grain drop into Molly's trough.

"You'd think they were starving," Whit said as she filled the feeder. She watched Eli count each of them. "They are all accounted for if you include Tomboy, who's saving your spot on the couch."

Eli took a seat on the barn floor, and it didn't take long for her lap to fill with black cats. She petted each one as they rotated from the food dishes to her lap. Cajun had climbed into the hayloft and took another ride down the slide just to make sure she noticed he had mastered the toy. Eli laughed. "Yes, I see you, big boy."

Whit took a seat beside Eli. She elbowed her and nodded toward the barn door when she saw Walter and Oscar come trotting in to join the party. "The family is all present now," she told Eli.

"Do you think they will stay the night?" Eli asked.

"It's a good possibility. Do you mind if Oscar and Walter stay in the house?"

"Not at all. We may need to consider putting in a cat door soon."

"They are both good at holding it until they go outside," Whit said. Oscar trotted over to the food dish. "He likes the unlimited supply too."

Eli chuckled as Oscar's head disappeared into the food bowl while Walter curled in Whit's lap. "I can't believe no one ever adopted him. He's such a sweet cat."

"I think he was just waiting for us," Whit answered.

"I like the way you think," Eli said and leaned over to kiss Whit. Her phone pinged, and she looked at it to find a message from Mitch.

We are leaving at 5, so we should be there before lunch.

Sounds great. We can't wait to see y'all.

We?

Yes, Whit and me.

Well, hot damn, about time.

I'll fill you in when you get here. Y'all be careful. Love ya.

Most.

Eli chuckled and handed her phone to Whit to read Mitch's message. "You've got a Fortner fan club."

"Remind me to pay Mitch when he gets here," Whit teased. "Is he okay with us as a couple?"

"He and the others in my family are fine with my lifestyle. All they ask is you love me and treat me well."

"I have every intention of doing just that." Whit handed Eli the phone, then kissed her. "You ready to head inside?"

"Yes, I think I hear the couch calling my name."

Whit stood and helped Eli to her feet. "Is there anything else we need to do before the family arrives?"

"Not that I can think of. I think we've made some great progress. We'll let Evan, Mitch, and Brad bring in some firewood."

"Evan could be a good friend for Mitch. He's a smart, level-headed kid. A few years older, but he can help him learn some new stuff. He also has a cute younger sister."

"Are you going to turn the tables on Mitch and play matchmaker for him?"

Whit shrugged. "Maybe."

"This will be an interesting summer."

"What do you want to have for lunch tomorrow? The crew will be hungry when they arrive."

"I'll grill some chicken if you'll raid your garden for some fresh vegetables."

"That sounds good. I'll go early so we can get stuff cooking after breakfast. I think I need one of your omelets."

"Not a problem. Easy to make and filling."

When they reached the cabin door, Eli stopped and called for Oscar and Walter, who trotted to the door and pranced in like they owned the place. "I think I can go upstairs tomorrow night. We can make some beds and perches for the boys in the loft next week."

"I'll change the sheets on Mitch's bed and do some laundry while we cook tomorrow," Whit said.

"I don't know about you, but I think I'm ready to go to bed," Eli said. "Today was a lovely day, but I'll admit, I'm whipped."

"Me too. I just want to strip down and snuggle into you," Whit replied.

CHAPTER SIXTEEN

Whit crept from the bed and slipped into some clothes before walking outside. Cruz and the cats followed her out and went into the barn as she continued on to the log bridge to cross over to her property. She picked out a large basket and walked to her garden to begin harvesting. Whit filled her basket and started the trip across the creek. She was excited about meeting Eli's family and also a little nervous. She wanted to make a good impression on them, especially Mark, who was so close to Eli. If Mitch were anything like his dad, she felt she would be okay. *Just be myself. I'm enough for Eli, and that's all that matters.*

Eli was in the shower when Whit entered the cabin. She placed her basket on the counter and started rinsing the vegetables. She flipped the switch on the coffee pot when she heard the shower turn off and had a cup ready for Eli when she walked in wearing a robe.

"Good morning," Eli said as she took the coffee and kissed Whit. "Are you okay with me kissing you in front of others?"

"I'm okay with anything you're comfortable with," Whit answered.

"Good, I'm finding it hard to keep my hands off of you." Eli smiled. She looked over at the sink, filled with vegetables. "You've been busy."

"I woke and thought I'd get a jump start on the morning. It will be a beautiful day today. Do you think you are ready to try a slow ride in the Gator? I'm sure you want to show Mark the property."

"I think if I take it slow, I'll be okay. I'll drive, so if I hit too many bumps, it'll be my fault."

"I'll ride with the boys, so you can tour Mark and Laura."

"Sounds like a plan. You still up for omelets this morning?"

"Yes, please."

"Ham and cheese or bacon?"

"Ham and cheese are fine with me."

They worked side by side in the kitchen until breakfast was ready, and took their food onto the deck to enjoy the crisp morning by the water. "You were right, this will be a beautiful day."

When they finished eating, Eli asked, "Do you want to shower now or get some veggies cooking first?"

"Let me get some food started, then I'll shower."

"Do you want me to slice the tomatoes and onions after I get the chicken marinated?"

"That would be great. I want to sauté some of those squash, so dice some onions for me if you would, please."

"No problem."

"I'm hoping you saved some bacon grease to help season these green beans. I dug a few potatoes to go with them too."

"There's a jar in the refrigerator door. There may even be a few chunks of ham left if you want to toss those into the pot."

"Great idea," Whit answered as she snapped the beans into a pot. "Do we need to make a few pitchers of tea?"

"I can handle those," Eli said as she filled a pot with water.

Whit rinsed her hands. "Beans are cooking, squash sliced, and corn shucked. I think I'll go hit the shower and get laundry started."

"I've got the sheets changed and the soiled ones in the laundry," Eli said.

"You must have gotten up right after I left," Whit said.

"The bed felt empty without you in it." Eli grinned. "Go shower. I've got this. I'll check on the travelers to see what time they expect to be here and tell them to not eat lunch."

Whit stripped out of her clothes and walked into the shower. The morning was passing and soon she would meet Eli's family. She dressed in a new pair of shorts and a polo-style shirt. *Not bad if I say so myself.* She added a spritz of perfume and took the clothes basket into the living room. "I'll get this laundry started and change over the sheets."

"Okay, sweets. Mark and the family will be here in about thirty minutes."

"Wow, they made fantastic time. How are the beans coming along?"

"They should be ready just in time. I've got your squash started, and I'll put the chicken on in a few. The tea's chilling, and the corn is boiling."

"We make a great team," Whit said. "I'll be right back."

†

Eli had just taken the last chicken breast off the flat top when she heard vehicles approaching. She grinned at Whit. "They're here." She reached for Whit's hand, and they walked out to greet the family.

Mitch had pulled to a stop when Brad came bundling out of his truck.

"Aunt Eli," he called and rushed to hug her. He grinned at Whit. "You must be Whit. Mitch hasn't stopped talking about you for the last half hour." He stepped closer and offered her a hug.

"It's nice to meet you, Brad. I'm glad y'all have made it."

"Especially with Mitch driving." Brad chuckled.

"Hey, I got us here," Mitch said. He hugged Whit first. "It's good to see you again."

"You, too. I hope you're ready to work."

"Always. Hey, what's with the bandage?" Mitch asked Eli.

Mark and Laura walked up just as Mitch asked his question.

"Okay, now everyone is here, I can say this once. My clumsy feet got twisted in the pedals on the tractor, and I smacked my head. I ended up with a slight concussion and a few stitches."

"Still as graceful as ever." Mark chuckled and hugged his sister close.

"A concussion is severe, should you be lying down and resting?" Laura asked.

Whit came to her rescue. "She's been doing pretty well. It wasn't easy at first, but overall she's been a compliant patient."

"You must be a miracle worker. I know how stubborn my sister can be," Mark said. "You must be Whit." Mark pulled her into a hug. "I'm Mark, and this is my wife, Laura. Brad's the skinny one, and you already know Mitch. He has been raving about your tomatoes for days."

"Well, we hope you brought your appetites. We have lunch just about ready," Whit said.

Brad had knelt down and was petting Cruz.

"Hey guys, watch this. Cruz, go get Molly," Eli said.

Cruz raced to the barn and disappeared. "Wait until you see this."

Mark broke out laughing when Cruz raced from the barn with a small goat hot on her tracks. "She is adorable," he said as Molly rushed right to him.

"They play so hard. It's hilarious watching them." Eli smiled at her brother. "I'm happy y'all are here."

"This place is beautiful," Laura said.

"Come in, and Mitch can give you the grand tour of the cabin while we set out lunch."

Eli reached for Whit's hand as they walked to the cabin. "Take it away, Mitch," Eli said when they walked inside.

Eli smiled with pride as Mitch gave them the tour of the cabin. She and Whit placed the food on the table and poured drinks while they waited for Mitch to lead them to the dining room.

"Y'all have it smelling so good in here," Mark said as they entered the room.

"We figured you might be hungry. Everything except for the chicken came out of Whit's garden."

"This looks fantastic," Laura said.

"The cabin is beautiful," Mark said as he took a seat beside Laura.

"Thanks, I can't wait until you see the location, I've picked out for y'all. The view is breathtaking."

"The photos look amazing." Laura took a sip of her tea. "I'm sure they don't do justice to the real view."

"When we finish lunch, we'll take the Gators and tour the property. I've got a project for Mitch and Brad later today."

"What do you need us to do?" Brad asked.

"Evan is a young man from town who has been coming out to help with the planting and stuff since my injury. He's coming out after lunch to help you guys bring in some firewood so we can have some campfires down by the creek while you're here."

"Sweet!" Brad cried out, and his braces flashed.

†

"It's been a long time since I've had vegetables this fresh," Mark said as he pushed his plate away.

"Whit just picked them this morning. She has a fabulous garden," Eli praised.

"You will have one too," Whit replied. "The spot you've picked out is some of the best soil on this mountain."

"It looks like you've been busy since I left," Mitch said.

"We've got fruit and nut trees planted and some berry bushes. The ground has been broken for the garden plot, but there's still a lot of work to do before we can plant anything." She looked at Whit. "Whit has already installed irrigation systems to both areas, so watering is not an issue."

Whit smiled at Eli. "We've also made a rock wall and put in an enclosed fire pit down by the creek and finished the laundry room."

"Do you ever sleep?" Mitch teased.

"Like a rock. All this exercise and fresh air kicks my butt." Eli grinned at her oldest nephew. "Will you and Brad get the Gators from the barn while we clear the table?"

"Oh, heck yeah," Brad said.

"Be mindful of the cats. Will you ride down and check the mail for me, too?" Eli asked.

"You got it, Aunt Eli," Mitch replied as he stood from the table. "Thanks for a great meal."

"You're welcome. I've got steaks for your dad to cook to break in the Green Egg, unless you boys want to do some fishing, and we can have fresh trout."

"The ones Mitch brought home sure tasted good," Mark praised his son.

"We picked up several more fly rods for you and Brad," Eli told her brother.

"When we get done with the tour, we can pitch in to get the trucks unloaded, and then we can wet some flies. Sound good to you, boys?"

"Yes, sir," Mitch replied. "C'mon, Brad, let's get a move on."

"Your mom and I will unload my truck to bring our bags in while the kitchen is being cleaned. Hurry back from the mailbox, and you can help, so we'll have one vehicle done."

"Brad can get the mail, and I'll help you with the bags, Dad," Mitch offered.

"Let's get to it then," Eli said, and began carrying dishes to the kitchen.

"Can I load the dishwasher or store the leftovers?" Laura asked.

"I'll rinse if you'll load," Eli answered.

"I've got the leftovers," Whit replied.

"Sounds great." Eli grinned with excitement for having her family surrounding her.

"Do you want us to set up the air mattress in the open loft area?" Mark asked.

"It would be better than the living room," Eli agreed.

"Brad would sleep outside if we let him." Mark chuckled.

"Maybe I'll pick out one of those cot tents for future visits then," Eli said.

"If you do, you may end up with both boys for the summer," Laura teased.

Eli started rinsing dishes. "I wouldn't mind at all."

"I can't get over the change in Mitch this last month," Laura said. "I've never seen him so excited and motivated. He's only got about a week left of assignments before he can test online."

"We'll make sure schoolwork gets done before anything else. That should keep Mitch motivated," Eli said.

Mitch came bounding through the door, pulling two large suitcases, and Mark followed him with two more. "Mom and Dad in the back, Aunt Eli?"

"Yes, please. Brad will get set up in the loft on the air mattress," Eli answered.

"I've got those bags, Mitch, if you'll carry Brad's duffle and the air mattress upstairs."

"I'm all over it, Dad," he answered, took the duffle and box from Mark, and raced up the stairs.

"What I wouldn't give to have his energy and knees," Mark said as he watched Mitch disappear upstairs.

"That's what I'm talking about," Laura said. "He usually moves at a sloth's pace."

"No offense, but you don't have Gators to drive and fish to catch in your yard." Eli chuckled. She looked at Mark. "Will you fish with the boys?"

"I'd love to. It's been a while since I've used a fly rod, though."

"Mitch will give you a refresher course if needed. The ladies and I'll watch y'all from the deck."

Brad walked in, carrying a handful of mail, and placed it on the kitchen counter. "The Gator is sweet, Aunt Eli," he said.

"Thanks, they are great for getting around here. You and Whit will ride with Mitch, and I'll follow with your parents."

She noticed the frown on his face. "Don't worry, you'll have plenty of time to drive and explore later."

"Yes, ma'am." He perked up.

†

Driving the Gator was a challenge for Eli, but she managed to miss most of the bumps as Mitch and the others raced ahead.

"Does this make your head hurt?" Mark asked from the passenger seat.

"Not too bad. Much better than walking, and I want to see what you think of the building site I picked out for you."

"This place is gorgeous," Mark said. "You chose well. I love what you've managed so far. You realize I will claim the workshop, right?" he asked.

"Mitch and I already plan to put a cot out there for you." Eli chuckled.

When the rock outcroppings came into view, Mitch pulled to a stop ahead of them. He and Brad jumped out of the Gator as Eli drove by.

"Right there," she said as she pointed to a level clearing which opened into a beautiful view. When she pulled to a stop, Mark looked at her, and she could see the tears in his eyes.

"This is perfect," he said. He stepped out of the Gator and waited for Eli and Laura to join him. "I can see the cabin of my dreams here," he said.

"Have you come up with a design yet?" Eli asked.

"Yes, I have, and it will be perfect for this spot."

"We have a creek, too?" Laura said.

"Yes, you do. I thought we'd build a bridge across it and cut a road down the mountain, so you'd have easier access," Eli explained. "There's a spring at the rear of the site we can

332

use for your water source. I can't wait for you to taste the water." She grinned.

"As good as the old homeplace?" he asked.

"Even better if you can believe it," she answered and handed him an empty water bottle. "Try it."

He took the container from her and walked over to the spring, filling the bottle with the cold water. He took a long drink and smiled. "You're right. This is great water." He handed Laura the bottle.

"I could get used to this," she said after tasting the water.

"Dad," Brad called out from atop the rock formation. "Whit says we can find gemstones here," he hollered out.

"She says there are sapphires and rubies in this area. Whit promised to show the boys the best spots to search this summer."

"I like her," Mark said. "She seems good for you."

"I do too. We'll see where things go for us." She watched Whit with the boys and smiled when she turned to wave to them.

"I hope it goes well. You deserve happiness," Mark said. "Let's go look at the creek."

They walked over to the creek and stopped at the bank. "I bet there is some great fishing here, too," Mark said.

"Mitch hasn't even tried out this site yet. He said there wasn't a need as long as he was catching them on the other creek."

"He said you were thinking about a trout pond," Mark said.

"We've got the land for it, and was told the local restaurants would buy as many as we could harvest. I've got an appointment with the state fishery to do a survey for us and let us know what we would need to do to get set up and certified."

Mitch trotted over to where they were and looked at Mark. "We're going to the top so I can show Brad the trailhead and the camp shelter. Do you want to go?"

Mark looked at Eli. "Go ahead, Laura, and I will start down the mountain."

They walked to the Gators and separated at the path. "Everything about this place is perfect," Laura said as they turned toward the cabin.

"I think so, too," Eli said and then laughed at Cruz and Molly racing up the trail. "I guess they felt left out."

"You made a wise choice with Molly. They seem to enjoy playing together."

"They wear each other out." Eli chuckled as she pulled to a stop. "Let's head home," she said to Cruz, who trotted in front of the Gator, with Molly at her side.

When they crested a hill and saw the cabin, they saw Evan had arrived. Eli did not see him until they pulled into the yard, and she heard a drill. Eli looked at the garden plot and saw Evan installing the gate. She drove over to see if he needed any help.

"Good afternoon, Evan. This is Laura. Whit and the boys will be down shortly."

"Nice to meet you, ma'am," he said to Laura. He turned to Eli. "How are you feeling?"

"Better thanks. Do you need some help?"

"No, ma'am, two more screws, and the gate will be hung. You still want some firewood brought in?"

"Yes, I do. As soon as the boys get here, they need to unload Mitch's truck, and then y'all can cut some wood. Afterward, they will do some fishing if you want to join them."

"I'd like to, but I promised Erin we'd go to dinner and a movie tonight."

Eli chuckled. "I promise we won't keep you long then. I'll park this Gator by the shop so you can load the chainsaw and supplies while we wait for the others to return."

"Thanks, Eli. How much do you want?"

"Enough for campfires this weekend, so maybe a load in each of the Gators? Hop on, I'll give ya a ride."

Eli parked, and Evan loaded the supplies he would need. "I'll concentrate on the downed trees along the path if it's okay."

"That's perfect. We can select a few others later to remove to widen the path, but for now, they should be all we need. Do you want some water to take with you?"

"Thanks, that would be great."

Eli and Laura returned to the cabin while Evan tossed a ball for Cruz. Eli grabbed a bottle of water and a pair of sunglasses before returning to the porch. "I think I hear the boys coming now," she told Laura, who was sitting on the steps and petting Molly.

When the others arrived, Eli made introductions, and the guys pitched in and soon had Mitch's truck unloaded.

"You boys ready to cut some wood?" Mark asked.

"You coming with us, Dad?" Mitch asked.

"Only to supervise. I'm gonna let you young'ns do all the work."

"I'll cut, and you two can tote," Evan said. "Let's do this."

They watched the two Gators disappear, and Whit turned to Eli. "How are you feeling?"

"I should have remembered the glasses. I've got a bit of a headache."

"I'll grab you a pill, and you can relax until the boys return. I don't think it will take them long as excited as they are. Oh, I'm stealing them for a bit later tonight."

"Really? What's up?" Eli asked.

"I promised I'd show them the lab," Whit said.

Laura looked puzzled.

"Whit has built a treehouse laboratory for her astronomy work. The boys will love it," Eli explained.

"Don't be surprised if Mark goes too. He's a big kid and would love to see it," Laura said.

"I'll invite him along, too." Whit smiled. "You want to sit out on the deck?"

"Sounds good," Eli answered.

"I'll be right back then. You need anything, Laura?"

"Some water would be great."

"Done," Whit answered.

Laura and Eli walked onto the deck. "It's so peaceful out here," Laura said.

Even though they could hear the chainsaw in the distance, it was quiet. The rippling of the creek and the cool breeze welcomed them. Whit returned with water and a pain pill. "Are you okay out here, or do you need to stretch out for a bit?"

"I'm okay here. I want to toss a salad to go with the fish the guys will catch. We can also have leftovers from lunch," Eli said.

"I'll toss the salad while you relax," Whit offered.

"I can help, too, and that way, we'll finish and let you rest in peace," Laura said.

"See, we got this," Whit said and leaned down to kiss Eli.

"Thanks, I promise I won't move from this spot," Eli answered. She propped her feet on the railing. Tomboy took it for an invitation and climbed in her lap.

"Your babysitter has arrived, so we're good to go," Whit teased. "Enjoy the sun, and we'll be back in no time."

Eli relaxed into the chair, her hand stroking Tomboy's soft fur. Feeling warmed by the sun, she closed her eyes. *Perfect.*

†

"Is she really okay?" Laura asked Whit.

"I think so. The bright sun gives her a headache, and I didn't think to remind her to take her glasses. Eli's been doing well, though, and the medicine should knock her headache out."

"She appears so happy with you."

"Eli's in love with this place. It's been a dream for so long. I'm happy to be a part of it. She's looked forward to your visit for weeks and wanted to have some projects already completed."

"Y'all have done a lot in a short time," Laura said.

"I think so too. Eli has worked hard to get to this point, and is excited to have Mitch here."

"Is it going to be a problem having him here as you two start a new relationship?" Laura asked.

"Not in the least. Mitch and I have several projects already planned, and he seems fine with Eli and me in a relationship. He played a bit of a matchmaker for us."

"He did, did he? Somehow it doesn't surprise me. He loves Eli and would move mountains to please her."

"She thinks the same of him."

When they had the salad tossed and stored in the refrigerator, Laura and Whit returned to the deck. Eli was dozing with Tomboy curled in her lap. "Why don't we sit on the front porch until the boys return and let her sleep," Laura suggested.

Whit nodded, and they walked through the house to sit in the rockers on the front porch.

They made small talk about work and the plans for the homestead until they heard the Gators coming down the mountain.

"Sounds like our menfolk are returning." Laura smiled.

Cruz was the first to arrive, and she rushed to Whit. "Hey, baby girl, did you have fun?" Cruz wiggled her back end with excitement.

The boys stacked the firewood while Evan laid a fire in the pit.

"Where's Aunt Eli?" Mitch asked.

"She's dozing on the deck, so hold the noise down," Laura told him as they finished stacking the wood.

"Is she okay?" Mark asked Whit.

"Yes, she had a bit of a headache from the bright sun. I gave her some medicine, and she should be fine." Whit smiled at him. "You want to go check on her while we get the tools and the Gators stored?"

"Sure," Mark answered and walked inside.

Evan stored the tools, and the boys drove the Gators into the barn. "I'll see you next week," he told Whit as he headed to his truck. "Have fun fishing," he said to Mitch and Brad.

"We will. Have a great weekend, and I'll see ya," Mitch said.

"Nice to meet you," he told Laura and then climbed in his truck and drove away.

"Ready to fish?" Mitch asked Brad.

"Oh, yeah," Brad answered. "Where's Dad?"

"Inside checking on Eli. You two start fishing," Laura told her sons.

†

Mark stepped out on the deck to check on Eli and saw Tomboy curled in her lap. He couldn't hold back a chuckle. Tomboy opened his eyes at the sound and stood to stretch before jumping down. "Hey there, pretty boy," Mark said as Tomboy wound around his legs. He knelt down to pet the cat.

"Don't even think about stealing him," Eli told her brother as she sat up in the chair.

"What about the other dozen?" Mark asked.

"Trust me, there will always be black cats at the clinic to adopt once you get here," she answered.

"How's your head?"

"Feeling much better. Forgot my sunglasses, and the bright sunlight kicked my butt."

"I like what you've accomplished so far, and it sounds like you have fantastic plans in place. I can't wait to get back here."

"The sooner, the better," Eli answered.

"Hey, Sleeping Beauty," Mitch called out as he and Brad walked by. "How are you feeling?"

"Better thanks. Go get them, tiger."

"You coming, Dad?" Brad asked.

"I'll be there in a few. I'll let you two get warmed up before I come to show you how it's done."

"Bring it on, old man," Mitch teased.

"I got your old man." Mark chuckled. "Are you going to stay here or move down by the firepit? We've got enough wood stacked for a week."

"I think I'll join the others by the firepit, but let me grab my camera first. I'll see you in a few."

"Love ya, Sis." Mark grinned.

"More," Eli said and walked him to the door.

†

Eli used the restroom and then walked out to join Whit and Laura by the firepit. She handed Whit the camera. "Will you do the honors? I'm sure the fish are about to start flying out of the creek."

"Sure," Whit answered. "You okay?"

"Much better, thanks."

Eli had just taken her seat when Mitch hollered out. "I got the first one."

"I guess that's my cue," Whit said and walked over to take a picture and then sat on a nearby boulder. Brad was fishing just above Mitch and Mark had just arrived on the scene.

"Only one fish?" he teased. "Let me show you how it's done, boys."

It didn't take long for all three to hook fish, and less than an hour to catch enough for dinner. Mitch was beaming with joy as he carried the bucket of fish to show to Eli.

"Y'all did great. Who got the biggest?" Eli asked.

"I did," Mark said with a grin. "It was the only one I caught."

"He got lucky," Mitch said. "C'mon, you two can help me dress these," he said, holding up the bucket. "You want me to drop the carcasses in the compost bin?"

"If you don't get swarmed by a herd of cats." Eli chuckled.

†

After a great dinner, cooked by Mitch and Mark, the group sat around the fire pit to relax. The evening had turned cool as the sun set, and the warmth from the pit was comforting to Eli.

Laura and Eli sipped on coffee as they enjoyed the fire. "Are you boys ready for a hike?" Whit asked.

"For sure," Mitch answered. He and Brad jumped to their feet.

"Would you like to join us?" Whit asked Mark.

"I'd love too," he said and stood to join them.

340

"Are you boys ready for s'mores when you get back?" Eli asked.

"I'm sure we'll work up an appetite hiking the mountain," Mitch replied.

Eli nodded. "Okay, we'll get things set for your return. You'd better take some flashlights if you plan to cross the log. I'd hate for someone to get a free ride into the creek."

"This should be fun," Mark said. "Is it strong enough to hold a fat old man?"

"It held up for me to cross." Mitch grinned.

"Enough said, let's go," Mark said and slapped his son on the back.

Mitch ran inside to get three flashlights. Laura and Eli watched the beams until they disappeared into the trees. Several minutes later, the lights reappeared on the other side of the creek. Eli smiled at Laura. "I didn't hear any screams, so I think it's safe to assume they made it across."

"We would know if they didn't. Why don't you sit tight, and I'll make a tray of s'more supplies."

"Everything we need should be in the pantry."

"I think I can find what we need. More coffee while I'm inside?"

Eli handed her the empty cup. "Yes, please, that would be great."

Cruz trotted down from the trail to sit beside Eli at the fire. She reached down to stroke her companion. "I don't blame you. I wouldn't want to cross the log at night, either."

†

Mark was groaning by the time they reached the lab. "I have to get in better shape to survive here," he said as they walked inside.

"The mountain will whip you into shape," Whit assured him.

"Wow," Mitch said as he looked around at all the electronic equipment.

"Wait until you see this," Whit said, and turned on a large monitor and then adjusted the viewfinder on the telescope. An enhanced view filled the screen, and she showed the boys how to change the focus and field of view on the telescope.

"That's freakin' awesome," Brad said as he took a seat and began maneuvering the lens across the heavens.

"So, you write college textbooks?" Mark asked.

"Yes, for astronomy and advanced physics courses," Whit answered. "I sometimes work with NASA on projects."

"Amazing," Mark mirrored the awe of his two sons. "I could watch this all night long," he said, indicating the large screen view.

"There have been many nights I have fallen asleep here," Whit confessed.

"I bet watching meteor showers would be incredible from this view," Brad said.

Whit reached for the keyboard and pushed several keys. "This was the last Leonid shower," she said as the video began playing on the monitor.

"Do we have to go home to Alabama, Dad?" Brad asked. "It is so cool here."

"Yes, Son, we do, but it won't be long before we can all live here."

"If you can come up some this summer, I'll show you some great spots in the heavens and on this mountain. There is so much to explore," Whit promised.

Brad looked at his dad, and Mark nodded. "I think you'll be spending several weeks here between baseball camps and school starting."

"Yes," Brad said and pumped his fist. "I can't wait."

"Are you ready to head home for some s'mores?" Whit asked.

"Not really, but yes," Mitch said. "This is neat. To think this was what you were doing when Aunt Eli thought you were moonshining or growing pot." He broke out in a laugh.

"Say what?" Mark said.

"Eli told me she had seen a flashlight beam going up the mountain at night, and she wondered if I was making moonshine or had a secret pot garden," Whit explained.

"I sure wouldn't have thought this was here," Mitch said.

"I can see why Eli might think that, but I'm glad you're legit," Mark teased.

"Top Secret clearance, so I reckon you can trust me." She grinned at Mark. She locked the door behind them as they started down the steps.

†

Brad was still talking excitedly as they reached the fire pit. "Mom, you won't believe her lab. It was totally awesome," he told Laura.

"See, I told you. You may end up with both boys this summer," Laura said to Eli.

"Bring it on," Eli answered.

"At least for a few weeks," Mark replied. "Whit has already promised him some grand adventures, so I'm sure we won't hear the end of that." Mark shot a wink to Whit.

"Grand adventures, huh?" Eli said.

"So much to do and see in the mountains," Whit said.

"For sure," Eli agreed. "Who's ready for s'mores?"

"Me," both boys said in unison.

Laura uncovered the tray of goodies, and the boys started creating the sugary treats.

343

†

Laura and the boys decided to call it a night, leaving Mark, Eli, and Whit by the campfire.

The barn owl hooted in the distance as they watched the shadows of the flames dance against the stone wall. Eli had reached over and was holding Whit's hand as midnight approached.

"What do you think of Cast Iron Farms?" Eli asked Mark.

He grinned. "I can't believe you remembered that conversation. It had to be at least two years ago."

"The name has been burned in my memory ever since," Eli answered.

"I love it," Mark said. "You've picked the perfect spot."

"Yes, I think I have. There's so much potential."

Mark nodded and appeared lost in thought as they enjoyed the warmth of the fire.

"I think we'd better turn in," Eli said. "You know those boys will be up at the crack of dawn."

"Normally, they'd sleep in until we drug them out of bed, but you're right, they will be ready to be out and exploring." Mark smiled at them. "I might sleep in a bit, though."

"Uh-huh, right. You're gonna be right there with the boys," Eli teased.

"Probably so." Mark closed the lid on the fire pit to extinguish the flame. "What a great system," he said.

They walked into the cabin together, and Mark hugged them both. "Goodnight, see you in the morning."

"Goodnight, Mark," Eli answered and took Whit's hand to climb the stairs. Cruz had disappeared earlier and was sleeping with Brad in the loft as they topped the stairs.

Tomboy was curled into a ball on the end of the bed. "I guess we are late to the party tonight," Eli said as she closed the door behind them.

"How are you feeling?" Whit asked.

"A bit of a dull headache, but I'm okay. Ready to snuggle into you for a good night's sleep."

"You need a pill?"

"Nope, the only thing I need is a kiss."

Whit walked over to Eli and kissed her. She lifted her shirt over her head and tossed it toward the hamper. "Clothes?" she asked.

"No, I want to feel you next to me," Eli answered.

CHAPTER SEVENTEEN

The weekend flew by and Eli hated to say goodbye to Mark. "It was great having you here. I just wish you didn't have to leave."

"Me too, but you can bet I'll be back as quick as possible. I love it here. I wish we could have gotten the garden ready for you to plant, but we came close."

"I didn't intend for y'all to work at all this weekend. It was supposed to be fun and relaxing."

"I had loads of fun and I now know where my new home will be on the mountain."

"The plan you have picked out will be perfect for that spot. I'll start shopping around and see if I can find the right builder for us. It's never too early to start looking."

"That's true." He walked back to the cabin with Eli. "Laura asked last night if we could spend Christmas with you. I told her we would be here."

"Thanksgiving, too. You all are always welcome."

"We have already committed with her family in Kentucky, so Christmas is ours."

"Maybe we can order up a white one." Eli grinned.

"The boys would go nuts." He chuckled. "It's been a long time since we had one."

They stopped to look across the mountain. Mark let out a soft sigh. "No promises, but I'll try for long weekends over Memorial Day and the fourth."

"Either weekend would be great to explore the area with the boys. They are both dying to go to Sliding Rock and see some of the waterfalls."

"I remember our trips to Sliding Rock. It was so much fun, but damn, that was some cold water. Maybe if you're game, we could do some rafting?"

"Right up my alley. I'll do some research and make reservations for both weekends. That way nothing gets booked before we make up our minds," Eli said.

Brad walked out carrying the last of the suitcases and placed it in the truck. "I can't wait to get back here," he said as he picked up Cruz's frisbee and let it sail across the yard.

"It won't be long. I'll come down and kidnap you if I have to," Eli told him.

"As soon as baseball season is over, I'd like to spend a few weeks here," Brad said.

Eli looked at Mark and nodded. "I'm serious. I'll come down and get him if you want me to."

"I'm hoping I can get the time off, but I'll let you know."

Mitch, Whit, and Laura walked out to the truck. Laura turned to Whit. "I know Eli will spoil him rotten, so I'm hoping you will keep Mitch on his toes."

"I promise he will finish his school and stay so busy he won't know what hit him." Whit chuckled. "Between our two homes, he will have a ton of projects."

"Not so many we can't have some fun in between though," Eli was quick to interject. She grinned at Mitch. "Someone has to keep the trout population under control here."

Mark chuckled and hugged Whit, and then Eli. "Love y'all."

"We love you more," Eli answered.

"Most," Mitch said, and gave his dad a bear hug.

"I'll text to let you know we made it home," Mark said and climbed in behind the wheel.

Mitch, Whit, and Eli watched them drive out of sight. "That time went by all too fast," Eli said.

Whit slipped her hand into Eli's. "Your head hurting?"

"Yes, how could you tell?"

"Your eyes give you away. Why don't you kick back on the couch and rest? Mitch and I have a solar panel system to plot out. I promise we'll be as quiet as we can."

"I think a nap and a pain pill is in order. You sure you don't mind me crashing on you?"

"We've got this, Aunt Eli," Mitch assured her.

Whit got her a pill and settled Eli onto the couch while Mitch took their laptops and notepads to the kitchen table.

"I love you," Whit said and kissed her forehead.

"Most," Eli answered with a grin. The last thing Eli heard in the room before she drifted off to sleep was the quiet laughter of her two most favorite people.

ABOUT THE AUTHOR

ALI SPOONER

Ali Spooner, lives in beautiful Northwest Florida with her long-term partner and several fur babies. Ali's writing began as a hobby, and with the assistance of the Affinity Rainbow Publishing team has taken her love of storytelling to a new level.

Ali's characters are primarily everyday people, from cowgirls to psychics. Ali also has created a few supernatural characters in her paranormal series. Several of her twenty plus books have been Amazon rated number one choices and always includes a happily ever after. Ali's hobbies include photography, reading, travel, college sports and spending time with family and friends.

OTHER AFFINITY BOOKS

Charlie by Erin O'Reilly
At fourteen, Hannah Garvin met 'the one,' Charlene Gaines and her life was never the same. They were inseparable and spent every moment they could together. One day, Charlie left without a word and again, Hannah's life took a dramatic change. Hannah vowed to never fall in love again. When she meets Mick, a new arrival to the small Texas panhandle town near her family's farm, her heart remembers what being in love was like, and yearns for more. Will Hannah let the memory of Charlie go so she can start a new life with Mick? Or will her heart betray her and hold on to her love for Charlie?

Misha's Promise by Renee MacKenzie
Misha Wyatt has settled into a peaceful existence as a healer in Karst, New America. When an airplane crashes in the meadow outside of Karst, Misha hurries to help the pilot. Misha is not expecting the pilot to be alive...or so beautiful. Will her uncontrollable desire to keep the pilot safe be her downfall? Can *they* survive their journey? The last book in the Karst series brings our characters to their physical and

emotional limits. Don't miss the culmination of this exciting series!

Heart Strings Attached by Ali Spooner & Annette Mori
Socialite Remy has her world shaken. Bartender Chancy has her orderly life turned around. When a mutually beneficial business agreement between Remy and Chancy turns into undeniable attraction. Will the two ignore culture norms to explore their intense desire for each other?

The Panty Thief by Annette Mori
Someone is stealing panties, but who? And why? Joey Hartford is a fourth-year medical student who insists she doesn't have time for a relationship. A new tenant in her apartment building is proving too tempting to ignore. Sabrina is in her final year of her doctoral program focused on completing her dissertation. Meeting Joey is dangerous for so many reasons. Add a suicidal ex-girlfriend who suddenly reappears in Sabrina's life and Joey's jealous friend-with-benefits, and things get complicated quickly.

Country Living by Jen Silver
Peri Sanderson achieves her dream of moving from London to a cottage in the English countryside with her wife, Karla. Peri sees their future as pastoral while chatting with the locals in a quaint village pub. Sexy urbanite, Karla, has other ideas. Secrets are everywhere. Peri quickly senses something not quite right among her rural neighbours and Karla. Temptation, betrayal, and intrigue combine to change the lives of both women beyond anything they could have imagined.

Before the Light by Samantha Hicks
One year after, her long-time partner Meredith's abduction, and their subsequent break-up, Kathleen Bowden-Scott's life

is spiralling out of control. She meets Bethany Jones and despite an instant attraction Kathleen shies away. In this fast-paced, romantic suspense, lies are exposed and hearts unite as Kathleen and Beth fight for their future.

Wanted for Christmas by JM Dragon
Belle Farrow knew what she wanted for Christmas–work. She had little to offer but a minor degree in cookery and household management. Certainly not enough for a decent chef or housekeeper position. Then she saw an advert in the local newspaper. Wanted: Housekeeper/cook/nanny for the period of Christmas until the New Year. This is Christmas. Perhaps Santa reads the ad column too and pushes a little spirit of the season to that request.

Dreams in a Jar by JM Dragon
When you believe your life is a never-ending spiral of despair and the only personal joy you have is inside of a novel, would you grab a chance to hide away in the local bookstore and dream of adventures? Thea's life is about to embark on a journey she never envisioned when local bookstore owner, Marion, is taken ill. Her niece, Sheryl Appleby, takes over the reins and her presence provides Thea the courage to take a leap of faith. Can she embrace the butterfly effect, or are Thea's dreams bottled in a jar forever?

Pleasure Workers by Annette Mori
Alex Cortez is accomplished at two things, fixing broken equipment and pleasuring women. She is happily doing both at the Ranch in Nevada. Danna Nichols, newly widowed, feels lost and alone. When her good friend Lindy invites her to check out the newly established Trophy Wives Club, it awakens dormant feelings and desires. An instant attraction happens and the two form a bond under unlikely

circumstances. Will the challenges of their social status tear them apart before they can enjoy the pleasures of their new love?

The Trophy Wives Club by Ali Spooner
What happens when under-appreciated professional women are offered their dream jobs? When one of Atlanta's elite businesswomen and wife of a prominent judge sets her sights on a goal, life begins to change for these women. Friendships and romance bloom in a unique fitness club on the outskirts of Atlanta, where more than a workout is offered.

Unknown Forces by Samantha Hicks
Jennifer Wilson spent the last seventeen years raising her younger sister Kelsey after a boating accident killed their parents. Riley hasn't had an easy life either and her friendship with Kelsey is the only thing steadfast in her life. When tragedy and secrets emerge, Jennifer and Riley must learn to lean on each other. The growing attraction between them only complicates matters. When events conspire to keep them apart, will they trust the unknown forces that keep pushing them together, or hide from their feelings forever?

A Window to Love by Annette Mori
Two life events, two paths colliding, two souls destined to meet. Mandie Carter lives an uninspired life. No passion, no romance, and just when she thought things couldn't get worse, life throws her a curve. Gail Forrester is barely hanging on. Buried under mountains of debt, only her much in demand architectural designs keep her afloat. Now, they must find a way forward together through what life and destiny has in store for them. Only then can they hope to step into that window to love.

Affinity
Rainbow Publications

eBooks, Print, Free eBooks

Visit our website for more publications available online.

www.affinityrainbowpublications.com

Published by Affinity Rainbow Publications
A Division of Affinity eBook Press NZ LTD
Canterbury, New Zealand

Registered Company 2517228